12/12/20

B15

Longer and Longer and *The Deal of a Lifetime*, he is also the author of a collection of heartfelt and humorous essays about fatherhood: *Things My Son Needs To Know About The World*.

Fredrik Backman's books are published in more than forty countries and have

He

528 529 86 3

Also by Fredrik Backman

A Man Called Ove

My Grandmother Sends Her Regards and Apologises

Britt-Marie Was Here

And Every Morning the Way Home Gets Longer and Longer

Beartown

The Deal of a Lifetime

Us Against You

FREDRIK BACKMAN

Translated by Neil Smith

PENGUIN BOOKS

PENGUIN BOOKS

UK | USA | Canada | Ireland | Australia
India | New Zealand | South Africa

Penguin Books is part of the Penguin Random House group of companies
whose addresses can be found at global.penguinrandomhouse.com

Published by arrangement with the Salomonsson Agency
Originally published in Sweden as *Vi mot er* by Bokforlaget Forum 2017
Published in USA as *Us Against You* by Atria Books 2018
Published in Great Britain by Michael Joseph 2018
Published in Penguin Books 2019

001

Set in 11/13 pt Bembo Book MT Std
Typeset by Jouve (UK), Milton Keynes
Printed and bound in Great Britain by Clays Ltd, Elcograf S.p.A.

A CIP catalogue record for this book is available from the British Library

ISBN: 978-1-405-93023-9

www.greenpenguin.co.uk

For Neda.
I'm still trying to impress you.
Just so you know.

I

It's Going to Be Someone's Fault

Have you ever seen a town fall? Ours did. We'll end up saying that violence came to Beartown this summer, but that will be a lie; the violence was already here. Because sometimes hating one another is so easy that it seems incomprehensible that we ever do anything else.

We're a small community in the forest; people say that no roads lead here, just past. The economy coughs every time it takes a deep breath; the factory cuts its workforce each year like a child that thinks no one will notice the cake in the fridge getting smaller if you take a little bit from each side. If you lay a current map of the town over an old one, the main shopping street and the little strip known as 'the centre' seem to shrink like bacon in a hot pan. We have an ice rink but not much else. But on the other hand, as people usually say here: What the hell else do you need?

People driving through say that Beartown doesn't live for anything but hockey, and some days they may be right. Sometimes people have to be allowed to have something to live for in order to survive everything else. We're not mad, we're not greedy; say what you like about Beartown, but the people here are tough and hardworking. So we built a hockey team that was like us, that we could be proud of, because we weren't like you. When people from the big cities thought something seemed too hard, we just grinned and said, 'It's supposed to be hard.' Growing up here wasn't easy; that's why we did it, not you. We stood tall, no matter the weather. But then something happened, and we fell.

There's a story about us before this one, and we're always going to carry the guilt of that. Sometimes good people do terrible things in the belief that they're trying to protect what they love. A boy, the star of the hockey team, raped a girl. And we lost our way. A community is the sum of its choices, and when two of our children said different things, we believed him. Because that was easier, because if the girl was lying our lives could carry on as usual. When we found out the truth, we fell apart, taking the town with us. It's easy to say that we should have done everything differently, but perhaps you wouldn't have acted differently, either. If you'd been afraid, if you'd been forced to pick a side, if you'd known what you had to sacrifice. Perhaps you wouldn't be as brave as you think. Perhaps you're not as different from us as you hope.

This is the story of what happened afterward, from one summer to the following winter. It is about Beartown and the neighbouring town of Hed, and how the rivalry between two hockey teams can grow into a mad struggle for money and power and survival. It is a story about hockey rinks and all the hearts that beat around them, about people and sports and how they sometimes take turns carrying each other. About us, people who dream and fight. Some of us will fall in love, others will be crushed; we'll have good days and some very bad days. This town will rejoice, but it will also start to burn. There's going to be a terrible bang.

Some girls will make us proud; some boys will make us great. Young men dressed in different colours will fight to the death in a dark forest. A car will drive too fast through the night. We will say that it was a traffic accident, but accidents happen by chance, and we will know that we could have prevented this one. This one will be someone's fault.

People we love will die. We will bury our children beneath our most beautiful trees.

2

There Are Three Types of People

Bang-bang-bang-bang-bang.

The highest point in Beartown is a hill to the south of the last buildings in town. From there you can see all the way from the big villas on the Heights, past the factory and the ice rink and the smaller row houses near the centre, right over to the blocks of rental apartments in the Hollow. Two girls are standing on the hill looking out across their town. Maya and Ana. They'll soon be sixteen, and it's hard to say if they became friends in spite of their differences or because of them. One of them likes musical instruments; the other likes guns. Their mutual loathing of each other's taste in music is almost as recurrent a topic of argument as their ten-year-long fight about pets. Last winter they got thrown out of a history class at school because Maya muttered, 'You know who was a dog person, Ana? Hitler!' whereupon Ana retorted, 'You know who was a cat person, then? Josef Mengele!'

They squabble constantly and love each other unquestioningly, and ever since they were little they have had days when they've felt it was just the two of them against the whole world. Ever since what happened to Maya earlier in the spring, every day has felt like that.

It's the very start of June. For three-quarters of the year this place is encapsulated in winter, but now, for a few enchanted weeks, it's summer. The forest around them is getting drunk on sunlight, the trees sway happily beside the lakes, but the girls' eyes are restless. This time of year used to be a time of endless adventure for them; they would spend all day out in nature and come

3

home late in the evening with torn clothes and dirty faces, childhood in their eyes. That's all gone. They're adults now. For some girls that isn't something you choose, it's something that gets forced upon you.

Bang. Bang. Bang-bang-bang.

A mother is standing outside a house. She's packing her child's things into a car. How many times does that happen while they're growing up? How many toys do you pick up from the floor, how many stuffed animals do you have to form search parties for at bedtime, how many mittens do you give up on at preschool? How many times do you think that if nature really does want people to reproduce, then perhaps evolution should have let all parents grow extra sets of arms so they can reach under all the wretched sofas and fridges? How many hours do we spend waiting in hallways for our kids? How many grey hairs do they give us? How many lifetimes do we devote to their single one? What does it take to be a good parent? Not much. Just everything. Absolutely everything.

Bang. Bang.

Up on the hill Ana turns to her best friend and asks, 'Do you remember when we were little? When you always wanted to pretend that we had kids?'

Maya nods without taking her eyes from the town.

'Do you still want kids?' Ana asks.

Maya's mouth barely opens when she replies. 'Don't know. Do you?'

Ana shrugs her shoulders slightly, halfway between anger and sorrow. 'Maybe when I'm old.'

'How old?'

'Dunno. Thirty, maybe.'

Maya is silent for a long time, then asks, 'Do you want boys or girls?'

Ana replies as if she's spent her whole life thinking about this, 'Boys.'

'Why?'

'Because the world is kind of shitty towards them sometimes. But it treats us like that nearly all the time.'

Bang.

The mother closes the trunk, holding back tears because she knows that if she lets out so much as a single one, they will never stop. No matter how old they get, we never want to cry in front of our children. We'd do anything for them; they never know because they don't understand the immensity of something that is unconditional. A parent's love is unbearable, reckless, irresponsible. They're so small when they sleep in their beds and we sit beside them, shattered to pieces inside. It's a lifetime of shortcomings, and, feeling guilty, we stick happy pictures up everywhere, but we never show the gaps in the photograph album, where everything that hurts is hidden away. The silent tears in darkened rooms. We lie awake, terrified of all the things that can happen to them, everything they might be subjected to, all the situations in which they could end up victims.

The mother goes around the car and opens the door. She's not much different from any other mother. She loves, she gets frightened, falls apart, is filled with shame, isn't enough. She sat awake beside her son's bed when he was three years old, watching him sleep and fearing all the terrible things that could happen to him, just like every parent does. It never occurred to her that she might need to fear the exact opposite.

Bang.

It's dawn, the town is asleep; the main road out of Beartown is empty, but the girls' eyes are still fixed on it from up on the hilltop. They wait patiently.

Maya no longer dreams about the rape. About Kevin's hand over her mouth, the weight of his body stifling her screams, his room with all the hockey trophies on the shelves, the floor the button of her blouse bounced across. She just dreams about the running track behind the Heights now; she can see it from up here. When Kevin was running on his own and she stepped out of the darkness with a shotgun. Held it to his head as he shook and sobbed and begged for mercy. In her dreams she kills him, every night.

Bang. Bang.

How many times does a mother make her child giggle? How many times does the child make her laugh out loud? Kids turn us inside out the first time we realize that they're doing it intentionally, when we discover that they have a sense of humour. When they make jokes, learn to manipulate our feelings. If they love us, they learn to lie shortly after that, to spare our feelings, pretending to be happy. They're quick to learn what we like. We might tell ourselves that we know them, but they have their own photograph albums, and they grow up in the gaps.

How many times has the mother stood beside the car outside the house, checked the time, and impatiently called her son's name? She doesn't have to do that today. He's been sitting silently in the passenger seat for several hours while she packed his things. His once well-toned body is thin after weeks in which she's struggled to get food into him. His eyes stare blankly through the windshield.

How much can a mother forgive her son for? How can she possibly know that in advance? No parent imagines that her little boy is going to grow up and commit a crime. She doesn't know what nightmares he dreams now, but he shouts when he wakes up from them. Ever since that morning she found him on the running track, motionless with cold, stiff with fear. He had wet himself, and his desperate tears had frozen on his cheeks.

He raped a girl, and no one could ever prove it. There will always be people who say that means he got away with it, that his family escaped punishment. They're right, of course. But it will never feel like that for his mother.

Bang. Bang. Bang.

When the car begins to move along the road, Maya stands on the hill and knows that Kevin will never come back here. That she has broken him. There will always be people who say that means she won.

But it will never feel like that to her.

Bang. Bang. Bang. Bang.

The brake lights go on for a moment; the mother casts one last glance in the rearview mirror, at the house that was a home and the gluey scraps on the mailbox where the name 'Erdahl' has been torn off, letter by letter. Kevin's father is packing the other car alone. He stood beside the mother on the track, saw their son lying there with tears on his sweater and urine on his trousers. Their lives had shattered long before then, but that was when she first saw the shards. The father refused to help her as she half carried, half dragged the boy through the snow. That was two months ago. Kevin hasn't left the house since then, and his parents have barely said a word to each other. Men define themselves in more distinctive ways than women, life has taught her that, and her husband and son have always defined themselves with one single word: winners. As long as she can remember, the father has drummed the same message into the boy: 'There are three types of people: winners, losers, and the ones who watch.'

And now? If they're not winners, what are they? The mother takes her foot off the brake, switches the radio off, drives down the road, and turns the corner. Her son sits beside her. The father gets into the other car, drives alone in the opposite direction. The divorce papers are in the mail, along with the letter to the school saying that the father has moved to another town and the mother and son have gone abroad. The mother's phone number is at the bottom in case anyone at the school has any questions, but no one's going to call. This town is going to do everything it can to forget that the Erdahl family was ever a part of it.

After four hours of silence in the car, when they're so far from Beartown that they can't see any forest, Kevin whispers to his mother, 'Do you think it's possible to become a different person?'

She shakes her head, biting her bottom lip, and blinks so hard she can't see the road in front of her. 'No. But it's possible to become a better person.' Then he holds out a trembling hand. She holds it as if he were three years old, as if he were dangling over the edge of a cliff. She whispers, 'I can't forgive you, Kevin. But I'll never abandon you.'

Bang-bang-bang-bang-bang.

That's the sound of this town, everywhere. Perhaps you understand that only if you live here.

Bangbangbang.

On the hilltop stand two girls, watching the car disappear. They'll soon be sixteen. One of them is holding a guitar, the other a rifle.

3

Like a Man

The worst thing we know about other people is that we're dependent upon them. That their actions affect our lives. Not just the people we choose, the people we like, but all the rest of them: the idiots. You who stand in front of us in every line, who can't drive properly, who like bad television shows and talk too loud in restaurants and whose kids infect our kids with the winter vomiting bug at preschool. You who park badly and steal our jobs and vote for the wrong party. You also influence our lives, every second.

Dear God, how we hate you for that.

In the Bearskin pub a number of silent old men are sitting in a row. They're said to be in their seventies but could easily be double that. There are five of them, but they have at least eight opinions, and they're known as the 'five uncles' because they always stand by the boards and lie and argue at all the practices at Beartown Ice Hockey Club. Afterward they go to the Bearskin and lie and argue there instead, and occasionally they amuse themselves by trying to trick the others into thinking that senile dementia has crept up on them: they sometimes change one another's house numbers at night and hide their keys when they've had a few drinks. One time four of them towed the fifth one's car out of his driveway and replaced it with an identical rental, just so he would end up terrified that it was finally time to go into a home when he couldn't get the car started the next morning. When they go to games they pay with Monopoly money, and for almost an entire season they all pretended to believe that they were at the 1980 Winter Olympics.

Every time they caught sight of Peter Andersson, the general manager of Beartown Ice Hockey, they spoke to him in German and called him 'Hans Rampf.' It slowly drove the GM mad, and that made the five uncles happier than an overtime win. People in the town often say that it's entirely possible that the uncles are in fact senile now, all five of them, but how the hell would anyone ever be able to prove it?

Ramona, the owner of the Bearskin pub, lines up five whiskies on the bar. There's only one sort of whisky here, but several types of sorrow. The uncles have followed Beartown Ice Hockey all the way to the top and right down to the bottom of the league system. All their lives. This is going to be their worst day.

Kira Andersson is sitting in her car on her way to the office when her phone rings. She's feeling stressed for a lot of different reasons. She drops the phone under her seat and swears with a level of anatomical precision that Kira's husband usually points out would embarrass a gang of drunken sailors. When Kira finally gets hold of the phone it takes the woman at the other end a couple of seconds to recover from the range of expletives.

'Hello?' Kira snaps.

'Yes, sorry, I'm calling from S Express. You emailed to ask for a quote . . . ,' the woman says tentatively.

'From . . . who did you say you were? S Express? No, you must have the wrong number,' Kira says.

'Are you sure? I've got the paperwork in front of me here and –' the woman says, but then Kira drops her phone again and launches into a spontaneous description of exactly what sort of genitalia the designer of the phone's head resembles, and by the time she manages to get hold of it again the woman at the other end has done herself a favour and hung up.

Kira doesn't think much more about it. She's expecting a call from her husband, Peter, who's got a meeting with the regional council about the future of the hockey club today, and her anxiety about the consequences of the meeting is like a band around her stomach being pulled tighter and tighter. When she tosses the phone onto the passenger seat, the background picture of her daughter, Maya, and son, Leo, glows briefly before the screen goes dark.

Kira drives to work, but if she had stopped the car and looked up 'S Express' online she would have seen that it's a moving company. In towns that don't care that much about their hockey team, that might have looked like a harmless joke, requesting a quote in the name of the Andersson family, but Beartown isn't that sort of town. In the silence of the forest you don't have to scream to be threatening.

Kira will figure it out soon enough, of course. She's a smart woman, and she's lived here long enough. Beartown is known for many things: dizzyingly beautiful forests, a last area of wilderness in a country where national politicians only want the big cities to grow. It has friendly, humble, hardworking people who love nature and sports, spectators who fill the stands no matter what league the team is playing in, pensioners who paint their faces green when they go to games. Responsible hunters, competent anglers, people as tough as the forest and as unyielding as the ice, neighbours who help anyone in need. Life can be hard, but they grin and say, 'It's supposed to be hard.' Beartown is known for that. But . . . well. The town is also known for other things.

A few years ago an old hockey referee talked to the media about his worst memories from his career. The second, third, and fourth places were occupied by games in the big cities where angry fans had thrown tubs of chewing tobacco, coins, and golf balls onto the ice when they didn't like a decision. But in first place was a small rink way out in the forest, where the referee had once awarded a power play to the visiting team in the closing minute of a game. They had scored, Beartown had lost, and the referee had glanced up towards the infamous standing area in the arena reserved for 'the Pack,' which was always full of men in black jackets singing at deafening volume or bellowing in a terrifying manner. But on that occasion they hadn't raised their voices. The Pack had just stood there, completely silent.

Kira's husband, Peter Andersson, general manager of Beartown Ice Hockey, was the first to realize the danger. He raced towards the scorekeeper's box, and as the buzzer rang out to signal the end of the game, he managed to switch all the lights off. In the darkness the security guards led the referees out and drove them away. No one needed to explain what would have happened otherwise.

That's why softly spoken threats work here. A call to a moving company is enough, and Kira will understand the reason soon.

The meeting in the regional council building isn't yet finished, but a few people in Beartown already know the result.

There are always flags fluttering outside the council building: the national flag and one bearing the council's coat of arms. The local politicians can see them from the conference room. It's a few days before the Midsummer holiday, three weeks after Kevin and his family left town. They changed history when they did that: not the history that was yet to come, but the history that had already happened. But not everyone has realized that yet.

One of the councillors coughs nervously, makes a brave attempt to button his jacket, even though as a rough guess half a dozen Christmas buffets must have passed since that was even theoretically possible, and says, 'I'm sorry, Peter, but we've decided that the region would be best served if we focus the council's resources on one hockey team. Not two. We want to focus on . . . Hed Hockey. It would be in everyone's best interests, yours included, if you could just accept that. Bearing in mind the . . . situation.'

Peter Andersson is sitting on the other side of the table. The realization of how he has been betrayed sends him tumbling into the darkness, and his voice is barely audible when he manages to say, 'But we – we just need a bit of help for a few months, until we find more sponsors. The council just has to stand as guarantor for the loan from the bank.'

He falls silent, immediately embarrassed at his own stupidity. Obviously the councillors have already spoken to the bank managers—they're neighbours, they play golf and hunt elk together. This decision was made long before Peter walked into the room. When the councillors asked him to come, they were careful to stress that this would be an 'informal meeting.'

There won't be any minutes. The chairs in the meeting room are extra narrow, enabling the men with all the power to sit on more than one chair at the same time.

Peter's phone buzzes. When he opens it, he finds an email telling him that the director of Beartown Ice Hockey Club has resigned. He must have known what was going to happen here and has probably already been offered a job in Hed instead. Peter is going to be left to deal with the blow on his own.

The politicians on the other side of the table squirm uncomfortably. Peter can see what they're thinking: 'Don't embarrass yourself. Don't plead, don't beg. Take it like a man.'

Beartown lies beside a large lake, with a narrow strip of beach along the whole of one side. At this time of year the beach belongs to the town's teenagers, when it's so warm that you almost manage to forget that winter in Beartown is nine months long. Among the profusion of beach balls and hormones sits a twelve-year-old boy in sunglasses. His name is Leo Andersson. Not many people on the beach knew that last year, but they all know it now and keep glancing at him as if he were primed to explode. A couple of months ago, Leo's older sister, Maya, was raped by Kevin, but the police were unable to prove anything, so Kevin got off. The townspeople divided, most of them taking Kevin's side, and the hate escalated until they tried to drive Leo's family out of town. They threw stones with the word BITCH painted on them through his sister's window, they bullied her at school, they called a meeting at the rink and tried to get her and Leo's dad fired as general manager of Beartown Ice Hockey.

A witness came forward, a boy the same age as Maya who had

been in the house when it had happened. But that didn't make any difference. The police did nothing, the town kept quiet, the adults did nothing to help Maya. Then one night, not long after that, something else happened. No one knows exactly what. But all of a sudden Kevin stopped going out. Rumours that he was mentally ill started to circulate; then, one morning three weeks ago, he and his family just up and left town.

Leo had thought everything would get better then. But it got worse instead. He's twelve years old, and this summer he learns that people will always choose a simple lie over a complicated truth, because the lie has one unbeatable advantage: the truth always has to stick to what actually happened, whereas the lie just has to be easy to believe.

When a vote of the club's members had decided by the smallest possible margin to let Peter Andersson stay on as general manager back at that meeting in the spring, Kevin's dad had immediately seen to it that Kevin changed clubs, from Beartown to Hed. He had persuaded the coach, almost all the sponsors, and almost all of the best players from the junior team to move with him. When Kevin's family suddenly left town three weeks ago, everything was turned upside down again, but – weirdly enough – nothing changed.

And what had Leo expected? That everyone would suddenly realize that Kevin was guilty and apologize? That the sponsors and players would come back to Beartown with their heads bowed? Like hell they did. No one bows their heads around here, for the simple reason that many of our worst deeds are the result of our never wanting to admit that we're wrong. The greater the mistake and the worse the consequences, the more pride we stand to lose if we back down. So no one does. Suddenly everyone with power and money in Beartown chose a different strategy: they stopped admitting that they had ever been friends of the Erdahl family. People started to mutter, very quietly at first, then with increasing assurance, that 'that boy was always a bit odd,' and 'his dad put way too much pressure on him, anyone could see that.' Then, weirdly, it slipped into comments like 'that whole family, they were never . . . you know . . . like us. The father wasn't from around here, not originally, he was a newcomer.'

The story when Kevin transferred to Hed Hockey Club was that he had been 'the victim of a malicious accusation,' and 'the subject of a witch hunt,' but now there's a different version: that the sponsors and players didn't move to Hed because they were following him but because they wanted to 'distance themselves' from him. His name has been erased from Hed's membership register, but it's still on Beartown's. That way everyone was able to move far enough away from both perpetrator and victim, so now all Kevin's former friends can call him a 'psychopath' while still calling Maya a 'bitch.' Lies are simple; truth is difficult.

Beartown Ice Hockey started to be called 'Kevin's club' by so many people that Hed automatically began to feel like the opposite. Emails were sent from players' parents to local councillors about 'responsibility' and 'insecurity,' and when people feel threatened a self-fulfilling prophecy occurs, one tiny incident at a time: one night someone wrote 'Rapists!!!' on one of the road signs on the outskirts of Beartown. A couple of days later a group of eight-year-olds from both Beartown and Hed were sent home from summer camp after a violent fight, caused by the kids from Hed chanting 'Beartown Rapists!' at the kids from Beartown.

Leo is sitting on the beach today, and fifty feet away sit Kevin's old friends, big, strong eighteen-year-olds. They're wearing red Hed Hockey caps now. They're the ones who wrote online that Maya had 'deserved it' and that Kevin was obviously innocent because 'who the hell would want to touch that slut even with a shitty stick?' As if Maya had ever asked any of them to touch her with anything at all. Now the same boys claim that Kevin was never one of them, and they'll go on repeating the same lie until he's associated only with Beartown, because however this story gets distorted these boys will make themselves the heroes. They always win.

Leo is six years younger than most of them; he's an awful lot smaller and an awful lot weaker, but some of his friends have still started to tell him that he 'ought to do something.' That one of those bastards 'needs to be punished.' That he has to 'be a man.' Masculinity is complicated when you're twelve. And at every other age, too.

Then there's a noise. Heads look down at towels. All over the beach cell phones start to vibrate. First one or two, then all at once, until the buzzing blurs together into an invisible orchestra where all the instruments are being tuned at the same time.

The news is arriving.

Beartown Ice Hockey no longer exists.

'It's only a sports club, there are more important things.' It's easy to say that sort of thing if you believe that sports is merely a matter of numbers. But it never is, and you can only understand that if you start with the simplest question: How does it feel for a child to play hockey? It's not so hard to answer that. Have you ever been in love? That's how it feels.

A sweaty sixteen-year-old is running along the road outside Beartown. His name is Amat. In a garage out in the woods, a dirty eighteen-year-old is helping his dad fetch tools and stack tires. His name is Bobo. In a garden a four-and-a-half-year-old girl is firing pucks from a patio into a brick wall. Her name is Alicia.

Amat hopes that one day he's going to be good enough for hockey to take him and his mother away from here. For him sports are a future. Bobo just hopes he can have another season of laughter and no responsibilities, seeing as he knows that every day after that will be like all his dad's days. For Bobo sports are a last chance for play.

For Alicia, the four-and-a-half-year-old girl firing pucks on a patio? Have you ever been in love? That's what sports are for her.

Cell phones buzz. The town stops. Nothing travels faster than a good story.

★

Amat, sixteen years old, stops out on the road. Hands on knees, chest heavy around his heart: *bang-bang-bang-bang-bang*. Bobo, eighteen years old, rolls another car into the workshop and starts to beat out a dent in the plate: *bang-bang-bang*. Alicia, four and a half years old, stands on a patio in a garden. Her gloves are too big and the stick is too long, but she still fires a puck at the wall as hard as she can: *bang!*

They've grown up in a small town in a big forest. There are plenty of adults around here who say that work is getting harder to find and the winters are getting worse, that the trees are denser and the houses sparser, that all the natural resources may be out in the countryside but all the money still ends up in the big damn cities. 'Because bears shit in the woods, and everyone else shits on Beartown.' It's easy for children to love hockey, because you don't have time to think when you're playing it. Memory loss is one of the finest things sports can give us.

But now the text messages arrive. Amat stops, Bobo lets go of the hammer, and soon someone is going to have to try to explain to a four-and-a-half-year-old girl what it means when a hockey club 'goes bankrupt.' Try to make it sound like it's just a sports club collapsing, even though sports clubs never really do that. They just cease to exist. It's the people who collapse.

In the Bearskin pub they usually say that the door should be kept closed 'so the flies don't get cold.' They usually say other things too: 'You've got an opinion about hockey? You couldn't even find your own arse with both hands in your back pockets!' 'You want to talk tactics? You're more confused than a cow on AstroTurf!' 'You think our defence is going to be better next season? Don't piss on my leg and tell me it's raining!' But today no one is arguing; today everything is quiet. It's unbearable. Ramona pours whisky into all the glasses, one last time. The five uncles, seventy years old, maybe more, raise their glasses in a perfunctory toast. Five empty glasses hit the bar. *Bang. Bang. Bang. Bang. Bang.* The uncles stand up and leave, go their separate ways. Will they call each other tomorrow? What for? What on earth are they going to argue about, if not a hockey team?

There's a lot that isn't talked about in a small town, but there are no secrets when you're twelve years old, because at that age you know where on the Internet to look. Leo's read everything. Now he's wearing a long-sleeved top, in spite of the heat. He says it's because he got sunburned, but he just doesn't want anyone to see the scratch marks. He can't stop scratching himself at night; the hate has crept under his skin. He's never been in a fight, not even about hockey. He often wonders if he's like his dad and just doesn't have violence in him. But now he just wishes someone would pick a fight with him, bump into him accidentally, give him one single reason to pick up the nearest heavy object and smash his face in with it.

'Brothers and sisters should look out for each other,' that's what everyone says when you're growing up. 'Don't argue! Stop fighting! Brothers and sisters should look out for each other!' Leo and Maya were supposed to have a big brother; perhaps he would have been able to protect them. His name was Isak, and he died before they were born of the sort of illness that makes it impossible for Leo to believe that there's a god. Leo barely understood that Isak had been a real person until he was seven years old and found a photograph album with pictures of him with their parents. They laughed so much in those pictures. Hugged each other so tightly, loved each other so infinitely. Isak taught Leo an unbearable number of things that day, without even existing. He taught him that love isn't enough. That's a terrible thing to learn when you're seven years old. Or at any age.

He's twelve now, and he's trying to be a man. Whatever that means. He tries to stop scratching his skin raw at night, tries to sob silently, curled up tightly under the covers, tries to hate without anyone else seeing or realizing. Tries to kill the thought that won't stop thudding at his temples. Brothers and sisters should look out for each other, and he wasn't able to protect his sister.

*

He wasn't able to protect his sister he wasn't able to protect his sister he wasn't able to protect his sister.

Last night he scratched his chest and stomach until a long wound opened up in his skin and blood started to seep out. This morning he looked at himself in the mirror and thought that the wound looked like a fuse leading to his heart. He wonders if it's burning inside him. And how long it's got left.

4

Women Are Always the Problem

The older generation used to call Beartown and Hed 'the Bear and the Bull,' especially when the towns were due to play each other at hockey. That was many years ago now, and no one really knows if Hed already had the bull as the emblem on their jerseys at the time, or if they put it there after being given the nickname. There was a lot of livestock around Hed in those days, more open countryside, so when industry arrived it was easier to build factories there. The people in Beartown were known to be hard workers, but the forest was denser there, so the money ended up in the neighbouring town to the south. Older generations used to speak metaphorically about the struggle between the Bear and the Bull and how that kept things in balance, stopped one of them from having all the power. Perhaps it was different back then, when there were still enough jobs and resources for both towns. It's harder now, because the idea that violence can ever be controlled is always an illusion.

Maya is over at Ana's. These are the few minutes of peace and quiet before the text message arrives, the last moments between Kevin leaving town and all hell breaking loose again. They had three weeks when people almost seemed to forget that Maya existed. It was wonderful. And it will soon be over.

Ana checks that the gun cabinet is locked, then fetches the key and makes sure the weapons inside aren't loaded. She lies to Maya and says she's going to 'clean them,' but Maya knows she does that only when her dad has started to drink again. The final sign that a hunter's alcoholism has crossed the line is when he forgets to lock the cabinet or leaves a loaded weapon inside. That's happened only once, when Ana was little and her mum had just moved out, but Ana has never quite stopped worrying.

Maya is lying on the floor with her guitar on her chest, pretending not to understand. Ana carries the burden of being the child of an alcoholic, and it's a lonely struggle.

'Hey, idiot?' Ana eventually says.

'Yeah, what, you moron?' Maya smiles.

'Play something,' Ana demands.

Maya giggles. 'Don't give me orders, I'm not your musical slave.'

Ana grins. You can't cultivate that sort of friendship, it only grows in the wild. 'Please?'

'Learn to play yourself, you lazy cow.'

'I don't need to, you idiot, I'm holding a rifle. Play or I'll shoot!'

Maya roars with laughter. They had promised each other that. That when summer came, the men in this stupid town weren't going to take their laughter away from them.

'Nothing miserable, though!' Ana adds.

'Shut it! If you want to listen to your stupid, bouncy blippety blip music you can get a computer,' Maya says, giggling.

Ana rolls her eyes.

'Okay, I'm still holding a gun! If you play your junkie music and I shoot myself in the head, it'll actually be your fault!'

They both roar with laughter. And Maya plays the happiest songs she knows, even if in Ana's opinion they're really not that happy at all. But this summer she takes what she can get.

They're interrupted by two short buzzing sounds from their phones. Then two more, followed by another two.

Being the general manager of a hockey club isn't a full-time job. It's three. When Peter's wife, Kira, can't be bothered to hide her irritation, she usually says, 'You've got two marriages, one with hockey and one with me.' She doesn't add that half of all marriages end in divorce. She doesn't have to.

The local politicians in the conference room will downplay this meeting, say it was 'only about sports.' The biggest lie Peter has ever managed to make himself believe is that hockey and politics aren't linked. They always are, but when politics work in our favour we call it 'cooperation,' and when it favours others we call it 'corruption.' Peter looks out of the window. There are always flags raised in front of the council building so the bastards inside can see which way the wind is blowing.

'The council . . . we . . . it has been decided that we should apply to host the World Skiing Championships. Beartown and Hed together,' one of the councillors says.

He's trying to look authoritative now, which is hard when you're simultaneously picking muffin crumbs from your jacket pocket. Everyone knows that he's been trying to get funding for a conference hotel for years, and the World Championships would give him the chance. As luck would have it, this particular councillor's brother-in-law works at the Ski Federation, and his wife runs a business that arranges hunting trips and 'survival courses' in the forest for wealthy businessmen from the big cities who evidently can't survive without a minibar and spa centre. Another councillor adds, 'We need to think about the region's image, Peter. The taxpayers are worried. All this negative publicity has created insecurity . . .'

He says it as if insecurity is the problem. As if it isn't THE PROBLEM that's the problem. He pours Peter some coffee; a different sort of man might have thrown the cup at the wall, but Peter has no violence in him. He never even fought on the ice when he was a player. These men used to sneer at him for that behind his back, but they really can't be bothered to do it out of sight anymore.

They know that Peter's weakness is loyalty, that he feels he owes his town. Hockey here has given him everything, and it's good at reminding him about that. A poster in the changing room at the rink says, 'A great deal is expected of anyone who's been given a lot.'

Another councillor, who prides himself on being the sort of man who 'tells it like it is,' says, 'Beartown has no junior team, and not much of an A-team! You've already lost all your best players and almost all your sponsors to Hed. We have to think of the taxpayers!'

One year ago the same councillor was asked a critical question by the local paper about the council's plans to finance an expensive new arena. He answered without a trace of hesitation, 'You know what Beartown's taxpayers want? They want to watch hockey!' They're so easy to blame, no matter what your opinion might be: taxpayers.

The same money will end up in the same pockets, the pockets are just moving town to Hed. Peter wants to protest but can't bring himself to. There's always been graft involved in council funding of sports, not just as straightforward 'grants' but also tucked away as 'loans' and 'subsidies.' Like when the council 'rented' the parking spaces outside the rink, even though the council already owned the land. Or when the council paid to 'rent the ice rink for the use of the general public' for all the members of the 'general public' who were desperate to skate between 2 am and 5 am every Wednesday. At one point, one of the hockey club's board members was simultaneously on the board of the council's property company and got the company to buy expensive 'sponsorship packages' for hockey games that were never played. Peter knew all about it. The former management of the hockey club was always corrupt. Peter had argued about it at first but eventually had to accept that those were just 'the rules of the game.' In a small town, sports doesn't survive without the support of the regional council. He can't start shouting about corruption now, because the politicians know exactly how much he knows.

They're going to liquidate his club. They just want to make sure he's going to keep his mouth shut.

The red hats of the well-built eighteen-year-olds carry the emblem of a charging bull. They're taking up more and more space on the beach, stretching the boundaries to see if anyone dare try to stop them. Leo's hatred for them knows no limits.

When Kevin left town, the story changed, but his old friends quickly adapted to new truths. All they needed was a new leader. And William Lyt, a forward on the first line and Kevin's former neighbour, put himself up and gave them the version of history they were longing for. He'd heard his parents repeat it at the kitchen table for several months: 'We're the victims here, we had victory in the final stolen from us. We would have won if Kevin had played! But Peter Andersson insisted on bringing politics into it! And then he tried to blame *US* for the fact that that psychopath raped that girl, even though we haven't done a damn thing! And you know why? Because Peter Andersson has always hated us. Everyone listens to him just because he was once a pro in the NHL, as if that makes him so morally superior. But do you think Kevin would have been prevented from playing in the final if it hadn't been Peter's daughter? If any of our sisters had been raped, do you think Peter would have called the cops to pick Kevin up the same day as the final? Peter's a hypocrite! Kevin's just an excuse, Peter never wanted boys from the Heights in Beartown Hockey, and you know why? Because some of us happened to be born into families with money, and that doesn't suit the myth of Peter Andersson as the great saviour!'

William's parents' words echo from his lips. Every season his mum, Maggan Lyt, gets annoyed that the club promotes kids from the poor parts of town as figureheads but when it's time for the bills to be paid it's always the parents from the Heights who are expected to open their wallets. 'When are people going to get tired of paying for Peter Andersson's social experiments?' she complained to anyone who would listen back in the spring, when news spread that the club was starting a hockey school for four-and five-year-old girls.

'They want a girls' club!' William bellows on the beach.

The words work because they're easy to understand. Everyone in his team has felt under attack and misunderstood since the rape. So it's a relief to hear that Peter Andersson hates them, because the easiest reason to hate him back is the conviction that he started it.

★

Peter looks around the table. He's expected to 'take it like a man,' but he's no longer sure what the politicians see him as: the boy who was raised by Beartown Ice Hockey Club? Who became team captain and led a dying backwoods team all the way to become second best in the country twenty years ago? Or the NHL professional he later became? Before he was persuaded to come back home and become general manager of the club once it had tumbled through the leagues, where, against all odds, he built up one of the best junior teams in the country and made the little club big again. Is he any of those men?

Or is he just a dad now? Because it was his daughter who was raped. He was the one who went with her to the police that morning back in March. He was the one who stood in the parking lot outside the rink and watched as the police pulled the junior team's star player off the bus just before they set off for the biggest game of their lives. He knows what all the men in here think, what men everywhere are thinking: 'If it had been my daughter, I'd have killed the man who did that to her.' And not a night goes by without Peter wishing he was that sort of man. That he possessed that violence. But instead he accepts the cup of coffee. Because masculinity is hard at any age.

One of the politicians begins to explain, and his tone veers between sympathetic and patronizing: 'You need to be a team player now, Peter. We have to act in the best interests of everyone in the district. A good reputation is vital to our hopes of attracting the World Skiing Championships. We're going to build a new arena in Hed and establish the hockey school there . . .'

Peter doesn't need to hear the rest; he's heard this vision of the future, he was there when it was written. First the rink and hockey school, then the shopping centre and better links to the highway. A conference hotel and a ski competition that gets shown on television. And then who knows? Maybe an airport? Sports are only sports until someone who doesn't give a damn about sports has something to gain from them; then sports suddenly become economics. The hockey club was going to rescue the entire council district, and that remains the case. Just not Peter's hockey club.

Another of the men, whose brain has evidently been on holiday for at least the past couple of hours, throws his arms out. 'Yes, obviously we're very sorry about . . . the situation. With your daughter.'

That's what they say: 'Your daughter.' Never 'Maya,' never her name. Because that allows them to insinuate what they really want him to think about: If it had been anyone else's daughter, would Peter have let Kevin play in the final? The politicians call it 'the situation,' but the PR consultants the council has brought in call it 'the scandal.' As if the problem wasn't that a girl was raped but that it happened to become public knowledge. The PR consultants have explained to the politicians that there are other communities that have 'been afflicted by similar scandals that have negatively impacted the town's brand.' That's not going to happen here. And the easiest way to bury the scandal is to bury Beartown Ice Hockey. Then everyone can point to the 'raft of measures' and show how they're building a bigger club in Hed, with 'better morals and greater responsibility,' without having to answer for the fact that it's the same men as always who are building it.

'All the damn journalists who keep calling, Peter. People are getting nervous! The council needs to turn the page!'

As if the journalists weren't calling Peter's family. Neither he nor Maya has spoken to them. They've done everything right, they've kept their mouths shut, but it doesn't make any difference. They didn't keep their mouths shut enough.

While eighteen-year-old William spent the summer gathering his team at Hed Hockey beneath the banner of a shared hatred of Peter Andersson, other conversations have been taking place in other parts of the district. William Lyt's father is on the board of the golf club; he plays with bank managers and politicians and is popular not only because he knows people with money but also because he's the kind of man who 'speaks his mind.' The council needs the business community's support to bid for the World Skiing Championships, so the business community has made one serious condition: one hockey club, not two. They say it's a question of 'responsible economics.' They stress the word 'responsible.'

So now, down on the beach a few days before Midsummer's Eve, all the young people's phones start to buzz at the same time. First the beach falls silent; then a group of muscular eighteen-year-olds burst into loud, malicious roars of laughter. None louder than William Lyt. He climbs into a tree and hangs up two red Hed Hockey flags so that they billow out like bleeding wounds over the green leaves, the colour of Beartown.

His team gathers in a semicircle beneath the trees, waiting for trouble. But they're too big, too strong; everyone on the beach goes to the same school, so nobody dares. The beach belongs to Lyt after that. It is divided in the way that all worlds are divided between people: between those who are listened to and those who aren't.

And the teenagers on the beach who see those young men and hate them without being able to do anything, the ones who love Beartown Hockey but aren't strong enough to take on William Lyt's gang, they now have to direct their fury towards someone else. Someone weaker.

Maya and Ana read the first anonymous texts, then they switch off their phones. 'This is your fault.' 'If the club dies so do you, slut!' 'We'll get your dad, too!' Ana and Maya know what's happening now, know who's going to bear the brunt of the hatred and threats.

Maya goes to the bathroom and throws up. Ana sits on the floor of the hall outside. She has read that support groups for victims of rape call themselves 'survivors.' Because that's what they do each day: they survive what they've been subjected to, over and over again. Ana wonders if there's a word for everyone else, the people who let it happen. People are already prepared to destroy each other's worlds just to avoid having to admit that many of us bear small portions of a collective guilt for a boy's actions. It's easier if you deny it, if you tell yourself that it's an 'isolated incident.' Ana dreams of killing Kevin for what he's done to her best friend, but most of all she dreams of crushing the whole town for what it's still putting Maya through.

The idiots won't say it was Kevin who killed Beartown Ice Hockey; they'll say that 'the scandal' killed the club. Because their real problem isn't that Kevin raped someone but that Maya got raped. If she hadn't existed, it wouldn't have happened. Women are always the problem in the men's world.

Maya and Ana pack their backpacks, walk out through the door and into the forest without even knowing where they're going. Because anywhere at all is better than here. Ana doesn't take her rifle. It's a decision she'll regret.

Leo waits until it starts to get dark. He hides alone at the edge of the forest until the beach is empty. Then he creeps back down to the lake, climbs up into the tree, and sets fire to the red flags. He films the flames consuming the words and the Hed Hockey logo burning. Then he posts the clip anonymously online where he knows everyone in the school will see it.

People will say that violence came to Beartown this summer, but that won't be true, because it was already here. Because people are always dependent upon other people, and we can't ever really forgive one another for that.

5

Everyone Is a Hundred Different Things

A young man with a bare chest and a backpack is walking alone through the forest. He has a tattoo of a bear on his arm. A well-dressed lawyer is sitting in an office. She has photographs of her family on her desk and is just fielding another call from a moving company without understanding why. At the same time a stranger in a Jeep is driving along a main road with a list of names in the glove compartment.

Their cell phones buzz. Peter Andersson hasn't even left the meeting in the council building, but the politicians have already leaked the news that Beartown Ice Hockey Club is going into liquidation. The politicians are learning things like that from their expensive PR consultants: that you have to 'control the narrative.'

The young man in the forest, the lawyer in her office, and the stranger in the Jeep all pick up their phones. They are all involved.

Everyone is a hundred different things, but in other people's eyes we usually get the chance to be only one of them. Kira Andersson is a lawyer, highly educated in two different countries, with two university degrees, but in Beartown she will always be 'Peter Andersson's wife.' There are days when she hates herself for hating that so much. For that not being enough for her, just belonging to someone else.

She eats lunch at her desk, surrounded by pink Post-it notes relating to work and yellow Post-it notes reminding her of things to buy and errands she has to run for various members of her family. Beside her computer stand photographs of Leo and Maya. The guilt she feels from their eyes could have destroyed her had she not been interrupted by the stamping sound in the corridor.

Kira almost smiles then, in spite of this hellish summer, because she knows which of her colleagues is about to storm in. Partly because she's the only other workaholic still in the office just before Midsummer and partly because a door never opens when she passes through it; it throws itself out of her way. Her colleague is over six feet tall and makes enough noise to be the same size in width. She's the worst loser Kira has ever known, and her standard reply whenever anyone complains about work is 'Shut up and send an invoice!' As usual, she starts the conversation in the middle of a sentence, as if it's Kira's fault for having the gall not to have been present when it started:

'. . . and now the pizzeria's closed, Kira! "Closed for the holidays." What the hell? What sort of person takes a holiday from a pizzeria? That ought to be classed as a vital public service, like . . . doctors and . . . firemen, and . . . shoe shops! And there I was, thinking I might have sex with the guy behind the counter, he always looks so sad, and the sad ones are always the best in bed! What are you eating? Have you got much left?'

Kira sighs as if she were about to blow out the candles on her very last birthday cake. She holds up the plastic tub containing her lunch. Her colleague pretends to throw up.

'Very mature,' Kira says.

'What *is* that?' her colleague whimpers.

Kira bursts out laughing. She didn't mean to, which makes it wonderful, a few seconds of normality. Her colleague has the eating habits of a teenager; she never asks 'What's good?,' just 'What do you get the most of?' She reads menus as if they were declarations of war. Kira gestures encouragingly with her fork. 'This is called "salad." It's a bit like meat, but you don't have to kill any animals. Here, try it!'

Her colleague flinches. 'No way, it smells like something you dragged out of the ass of a corpse.'

'Oh, come on, seriously?' Kira says, disgusted.

'What?' her colleague asks in surprise.

'You're like a little kid!' Kira says.

'*You're* like a little kid! Shut up and send an invoice!' her colleague mutters, then lands on a chair as if she'd been thrown off a rooftop.

30

Kira is about to say something but gets distracted by the ring of the phone on her desk. She's expecting it to be Peter, but the voice at the other end exclaims cheerfully, 'Is that Kira Andersson? I'm calling from Johansson's Movers, we've got an order in your name for fifty new removal boxes. Is it okay to leave them in your garden?'

Kira doesn't even hear the end of the sentence. She just sees her colleague open her laptop, read something, and go white. The next moment Kira's cell phone buzzes.

Peter gets up from his chair. Most of the politicians on the other side of the table don't humiliate him by shaking his hand, they just walk out. But one of them stops and says with fake benevolence, 'It was impressive, Peter, what you managed to do with the juniors back in the spring. A unique achievement, frankly, our lads from our little town putting up a fight against the big teams. If only they'd . . . won. Then maybe . . . you know.'

Peter knows. All too well. In a sport where Cinderella stories are under threat of extinction, where the big clubs' hockey schools vacuum up all the talent from the smaller clubs, Beartown managed to get its best and brightest boys to stay and fight for their home team. They made it all the way to the final but had to play that game without their biggest star. So they almost won. And that's not enough.

Beartown is a hockey town, and kids are raised with the philosophy 'The stats never lie.' Either you're the best or you're everyone else, and the best don't make excuses, they find a way to win. With all available means, at any cost. People talk about a 'winner's mentality,' because a winner has something that others lack, a special brain that takes for granted that it was born to be heroic. When a game comes down to the last decisive seconds, the winner bangs his stick down on the ice and yells to his teammates to pass to him, because a winner doesn't ask for the puck, he demands it. When thousands of spectators stand up and roar, most people become uncertain and back away, but the winner steps up. That's the sort of mentality we're talking about. Everyone dreams about being the best, about being the one who fires the final shot in the last crucial moments of the season, but there are desperately few of us who actually dare to take the chance when absolutely everything is at stake. That's the difference between us.

Just over twenty years ago, Beartown's A-team could have been the best in the country. All season everyone in town kept repeating the same thing: 'Beartown against the rest!' Journalists in the big cities thought Beartown had no chance. Their well-paid opponents underestimated the team, but when they came to Beartown something happened: when their team bus drove mile after mile straight through the forest, when they stepped into a shabby building and were confronted with stands that had been transformed into roaring green walls on all sides, the giants trembled. The rink was a fortress that season; the whole town would march there, the team played with an entire community behind it. No one cared if the big clubs had the money, because this was the home of hockey. 'Beartown against the rest.'

But the very last game was an away game, in the capital. In the dying seconds, Peter Andersson got the puck. Deep in the forest lay an entire community that was going to live or die on the actions of his stick, and how tiny are the margins for a sports club at a time like that? The gap between the elite and the rest is immense in hockey: the teams at the top of the league get all the television money and the millions in sponsorship, while those lower down have to learn that 'the best team always wins.' So when Peter got the puck it was more than a shot, more than a game; it was a chance for the little town to fell a giant. What a fantastic story that would have been. For one single evening, after all the crap the people in this forest had been through, Beartown finally had a chance to feel that its turn had arrived. It would have been the sort of story that makes everyone love sports: that the biggest and richest don't always win.

So Peter took the shot. And missed. A town held its breath, and then it couldn't breathe. The end-of-game buzzer sounded, its opponents won, the following season Beartown tumbled out of the top division and never managed to fight its way back.

Peter moved to the NHL and turned professional but got

injured. His career passed as quickly as a dream. Then he came home and against all the odds built up a junior team that became the best in the country. Almost.

The politician in the doorway shrugs. 'Winning cures everything, Peter.'

He might as well have said what he meant: 'You're not a winner, Peter. Because winners win. That's how we know who they are.' Winners always get that last shot right. Winners don't mix up what's going on off the ice with what happens on it. Winners don't ask the police to drag the team's biggest star off a bus on the way to the biggest game. Winners know that winning cures everything in this community but that a second place doesn't cure anything.

The politician pats him half-heartedly on the shoulder. 'Listen, Peter, maybe you could see this as an opportunity? A chance to try a different job? Get a bit more time with your family!'

Peter feels like telling him to go to hell but instead walks in silence out of the council building. He walks around the building, stops below a staircase, and leans over a flower bed. When he's sure that none of those bastards can see him standing there alone, he throws up.

His phone rings. It's Kira. He realizes that the rumour is making the rounds but can't bring himself to answer. He doesn't want to hear the disappointment in his wife's voice and is worried that she'll hear the sob in his. She calls again and again until he switches his phone off. The problem with living your whole life for a hockey club is that he hasn't got a damn clue who he is without it. He gets into the car and drives, his fingers clutching the wheel so tightly that blood starts to seep from his torn cuticles.

There's a stranger sitting in a Jeep, watching the road silently and intently through sunglasses, inhaling deeply from a cigar and letting the smoke roll out from the open window. The Jeep is parked in the shade of some trees and is rusty and nondescript enough for no one to pay any attention to it. The list of names is in the glove compartment. 'Peter Andersson' is written at the top. When Peter gets into his car and drives off, the stranger follows him.

6

If There Isn't a War, They Start One

The eighteen-year-old man in the forest takes off his backpack, puts it down on the grass, and climbs up into a tree. Summer has started to make his long hair fairer and his skin darker around the bear tattoo. His name is Benjamin, but only his mum and sisters call him that, everyone else knows him as Benji. His name is rarely associated with memories of a positive childhood – ever since preschool people have been saying that the boy would end up in prison or the cemetery. Hockey was both his salvation and damnation, because all his worst characteristics off the ice made him admired on it. Kevin was the star, Benji his protector. Brothers. The town loved Kevin's hands, but they worshipped Benji's fists. Whenever anyone in Beartown tells the old joke 'I went to see a fight, and suddenly an ice hockey game broke out,' they're always telling it about him.

So the town was shocked when Kevin was accused of rape, but it was shocked almost as much when Benji took Maya Andersson's side against his brother. He stayed in Beartown rather than move to Hed Hockey Club. Benji Ovich did the right thing. And for what? Mocking text messages from anonymous senders arrive one after the other, telling him that his club is dead now. He made the wrong choice. He's got nothing. A few months back, he was playing alongside his best friend in one of the best teams in the country. Now he's sitting alone in a tree, smoking and getting high, and is on his way to proving everyone who doubted him right: 'Sooner or later that boy is going to do himself or someone else some serious damage.'

Every time Kira Andersson looks at the pictures of Peter, Maya, and Leo on her desk this summer, she feels endlessly ashamed at the fact that when she's here at work it's easier to imagine that they're a normal family. That the four of them aren't burning to ashes inside, that the house they share hasn't long since fallen silent because none of them has any words left.

Maya asked her family to stop talking about the rape. They were sitting at the breakfast table at the start of the summer, and she said it without any drama: 'I need to move on now.' Peter and Kira tried to smile and nod, but their eyes bored holes in the parquet floor. You have to be supportive, you can't grab hold of your daughter and yell that *we* need to talk about it, that it's her parents who feel scared and abandoned and . . . selfish. Because that is what they're being, isn't it? Selfish.

Kira knows people don't understand that she can go on working or that Peter can go on caring about hockey, but the truth is that sometimes they're the only things they have the strength to care about. When everything else is collapsing, you throw yourself into the only thing you know you can control, the only place you feel you know what you're doing. Everything else hurts too much. So you go to work and hide there, the way mountain climbers dig holes in the snow when a storm hits.

Kira isn't naive, but she's a parent, she's been trying to see a way forward. Kevin is gone; the psychologist said Maya was making progress in her treatment for the trauma, so perhaps everything could still be okay. That's what Kira has been telling herself. Peter was going to meet the council, the club would get the money it needed, everything would sort itself out.

But now she hangs up on the moving company that has received an order for packing boxes in her name. She reads the text that has just arrived. It's from a journalist: 'We're trying to get hold of your husband for a comment about Beartown Ice Hockey going into liquidation.' The next text is from a neighbour, saying 'Didn't know you were moving??' There's a screenshot attached from a real estate agent's website, where someone has put the Anderssons' house up for sale. The photographs are very recent. Someone has been in their yard that morning.

Kira calls Peter, but he doesn't answer. She knows what's going to happen now; if the hockey club collapses, it won't matter whose fault it really is, because some people in this town have already started to look for scapegoats. It will be Peter's fault. Maya's fault. The general manager's. The slut's.

Kira calls Peter again. Again. Again. The last time she tries, the call doesn't even go through. Her colleague backs away when Kira slams her fist onto her desk as hard as she can; she hears her fingers crunch but goes on punching with all the strength the hundred different women inside her can summon up:

BANG. BANG. BANG-BANG-BANG.

Benji curls up, smoke seeping from his nostrils. He's heard people say that drugs lift them up into the skies, but for Benji it's the sea: he doesn't fly, he just floats. Drugs keep him on the surface without his having to make any effort, and the rest of the time he feels he has to swim for his life the whole time.

As a child he always loved the summer, when the foliage lets boys hide in trees without being seen from the ground. He's always had a lot to hide from, as anyone does who's different in a locker room where everyone learns that you have to be a single unit, a clan, a team, in order to win together. So Benji became what they needed: the wild one. So feared that once, when he was wounded, the coach put him on the bench anyway. He didn't play a single minute, but the opposing team still didn't dare lay a finger on Kevin.

Benji taught himself some of that hardness: he climbed trees in a way that his coach used to laugh and say made him 'half tank, half monkey,' and he chopped wood out at his sister's boarding kennels and punched the stack of wood into shape to harden his knuckles. But some of the hardness was just there inside him, it couldn't be injected or driven out, and it made him unpredictable. One winter when he was little, some of the boys on the team called him 'sledge,' because he wasn't driven to training by his parents but came on his bike with his hockey bag on a sledge behind him. The nickname lasted a few months, until one of the boys went too far and Benji came into the locker room with the sledge in his hands and knocked out two of his teeth. There weren't many nicknames after that.

He's sitting quietly in the tree now, but inside him everything is chaos. When a child gets a best friend, it's like a first infatuation; we want to be with them all the time, and if they leave us it's like an amputation. Kevin and Benji came from such different parts of town that they could easily have been different species, but the ice became their dance floor. Kevin had the genius and Benji the violence. It took a decade before everyone realized that there was a bit of genius in Benji, too, and a lot more violence in Kevin.

How much can you forgive your best friend for? How can you know in advance? One night back in the spring Kevin stood shaking in the forest, not far from here, and asked Benji to forgive him. Benji turned and walked away from him. They never spoke again.

That morning three weeks ago when Kevin left town, Benji was sitting in the same tree as he is now. Hitting the back of his head against the trunk, harder and harder. *Bang. Bang. Bang*. He's high on drugs and heavy with hatred; he hears voices and at first isn't sure if he's imagining them. Then he sees them, they're coming closer, he sees them through the trees. His muscles tighten.

He's going to hurt someone.

If you want to know why people sacrifice everything for love, you have to start by asking how they fell in love. Sometimes it doesn't take anything at all for us to start loving something. Just time. All adults know, deep down, that hockey is make-believe, an invented game, but when you're five years old your heart is fairly small. So you have to love with all of it at once.

Peter Andersson's mum was ill, and his dad used to get so drunk that he would shout as if his son didn't have ears and would hit him as if they were complete strangers. Peter grew up with a head full of voices whispering that he was no good at anything, and the first time they fell silent was when he pulled on a pair of skates. You can't give a boy what he found in hockey classes and then take it away without there being consequences. Summer came, the rink closed, but five-year-old Peter marched around to the home of the A-team coach and banged on the door. 'When does hockey start?' he demanded to know.

Sune, the A-team coach smiled. 'In the autumn.' He was already an old man, and his stomach was so round that he could talk only in circular arguments. 'How long is it until then?' the five-year-old asked. 'Till the autumn?' The coach grunted. 'I can't tell time,' the five-year-old said. 'It's several months,' the coach muttered. 'Can I wait here?' the five-year-old asked. 'Until autumn?' the coach exclaimed. 'Is that a long time?' the five-year-old asked. It was the start of a lifelong friendship.

Sune never asked about the bruises, the five-year-old never talked about them, but every blow he received at home was visible in his eyes the first time he learned to shoot a puck in the coach's small garden. The coach was aware that hockey can't change a child's life, but it can offer a different one. A way out and up.

Sune taught Peter what a club is. It's not something you blame nor something you demand things of. 'Because it's us, Peter, Beartown Ice Hockey is you and me. The best and worst things it achieves demonstrate the best and worst sides of us.' He taught Peter other things, too, such as standing tall both when you win and when you lose, and that the most talented players have a duty to elevate the weakest because 'a great deal is expected of anyone who's been given a lot.'

That first evening, Sune walked home with the five-year-old. They stopped a few hundred feet from the boy's house, and the coach said that if the boy came around the next day, he could carry on shooting practice. 'You promise?' the boy asked. Sune held out his hand and said, 'I promise. And you have to keep promises, don't you?' The boy shook his hand and nodded. Then the old man sat down on a bench with the boy and taught him how to tell time, so he could count the minutes until tomorrow.

Sometimes it doesn't take anything at all for us to start loving something, just time. Young Peter Andersson dreamed about the same thing every night for several years, the sound of a puck leaving a stick and flying into the side of a house:

Bang.

Benji Ovich's mother hardly ever talks about his father, but on the rare occasions when it does happen, she always closes her eyes and whispers, 'Some people are just like that. If there isn't a war, they start one.'

Benji has been told that he resembles him, his father, but he doesn't know how. Maybe more inside than out. He knows his dad was in pain, so much pain that one day he couldn't bear it any longer. Hunters in these parts never use the word 'suicide,' they just say, 'Alain took his rifle and went into the woods.' Benji has always wondered if he had been planning it for a long time or if he just suddenly did it. He wonders the same thing when he sees pictures of lonely men who have done terrible things on the news: Why that day in particular? Why not another day? Did you make a choice, or did it just happen?

Benji knows that grief and anger can reprogramme a brain like chemicals and drugs do. Maybe there's a time bomb inside some people's heads the whole time, just waiting for a switch to be thrown. Maybe his mum's right, some people are just the sort who start wars.

From the tree he sees Maya and Ana come through the forest. He will never be able to explain what happened to him then; it was just an instinct being awakened. Something gets switched off, something else gets switched on. He climbs down and picks his backpack off the ground, takes something from it, and holds it in his hand as he starts to move through the trees.

Stalking them.

★

Maya and Ana are walking aimlessly through the forest, slower and slower the farther they get. They're not talking; they already know everything each other might want to say anyway. They've always known that Beartown isn't an easy place to grow up in if you're different, and one of the worst things about becoming an adult is starting to realize that perhaps nowhere is. There are bastards everywhere.

The two young women have never really had much in common, the princess and the child of nature, the musician and the hunter. The first time they met was when Ana pulled Maya out of a hole in the ice when they were children. Maya had only just moved here at the time, and Ana had never had a friend, so they had saved each other's lives. Ana used to tease Maya for never being able to walk quietly in the forest, saying she moved like an elk in high heels. Maya used to joke that Ana was the way she was because Ana's mum had had an affair with a squirrel.

She stopped saying that when Ana's mum moved away. In return Ana stopped teasing Maya about being dependent on decent Wi-Fi. For a few years they were equals, but teenage years always change the balance of power in friendships between girls. When they started high school, Ana's knowledge of how to survive in the forest wasn't worth anything, whereas Maya knew how to survive in the school corridors. But this summer? They're not safe anywhere now.

Ana is walking ahead, and Maya is following, looking at her hair. She often thinks that Ana is simultaneously the strongest and weakest person she knows. Ana's dad is drinking again; it's no one's fault, that's just the way it is. Maya wishes she could take the pain away from Ana, but she can no more do that than Ana can take the rape away from Maya. They're falling into different chasms. Maya has her nightmares, and Ana has her own reasons for not being able to sleep. She sleeps with the dogs on the nights her dad comes home late and rages about in the kitchen like a monster made up of sorrow and unspoken words. The dogs lie in a protective circle around Ana without her asking them. Beloved creatures. Her dad has never, not so much as once, raised his hand against his daughter. But she's still frightened of him when he's been drinking. Men don't know their own weight, they don't understand the physical terror they can instil in another person simply by tumbling through a door. They're hurricanes tearing through a forest of saplings as they get up drunkenly from the kitchen table and stumble from room to room without being aware of what they're trampling on. The next morning they don't remember anything; the empty bottles have been cleared away and the glasses washed in secret, and the house is silent. No one says anything. They must never see the destruction they've left behind them in their children.

Ana stops and turns around. Maya looks at her and smiles weakly. 'God, I love you so much,' she thinks, and Ana knows. So she asks, 'Forced to have an operation to have a pig's snout or one to have a pig's arse?'

Maya laughs loudly. This is their game, has been ever since they were little. Either-or. 'Snout. That curly tail would be way too lumpy to sit on when I'm playing guitar.'

'You're so stupid!'

'I'm stupid? Do you even hear the stuff that comes out of your mouth?'

Ana snorts. She looks off through the trees. 'Okay, how about this one: Be unhappy and live for a hundred years or be happy for a single year and then die?'

Maya thinks in silence. She never gets to answer. By the time she reacts, Ana has already spun around, staring at the trees. She should have noticed sooner, but Ana is used only to tracking and hunting, not to being stalked.

A quick cracking sound, dry branches snapping under a solid weight. They're far away from the town; this is a dangerous place to encounter an animal.

And those branches weren't broken by an animal.

★

The rink in Beartown is closed and dark when Peter gets there. He doesn't switch the lights on; there are yellowing sheets of paper on the walls, and he knows what they say without needing any light. Small words written in a loud voice: 'Team before individual.' Farther away: 'The only time we're not moving forward is when we're taking aim.' Above that: 'Dream – Fight – Win!' And nearest the door, in his own handwriting: 'We stand tall when we win, we stand tall when we lose, we stand tall no matter what.'

People with logical minds might think notes like that are silly, but you don't get to be best at a sport by being logical. You have to be a dreamer. When Peter was in primary school, a teacher asked the pupils what they wanted to be when they grew up. Peter said, 'A pro in the NHL.' He can still remember the way the whole class laughed, and he's spent his whole life proving them wrong. People with logical minds realize it's impossible for a small boy from little Beartown to play with the best in the world, but dreamers work differently.

The only problem is that you're never finished, you can never prove enough, the people laughing just move the boundaries. There's a clock on the wall of the changing room; it's stopped, no one will bother to change the battery. It takes time to learn to love something but much less to kill it: a single moment will do. Sports is merciless: a big star becomes a has-been during a ten-second walk from the ice to the locker room, a club that has survived more than half a century is condemned to collapse during a few minutes in a council building. Peter wonders if they'll demolish the rink now, build their conference hotel or some other crap the people with money and power dream about. They never love anything, they just own things. For them this is nothing more than bricks and mortar.

He goes up into the stands, stops in the narrow corridor outside the offices on the upper floor. How many of his lives are in this building? What are they worth now? There are framed photographs on the wall from the club's biggest moments, the founding of the club in 1951, the magical season twenty years ago when the

A-team became the second best in the country, and then the junior team that took silver this spring. A lot of the pictures are of Peter.

In one furious movement he sweeps them all off the wall. He starts at one end of the corridor and pulls every frame off every hook. Glass shatters across the floor, but Peter is already walking away. The rink is still in darkness when he slams the outside door.

The stranger sits in the darkness in the stands and watches Peter leave. As he starts up his car out in the parking lot, the stranger goes up to the offices and looks at the destruction. Sees the old photographs of Peter among the shattered glass, along with more recent pictures of the junior team. Two players are in almost every picture. The stranger pushes the glass aside with a sturdy boot and bends over an older photograph of the same boys, long before they became the entire town's big stars. An award ceremony when they're maybe ten or eleven, arms around each other like brothers, their numbers and surnames on their backs: '9 ERDAHL and 16 OVICH.'

Best friends, a sport they loved, and a team they've given their lives for; what's a young man capable of if you take all that away from him at the same time? The stranger carefully draws a circle on the pad, around the name 'Benjamin Ovich,' then walks back down the stand and out of the rink. Lights a fresh cigar. It's warm and there's no wind, but the stranger still cups the flame, as if a storm were brewing.

Ana and Maya hear their hearts pounding as they turn around and see Benji walking between the trees. Not long ago a boy who loved his hockey team and his best friend, now a grown man with eyes in which the pupils have drowned. One fist is clenched, the other is clutching a hammer.

Ask anyone in Beartown, and they'll tell you that that boy has always been a ticking time bomb.

7

Start by Eating Lunch

There's an old saying in Hed: 'Tell a stranger you hate Beartown, and you'll have a friend for life.' The smallest child in Hed is quick to learn that it's important for Hed Hockey to do well but that it's even more important that things go really badly for Beartown. Partly in jest, obviously. The stands are full of screamed threats about 'hating' and 'killing' each other, but of course they aren't serious. Until all of a sudden they are.

When we describe how the violence between the two towns started, most of us will no longer remember what came first: the burning flags that twelve-year-old Leo filmed and posted online or another video clip that someone over in Hed posted almost simultaneously. Because nothing travels faster than a good story, and obviously no one who has grown up in Hed loving a red team and hating a green one can conceal his *schadenfreude* when the council, money, and power all pick a side.

So one member of Hed's fan club stops a councillor on her way home from work and films himself asking, 'Okay, so what's everyone in Beartown who likes hockey supposed to do now?' The politician, a nervous middle-aged woman, doesn't appear to know what to say. Unless she knows exactly. Because she replies, 'They can start supporting Hed, can't they?'

That night she is woken by a loud bang. When she walks out of her front door the next morning, there's an axe sticking out of the hood of her car.

When she walks to the bus stop, a car drives past containing two men in black jackets. They don't need to look at her. She knows she's being watched anyway.

*

The Bearskin pub is where it's always been, in the middle of Beartown. It's the sort of pub that used to smell better when smoking was permitted indoors. Its owner, Ramona, has a face that resembles the floorboards: life has left its mark on her like the chairs being dragged back and forth too many times over the years, as well as all the cigarettes that earned her the nickname 'the Marlboro Mum' from the young men who have made the Bearskin their second home, and sometimes their first. Ramona is past retirement age, but no one who values the shape of his nose mentions the fact out loud. She's pouring herself a late breakfast in a tall glass when a stranger walks in. Ramona raises a surprised eyebrow.

'Yes?'

The stranger looks around at the empty bar uncomprehendingly. 'Sorry?'

'Can I help you?' Ramona asks suspiciously.

The stranger has unkempt hair, jeans, a tracksuit top, and thick socks in the sort of heavy boots you wear if you regard temperatures above freezing as unnatural.

'This is a bar, isn't it?'

Ramona's lips curl warily. 'Yep.'

'Does it come as a surprise for the bar to have a customer?'

'Depends on the customer.'

The stranger seems to agree that this is a valid observation.

'I've got some questions.'

'Then you've come to the wrong town.'

The door behind the stranger opens. Two young men walk in.

They're wearing black jackets.

Ana and Maya can feel their heartbeats pulsing in their necks. They haven't considered Benji an enemy; he was one of the few who stayed in Beartown when Kevin and all the others went off to Hed Hockey. But if Ana and Maya have learned anything, it's that loyalty around here can switch in an instant, and that they can never trust that a man won't try to hurt them.

But Benji stops a few yards away with the hammer swinging gently in his hand. He seems to be waiting for them to react. He's always been muscular, but this summer has given his body something else, an aura of cruelty. Ana didn't bring her rifle with her; she regrets that now. She's seen Benji play hockey; she knows that what makes him better and more dangerous than the others is that he's unpredictable. On the occasions when it has gone wrong and he hurt someone, no one ever saw it coming in advance.

But his upper body is barely moving now. When he finally opens his lips, the words come quietly and jerkily from a larynx that sounds as though it hasn't been used in weeks. He drops the hammer in front of Ana's feet with a dull thud and says, 'You'll need this. I've got something. For you.'

It will take a long time for the young women to realize that he had the hammer with him because he knew Ana and Maya would need to be armed before they dared go with him. It can be an unbearable sorrow for someone to know that he's regarded as such a wild animal in other people's eyes.

The men in black jackets stop inside the door, accustomed to their presence alone being enough to suddenly remind a stranger that he's left his clothes in a machine at the laundromat or has to give blood at a medical centre three or four hundred miles away. Over the next few months the stranger will realize that there are plenty of stories about the people who usually drink in the Bearskin, just not many people who are prepared to tell them. They have no symbols, no website; when it's game day in Beartown, there's no way to tell them apart from other men on their way to the rink. But the stranger will learn that 'the Pack' make sure that no one runs their hockey club without their blessing or curse, and you don't notice how many of them there are until they've become your enemies. The stranger seems either too smart or too crazy to care.

'Are you a journalist?' Ramona asks.

She isn't sure if the stranger simply chooses to ignore her aggressive tone or has some sort of condition that prevents it registering.

So she adds, 'We've had a few journalists here before you with "questions," and they always go home with them unanswered. But they usually end up getting better home insurance.'

The direct threat seems to fly straight over the stranger's untidy hair; who calmly spins around on the barstool and looks at the decor, the walls covered with photographs and pennants and jerseys.

'I don't suppose you serve lunch here?'

The men by the door don't know if this is a veiled insult or a polite question. But Ramona suddenly starts to laugh. She makes a slight gesture, and the men disappear through the door.

'You're no journalist,' she declares to the stranger with her head slightly tilted.

Then her tone shifts quickly to one of displeasure again. 'So what the hell are you doing in Beartown?'

The stranger's hands settle neatly on the bar. 'I thought I might start by eating lunch.'

Kira calls Peter again but gets no answer. Seriously? She's had a feeling that something like this would happen, that the council would find a way to turn against Peter. He's a romantic, but Kira's a lawyer, and she figured out a while back that the easiest way for the council to bury the scandal would be to bury the club.

The whole of the Andersson family, Peter and Maya and Leo and she herself, agreed at the start of the summer that they were going to stay in Beartown. Stay and fight. But she is no longer feeling so sure. How long can you stay in a place that keeps trying to reject you like a hostile virus? And if Peter doesn't even have a club here anymore, what have they got left?

Her colleague is back, sitting quietly on the other side of the desk, but of course Kira can remember all the things she's said about Peter. 'He's an addict, Kira. You might think addicts always drink or take drugs or gamble on the horses, but your husband hasn't got a problem with alcohol or gambling. He's got a problem with competitiveness. He can't stop trying to win. He can't live without that rush.'

47

How many times has Kira lain awake wondering if that's true? She calls again, again, again. Eventually Peter answers. Angry, even if that isn't audible in his voice. Only to her. The tiniest little change in the way he says her name. She whispers, 'I've been trying to call, darling, I . . . heard what happened . . .'

He doesn't reply. So she asks, 'Where are you?'

And then it comes: 'In the office, Kira. I'm in a meeting. Let's talk later.'

She can hear from the noises in the background that he's in the car. He always used to do that when he lost games as a player: get into the car and drive for hours. He never used violence against anyone else, only himself. So he would drive out into the darkness without considering that there was someone sitting at home waiting for him, someone who was terrified that this would be the evening when the phone rang and it wasn't his voice at the other end. That a police officer's voice would ask, 'Are you Peter Andersson's wife?,' and she would hear the voice take a deep, sympathetic breath when she whispered 'Yes.'

'I don't know what to say, darling. I'm so very sorry,' Kira says now.

'There's nothing to say,' he replies bluntly.

She hears the background noise, wonders how fast he's driving. 'We need to talk about it . . .'

'There's nothing to say. They won. They wanted to kill the club, and they found a way to win.'

She takes a cautious breath, the way she always does, as if she's done something wrong. 'I . . . maybe . . . I know it feels like the end of the world right now, but –'

'Don't start, Kira.'

'What do you mean, "Don't start"?'

'You know what I mean!'

'I'm just saying that this could finally be a chance for us to talk about doing something . . . else.'

How many times has she asked him that? 'When does hockey stop?' How many times has he said 'Next year'? Next year he'll cut back, next year he'll work less, next year it will be her turn to really focus on her career. She's been waiting twenty years for next year. But something always happens that makes him indispensable, a crisis that makes him essential and her selfish for demanding something so unreasonable as normal office hours, as his actually coming home.

He flares up now. It probably isn't intentional. 'What am I supposed to do, Kira? Become a house husband or what?'

So she gets defensive. That probably isn't intentional either. 'Stop taking your frustration out on me! I'm just saying that perhaps there's . . .'

'There's what, Kira? This club is my whole life!'

Peter can hear nothing but the sound of her breathing. She bites her cheek to stop herself screaming. He tries to calm down and apologize but is suffocated by everything else he's feeling, and the only thing that comes out is 'You know what I mean . . .'

How many years has she given it? They moved to Canada for his hockey career, they moved to Beartown for his hockey career, how many times has she thought that he of all people ought to understand her? All hockey players are driven by the need to find out how good they can become, but the same thing applies to lawyers. After they moved to Beartown she drank too much wine one evening and blurted out the truth: 'Living here basically means accepting never reaching your full potential.' Peter thought she was talking about him, so he felt hurt. *He* felt hurt.

'You know what I mean!' he repeats now, and yes, she knows exactly.

And that's the problem. Hockey is his whole life, so she hangs up.

Her colleague only just has time to duck before the phone hits the wall.

The stranger lays a creased sheet of paper on the bar, a list of names. 'Do you know these people?'

The old bar owner looks at the list without touching it. 'Today's lunch is meat, potatoes, and sauce. When you've finished, you're welcome to leave in any direction of your own choosing.'

The stranger's nose wrinkles. 'Do you have a vegetarian option?'

Ramona swears and disappears into the kitchen. A microwave oven pings; she comes back and carelessly puts a plate down on the counter. Meat, potatoes, and sauce.

'I'm vegan,' the stranger says, as if it were perfectly natural and not something a normal person should ever have to apologize for.

'You're what?' Ramona grunts.

'Vegan.'

'In that case we've got potatoes and sauce,' Ramona says. She picks up a knife and starts pulling the pieces of meat off and putting them down directly on the counter, like an irritated mother.

The stranger watches this process, then asks, 'Is there cream in the sauce?'

Ramona finishes her beer, swears again, snatches up the plate, and vanishes into the kitchen again. She returns with a different plate, one that contains nothing but potatoes.

The stranger gives an unperturbed nod and starts to eat. Ramona looks on irritably for a while before putting a glass of beer down next to the plate. 'On the house. You need to get some sort of nourishment inside you.'

'I don't drink alcohol,' the stranger says.

'Nor do I, I've given up!' Ramona says, pouring herself another beer and hissing defensively, 'This? Not even five percent alcohol! It's practically milk!'

The stranger appears to ponder asking Ramona what sort of cows she gets her milk from but decides not to. Ramona pours two shots of whisky and downs one of them. The stranger doesn't touch the other glass.

'It's not for the alcohol. It's good for the digestion,' Ramona declares.

When the stranger still doesn't touch it, Ramona downs that one, too. Twice as good for the digestion. The stranger glances at the pennants and jerseys on the walls. 'Have you always been this fond of hockey in this town?'

Ramona snorts. 'We're not "fond" of hockey here. People in the big cities with their bloody popcorn and VIP boxes, they're "fond" of hockey. Then the next day they're fond of something else. This isn't a big city.'

The stranger doesn't react. That frustrates Ramona, because she's usually better at reading people. The stranger finishes eating and stands up, puts some money on the counter, tucks the list of names away in a pocket, and is halfway out of the door when Ramona bellows, 'Why are there only men on that list?'

The stranger turns around. 'Sorry?'

'If you've come to Beartown to ask about hockey, why have you only got men on that list of yours?'

'I haven't. You were on the list as well.'

The door opens and closes. The stranger pushes past the men in black jackets outside. Ramona stays where she is, confused. It's not a feeling she's used to and certainly not one she likes.

8

When a Relationship Breaks Down

When he was younger, Benji was always running away from home once the trees had turned green, and he would walk for hours before climbing up into one of them. If the wind was coming from the town, he would scream as loudly as he could, roaring out everything that hurt. If the wind was coming from the other direction, he would sit still until it numbed his cheeks so much that he could no longer feel the tears.

It was his three older sisters who taught him to hunt. Not because they wanted to, but when their mum was working, the boy clearly couldn't be left alone at home without causing all sorts of chaos. The only reliable thing about Benji has always been that he's unreliable. But to everyone's surprise, nature managed to get through to him where people failed. When someone learns to be in the forest as a child, it's like gaining an extra language. The air talks here, and Benji understands. It's mournful and wild.

His sisters were taught to hunt by their father, and Benji hated them for that, for being able to remember him. So when he met Kevin, it was the first time he had anything in his life that was his and his alone. In the summer they would disappear to their secret place, a small, overgrown island in a lake that not even the hunters went to. The boys could be themselves there. They swam naked and let themselves dry in the sun on the rocks, they fished for their supper and slept under the stars, sometimes not saying a word to each other for several days. The first summer they spent twenty-four hours there, but by the time they were teenagers, that had stretched to weeks, every moment until hockey training started again.

During the first years of their friendship Benji still wet the bed when he dreamed about his father. But never on the island. Once he'd rowed out and knocked a stake between the rocks and made the boat fast, the dreams couldn't reach him there. Kevin meant everything to Benji. The best friends of our childhoods are the loves of our lives, and they break our hearts in worse ways.

Benji leads Ana and Maya to the tangled, overgrown shore. There's no jetty in the lake, but he pulls out a rowboat hidden under the bushes and throws his backpack into it. Then he dives into the water and swims.

At first the girls don't understand what they're rowing towards; there are just some overgrown rocks in the middle of the lake, a few low trees, and from the water it doesn't even look possible to go ashore. But Benji appears behind some big rocks and pulls the boat towards the island with water dripping from his arms and his bare feet pressed hard against the ground.

Ana finds some metal stakes in the backpack and uses the hammer Benji gave her to knock them into a crevice in the rocks and ties the boat fast. Maya gets out after her, and only then do the girls realize what they're looking at. In the middle of the little island is a cleared rectangle in the grass, impossible to see from anywhere on the water, just large enough for a two-man tent.

'It's a good place to hide,' Benji mumbles quietly, looking down at the ground.

'Why are you showing it to us?' Maya asks.

'I don't need it anymore,' he says.

He's lying, she can see that. For a fleeting moment he looks as though he's about to admit it. But instead he points, almost shyly, and adds, 'If you swim over there, you can't be seen from the forest.'

Maya and Ana don't ask who he used to share the island with. It's theirs now. The best thing about nature is that it isn't nostalgic; rocks and trees don't give a damn about their previous owners. Benji walks towards the water, but just before he jumps from the rocks Maya calls after him, 'Hey!'

He turns around. Her voice breaks. 'I hope you're one of the people who gets a happy ending, Benji.'

The young man nods quickly and turns away before she has a chance to realize how much that means to him. The young women stay on the island as he dives into the lake and swims away.

Ana follows his arms as they break the water, peering at the taut body as it climbs up into the forest on the other side. Mournful and wild. She bites her bottom lip happily. When Maya shoots her an accusing glare, Ana snaps, 'What? I was just thinking . . . he didn't have to go off right away, did he? I mean, *he*'s welcome to watch while I go for a swim . . .'

Maya taps her temple. 'You've got serious mental problems.'

'What? Did you see his arms? All I'm saying is that he's welcome to watch when . . .'

'Thanks! That's enough! If you keep going on about it, you can't stay on my island!'

'What? So now it's your island all of a sudden?'

Maya bursts out laughing. Her best friend is the craziest, smartest person she knows, and in her own screwed-up way Ana is struggling to get everything back to normal again: boys, sex, life, the world. She starts where she always does when it comes to survival: with humour.

They stay on the island almost all summer. Ana makes sporadic trips home to fetch supplies but mainly to clear away the empty bottles from her dad's kitchen. She always comes back before it gets dark, and she always makes sure that Maya has enough to eat. One morning Maya wakes up to find her friend standing naked at the edge of the water, swearing as she tries to catch fish with her bare hands, because she's seen some idiot in a survival programme on TV do it; from then on Maya refuses to call her anything but 'Gollum.' In return, Ana watches Maya the first time she takes her clothes off and, noting the tan line made by her T-shirt and shorts, says, 'You're going to make a great dad someday. You've already got every dad's beach holiday T-shirt tan.' They spend one last summer singing loudly and dancing badly, sleeping without nightmares beneath the starry sky. Maya plays her guitar, calm and free. She doesn't know it yet, but in ten years' time one of the songs she writes here will be the first thing she plays at every concert when she goes on tour. She will have tattoos on both arms then, a guitar and a rifle, and will dedicate the song to her best friend. Its title is 'The Island.'

Benji is running alone in another part of the forest. He finds new hiding places; he's had a lot of practice over the years. He's become a man who doesn't take anything for granted; only children think certain things are self-evident: always having a best friend, for instance. Being allowed to be who we are. Being able to love who we want. Nothing is self-evident to Benji anymore; he just runs deeper into the forest until his brain is gasping for oxygen and he can no longer feel anything. Then he climbs up into a tree. And waits for the wind.

You have to keep your promises. That's one of the first things children learn when they start to talk. When Maya was little, she made her dad promise that she could be an astronaut, and Peter promised, because that's what parents do. He promised everything else as well: that no one would ever hurt her. That everything would be all right. Even though it isn't true.

After everything that happened in the spring Peter asked his daughter if she wanted to move away from Beartown. She said, 'No. Because this is my town, too.' He asked what he could do for her, and she said, 'Build a better club, for everyone.' So he promised.

He's never been good with words. Never been the kind of dad who could tell his kids and his wife how much he loves them. He's always hoped that just showing them he did would be enough. But how can he show them anything now? Beyond the fact that he's a loser?

He pulls up at a pedestrian crossing. A young father is crossing the road with his daughter, eight or nine years old. The father is holding her hand, and the girl is making it very plain that she thinks she's way too old for that. Peter has to stop himself getting out of the car and shouting at the father to never let go. Never let go! Never!

When Peter and Kira had their first child, Isak, Kira said to him, 'This is what we are now. Everything else comes after this. First and foremost, we're parents!' Peter already knew, of course. All parents know. It's not a voluntary process, it's an emotional assault; you become someone else's property the first time you hear your child cry. You belong to that little person now. Before everything else. So when something happens to your child, it never stops being your fault.

Peter feels like leaping out of the car and shouting at that father, 'Never let her out of your sight, never trust anyone, and don't let her go to that party!'

When Isak died, people asked, 'How does anyone get over that?' Peter's only response is that you don't. You just carry on living. Some of your emotional register switches to autopilot. But now? He doesn't know. He just knows that when something happens to your child, it doesn't make any difference whose fault it is, because it never stops being your fault regardless. Why weren't you there? Why didn't you kill him? Why weren't you enough?

Peter wants to shout at the dad crossing the road, 'NEVER LET GO BECAUSE THOSE BASTARDS WILL TAKE YOUR WHOLE LIVES AWAY FROM YOU!'

Instead he just cries quietly, his fingernails embedded in the steering wheel.

The Island

It was summer
And the island was ours
We had had winter
For a thousand years

You were broken
I was cracked

You hung the rope
I tied the knot

How many times did we have time to die
Before we turned sixteen
How many songs about saying good-bye
That only you know what they mean

But this was summer
And the island was ours
And you were mine
For a thousand years

Kira used to fall asleep on the sofa when Peter got home late. An unopened bottle of wine and two glasses on the table, a silent little dart of guilty conscience to remind him that she'd been waiting for him. That his not coming home actually hurt someone. He used to pick her up gently and carry her to bed, then fall asleep, breathing hard against her back.

A long marriage consists of such small things that when they get lost we don't even know where to start looking for them. The way she usually touches him, as if she didn't mean to, when he's washing up and she's making coffee and her little finger overlaps his when they put their hands down on the kitchen counter together. His lips brush her hair fleetingly as he passes her at the kitchen table, the two of them looking different ways. Two people who have loved each for long enough eventually seem to stop touching each other consciously, it becomes something instinctive; when they meet between the hall and kitchen, their bodies somehow find each other. When they walk through a door, her hand ends up in his as if by accident. Tiny collisions, every day, all the time. Impossible to construct. So when they disappear, no one knows why, but suddenly two people are living parallel lives instead of together. One morning they don't make eye contact, their fingers land a few inches farther apart along the counter.

They pass each other in a hallway. They no longer bump into each other.

It's past midnight by the time Peter opens the front door. Kira knows he's hoping she's asleep, so she pretends to be. The wine bottle on the table is empty; there's only one glass beside it. He doesn't carry her to bed, just covers her clumsily with a blanket where she lies on the sofa. He stands there for a few moments; perhaps he's waiting for her to stop pretending. But when she opens her eyes, he's in the bathroom. He locks the door, stares down at the floor; she lies on the sofa, stares at the ceiling. They don't know if they have anything to say to each other anymore. Everything has a breaking point, and even though people always say that 'a joy shared is a joy doubled,' we seem to insist on believing that the opposite is true of sorrow. Perhaps that isn't actually the case. Two drowning people with lead weights around their ankles may not be each other's salvation; if they hold hands, they'll just sink twice as fast. In the end the weight of carrying each other's broken hearts becomes unbearable.

They sleep out of reach of each other's fingertips. With no lips against hair, no breath against back. And night after night a single question slowly takes root inside both of their heads: Is this how it starts? When a relationship breaks down?

9

He's Going to Need Someone to Fight Tonight

Everyone who loves sports knows that a game isn't decided only by what happens but just as much by what doesn't. The shot that hits the post, the bad call by the referee, the pass that didn't quite connect. Every discussion about sports dissolves sooner or later into a thousand 'ifs' and ten thousand 'if only that hadn'ts.' Some people's lives get stuck the same way, year after year passing by with the same story being repeated to strangers at an ever more deserted bar counter: a doomed relationship, a dishonest business partner, an unfair dismissal, ungrateful kids, an accident, a divorce. One single reason why everything went to hell.

When it comes down to it, everyone has something to say about the life he should have had instead of this one. Cities and towns work the same way. So if you want to understand their biggest stories, first you have to listen to the smaller ones.

The council building is left almost empty after Midsummer as the politicians take their holidays or spend time at their regular jobs. If you want to understand how the local council is run, that's where you have to start: politics here is a part-time occupation, and the salary of just a few thousand kronor a month makes it almost an act of charity when seen in relation to the number of hours worked. So most councillors are employed elsewhere or have their own businesses, meaning that they have customers and suppliers and bosses and colleagues. Naturally this makes it difficult to claim to be truly independent, but no man is an island, especially not this deep into the forest.

One single councillor goes on working eighteen hours a day in the council building throughout the summer, and he doesn't owe anything to anyone around here. His name is Richard Theo, and he sits in his office in a black suit, making a stream of phone calls. He is hated by some and feared by many, and soon he will change the direction of one hockey club and two towns.

Several days of rain follow, and Beartown becomes a different place: the town isn't as used to this sort of precipitation as it is to snow. People stay indoors, quieter and more irritable than usual.

The Jeep drives through the mud up into the forest, and the stranger stops outside a small garage beside a shabby-looking house. Cars are parked on the grass, waiting to be repaired. One of them is difficult to avoid: it has an axe sticking out of the hood.

The stranger sees an eighteen-year-old youth with fists the size of piglets jump up onto the chassis and pull the axe out of the metal, his shoulders so tense that his neck seems to retract into his guts.

A gruff-looking man in his forties, so similar to the young man that there's no way the postman would ever have to take a paternity test, walks over to the Jeep and taps on the window. 'Tires?' he grunts.

The stranger winds the window down and repeats uncomprehendingly, 'Tires?'

The man kicks the front wheel. 'They're worn smooth, this one's got grooves no deeper than an old LP, so I assume that's why you're here?'

'Okay,' the stranger says.

' "Okay"? Do you want new tires or not?' the man wonders.

'Okay,' the stranger says and shrugs as if the man was asking about ketchup on a burger.

The man grunts something inaudible and yells, 'Bobo! Have we got tires for this one?'

The stranger obviously isn't here to get the tires changed but to assess the quality of a defensive player. But if that's going to require a change of tires, then so be it. So the stranger watches the eighteen-year-old, Bobo, whose efforts pulling the axe from the car hood remind the stranger of a cut-price King Arthur. He disappears into the workshop, where there are no pictures of scantily clad women on the walls, from which the stranger concludes that there's a woman in the house whom the father and son are unwilling to cross. There are, however, pictures of ice hockey teams, new and old alike.

The stranger nods to them, then at Bobo when he comes back with a tire under each arm, and asks the father, 'That lad of yours, is he any good as a player?'

The father suddenly lights up with the sort of pride you only have if you've been a defenceman yourself:

'Bobo? Yes! Toughest defenceman in town!'

His choice of the word 'toughest' doesn't surprise the stranger, because both father and son give the distinct impression of being the sort of men who can skate in only one direction. The father holds out a grease-stained hand, and the stranger shakes it with the enthusiasm of someone invited to take hold of a snake.

'People call me Hog,' the father grins.

'Zackell,' the stranger says.

The stranger leaves the workshop with an improved set of secondhand tires for a little more than the going rate and a scrap of paper: 'Bobo. If he can learn to skate.'

The sheet of paper isn't just a list. It's a team sheet.

Amat runs alone along the road with his shirt black with sweat until his eyes are streaming and his brain is empty of all thought.

He's one of the brightest hockey talents this town has ever seen, but no one realized it until this spring. He lives with his mum in one of the cheapest apartment blocks at the far end of the Hollow in the north of Beartown; he's always played with secondhand equipment, and he's been told he's too small, but no one is faster on skates than he is. 'Kill them!' his best friends usually say instead of 'Good luck!' His speed is his weapon.

Hockey is the sport of bears around here, but Amat taught himself to play it like a lion. The sport became his way into the community, and he thought it could be his ticket out as well. His mother works as a cleaner in the ice rink in the winter and in the hospital during the summer, but one day Amat hopes to turn professional and take her away from here. Back in the spring he got his chance, with the junior team. He grabbed it. He showed everyone in town that he was a winner, and the path to his dreams lay open. It was the best day and the worst night of his life. After the game he was invited to a party that Maya Andersson was also going to, and the only thing Amat had ever dreamed of more than playing was being allowed to kiss her.

He was drunk, but even so he will never forget every detail of how he stumbled through room after room of drunk and high teenagers singing and laughing, went upstairs, and heard Maya calling for help. Amat opened a door and saw the rape.

When Kevin realized what Amat had seen, he and William Lyt and some of the other boys in the junior team offered Amat everything the boy had dreamed of — a place on the junior team, star status, a career — in exchange for keeping his mouth shut. Kevin's father gave him money and promised to get his mother a better job. If anyone condemns Amat for giving the offer serious consideration, that person has lived a life where morality is easy. It never is. Morality is a luxury.

Kevin's parents and the club's sponsors called a meeting and tried to force Maya's father out of the club. In the end Amat went to the meeting, stood up at the front, and told everyone what he had seen Kevin do. Peter Andersson won the vote of confidence and kept his job.

And then what? Amat is running faster now, his feet hurt more, because what the hell happened next? Kevin was never punished. Maya never got justice, and Amat left that meeting with hundreds of enemies. Lyt and his friends found him and beat him up, and if Bobo hadn't changed sides at the last minute and defended Amat, they would have killed him.

Neither Amat nor Bobo is welcome at Hed Hockey Club now. Amat is a snitch and Bobo a traitor. And Beartown Ice Hockey? Soon it won't exist anymore. Amat is on his way to becoming one of those people who sits at a bar counter in thirty years' time with a story full of 'ifs' and 'if only that hadn'ts.' He's seen them in the rink, shabby men with three days' worth of stubble and four days' worth of hangover, whose lives peaked while they were still teenagers.

Amat could have turned professional, his life could have changed, but instead he's on his way to becoming a has-been at the age of sixteen.

His gaze is focused inward. He doesn't even notice the Jeep behind him. When it passes him, he doesn't know it was fifty yards behind him for several minutes, so that the stranger could make a note of how far he is from Beartown and how fast he's running. The stranger writes, 'Amat. If his heart is as big as his lungs.'

Benji is sitting with his back against his father's headstone. His body is full of moonshine and grass, and the combination acts as a circuit breaker. He's closing down. Can't bear it otherwise.

He has three older sisters, and you can tell the difference between them if you mention his name. Gaby has young children; she reads them bedtime stories, goes to bed early on Friday nights and still watches TV programmes on TV instead of a computer. Katia is a bartender at the Barn in Hed; she spends her Friday nights pouring beer and shepherding three-hundred-pound drunks through the door when they decide to try to relieve other three-hundred-pound drunks of their front teeth. Adri is the eldest; she lives alone at her boarding kennels outside Beartown, she hunts and fishes and likes people who keep their mouths shut. So if you say 'Benji,' Gaby will exclaim anxiously, 'Has something happened to him?' Katia will sigh and wonder, 'What's he done now?' But Adri will force you up against a wall and demand, 'What the hell do you want with my brother?' Gaby worries, Katia solves problems, Adri protects: that's been the division of responsibilities since their father took his rifle and went out into the forest. They know they can't teach a heart like Benji's, but they might be able to tame it. So when he lives like a nomad, staying sometimes at his mother's, sometimes out in the forest, sometimes with one of his sisters, they fall into their old roles. If he's at Gaby's, she still gets up at night to check that he's breathing, even though he's eighteen years old. When he sees Katia, she still spoils him, lets him get away with way too much shit, because she doesn't want him to stop coming to her with his problems. And when he's staying out at the kennels with Adri, she sleeps with the key to the gun cabinet under her pillow. To make sure her little brother doesn't do the same thing as their father.

There have always been adults in this town who have thought that Benji is a rebel. His sisters know that the exact opposite is true. He became precisely the person everyone wanted him to be, because a young boy carrying a huge secret soon learns that sometimes the best place to hide it is where everyone can see you.

As a child Benji was the first person to recognize that Kevin could be a star. In Beartown players like that are called 'cherry trees.' So Benji saw to it that Kevin got enough space on the ice to blossom. Benji could give and take so much rough treatment that men in the stands used to say, 'Now, there's a real hockey player. This isn't a sport for fags and weaklings, it's for guys like Benji!' The more he fought, the better they thought they knew him. Until he became the person they wanted him to be.

He's eighteen now. He gets up and leans on the headstone, kisses his father's name. Then he takes a step back, clenches his fist as tightly as he can, and punches the same place with full force. Blood drips from his knuckles as he makes his way through the forest towards Hed. Tomorrow would have been Alain Ovich's birthday, and this is the first time that Benji is celebrating it without Kevin. He's going to need someone to fight tonight.

He never sees the Jeep. It's standing parked beneath a tree. The stranger walks through the rain to the grave, looks at the name engraved in the stone. Back in the Jeep a pen scratches on a sheet of paper, 'Ovich. If he still wants to play.'

★

64

Benji. Amat. Bobo. Inside every large story there are always plenty of small ones. While three young men in Beartown thought they were in the process of losing their club, a stranger was already constructing a team with them.

Richard Theo, the politician, is alone in the council building when evening falls. He looks younger than his forty years, a genetic quirk he used to hate when he inspected his impassively hairless testicles as he waited for the onset of puberty but from which he is now reaping the rewards as his contemporaries pluck grey hairs from their beards and curse the law of gravity every time they pee. Theo is wearing a suit. At best his colleagues wear jeans and a jacket, so he's used to being mocked for 'looking like a government minister even though he's just a nobody from the provinces.' It doesn't bother him. He doesn't dress for the job he's got but for the one he wants.

He grew up in Beartown but was never one of the popular kids, never played hockey. He went abroad to study, and no one noticed he was gone. He worked in a bank in London and was gone for years before he suddenly came home with expensive suits and political ambitions. He joined the smallest political party in the area. It isn't the smallest anymore.

Not long ago Theo was the sort of face that former classmates would see in old school photographs and not remember his name, but that changed when the local paper shone a negative light on his politics. But how they learned his name is unimportant to Theo. As long as they know it. Opinions can be changed.

He wasn't at the meeting where Peter was informed of the fate of Beartown Ice Hockey Club, because Richard Theo isn't part of the establishment. All councils have a political elite that you either belong to or you don't, and the establishment here has chosen to freeze Theo out. Naturally they claim it's because of his politics, but he's convinced that the real reason is that they fear him. He can get the people on his side. They call him a populist, but the only difference between him and the other parties is that he doesn't need flags: they have their offices on the top floor of the council building and play golf with business leaders, whereas Richard Theo has his office on the ground floor. He collects his information from people who have lost their jobs rather than from the people firing them, from the people who are angry instead of the ones who are happy, so he doesn't need flags to tell him which way the wind is blowing. While all the other politicians are running in the same direction, men like Richard Theo go the other way. And sometimes that's how they win.

There's a knock on his office door. It's late, no one has seen the stranger arrive.

'There you are at last! Well? Have you finished thinking about it? Are you going to take the job?' Richard Theo asks without further ado.

The stranger stands in the doorway with a pocket containing the sheet of paper with the names of the team players on it, but Zackell's reply is so apathetic that it's hard to tell if it's because of a lack of enthusiasm about the job, or life in general. 'When you called me, you offered me the job of coach of Beartown Ice Hockey's A-team. But the club's going into receivership. And even if it weren't, it already has a coach. And even if it didn't, you're still a politician rather than the club's general manager, so unless I've seriously misunderstood the democratic process, you can't offer me a job as a coach any more than you can offer me a unicorn.'

'Yet you're still here,' Richard Theo says simply.

'I happen to be very fond of unicorns,' Zackell confesses in a way that makes it impossible to tell if the remark is supposed to be funny or not.

Theo tilts his head to one side. 'Coffee?'

'I don't drink coffee. I don't like hot drinks.'

Theo jerks as if he's trying to avoid a dagger. 'You don't drink coffee? You're going to have trouble fitting into this town!'

'This town isn't alone in that,' Zackell replies.

Theo chuckles. 'You're a very strange person, Zackell.'

'So I've been told.'

Theo slaps his hands on his desk and stands up cheerfully. 'I like that! The media will like it, too! The coaching job is yours; let me worry about the general manager. I look forward to the two of us working together.'

He looks as though he's considering attempting a high five. Zackell looks very much as though that isn't going to happen. 'My main ambition is that you and I will never have to "work together." I'm here for the hockey, not politics.'

Theo throws his arms out brightly. 'I hate hockey; you can have that all to yourself!'

Zackell's hands are firmly embedded in the pockets of the track-suit. 'For someone who hates hockey, you seem to be very involved in it.'

Theo's eyes narrow contentedly. 'That's because when every-one else runs the same way, I go the other way, Zackell. That's how I win.'

10

How Do You Tell Your Children?

The lights in the law firm are switched off, except for in one office. Kira Andersson is working while her colleague is lying across two armchairs looking for package holidays on her computer.

'A package holiday? You don't even like taking time off,' Kira points out.

Her colleague stretches like a cat that's been told off. 'I don't. But with this body, Kira, it would be a crime against humanity if it didn't get shown off in a bikini at least once a year!'

Kira laughs. How wonderful that her colleague can still make her do that so easily. That she has a friend like her. 'Tell me when you've booked so I can call and warn the country in question to keep all its husbands locked away.'

Her colleague nods seriously. 'And sons. And dads, if I've drunk enough Fernet.'

Kira smiles. Then she blinks slowly and mutters, 'Thanks for being here . . .'

Her colleague shrugs her shoulders. 'The Wi-Fi at home is bad.'

Which is rubbish, of course. She's still at work because she knows Kira doesn't want to go home early tonight and sit in an empty house waiting for Peter. She doesn't judge, she doesn't go on about it, she just stays behind in the only office where the lights are still on.

How wonderful to have a friend like that.

'Never love a hockey club. It can never love you back.' Peter's mother told him that. She was softer than his dad, although some-times Peter thinks his dad might have been softer, too, before she got sick. 'Never believe you're anything special,' his dad said. Peter evidently didn't listen to either of them.

He's called everyone he knows. Everyone he's played with. Asked for advice, asked for money, asked for players to save the club. Everyone understands, everyone sympathizes, but hockey is built on statistics and figures. No one gives you anything for nothing.

His phone rings: it's his childhood friend Tails, the supermarket owner and Beartown Ice Hockey's last real sponsor. Tails's voice is trembling when he says, 'This is so fucked, Peter. It's so fucking fucked . . . it . . . they've posted something . . .'

'What?' Peter asks.

'I wanted to call so you can stop the kids seeing it. They've . . . the bastards, there's a death notice in the local paper today. Your name.'

Peter says nothing. He understands the message. You can tell yourself as much as you like that 'the criticism belongs to the job' and that you 'shouldn't let it bother you.' But we're all only human. If your name appears in a death notice, it bothers you.

'Ignore them,' Tails advises, even though he knows it's impossible.

It might be possible to save a hockey club in Beartown even if you don't have everyone on your side. But not if everyone's against you.

Peter hangs up. He ought to go home, but Maya's camping with Ana and Leo is sleeping over at a friend's. Peter and Kira will be alone in the house, and he knows what she's going to say. She's going to try to persuade him to give up.

So Peter turns the Volvo around and drives. Out of Beartown, off along the road, faster and faster.

On the wall of Richard Theo's office hangs a picture of a stork. Theo has studied statistics and knows that the simplest way to influence people's opinions is to demonstrate a connection: bad diet leads to illness, alcohol causes road accidents, poverty generates crime. He also knows that numbers can be massaged to suit a politician's needs.

In a book by a British statistician, Theo learned, for instance, that there are statistics showing that the number of children born each year is much greater in towns where there are storks than in towns where there aren't many storks. 'What does this prove? That storks deliver babies!' the statistician wrote sarcastically. Of course that isn't the case; there are more storks in towns with a lot of chimneys, because that's where they build their nests. A lot of chimneys means a lot of houses, which means more people, which means more babies.

So Richard Theo has a picture of a stork on the wall of his office to provide him with a daily reminder that whatever is happening isn't important. The important thing is how you explain it to people.

He's interested in other animals, too, such as bears and bulls. Like all the other children around here, he grew up knowing that those were the names of the hockey clubs, but when he started to study economics abroad, he learned a different story. On Wall Street brokers call an optimistic market with rising share prices a 'bull' market, and the slow, remorseless downward movement of the market in a recession is a 'bear' market. The idea is that both are necessary, that the conflict between the two keeps the economy in balance.

Richard Theo has the same idea about the hockey clubs, but his goal is to alter the balance. Because political elections are simple: When everything is going well, when people are happy, the establishment wins. But when people are angry and arguing, people like Richard Theo win. Because for an outsider to win power requires a conflict. But if there's no conflict? You have to create one. He dials the number of an old friend in London. 'Is everyone agreed?' he asks.

'Yes, everyone's on board. But you appreciate that the new owners require certain . . . political guarantees?' his London friend says.

'They'll get what they want. Just make sure they show up here and look happy in the pictures for the local paper,' Theo says.

'And what do you want?'

'I just want to be their friend,' Theo insists.

His London friend laughs. 'Yeah, right, as usual.'

'It's a good deal for the new owners,' Richard promises.

His London friend agrees. 'A very good deal, no doubt about it, and it couldn't have happened without your specialist knowledge and political contacts. The new owners appreciate your help. But seriously: Why are *you* so interested in the factory?'

Theo's voice is gentle. 'Because the factory's in Beartown. I need it because it's going to give me a hockey club.'

His London friend laughs again. When he and Theo met at university in England, Theo had only a small academic grant and empty pockets. His mother was a teacher and his father a factory worker, but his dad was active in the union and had gained a reputation as such a tough negotiator that legend has it that the factory managers gave him a job in middle management simply so they wouldn't have to negotiate with him. His dad grew fat and comfortable, and soon he wasn't at all dangerous. That taught Richard Theo what it was possible to do with power. So when he got to university, he consciously sought out a particular type of man: those from wealthy families who were also weak and bullied and had low self-confidence. Theo was quick-witted and funny, a good friend and excellent company at parties, as well as being pretty good at talking to girls. Those are valuable qualities anywhere. In return he acquired loyal friends who soon inherited money and power from their parents. That taught Theo the value of contacts.

When he got home to Beartown, he could have joined any political party, but he chose the smallest, for the same reason he had chosen to start his political career in Beartown instead of a larger city: sometimes it's more effective to be a big fish in a small pond than a small one in a big pond. Political affiliations and colours were unimportant to him; he would have been just as happy on the extreme right or extreme left. Some people are driven by ideals, but Richard Theo was driven by results. Other politicians say he's an 'opportunist' with 'simple answers to difficult questions,' the sort who one moment is standing with unemployed men in the Bearskin pub promising council investment, the next is hobnobbing with the bosses on the Heights promising lower taxes. He seeks out simple scapegoats every time a crime is committed in the Hollow so that he can call in the local paper for 'more police' while simultaneously criticizing the establishment for 'not sticking to the council budget.' He sits with environmentalists and promises to stop the hunting lobby's influence on local politics, but when it suits his agenda he sits in other rooms and fans the hunters' frustration with the wolf huggers in the big cities and the gun haters in government agencies.

Theo is, of course, supremely ambivalent about the criticism, because it's just another way of saying that he doesn't need flags. Politics is about strategy, not dreams. So what situations can he exploit this summer?

There have long been rumours that the hospital in Hed is going to be shut down. The factory in Beartown has been cutting its staff for years. And now Beartown Ice Hockey is threatened with bankruptcy. You need to know a good deal about wind to understand how to win something from all three of those.

'A hockey club? I didn't think you liked sports,' his London friend says in surprise.

'I like things that are useful to me,' Richard Theo says.

Two women, Fatima and Ann-Katrin, are sitting in a small car on their way through the forest. Their sons, Amat and Bobo, became teammates in the spring, and the bear on their sons' jerseys brought the mothers together as well. Ann-Katrin works as a nurse in the hospital that Fatima cleans in the summers, so they started having coffee together, and realized that although the places of birth in their passports may have been a very great distance apart, they share the same mentality: work hard, laugh loud, and love your children with everything you've got.

To start with, of course, much of their conversation revolved around the rumours that the hospital was going to be closed. Fatima told Ann-Katrin that one of the first things she learned to say in the Beartown dialect, where she had just arrived with a little boy in her arms, was 'That's going to be difficult.' Fatima loved the people here because they didn't try to pretend that the world was uncomplicated. Life is tough, it hurts, and people admitted that. But then they grinned and said, 'What the hell? It's supposed to be hard. Otherwise every bugger in the big cities would be able to do it!'

Ann-Katrin related stories of her own. About her parents, who died young, and about growing up in the forest as the economy was getting worse, and about falling in love with a big, clumsy man called 'Hog' because he played hockey like a wounded wild boar and could skate only in a straight line at full speed. Ann-Katrin had never travelled, had never seen the world, had never felt the need. 'The most beautiful trees are here,' she promised Fatima, adding 'And the men aren't too bad either, if you're patient.'

Hog and their three children – Bobo is the eldest – have kept Ann-Katrin busy. She gets up early, feeds and clothes them, helps Hog with the paperwork in the workshop, then goes to the hospital and works long shifts full of the worst days in other people's lives. Then home again, 'homework to be done and the house to sort out and tears to be wiped from cheeks from time to time.'

But in the evenings, she told Fatima, Hog creeps through the kitchen more softly than a man of his bulk ought to be able to. And when he holds her, when she turns around close to him and they dance, with her toes on his feet so that he's carrying her whole weight with every little step, it's all worth it. It becomes the whole world. 'Do you remember when the children were really small, Fatima? When you'd get to preschool and they'd run towards you and literally jump up into your arms? Jump with complete abandon because they trusted us to catch them, that's my favourite moment in the whole world.' Fatima smiles and says, 'Do you know what? When Amat plays hockey, when he's happy, I still feel like that. Do you know what I mean?' Ann-Katrin knows exactly. That was how they became friends.

When Ann-Katrin collapsed in the cafeteria of the hospital one afternoon a few weeks ago, it was Fatima who caught her. She was one of the first people Ann-Katrin told about her illness. Fatima went with her to doctors appointments, drove her to see specialists at another hospital so that Hog could stay at home and run the garage. They're sitting in the car now, almost home, and Ann-Katrin smiles tiredly. 'You do too much for me.'

Fatima replies firmly, 'Do you know what I learned when I came to Beartown? That if we don't look after each other, no one else will.'

'Bears shit in the forest, and everyone else shits on Beartown!' Ann-Katrin says in the voice of the drunk old uncles in the Bear-skin, and the two women laugh out loud.

As they pull up on the grass in front of the workshop, Fatima whispers, 'You have to tell Bobo that you're ill.'

'I know,' Ann-Katrin sniffs with her face in her hands.

She wanted to wait until the hockey season had started so Bobo would have somewhere to take his feelings. But there isn't time. So how do you do it? How do you tell your children that you're going to die?

The Barn is a bar on the outskirts of Hed; it has live music and cheap beer and, like all similar places, it's become a natural meeting place for people who are trying to forget their problems, as well as for the people who are looking for them. Katia Ovich is sitting in the office huddled over the accounts when one of the bouncers knocks on the doorframe.

'I know you didn't want to be disturbed, but your little brother's sitting in the bar. In his T-shirt.'

Katia lowers her head and lets out a deep sigh. Then she gets up, pats the bouncer on the shoulder, and promises to take care of it.

Sure enough, Benji is sitting in the bar, which in itself isn't a problem. He's pretty much grown up in the Barn, and when it's been short of staff he's stood behind the bar serving beer long before he was old enough to buy it for himself. But things are different now. The regulars in the Barn support Hed Hockey, but they've let Benji come for three reasons: (1) The regulars like Katia. (2) Benji has been only a junior player in Beartown. (3) He's had the sense to wear long sleeves.

But he's eighteen now, and if he plays hockey this autumn he'll be on the A-team, and he's sitting at the bar wearing a T-shirt so that everyone can see the tattoo of the bear on his arm. The same week someone has posted a clip online of red Hed Hockey flags burning and a politician in Hed who spoke in public about the possible bankruptcy of Beartown Ice Hockey ended up with an axe in the hood of her car.

'Are you going to put a top on?' Katia asks when she arrives behind the bar.

Benji smiles. 'Hello, favourite sister.'

That was always his trick when he was little, and her weakness was that she could never get angry, because she wanted him to love her most. She sighs sadly. 'Please, Benji, can't you just do this somewhere else?'

She gestures towards his beer glass. Katia knows she can't stop anyone in her family from doing anything; she learned that early in life. Tomorrow would have been their dad's birthday.

'Don't worry, favourite sister,' Benji says.

As though she has a choice. She looks beseechingly at him. 'Finish your beer and then go home, okay? I just need to finish the accounts, I'll be done in fifteen minutes.'

Benji leans over the bar and kisses her cheek. She feels like both hugging him and hitting him, the same as usual. She looks around the bar; it isn't even a quarter full, and most of the people here are either too old or too drunk to worry about Benji's tattoo. Katia hopes she can get him out of here before that changes.

When Amat's legs have no strength left, he turns and runs back along the road more slowly. Halfway home he encounters a Volvo. It's Peter Andersson's. Maybe Amat should stop himself, maybe he should have more dignity, but he starts jumping up and down and waving frantically. The car slows down, almost unwillingly. Amat leans in through the wound-down window, and the words bubble out of him breathlessly: 'Hi, P – Peter, I just wanted to ask . . . all the talk about the club, is there going . . . I mean, is there going to be a junior team in the autumn? I want to play, I have . . .'

Peter shouldn't have stopped the car, should have known himself better than to take out his feelings on a sixteen-year-old boy. For a moment he forgets what Amat did back in the spring, that the reason why the junior player can't go to Hed now is that he testified on behalf of Maya. Saved Peter's job. But sometimes grief and rage can consume a grown man so completely that he can't actually consider the fact that other people have feelings too.

'Amat, I've got a lot on my mind, we'll have to talk about this another time.'

'When? I've got nowhere to *play*!' Amat blurts out breathlessly.

He may not have meant to sound angry, but he's frightened. Peter's guilty conscience threatens to suffocate him, and at times like that sometimes the right places in our hearts don't get enough oxygen, so he snaps back, 'Are you having trouble hearing me, Amat? I DON'T GIVE A DAMN ABOUT THE JUNIOR TEAM! I don't even know if I've got a CLUB!!!'

Only then does Amat see that Peter's been crying. The boy backs away slowly from the car. Peter drives away, utterly crushed. In the rain he didn't see the tears running down the boy's cheeks as well.

A man is sitting in the bar of the Barn, twenty-five, maybe twenty-seven. Blue jeans, polo shirt. He's drinking beer and has a book open in front of him. When Katia goes back to the office, he raises an eyebrow in Benji's direction and asks, 'Should I move?'

Benji turns towards him with the sort of carefree little quiver of the corners of his lips that people find very hard not to find infectious. 'What for?'

The man in the polo shirt smiles. 'Your sister seems to think you're going to get in trouble. So I'm wondering if I should move.'

76

'That depends how much you like trouble,' Benji replies and drinks some of his beer.

The man in the polo shirt nods. He glances at Benji's hand and sees the blood on his knuckles. 'I've lived here for four hours. How quickly is it reasonable to get into trouble?'

'Kind of depends how long you're thinking of staying. What's the book?'

The question comes so out of the blue that the man momentarily doesn't know what to say; then he realizes that perhaps that was the point. Benji has many ways of making other people feel uncertain.

'It was . . . I mean, it *is* a . . . it's a biography of Friedrich Nietzsche,' the man in the polo shirt says and clears his throat.

'The guy with the abyss?' Benji asks.

The man in the polo shirt looks surprised. ' "If you look long into the abyss, the abyss also looks into you." Yes, that's Nietzsche.'

'You look surprised,' Benji observes.

'No . . . ,' the man lies.

Benji drinks his beer. For many years his mother had a way of punishing him for fighting in school by forcing him to read the newspaper. He wasn't allowed to go to hockey practice until she'd tested him on everything: the editorial, the foreign news, culture, politics. After a few years that got too easy for him, so his mother started to use literary classics instead. She could hardly read them herself, but she knew her son was smarter than he let anyone believe. So his punishment for misbehaviour was also a reminder: you're better than this.

Benji sniggers at the man in the polo shirt. 'Were you expecting me to trot out "What doesn't kill you makes you stronger" when you mentioned Nietzsche? Or maybe "In heaven, all the interesting people are missing"? Or . . . how does it go? "And those who were seen dancing were thought to be insane by those who couldn't hear the music"?'

'I don't think that last one is Nietzsche,' the man replies cautiously.

Benji drinks his beer in a way that makes it impossible for the

77

man to know if it was a mistake or a test. Then he says, 'You still look surprised.'

'I . . . no . . . okay, to be honest, you don't look like someone who'd quote Nietzsche,' the man says, laughing.

'There are lots of things I don't look like,' Benji says.

The corners of his mouth are dancing again.

Bobo and his mother go for a long walk in the forest that evening. She wants to tell him how hard it is to be an adult, how complex the world is, but she doesn't know how. All the while Bobo was growing up, she tried to teach him that violence was wrong, but this spring he found himself in the worst fight of his life and came close to being seriously injured, and she's rarely been as proud of him as she was then. Because he defended Amat. Got beaten up for his sake. He stood up for something.

For many years she was pleased that Bobo was such a softie. Other boys were embarrassed when their mothers kissed them on the forehead in front of their friends, but not hers. He was the sort of boy who would say, 'Your hair looks nice today, Mum.' Now she wishes he was tougher. Colder. Maybe he'd have been able to handle it better.

'I'm not well, Bobo . . . ,' she whispers.

Bobo cries when she tells him, but she cries more. Bobo isn't the little boy who used to jump up into her arms anymore; he's big enough now to have space in his chest for the greatest sorrow and tall and strong enough to pick his mother up and carry her home after she's told him she's going to die. She whispers against his neck, 'You've always been the best big brother in the world. You're going to have to be even better now.'

That evening she hears him read Harry Potter to his little brother and sister. That night Hog makes some weak tea and Bobo comes into the bathroom and holds his mum's hair when she throws up. When she's lying on her bed, her son wipes her cheeks and says, 'Do you want to hear something silly? You know you're always telling me I'll never find a girlfriend because my demands are too high? That's your fault. Because I want someone who looks at me the way you and Dad look at each other.'

Ann-Katrin presses Bobo's big, dumb lummox's head tight to her forehead. She would have loved to see him get married. Become a dad. Life is so damn, damn, damn tough sometimes that it's almost unbearable. Even if that's the way it's supposed to be.

Katia is almost finished with her paperwork when the bouncer comes running in. She knows it's already too late. None of the clientele of the Barn could be bothered to argue with Benji about his tattoo, but someone has called some men who don't share the same tolerance of artistic freedom. One of them has a bull tattooed on his lower arm. As they walk through the door, Benji turns to the guy in the polo shirt and says, 'Now would be a good time to move away!'

He grins as he says this, like a naughty child who's left a whoopee cushion under the seat of a chair. None of the men in the doorway is in anything like as good shape as Benji, but there are four of them and he's on his own. He bounces enthusiastically down from his bar stool as if he's pleased that there are so many of them, to even things up. They don't rush at him; he's the one who walks straight towards them, and it makes them nervous just long enough to give him an advantage. The man with the bull tattoo grabs an empty beer bottle from a table, so Benji decides to tackle him first. But he doesn't get a chance.

The man in the polo shirt watches Katia come rushing out of the office and throw herself into the group of men. She pushes the man with the beer bottle up against the wall and yells, 'One single swing in here, and you'll be drinking at home for a year!'

Then she spins around towards Benji and sees a very familiar look in his eyes. The same as their older sister Adri's, the same as their father's: if there isn't a war, they start one.

'Benji . . . not here, not today, please . . . ,' she whispers.

She puts her hands on his chest, feels the beat of his heart. His pulse is calm, his breathing steady. Four grown men want to beat him up, and he isn't even scared. Nothing frightens Katia as much as that.

Benji looks her in the eye. She has their mother's eyes, and she doesn't often ask her little brother for anything. So he kisses her on the cheek and laughs scornfully at the four men in the doorway. 'Are you coming in or going out? I'm going home, so if you're not too busy feeling each other's dicks maybe you could get out of the way?'

The men glance at Katia and the bouncers, and eventually they step back. The point has already been made: it's no longer acceptable to show up in Hed with a bear tattoo. Beartown may have a 'Pack,' but there are men here who are prepared to take a stand, too.

As Benji walks through the door, he lets out a loud laugh. The men he's left behind are quivering with rage. One of them mutters to Katia, 'It's lucky for your brother that he's got you. You just saved his life.'

Katia glares at the man. 'You think? Really? You think I saved *his* life?'

The man tries to smile confidently, but his mouth is dry. Katia snorts. She goes and gets her things from the office, then fetches her car, but Benji has already disappeared into the night, where she won't find him.

All sports are silly. All games are ridiculous. Two teams, one ball, sweat and grunting, and for what? So that for a few baffling moments we can pretend that it's the only thing that matters.

That night Hog and Bobo clear the floor of the garage. They've never talked much as father and son, and perhaps they're both worried that they might take to the easiest alternative now. There are bottles of drink in that house, as in everyone else's. So they choose a different option, drive the cars out, move the tools and machinery until the garage is empty.

Then they fetch hockey sticks and a tennis ball. They play against each other all night, sweating and grunting, as if it were the only thing that mattered.

★

When the door closes behind Benji, he walks alone a couple of hundred feet into the forest. Then he stops with his hands in his pockets and looks around. As if he's considering whether or not to try to find another way of complicating his evening or if he should pick a tree to climb and smoke weed in until he falls asleep instead. The voice behind him is both expected and unexpected.

'I've never been in a fight, not once, so I won't be much use if that's what you're after. But I'd be happy to have a beer somewhere else,' says the man in the polo shirt.

Benji looks over his shoulder. 'Do you know any good clubs around here, then?'

The man laughs. 'Like I said, I've only been living here for the past four hours. But . . . I've got somewhere to stay. And a fridge.'

He's never done this before, asked someone home right away, it's never worked that way for him before. But Benji has a way of encouraging people to be spontaneous. Foolhardy, too.

They take the path through the forest. The man is renting a cabin at a campsite on the outskirts of Hed, in the direction of Beartown, far enough away not to be within sight of either town. They kiss for a long time in the hallway. When the man wakes up in bed the next morning, Benji is already gone.

The man finds his book where he dropped it, between the front door and the bedroom. He leafs through it until he finds the quote he's looking for: 'One must still have chaos in oneself to be able to give birth to a dancing star.'

Some distance away a young man is standing in a cemetery firing pucks at a gravestone. He has scraped knuckles, and worse things are going on inside him. Alain Ovich is dead, and Kevin Erdahl may as well be. Benji is a man who loves men, and he loses everyone he loves.

It's hard to have more chaos in oneself than that.

II

One Last Chance to Be a Winner

It's impossible to measure love, but that doesn't stop us coming up with new ways to try. One of the simplest is space: How much space am I prepared to give the person that you are so that you can become the person you want to become?

Kira once made a valiant attempt to discuss this with Peter in terms of ice hockey: 'A marriage is like a hockey season, darling, okay? Even the best team can't be at their best in every game, but they're good enough to win even when they play badly. A marriage is the same: you don't measure it by the holiday where you drink wine before lunch and have great sex and your biggest problem is that the sand is too hot and the sun is shining too brightly on the screen when you want to play games on your phone. You measure it from everyday life, at home, at its lowest level, from how you talk to each other and solve problems.'

Peter got cross, as if she were trying to spark an argument, and asked what she wanted. She said she wanted to have 'a grown-up conversation about our problems.' He considered this for an unreasonably long time before he finally said, 'I have a problem with you always leaving a tiny dribble of milk in the carton and putting it back in the fridge because you can't be bothered to rinse it and put it in the recycling bin.' She just stared at him and asked, 'You think *that's* the biggest problem in our marriage?' Insulted, he muttered, 'So why bother even *asking* if you're only going to criticize my answer?' She massaged her temples. He slammed the door behind him and went off to a hockey game. It's not without its complications, having a relationship that works like that.

Kira is sitting at the kitchen table this evening. She's seen the announcement of her husband's death in the newspaper. The bottle of wine in front of her is unopened; there are two glasses beside it. She spins her wedding ring, around, around, around, as if it were a nut she was trying to tighten. Sometimes she tries taking it off, just to see how it would feel. Cold, it feels cold, as if her skin has grown thinner there.

It's late when she hears the Volvo pull up outside. It's ridiculous, she knows it is, but she goes and stands right behind the door. Because when she hears Peter's footsteps outside she wants to know if he puts the key in the lock straight away or if he pauses first. If he hesitates. If he stands out there and takes some deep breaths before summoning up the courage to go inside.

Peter stops with his hand on the door handle. Rests his forehead gently against the door, as if he were trying to hear how the house is breathing, if anyone's awake inside. Not long ago, when she thought he was asleep, he heard Kira talking on the phone to someone in the kitchen: 'For twenty years he's said that next year it will finally be my turn to focus on my career. Next year. Does he really think he's the only person driven to find out how good he can be at something?'

For twenty years Peter has told himself that he's doing this not for his own sake but for other people's. He became a professional hockey player in Canada so he could provide for his family. He took the job as general manager in Beartown because the family needed a safe place after they'd lost Isak. He fought for the club because he was fighting for the town. Because Beartown Ice Hockey was the pride of the community, the only way for this whole chunk of the country to remind the big cities that there were still people living here. That they could still give them a thrashing.

But he isn't sure anymore. Maybe he's just being selfish? He tries to stop thinking about the death notice. He's always been prone to worrying, anxious about everything from bills to whether the coffee machine is switched off, but tonight is something different. Tonight he's scared.

He's just put the key in the door when a metallic click makes him start. A car door swings open out in the street.

A black-clad man gets out and walks towards him.

Two cars are driving through the forest. One of them drives all the way to the kennels, and a man in a black jacket that can't possibly be fastened over his muscular chest gets out. He shakes Adri's hand. Adri was in high school with him half a lifetime ago and has nothing against him, except for the fact that he's less sharp than someone suffering from rheumatism handling a disposable camera. Once she had to explain to him that south on the map didn't actually mean a downward slope and on another occasion that islands didn't float on the sea but were actually fixed to the ocean floor. He doesn't have many branches on his family tree. He's got himself a new tattoo on his hand, she notices, a spiderweb so uneven that it practically forces her to ask, 'What the hell . . . did you lose a bet or something?'

'What?' he answers uncomprehendingly, and stares at his hand, clearly not struck by the fact that it looks as though whoever did it was working in the dark.

Someone once called him 'Spider' at school because he had long, thin, hairy legs. He was the sort of boy who didn't care what anyone called him, as long as they knew who he was, so he embraced the insult. He's gotten himself at least a dozen spider-themed tattoos since then, all of them apparently done by drunks sitting on top of a tumble dryer.

Adri shakes her head wearily and opens the trunk of Spider's car, which is full of boxes of liquor. Adri notes that the other car is waiting as usual where the road ends, at the edge of the forest. The driver is sitting inside it so he can warn them if any unwelcome visitors are approaching, but the passenger gets out. Adri has known him for many years, too, and – unlike Spider – he definitely isn't an idiot. That's what makes him dangerous.

His name is Teemu Rinnius. He's not particularly thickset, and he's not particularly tall, and his hair is so neat that his best friends call him 'the accountant,' but Adri has seen him fight and knows that beneath that hair his head is made of concrete. His kick is so hard that in this town it's the horses that are frightened of standing behind him. When he was younger, he and his little brother were so notorious that the hunters used to joke, 'You know why you should never knock the Rinnius brothers off a bike? Because it's probably your bicycle!' Now that he's older they no longer tell jokes about him, and if anyone from outside comes to the town asking for Teemu Rinnius, even the smallest child has the sense to answer, 'Who?'

Teemu isn't wearing a black jacket; he doesn't need one. He opens the back door of the car and lets out two dogs. He bought them from Adri as puppies, so if anyone asks what he's doing here this evening, he can say he's thinking of buying another one. He has no delivery schedule, no fixed routine; Adri gets a phone call a couple of hours in advance, then he shows up once it's dark. She calls him 'the wholesaler,' half affectionately, half mockingly. She herself is the retailer. Two cars can't go from door to door in Beartown dropping off bottles of drink without attracting suspicion, whereas everyone knows that all the hunters in the area usually drop in at the kennels from time to time to check out the puppies and drink coffee. Perhaps they come a little too often, those hunters, especially before major holidays. But if you ask anyone around here about Adri, they'll all say the same thing: 'She makes very good coffee.'

The men in black jackets always have two cars, and Teemu never sits in the one containing the drink. There are police investigations that claim that he's the leader of a 'violent hooligan gang known as the Pack, who support Beartown Hockey.' There are plenty of stories of their influencing the club's affairs, that highly paid players on the A-team who don't perform well enough have voluntarily torn up their own contracts, but there's never been any proof. And naturally there's no proof that the Pack is involved in the organized smuggling of alcohol or trading in stolen cars and snowmobiles, either. There has never been any proof that the Pack has ever threatened anyone, the way criminal networks everywhere usually have to do in order to establish their violent credentials. Police investigations claim that the Pack don't need to do that because they use hockey games to advertise themselves. The theory goes that anyone who has seen the black jackets packed in the standing area of the rink, or who has heard what they've done to fans of other teams that have challenged them, would understand the seriousness of the situation if they appear on the doorstep.

But obviously that's all nonsense. Rumour and exaggeration by city types who've seen too many films. If you ask almost anyone who lives in Beartown about the Pack, they'll just reply, 'What pack?'

When Adri lifts the last crate of drink from the back of the car she notes that there's a large axe under it. She rolls her eyes.

'Seriously, Teemu, don't you think it looks a bit suspicious, having an axe in the trunk when every cop in the district has seen pictures of that councillor's car in Hed?'

There aren't many people who dare take that tone with Teemu, but he merely looks amused. 'Adri, think about it: after what happened to that poor woman's car in Hed, wouldn't it look more suspicious if we *didn't* have axes in our cars?'

Adri bursts out laughing. 'You're such an idiot. Except you're not.'

Teemu smiles. 'Thank you kindly.'

When Ana has fallen asleep out on the island, Maya lies awake and writes lyrics about hatred. Sometimes she carries on so long that she ends up writing about love. Not the earth-shattering falling-in-love kind but the boring, whole-of-your-life sort. She doesn't know why, but she's thinking a lot about her parents this summer. When you're a teenager, you want them to be sexless, but somewhere along the way the smallest memories of affection between our parents get imprinted on our DNA. Parents who divorce, like Ana's, can stop a child believing in eternal love. Parents who stick together for a lifetime can make a child take it for granted instead.

Maya remembers such insignificant things from her childhood. The way her mum laughs when she describes her dad's style of dress as 'plainclothes cop at high school disco.' Or the way her dad shakes the all-but-empty milk carton each morning and mutters, 'Welcome to today's Guinness World Record attempt, where we will try to make the smallest cup of coffee in the world.' The way her mum loses it if there are socks on the floor and the way her dad would like to take anyone who doesn't wipe the dish rack in front of a war crimes tribunal. The way her mum moved around the world twice for the sake of her dad's hockey and the way her dad sneaks admiring glances at her mum when she takes business calls in the kitchen. As though she were the smartest, funniest, most stubborn, most argumentative person he's ever met and that he still can't quite believe she's his.

The way Maya and Leo didn't know their parents' real names for years because they just called each other 'darling.' The way they've never mentioned the word 'divorce,' not even when they're having a row, because they know that's the nuclear option, and if you threaten it once, every argument from then on will end the same way. The way they suddenly seem to have stopped squabbling about little things now, the way the house has gotten quieter, the way they can hardly look each other in the eye anymore after what happened to Maya. The way they can't bring themselves to show each other just how badly they were broken by it.

Children notice when their parents lose each other in the very smallest ways, in something as insignificant as a single word, such as 'your.' Maya texts them each morning now and pretends it's to stop them worrying about her, even though it's actually the reverse. She's used to them calling each other 'Mum' and 'Dad.' As in 'Mum didn't really mean you were grounded for a thousand years, darling,' or 'Dad didn't demolish your snowman on purpose, he just tripped, darling.' But suddenly one day, almost incidentally, one of them writes, 'Can't you call your mum, she worries so much when you're not home?' And the other writes, 'Remember, your dad and I love you more than anything.' Four letters can reveal the end of a marriage. 'Your.' As if they didn't belong to each other anymore.

Maya sits on an island in a lake far out in the forest and writes songs about it, because she can't bear to be at home and watch it happen.

Minefield

This is a minefield you're walking on
Every word a bomb, but you go on walking
Until there's a quiet 'click' beneath a foot
And then it's too late to go back.

The worst thing about being a victim is the victims I turned you into
I can't mend you now, no matter how much I want to
It's like I was the one who died but you're the ones who were buried
Like I was the one he broke but you're the ones who snapped.

The men in black jackets shake Adri's hand and walk towards the cars, but Teemu stays where he is and lights a cigarette. Adri tucks a wad of chewing tobacco the size of a baby's fist under her lip. She isn't an idiot either; she knows who the Pack are and what they're capable of, but she's a pragmatic person.

One summer a few years ago, Beartown suffered a series of break-ins. A gang showed up at night with vans, and on one occasion an elderly man got beaten up when he tried to stop them. Another time a neighbour called the police while the burglary was in progress. One solitary police car appeared three hours later. Adri remembers how a few months earlier there had been reports of illegal hunting of wolves in the forest not far from here and the police had showed up with helicopters, the National Crime Unit, and a SWAT team. Whatever your views on that, when Adri sees wolves getting better protection than pensioners, she has more faith in the criminal standing beside her than in the criminals in the government and on the council. It has nothing to do with morals. Most people are like her: pragmatic.

When the gang came back, men in black jackets were waiting for them. Everyone else in Beartown closed their doors that night, turned up the volume on their televisions; no one asked any questions afterward. There were no more break-ins. Teemu is a lunatic, Adri won't argue with anyone about that, but he loves this town the same way she does. And he loves hockey. So now he's grinning like a fool. 'Benji's playing on the A-team this autumn, isn't he? You must be so goddamn proud! Have you seen the list of games? Is he stoked?'

Adri nods. She knows that on the ice Benji is everything Teemu wants in a Beartown player: tough, fearless, mean. And he's from here, a local boy made good, a boy next door. Men like Teemu love that. And yes, Adri's seen the game schedule, it was posted online that morning. Beartown is playing Hed Hockey in the first game of the autumn.

'He'll be playing – if there's a Beartown club for him to play in,' she says with a dry laugh.

Teemu smiles, but the look on his face is increasingly hard to interpret. 'We're relying on Peter Andersson to solve that.'

Adri peers at him. It was the Pack who made sure that Peter won the vote of confidence back in the spring and kept his job as general manager; no one can prove it, but everyone knows. Without their votes, Peter would have been out. Now the club has lost almost all its sponsors to Hed, so the Pack were taking a big risk. Ramona, owner of the Bearskin pub, usually says, 'Teemu may not know the difference between right and wrong, but he knows the bloody difference between good and evil.' Perhaps she's right. The Pack lined up behind a general manager and his daughter against the team's star player, Kevin. But that could be a dangerous burden for the general manager if he steers the Pack's club into bankruptcy.

'Are you really relying on Peter? I saw the announcement of his death in the paper,' Adri points out.

Teemu raises an eyebrow. 'Perhaps someone was trying to make a joke.'

'Perhaps someone from your part of the stand was trying to send a message?'

Teemu rubs his head with a fake look of concern. 'It's a big stand. I can't control everything.'

'If Benji gets caught up in any of this, I'll kill you.'

Teemu suddenly bursts out laughing, and the sound echoes through the trees. 'There aren't many people who talk to me like that, Adri.'

'I'm not many people,' she replies.

Teemu lights another cigarette from the butt of the last one. 'It was you who taught your brother to play hockey, wasn't it?'

'I taught him how to fight.'

The trees echo to the sound of Teemu's laughter again. 'Who wins if you fight now?'

Adri looks down. Her voice becomes thicker. 'I do. Because I have an unfair advantage. Benji can't hurt anyone he loves.'

Teemu nods appreciatively. Then he pats her arm and says, 'We only ask one thing of Benji out on the ice. The same thing we ask of everyone.'

'That he should do his best and have fun?' she suggests tartly.

Teemu grins. So does she, eventually. Because she knows what he means. Win. That's all anyone ever asks of you around here. Teemu hands her an envelope and says, 'Ramona heard that you and Sune have started a girls' team for five-year-olds. This is from the kitty.'

Adri looks up in surprise. 'The kitty' is a small box of cash Ramona keeps at the Bearskin for the regulars who lose their jobs and can't pay their bills. All the tips end up there, and people leave more tips at the Bearskin than you might think. Teemu always pays double for his beer, because once when he was younger and had thrown out another of his mother's more unpleasant boyfriends, someone came around and gave the family an envelope like this one. Teemu never let anyone hit his mother again, and when he got old enough to build up the Pack, he never forgot the generosity of the Bearskin's regulars. So now he says, 'For sticks and skates. Or whatever the girls need.'

Adri nods gratefully. When Teemu turns to walk back to the car, she calls after him, 'Hey! Give Peter Andersson a chance! He might yet find a way to save the club!'

Teemu closes the trunk of the car with the axe still inside. 'I am giving Peter a chance. If I wasn't, he wouldn't still be in town.'

Peter stands outside his house but lets go of the door handle, takes the key out of the lock, and turns anxiously towards the street. Richard Theo is walking towards him, dressed in a black suit even though it's the middle of the summer. They've never spoken to each other as far as Peter can remember, but obviously he's well aware of who Richard Theo is. He knows what sort of politics Theo represents, and he doesn't like it. It's aggressive, it sets people against each other, and – above all – Richard Theo has given Peter the impression several times that he really hates hockey.

'Good evening, Peter, I hope I'm not intruding,' Theo says.

There's something ominous in his friendly manner.

'Can I help you?' Peter asks, rather confused.

'No, but I can help you,' Theo replies.

'With what?'

The politician's mouth cracks into a smile. 'I can save your hockey club, Peter. I can give you one last chance to be a winner.'

12

I Am Prepared to Burn in Here

Anyone who devotes his life to being the best at one single thing will be asked, sooner or later, the same question: 'Why?' Because if you want to become the best at something, you have to sacrifice everything else. So the very first time Kira met Peter, that evening in the capital when Peter had just lost the biggest hockey game of his life and stumbled dejectedly into Kira's parents' restaurant, that was what she asked him: Why?

He could never answer it properly, and that drove her mad, but many years later, when they were married and had kids and a whole life together, she read a hundred-year-old quote from a mountaineer. He was asked, 'Why do you want to climb Mount Everest?' The mountaineer replied in bemusement, as if the question was ridiculous and the answer obvious, 'Because it's there.'

Kira understood then, because why had she wanted to go to university when no one else in her family had been? Why had she chosen law when everyone had told her it would be too hard? Why? To find out if she could do it. Because she wanted to climb that damn mountain. Because it was there.

So she knows what's happening now, possibly before Peter understands it himself. She stands behind the front door and hears enough of his conversation with Richard Theo. Her husband is going to find a way to save his club and make himself indispensable again. The way he always does. Kira sits in the hallway until she hears the Volvo start up and watches through the window as Peter drives off. The bottle of wine remains unopened. She puts the glasses back into the cupboard, and the skin beneath her wedding ring is cold when she goes to bed. A night will pass, and tomorrow she will wake up and try to pretend that everything is fine, even though she knows that each day that passes now means it will be even longer to next year.

Peter drives aimlessly for hours, alone. Constantly asking himself the same questions: 'How much is a hockey club worth? Who is it for? How much is it allowed to cost?' And somewhere beneath those are other questions: 'What can I do apart from hockey? What sort of man would I be without it?'

He's never loved anyone but Kira, and he knows she'd be delighted if he gave up ice hockey, but deep down: Would she really? She fell in love with a man with dreams and ambitions, so how will she look at him if the years just keep passing and he never amounts to anything?

When dawn breaks, the light pours over Beartown in the way Peter's mother always said about summer: 'As if the Lord God Himself were pouring orange juice over the treetops.' Peter is sitting outside the supermarket with his eyes closed, asking himself the same questions, over and over and over again.

The first thing Richard Theo said to him last night was 'You don't like my politics, do you?' Peter replied thoughtfully, 'With all due respect, I don't agree with what you stand for. You're an opportunist.' Theo nodded and seemed not to take offence: 'You're only an opportunist until you win, then you're the establishment.' When he saw Peter's look of distaste, he added, 'With all due respect, Peter, politics is about realizing that the world is complicated even though people like you would prefer it to be simple.'

Peter shook his head. 'You thrive on discord. Your type of politics creates conflict. Exclusion.' The politician smiled understandingly. 'And hockey? What do you think that does to everyone who isn't on the inside? Do you even remember me from school?' Peter cleared his throat awkwardly and muttered, 'You were a few years below me, weren't you?' Theo shook his head, not angrily, not accusingly, but almost sadly. 'We were in the same class, Peter.'

Peter doesn't know if Theo planned that, to get him off balance, but it worked. When Peter looked down at the ground, shame-faced, the councillor smiled happily and then explained very plainly why he had come to see Peter: 'I have certain contacts in London. I know which company is going to buy the factory in Beartown.'

'I didn't even know it was being sold!' Peter exclaimed, but the politician merely shrugged his shoulders modestly. 'It's my job to know things that no one else knows, Peter. I know a lot of things about you, too. That's why I'm here.'

Leo wakes up in an empty house the next morning. His mum has left a note on the kitchen table: 'I'm at work, your dad's at the rink, call if you need to. There's some extra money on the counter. We love you! Mum x.' Leo isn't a child anymore. He notices the word 'your' as well. Your dad. Not Mum's other half.

The boy goes into his big sister's room, closes the door, and curls up on the floor. Maya's notebooks are under the bed, full of poems and song lyrics, and he reads them through different types of tears. Sometimes hers, sometimes his own. Maya was never like other big sisters who yelled and threw their younger siblings out of their rooms. When Leo was younger, he was allowed to come in here. Maya let him sleep in her bed when he was frightened, when they eavesdropped on their parents in the kitchen and heard them fall apart when they talked about Isak. The floor next to Maya's bed was always Leo's safest place. But he's older now, and Maya is spending the whole summer out in the forest with Ana. Leo used to ask Maya's advice about everything, so he doesn't know who to ask now, about what a little brother is supposed to do for his big sister when she gets raped. Or what he can do for his parents when they let go of each other. Or what to do with all the hatred.

At the back of a notepad under Maya's bed he finds a page en-titled 'The Matchstick.' He very carefully tears it out and puts it into his pocket. Then he goes down to the beach.

*

He keeps scratching himself the whole time, hard and deep. He tugs his sleeves farther down over his hands.

Those rainy days could have been a chance for emotions in Beartown and Hed to cool off, but William Lyt has sweated his way through them. His coach once said to him that he had never seen anyone play with 'such an immense need for validation.' Maybe he meant it as an attempt to get William to talk about his complexes, but William took it as a compliment.

Throughout his childhood, William had fought to become Kevin's best friend again. He used to be, when they were little, driving pedal cars outside Kevin's house and playing hockey indoors in William's basement. Then they started playing hockey, and suddenly Benji appeared. Kevin never stood next to William in team photographs after that. William did what he could to break Benji, teased him about his cheap secondhand clothes and called him 'Sledge.' Until Benji whacked him in the face with the sledge, costing William both his front teeth and the respect of the changing room. William's mother demanded that Benji be punished for the 'assault,' but the club did nothing.

When they got older, William tried to outshine Benji by boasting about girls he claimed to have slept with, making himself out to be a better friend at parties than that tree-climbing pothead. He was lying, of course: he was a virgin longer than most of the team. But one day Kevin came into the locker room and shouted, 'William! Your girlfriends are waiting for you out here!' Confused, William got up and went out. The corridor was empty, but there was a pack of ten thick white socks on the floor. Kevin was roaring with laughter: 'That way your mum won't have to do the washing *every* time you "sleep" with one of your "girlfriends"!' William never forgot the way the team laughed at him. Especially the way Benji did. William has spent years playing with a desperate need for validation, so now what? Hed Hockey is a fresh start for him, a chance to finally become a leader. He's never going to let himself be the guy with the socks again.

While it's been raining this summer he has been weight training nonstop and watching the video online of his red Hed Hockey flags burning. Over and over again. He was hoping to find a tiny clue as to the identity of the cowardly bastard who had posted it, and eventually he thought he had spotted something: the hand holding the lighter in the video was small, a junior school kid's, and when his sleeve slipped back over his wrist his lower arm looked as though it was covered with scratch marks.

William calls the biggest guys in his team. They buy cigarettes and set off for the beach.

The Matchstick

If there is a darkened room and you lock up a child who is terrified of the dark
If they are left there with their blackest fears because life is a bastard
If it was you in that room and you found a single matchstick in your pocket
You would light the match, even if the room smelled of gas

Only a few degrees separate rain from snow
All houses are built up but burn down
You have shown me things I fear more than death
So I am prepared to burn in here if I can do it with you

When the sun returns to Beartown, the beach once more fills with teenagers pretending not to stare at each other's bodies. At first everything is cheerful and noisy, but soon a frightened silence creeps along the shoreline. Two youths climb into a tree and hang up new Hed Hockey flags. William Lyt is prowling between the towels, and he stops at every junior school kid and holds out a cigarette. 'Have you got a light?'

No one looks him in the eye. He grabs hold of each boy's arm and looks for scratch marks. It's possible that Lyt himself doesn't really know what he's hoping to find, because who would dare to confess anything to him here? But he wants him to be afraid, if nothing else. So that he doesn't challenge his team again. With each teenager who shakes his head as he stares down at the sand, William's heart feels a bit lighter, he feels a bit bigger.

Then he hears a scraping sound. First once, then once again, immediately afterward, and a slight hiss as the flame ignites. A thin voice behind William says, 'I've got a lighter!'

Leo's fingers aren't trembling. His sleeve slides up. The scars on his arm stand out vividly.

'What . . . what do you mean, you know a lot of things about me?' Peter managed to say the previous evening. Richard Theo replied in a carefree, almost cheery way, 'I know that Beartown Ice Hockey is at most just three months away from bankruptcy, even if your friend Tails sells another of his supermarkets. And I know that your A-team coach, Sune, is ill.'

Peter just gawped at him. At the start of the summer Sune had started to have trouble with his heart: Adri Ovich had found him on the floor of his row house when he had failed to show up at the newly formed girls' team's skating class. Adri had called Peter from the hospital, but Sune had asked the pair of them not to tell anyone else. It was just a 'little murmur,' and he didn't want to be 'some damn martyr.'

Naturally they kept quiet, but if Peter were honest, that was much for his own selfish reasons as for Sune's sake: he couldn't recruit a new coach without sponsors or money, he couldn't persuade the team's players to sign new contracts without a coach, and without players there was no way he could attract either sponsors or a new coach.

'As I said,' Richard Theo said quietly, 'it's my job to know things. I have friends at the hospital. I'd like to be your friend, too.' Then, very calmly and methodically, he went through his offer to Peter: the new owners of the factory would require political investment in order to rebuild the factory.

Theo could arrange that. But the owners also recognized that they 'needed to have the support of local residents,' so he had persuaded them that 'the quickest way to these people's hearts is through hockey.'

Peter squirmed and did his best to hold his voice steady as he replied, 'From what I've heard, the other parties don't want to work with you. What reason do I have to believe that you can actually achieve all this?'

Theo replied serenely, 'Yesterday the ice rink had a large, unpaid electricity bill, Peter. If you'd care to phone and check, you'll find that it's been paid. It that enough proof?'

Peter felt very uneasy. 'Why our club? Why not approach Hed Hockey instead?' The politician smiled again. 'Beartown is famous for being hardworking. And what you achieved twenty years ago, when the whole town lined up behind the club, there's a lot of symbolic power in that. What was it you used to say? "Beartown against everyone else"?'

Peter grunted defensively. 'I didn't think you liked hockey.' Theo adjusted his cufflinks and replied, 'My political stance will always be that taxpayers' money should go to health care and jobs, Peter, rather than sports.'

Peter scratched his head and did his best not to look impressed when he said, 'So you'll let taxpayers' money go to the factory instead, in return for the new owners' sponsoring the hockey club? And that way you get to be the politician who saved both jobs and hockey in Beartown. As well as appearing to save taxpayers' money . . . which can be spent on health care services instead . . . bloody hell. You'd win the next election on the back of that.'

Theo put his hands into his pockets, but without radiating any sense of smugness. 'You know, we have a lot in common, Peter. We just play different games. And in order for me to play mine, I need to win the next election. In order for you to play yours, you need a club.'

William is eighteen years old and probably weighs twice as much as the twelve-year-old boy standing in front of him. But Leo isn't backing down. He meets William's gaze with eyes that seem to think they have nothing left to lose.

The whole beach is watching, and even if William hadn't wanted to beat up a boy six years younger than him, there's no way he can back down now. His hand grabs Leo by the neck to hold the little bastard's head steady, but something happens to the twelve-year-old then: the strangulation prompts panic, his mouth opens instinctively as William's fingernails dig into the flesh beneath his chin. Leo starts to retch, and tears spring to his eyes. There are only two natural responses: desperately clutch at his attacker's hands or hit out furiously as hard as he can, directly upward.

Leo's first blow finds nothing but air, but he takes another wild swing and hits William's ear. No one tells you before the first time you get into a fight, but being hit on the ear is bloody painful. William's grip loosens for a fraction of a second, and Leo seizes his chance. He strikes out as hard as he can, hitting William under his chin, and hears the eighteen-year-old's teeth crunch together hard. William must have bit his tongue, because when he throws himself at Leo, blood is pouring from his mouth, and then it's all over. William is too big for the twelve-year-old to stand a chance.

Peter shook his head again at Richard Theo, but not as defiantly this time. 'You and I have nothing in common. You're only interested in power.' The politician laughed at that, for the first time in the conversation. 'Do you really think you're any less political than me, Peter? This spring, when your daughter accused Kevin Erdahl of rape and the sponsors tried to get you dismissed as general manager, you won that vote of confidence because this . . . "Pack" . . . took your side. That's right, isn't it?'

Tiny, cold drops of sweat let go of the hairs on the back of Peter's head and made their way down his spine. 'That wasn't . . . I had no influence . . . I never asked . . . ,' he stammered, but Theo dismissed his objections: 'Everything is political. Everyone needs allies.'

Peter's pulse was ringing in his ears when he asked, 'What do you want from me?' The politician replied frankly, 'When everything becomes official, you take part in a press conference. Just smile for the cameras and shake hands with the new owners. In return, you'll get an injection of capital and complete control over the club. No one will interfere with your job. You'll get the chance to build a winning team. All I want is your . . . friendship. That's not too much to ask, is it?'

He smiled again, and before Peter could answer, the politician moved on to his most important point: 'And one last thing: the new owners obviously don't want to be associated with any form of violence. So when you stand at that press conference, you have to distance yourself from the Pack. And say that you're going to get rid of the standing areas in the rink.'

Peter couldn't bring himself to say anything. Theo seemed to have expected that. He helpfully clarified a few more things, and after he left, Peter just stood there, he didn't know for how long.

When Peter eventually got back into his car and drove off into the night, one thought kept drumming through his head: Control of the club? With a decent budget? He had often been accused of seeing himself as slightly 'morally superior,' and perhaps there's been some justification for that. He considers a hockey club to be more than just sports: it should be an incorruptible force that is never governed by money or politics.

But how many of his ideals is he prepared to sacrifice? What enemies is he prepared to leave himself with? If he gets the power. If he gets to win.

He's on his way to finding out the answers.

Richard Theo got into his car and drove all night, all the way to a small airport where a friend had just landed. Theo shook hands with his friend, who said irritably, 'This better be worth my time.'

Theo offered his apologies. 'Some things are best not discussed over the phone.'

'Well, then,' his friend nodded.

Theo went on, 'I can guarantee our friends in London all the political investment in the land and factory that they require. But

I need a number of things in return. There's a violent gang of hooligans that's spoiling the club. One councillor can't do much to stop them, but a big new sponsor could . . . well, you understand. Exert a degree of influence.'

His friend nodded. 'The hockey club again? Why is that so important to you?'

Theo smiled. 'It's symbolic.'

'So what do you want?' his friend asked.

'The new owners need to set a precondition for their sponsorship agreement: that the general manager of Beartown Ice Hockey speaks out publicly and distances himself from violent fans, and that he gets rid of the standing areas in the rink.'

'That doesn't sound like a big deal.'

'It isn't. But it's important that it comes directly from the owners, not from me.'

His friend gave him his word. They shook hands. The friend got on board a plane.

Richard Theo got into his car and all the way back thought that only someone who had never set foot in Beartown could say that what they had just discussed wasn't 'a big deal.' That's why Theo was always one step ahead of everyone else. Nobody bothered to do any research anymore.

'William! William!' one of the guys on the team hisses somewhere. Leo is too dizzy to hear where the voice is coming from; he's lying on his back and can't see anything through the punches raining down on him.

William raises his arm one last time, but another teammate grabs hold of him and repeats, 'William!'

From the corner of his eye William sees his friend nod towards the road behind the beach. A car has stopped there. Two men in black jackets have gotten out. They're not walking towards the beach; they don't have to. The Pack has never gotten involved in the activities of the town's teenagers: there's always been a dividing line between the seriousness of A-team hockey and the games of the junior team. But William is no longer a junior, and this is no longer just hockey.

William lets go of Leo. Gets up hesitantly. The men in black jackets don't move. William spits blood, and red saliva dribbles onto his T-shirt. 'That's enough,' he mutters quietly, so that no one will hear his voice shaking.

He turns and walks away. His teammates follow him. The men in black jackets stand on the road until one of William's friends gets the hint, climbs up into the tree, and takes down the Hed Hockey flags. The men in black jackets disappear without a word, but the point has been made. No more Hed Hockey on Beartown territory.

Leo sits down on his blanket, without bothering to wipe William's blood from his face. His throat is so sore that he's sure something is broken. One of his friends pats him on the shoulder; another one gives him a cigarette. Leo has never smoked in his life, but he can't not start now. It hurts horribly and is incredibly good.

He didn't back down in the face of William Lyt, and no more red flags are hung from the trees this summer. Perhaps Leo could have made do with that, but his twelve-year-old heart is beating to a different frequency now, because he's discovered something. Adrenaline. Violence. It's like an infatuation. So tomorrow morning William Lyt's mother will open the mailbox outside their house and discover that it is full to the brim with cigarette lighters.

People like William Lyt can't ignore that sort of provocation. And people like Leo Andersson count on that.

13

So They Gave Him an Army

'Everything has its price, everyone will pay something!' Those were the most frequent words from Ramona's husband's mouth when he was alive. The first thing he asked anyone who had bought anything, regardless of whether it was a new car or a secondhand toaster, was 'What did you pay?' And whatever they replied, he would grunt, 'They saw you coming! I'd have gotten it for half that!' Ramona had been so sick of hearing it, but what she would have given to hear it one more time. He loved her, and he loved hockey and used to say that the centre circle of Beartown's rink was their wedding ring, so he didn't need one on his finger. When life was tough, he never said, 'It'll be okay,' he just said, 'Soon time for hockey.' If anyone said 'It's summer,' he would correct them and say, 'This is preseason.' He rearranged the pages of every calendar so that the year started in September, because that's when his year started, when Beartown played its first game.

Eleven seasons have passed since he left Ramona. Today a telemarketer is sitting somewhere and dialling a number without really caring whose number it is. 'Is that Holger? How are you doing today, Holger?' he says loudly when the call is answered.

'Holger's been dead eleven years. And he wasn't feeling particularly brilliant before that, either. What do you want, boy?' Ramona replies, standing at the bar with her second breakfast in her hand.

The caller taps anxiously at his keyboard. 'Is that the Bearskin pub?'

'Yes,' Ramona says.

'I see . . . sorry, but Holger is still listed as one of the owners on our files . . .'

'It's still our pub. It's just that I'm the one doing all the work these days.'

'Ah, what does it say here . . .? Is that . . . "Ramona"?'

'It is.'

The salesman takes a deep breath and starts again. 'Great! How are you doing today, Ramona?'

'Boy, these days there's technology that can help people like me find out where people like you live.'

'I'm . . . I'm sorry?'

'You heard me.'

A short silence follows. Then eventually the salesman clears his throat and for slightly unclear reasons summons up the courage to recite, a little too quickly, 'I'm selling subscriptions to our skin care products! Every month you receive eight different products through the post, but you only keep the ones you want and send the others back free of charge . . .'

'Eight?' Ramona wonders after two large gulps of breakfast.

'Yes!'

'And I'm supposed to have an opinion about that? Tell me, boy, do you honestly think a person has that much skin?'

The salesman doesn't have a scripted reply to that, so instead he tries, 'Right now we have a very attractive off –'

Ramona's voice is simultaneously apologetic and irritated, as if she's about to tell him that his cat has been run over but that it was actually something of a nuisance for her because the little bugger jumped out of the way the first two times she tried.

'Boy, the people you call probably have their hands full trying to hold their lives together. Eight different skin care products? People just want to make it through the day.'

The salesman replies in a voice scratchy with cough drops and despair, 'Me, too.'

'Have you had breakfast, boy? That's the most important beer of the day. Probably good for the skin, too, full of vitamins.'

'I'll give it a try,' the salesman promises.

'You know what, boy? If you're ever passing Beartown, you can have one on the house.'

' "Beartown"? I didn't even know there was a place called that.'

Ramona hangs up. 'Everything has its price,' Holger said before he left her, and when he was buried the priest said the same thing: 'Grief is the price we pay for love, Ramona. A broken heart in exchange for a whole one.' He was a bit drunk at the time, of course, that damn priest. But that didn't stop him being right. Everyone pays something, people and communities alike.

There was once a time when every telemarketer had heard of Beartown. 'Beartown? You're the ones with the hockey team, right?'

In the yard below the apartment blocks in the Hollow some children are playing hockey, using a wall as the goal and soda bottles as posts. Amat is standing at the window of his room watching them. He used to play with his best friends, Zacharias and Lifa. It was an easy game back then. A stick each, a tennis ball, two teams.

But they're sixteen now, almost men. The Hollow has gotten worse, unless they've just gotten big enough to see the truth about their surroundings. If you want to understand the Hollow, you need to know that everyone who lives here regards the rest of Beartown the way the rest of Beartown regards the big cities: 'We only exist for them in the form of negative newspaper headlines.'

Lifa once said to Amat: 'They love you if you're good at hockey, but they'll only say you're from Beartown when you win. When you lose, they'll say you come from the Hollow.' Lifa hasn't played hockey for years now; he's changed, become harder. He hangs out with his brother's gang now, does deliveries on his moped carrying a backpack whose contents Amat doesn't know anything about. They see even less of each other now.

Zacharias spends his nights at home playing computer games and sleeps all day. His parents are spending the summer with relatives, and Zacharias might as well be living in a different country because he lives his whole life online now. At the start of the summer Amat would stop at his apartment each day and ask if he wanted to join him for a run, but Zacharias just tried to lure him in to play games and eat toasted sandwiches, so Amat stopped going over to avoid the temptation of spending the summer doing nothing. Nothing leads to nothing, he knows that much.

So Amat has been training alone, putting weights on his bed and lifting it like a primitive bench press, doing push-ups until he cries, and running along the roads until he throws up. He goes down to the communal laundry room at night and practices stick handling pucks and balls between glass bottles, faster and faster. Every other evening, his mum, Fatima, comes home late because she's helping a friend who's ill, Amat doesn't know who. He doesn't tell her he misses her, because he doesn't want to make her feel guilty. Fatima is the sort of person who looks after everyone who needs her, and her son is big enough to take his place in line.

But this evening he isn't training. Or sleeping. The other kids of his age from the Hollow hang out on 'the Hill' at night, on the edge of the forest looking out over the old gravel pit. Amat can see them from the balcony, cooking hot dogs on barbecues and smoking weed, talking about nothing and laughing. Just being . . . teenagers.

Everything has its price. They say you have to spend ten thousand hours practicing to get really good at something, so how many more is it going to cost Amat to get away from here? He hasn't even got a team now. After everything he gave up in the spring to stand up and tell the truth about what Kevin did to Maya, he hasn't got anything left. Even Maya's father doesn't give a damn.

Amat pulls on a jersey, leaves the apartment, and heads up towards the Hill. Most of the teenagers around the fires have known him since he was little, but they still look at him like some captive animal that has just jumped out of its cage. He stops, embarrassed, and looks down at the ground until someone suddenly laughs and passes him a cigarette whose contents he doesn't bother to ask about.

'Here, superstar, party time!' the girl who hands it to him says with a grin.

She's sweet. So is the smoke. Amat closes his eyes and drifts away, and when she takes hold of his hand he thinks that maybe he could stay here after all. Everything else can go to hell: hockey, the club, the demands, the pressure. He's going to let himself be normal, just for one night. Smoke until he sabotages himself and fades away into the night air.

He finds himself holding a beer, doesn't know where it came from. Then when another hand comes out of nowhere and knocks his arm so hard that he drops both the beer and the joint, Amat yells, 'What the hell?' and turns instinctively to shove the idiot in the chest.

Lifa, his childhood friend, is big now. His chest doesn't budge an inch. Instead he grabs hold of Amat's jersey and throws him roughly down the slope.

Tails, the tall, thickset supermarket owner who's almost always in a better mood than a Labrador under a water sprinkler, just sits there in shock as Peter tells him the whole story. They're sitting in Tails's office at the back of the shop, full of files containing Beartown Ice Hockey Club's accounts. Tails is the club's last big sponsor and is spending all his time trying to figure out how long he can keep the club alive without the help of the council.

'I don't get it . . . why would Richard Theo want you to take a stand against . . .'

He stands up and closes the door before he finishes his sentence in a whisper: ' . . . the Pack?'

Peter rubs the dark rings under his eyes. 'The factory's new owners want to sponsor a "family sport." That looks better in the media. They've told Theo that they want to get rid of "hooliganism." And after that business with the axe in the councillor's car, well . . .'

'But how's that going to work?' Tails asks.

Peter closes his eyes in exhaustion. 'I have to say in a press conference that the club is getting rid of the standing area.'

'The Pack aren't the only people who use that . . .'

'I know. But everyone in the Pack uses it. Richard Theo doesn't care what happens, he's just bothered about how it looks.'

Tails's eyes open wide. 'He's a smart bastard, that Theo. Everyone knows the Pack voted to let you stay on at the meeting in the spring. So if *you* distance yourself from them in the paper it will be . . . more effective.'

'And Richard Theo gets everything he wants: the factory, jobs, the hockey club. He can take the credit for everything and won't be blamed for anything. Not even the Pack will hate him, they'll just hate me. And we'll be giving him everything he needs to win the next council elections.'

'You can't do it, Peter. The Pack will . . . you know what they're like . . . there are some crazy bastards in that gang, and hockey's the only thing some of them have got!' Tails says.

He knows because a few members of the Pack work in his warehouse. They work hard, and they make sure everyone else on their shift does, too, and if there's ever a break-in at the store, Tails never has to call a security firm, because it gets taken care of. In return, Tails arranges their shifts so they never have to take holiday in order to go to Beartown Ice Hockey's away games, but if the police show up a week later their names still appear on the rota, at precisely the time when the police are trying to prove that they were involved in 'hooligan-related violence.' 'Hooligans? There are no hooligans working here,' their employer exclaims uncomprehendingly. 'Pack? What Pack?'

Peter wrings his hands. 'What's the alternative, Tails? Richard Theo only cares about power, so putting the fate of the club in his hands and those of a bunch of utterly unknown investors is madness. But being realistic, if we don't, the club will be dead anyway in three months.'

'I can sell another store or take out a loan on this one,' Tails suggests.

Peter puts a heavy hand on his friend's shoulder. 'I can't ask you to do that, Tails, you've already done more than enough for the club.'

Tails looks insulted. 'The club? The club's you and me.'

Peter's stern face cracks into a gentle smile. 'You sound like Sune, the way he used to go on when we were little: "We are the club,"' he says, imitating the old coach.

Tails and Peter used to hate summer when they were children, because the hockey rink was closed. They became best friends in an empty parking lot, along with Hog and a few others, children who didn't care about swimming in the lake or playing war games in the forest. They used to play hockey on the tarmac with battered old sticks and a tennis ball until it got dark, then drag themselves home with scraped knees and ten World Championship wins in their hearts. They're sitting in that very same parking lot now, because that's where Tails built his first supermarket. He puts his hand on an old team photograph on the wall and says to Peter, 'I wouldn't be doing it for the club, you idiot, I'd be doing it for you. When we won silver twenty years ago and you got the puck at the end of the game to take the last shot, do you remember who made that pass?'

Does he remember? Everyone remembers. Tails made the pass, Peter missed the net. Tails may feel that they won silver, but Peter just thinks they lost gold. It was his fault. But Tails wipes his eyes with the back of his hand and says quietly, 'If I had a hundred chances to do it again, I'd pass the puck to you every time, Peter. I'd sell all my stores for you. That's what you do when you have a star in the team: you trust him. You give him the puck.'

Peter stares at the floor. 'Where can a man find friends as loyal as you, Tails?'

Tails flushes with pride. 'On the ice. Only on the ice.'

An ancient man shuffles into the Bearskin alone. Ramona has never seen him without the other four of the five 'uncles.' He looks as though he's aged half a lifetime, as if the years have hit him all at once.

'Have they been here?' he wonders, meaning the friends he's spent every day with for as long as anyone can remember.

Ramona shakes her head and asks, 'Have you tried phoning them?'

The old man looks miserable. 'I haven't got their numbers.'

Year after year, day after day, the five uncles have either been in the stands to watch hockey or here in the Bearskin pub to talk about hockey. They've all used the same calendar, where each year starts in September. Why would they need one another's phone numbers?

The old man stands for a while at the bar, lost. Then he goes home. He and his friends: five men who sat in a bar every day to talk about sports. They're not about to become five men who sit in a bar every day and just drink.

The youngsters around the fires have fallen silent. In a very short space of time Lifa has grown from a nobody to the sort of person nobody here messes with. He doesn't even have to raise his voice.

'Anyone who gives Amat another beer or cigarette will never enjoy another barbecue here. Understood?'

Farther down the slope Amat coughs as he gets to his knees. Zacharias is standing a short way behind him with melted cheese on his shirt. When Lifa came around to his apartment a short while ago, saying he'd heard that Amat was up on the hill, Zacharias tried to persuade Lifa to come inside and have a toasted sandwich instead, but Lifa just stared at him until Zacharias grabbed a pair of trousers and decided to keep his mouth shut.

'I'm partying, Lifa! Mind your own business!' Amat manages to say.

Lifa raises his fist but doesn't use it. He just walks disappointedly towards the apartment blocks. Zacharias helps Amat to his feet and mutters, 'This isn't like you, Amat . . .'

'What do you mean, "like me"? There isn't a "me"! I haven't even got a team to play for!'

Amat is aware how pathetic he sounds. Lifa comes back up the hill, trailing a group of kids with sticks in their hands. Lifa prods one of the kids on the shoulder. 'Tell him who you are when you're playing!'

The boy clears his throat shyly and looks through his bangs at Amat when he says, 'I'm . . . you.'

Pieces of grit fall from Amat's hair. Lifa pokes him in the chest. 'Are you feeling sorry for yourself?'

'I'm not –' Amat starts to say, but Lifa interrupts and points at their apartment block. 'Zach and I played hockey with you in that yard every day, and how much do you think we enjoyed that, all the damn time? Don't you think Zach would rather have been playing computer games?'

'Much, much rather,' Zach confirms, gently brushing cheese from his shirt.

Lifa's eyes are blazing. 'We played hockey with you every evening because we could see how crazy good you were, Amat. What you could become.'

'I haven't even got a *team* now, I –' Amat whimpers, but Lifa cuts him off.

'Shut up! You're going to get away from here, and you know why? Because whether you give up or not, these kids here are going to do what you do. So you need to get training! Because when you're playing in the NHL and get interviewed on TV, you can say you came from here. You came from the Hollow, and you did something with your life. And every kid in these blocks will know that. And they'll want to be like you, not me.'

Tears are running down Lifa's face, but he makes no attempt to hide them. 'You selfish bastard! Can't you see what everyone else here would give to have your talent?'

Amat's hands are shaking. Lifa walks over and hugs him as though they're eight years old again. He kisses his hair and whispers, 'We'll come running with you. Every mad sod here will come running with you all summer, if that's what it takes.'

He's not joking. Lifa runs up and down along the road beside Amat that night until he collapses, and after Amat has carried his friend home on his back, Zacharias starts running in his place. When he can't run anymore, other kids show up. Two dozen certifiable lunatics who promise Amat not to smoke and drink as long as he needs someone to train with.

In ten years' time, when Amat is playing hockey professionally, he won't have forgotten this. Some of the guys here will have died of overdoses, others will have died violently, some will be in prison, and some will just have made a mess of their lives. But some will have lives – big, proud lives. And they will all know that here, for just one summer, they were running for something. Amat will be interviewed on television in English, and the reporter will ask where he grew up, and he will say, 'I'm from the Hollow.' And every single bastard here will know that he remembers them.

He had no team. So they gave him an army.

14

A Stranger

Peter is walking alone through Beartown. Past the row house where he lost his mother and dodged his father's grief, past the rink where he found a new home, along the lake, and across the parking lots where he found his best friends, Tails and Hog. When Peter was given a professional contract, he played hockey with them that last evening before he went to Canada, with a tennis ball on the tarmac, just like when they were kids. He was almost paralysed by nerves, but his friends said, 'Come on, hockey's a simple game. If you strip away all the crap around it, the stands and the crowd and the rankings and the money, it's simple. Everyone gets a stick, there are two nets and two teams.'

Naturally it was Sune, their coach, who had drummed that into them. They always went to Sune for good advice, about both life and hockey: the coach was more of a father to them than their real dads ever were. So that's where Peter's going now. Through his town to the home of his old coach, to tell him that he's been given one last possibility of saving their club.

The old man has lost a lot of weight as a result of heart disease; his shoulders have slumped, the T-shirt with the bear logo on it is hanging lower over his stomach. He isn't married and has no children, like an aged general who has lived his whole life in the service of hockey. 'When did he get so old?' Peter wonders, and Sune seems to read his mind, because he grins wearily and replies, 'You don't look much like a sweet little rosebud yourself these days, you know.'

A puppy is yelping happily around the old man's feet, and he snaps at it, 'At least try to pretend you've been trained!'

'How are you?' Peter asks.

Sune pats him paternally on the shoulder and nods at the deep circles beneath Peter's eyes. 'You look like I feel. What can I do for you?'

So Peter tells him everything: how he can save the bear on Sune's T-shirt, but only with the help of a powerful sponsor he doesn't know anything about and a politician no one trusts. And only if he gets rid of the standing area and throws the Pack out of the rink, the men who saved his job in the spring.

Sune listens. Then he says, 'Do you want coffee?'

'I'm here for your advice,' Peter insists impatiently.

Sune shakes his head and snorts, 'Rubbish. When I was your coach and you were going to take a penalty, you always came back to the bench so that everyone would think you were asking my advice. That was kind of you, a way to show your old coach respect, but you and I both know that you'd already made your mind up. And you've made your mind up now as well. Come in and have some coffee. It tastes awful, but it's strong.'

Peter remains stubbornly where he is in the hall. 'But even if I *can* save the club . . . if you can't train the team, then I haven't got a coach!'

Sune replies with a rumble of laughter. Only when Peter follows him into the kitchen does he realize why. The two men aren't alone. There's a stranger sitting at the kitchen table. Sune blinks happily. 'This is Elisabeth Zackell, you probably recognize her. She came around a little while ago to tell me she's here to take my job.'

Kira Andersson is sitting on the steps outside the little house. Waiting for a man who never comes. She knows what her colleague would have said: 'Men! You know why you can never rely on men? Because they love *men*! No one loves men as much as *men* do, Kira! They can't even watch sports if it's not being played by *men*! Sweaty, panting men fighting against other men, with ten thousand men in the stands, that's what men want. I bet you they'll soon invent a type of porn featuring nothing but men but aimed at heterosexual men who don't really get turned on by men but don't think women are actually capable of having sex properly!'

Kira's colleague makes her laugh, a lot. Like the time a man in a suit sneezed in the middle of a meeting, deafeningly and shamelessly, without making any attempt to cover his mouth, and her colleague exclaimed, 'Men! Imagine if you had periods! You're incapable of keeping a single bodily fluid inside you in public.'

But today Kira's colleague didn't manage to make her laugh, just feel ashamed. Throughout their friendship, her colleague has kept on saying that they ought to start their own business together. Kira has never really needed to make any excuses because it's been just an entertaining fantasy, something to talk about once every few months over a box of wine and increasing amounts of hubris. But today her colleague thundered into Kira's office waving a sheet of paper: 'The premises are empty!' The premises they've fantasized about for years, in a location where Kira and her colleague wouldn't have any trouble luring the biggest clients away from their current firm. It would be perfect.

But Kira replied the way she always does: 'I can't right now, not with Peter's job and the children, I need to be there for Maya.' Her colleague leaned over her desk. 'You know our clients would come with us. I've got enough money saved up. If not now, *when*?' Kira tried to make excuses, but the only one she could find was time. Starting a new business would demand sixteen-hour days, seven days a week, and how could that work with picking up and dropping off at hockey practice and guitar lessons and lottery ticket sales and the volunteer parents' rotation in the coffee stand at the ice rink?

Her colleague looked her sternly in the eye. 'You're four different women, Kira. You're trying to be everything to everyone, the whole time. A good wife, a good mother, a good employee. How long are you going to carry on like that?'

Kira pretended to stare at an important document on her computer screen, but eventually gave up and muttered, 'You said four. Wife, mother, employee . . . who's the fourth woman?' Her colleague leaned over the desk and switched off the screen, tapped the glass sadly, and said, 'Her, Kira. When is it going to be that woman's turn?' Kira sat and stared into the eyes of her own reflection in the dark monitor.

Now she's sitting on the steps outside the house. Drinking wine. Waiting for a man who never comes.

Peter holds out his hand, and Elisabeth Zackell shakes it as if she doesn't really want to. Her body language is odd, as if there's a much smaller Elisabeth Zackell sitting inside her, trying to steer this one with a joystick.

'I saw you play in the Olympic Games . . . ,' Peter admits.

Zackell doesn't seem to know what to do with that information, so Sune jumps in. 'For God's sake, Peter, you've got two hundred and forty international appearances standing in front of you! Olympic and World Championship medals! And she's got her coaching licence! If she'd been a man, you'd be on your knees begging her to take my job!'

Peter takes the cup of coffee, sinks down at the kitchen table, and looks apologetically at Elisabeth Zackell.

'But if you were a man, you'd already have a job at one of the top clubs, wouldn't you?'

Zackell agrees with a curt nod. 'I've never been given a chance to coach a good team, so I've decided to take a useless team and make it good instead.'

Peter's eyebrows twitch in indignation, Sune bursts out laughing, and Zackell doesn't appear to know what she's said to warrant either response.

'You are useless, aren't you?'

Peter smiles reluctantly. 'How did you know we needed a new coach? Sune's kept very quiet about his illness . . .'

He breaks off when he realizes the answer. Zackell doesn't have to say 'Richard Theo.' Peter drinks some coffee, then exclaims, half to himself, 'He's smart, Theo. A female coach . . .'

'Was it your daughter who was raped?' Zackell interrupts.

Peter and Sune clear their throats uncomfortably. Zackell looks confused. 'Wasn't she? Raped, I mean. By a player the two of you had nurtured?'

Peter replies in a quiet voice, 'Is that why you're here? As Richard Theo's PR coup? A female hockey coach in what used to be a violent men's club? The media will love it.'

Zackell stands up impatiently. 'I'm not going to talk to the media. You can do that. And I don't give a shit about Richard Theo's PR coup. I'm not here to be a female hockey coach.'

Peter and Sune glance at each other.

'What do you want to be, then?' Sune asks.

'A hockey coach,' Zackell replies.

Sune scratches his stomach. As he always says, we only pretend hockey is complicated, because it isn't really. When you strip away all the nonsense surrounding it, the game is simple: everyone gets a stick; there are two nets, two teams. Us against you.

There's a sound from the garden, and Sune looks up and grins, but Peter is too distracted by his own thoughts to recognize the noise at first.

'I –' he begins, trying to sound like a grown man, a general manager, a leader.

But the sound interrupts him again. *Bang!* The boy Peter used to be, the dreamer, would have recognized the sound at once. He looks quizzically at Sune. *Bang-bang-bang!* comes from the garden.

'What's that?' Peter asks.

'Oh, yes! Did I forget to say?' Sune grins, the way you do when you haven't forgotten a damn thing.

Peter gets up and follows the noise, out through the terrace door. At the back of Sune's house stands a four-and-a-half-year-old girl, firing pucks against the wall as hard as she can.

'Do you remember when you used to come here and do the same thing, Peter? She's better than you were. She could already tell time when she got here!' Sune informs him happily.

Peter follows the pucks' movement towards the wall, and is thrown back in time, a whole lifetime. It's a simple game, really. The girl misses one of her shots and gets so angry that she hits her stick against the wall as hard as she can. It snaps, and only then does she spin around and catch sight of Peter. He sees the child shrink instinctively. All of Peter's childhood shatters inside his chest.

'What's your name?' he whispers.

'Alicia,' she replies.

Peter sees her bruises. He used to have similar ones. He knows she'll lie if he asks how she got them; children are so incredibly loyal to their parents. So Peter crouches down and promises her with all the despair of his childhood shaking in his voice, 'I can see that you're used to getting hurt if you make a mistake. But hockey will never treat you like that. Do you understand what I'm saying? Hockey will never hurt you.'

The girl nods. Peter fetches another stick. Alicia carries on firing pucks. Behind them Sune says, 'I know you've already decided to save the club, Peter. But it can be useful to be reminded of who you're saving it for.'

Peter blinks up at the old man, more than he needs to. 'You've coached the Beartown A-team all my life. Are you suddenly prepared to surrender the job to a . . . stranger?'

He does his best to hide the fact that 'stranger' wasn't his first choice of word. Sune's breathing sounds laboured as he replies, 'I've always known that Beartown Ice Hockey is more than a club. I don't believe in targets and tables, I believe in signs and symbols. I think it's more important to nurture human beings than to foster stars. And so do you.'

'And you think that this Elisabeth Zackell in your kitchen thinks the same?'

Sune smiles, but his chin moves slowly sideways. 'No, Elisabeth Zackell isn't like us. But right now that might be what the club needs.'

'Are you sure about that?' Peter wonders.

Sune pulls at his belt; his failing heart has made his trousers too big. Of course he doesn't want to give up his job; no one wants to do that. But he has given his life to the club, so what sort of leader would he be if he wasn't prepared to swallow his pride when the club's at risk of dying?

'When the hell can you be sure of anything, Peter? All I know is that the bear is supposed to symbolize the best of this town, but there are people around who want to bury it as a symbol of our worst qualities. And if we let those bastards get away with it, if we let them transfer all the money to Hed as soon as it suits their purposes, what signal are we giving the kids in this town then? That we *were* only a club? That this is what happens if you dare to stand up and tell the truth?'

'In what way is Zackell different from you?' Peter asks.

'She's a winner,' Sune says.

The men can't find any more words. They just stand there watching as Alicia fires pucks against the wall. *Bangbangbangbangbang*. Peter goes into the bathroom, turns the tap on, and stands in front of the mirror without looking at it. When he comes out, Zackell has already put her boots on.

'Where are you going?' Peter wonders.

'We're done, aren't we?' Zackell says, as if she has just employed herself.

'Surely we need to talk about the team?' Peter points out.

'I'll put more coffee on,' Sune says, pushing past them into the kitchen.

'I don't drink coffee,' Zackell says.

'You don't drink *coffee*?' Sune hisses.

'I told you that when I got here.'

'I assumed you were joking!'

Peter stands between them, rubbing his eyelids with his palms. 'Hello? The team! When are we going to talk about the team?'

Elisabeth Zackell looks as though a very small Elisabeth Zackell is running around inside the big Elisabeth Zackell's head, trying to find the correct switch. 'What team?' she asks.

The game may be simple, but people never are. *Bang bang bang.*

15

Vidar Rinnius

It won't be long before the staff at Beartown School hold their first planning meeting in advance of the autumn term. They will discuss budgets and teaching plans and the rebuilding of the gym, as usual. But then a teacher will ask about a pupil named Vidar who has suddenly appeared on the register for one class. The headmaster will clear his throat uncomfortably. 'Yes, he was a pupil here before, and now he's joining us again. We've only just been informed . . .' The teacher will wonder where this pupil has been in the meantime. Has he attended a different school? 'Well, Vidar has been in . . . an alternative educational system,' the headmaster will concede. 'You mean youth custody?' the teacher will ask. 'I think it's more of a . . . clinic,' the headmaster will say. The teacher seems neither to understand nor to care about the difference.

A teacher towards the back of the room will whisper, 'Assault and drugs charges. He tried to beat a police officer to death!' Another will snap, 'I don't want that psychopath in my class!' Someone will ask, in a louder voice, 'Wasn't Vidar given a longer sentence?' but will get no answer. Another will ask nervously, 'Vidar? What's his surname?' The headmaster's eyelashes will flutter like a hummingbird's wings when he replies, 'Rinnius. Vidar Rinnius. He's Teemu Rinnius's younger brother.'

Elisabeth Zackell scratches her head. It's hard to tell if her hair has been fashioned by a stylist or by mistake. She steps out through Sune's door in shoes made for freezing temperatures and feet at least two sizes larger and lights a cigar. Peter follows her, clearly worried now. 'What are you doing?' he asks.

Zackell, evidently not very good at reading people's intentions, assumes he means the cigar. 'This? Oh . . . I don't know. I'm a vegan, I don't drink alcohol or coffee. If I didn't smoke, no normal person would ever trust me,' she says, not as a joke but as if she's given the matter serious consideration.

Peter sighs deeply before he starts to cough. 'You can't just show up here and take for granted that you're going to get the job of coach without telling me what you'd do with our *team*!'

Zackell fills her mouth with smoke and tilts her head to one side. 'The team you've got right now?'

'Yes! That's the team you'd be coaching!'

'What, your A-team? Hopeless. A bunch of has-beens who are too old and useless for anyone else to want them.'

'But can you make them good? Is that what you're saying?'

Zackell chuckles. Not in a friendly or charming way, just patronizingly. 'No. Dear me, no. There's no way of making a useless team good. I'm not Harry Potter.'

Peter gets smoke in his eyes and loses his temper. 'What are you *doing* here? What do you *want*?'

Zackell pulls a crumpled sheet of paper from her pocket. She blows the smoke away from Peter, hesitantly, as if she doesn't really want to apologize for smoking and instead regrets that he doesn't smoke. 'Are you angry?'

'I'm not . . . angry,' Peter says, pulling himself together.

'You look a bit angry.'

'Well I'm *not* . . . just leave it, okay?'

'I've been told I'm not good at dealing with . . . people. Feelings, stuff like that,' Zackell concedes, but her face is still completely expressionless.

'You don't say? I can't think why!' Peter says sarcastically.

Zackell hands him the sheet of paper. 'I'm a good coach, though. And I've heard that you're a good general manager. If you can get the names on this list to give me their all on the ice, I can make a winning team out of them.'

Peter reads the names: Bobo. Amat. Benji.

'They're just teenagers. One of them is only sixteen years old. You're going to build the A-team out of them?'

'They're not going to build the A-team. They're going to carry it. That one's the new team captain,' Zackell says, cutting him off.

Peter stares at her, then at the name she's pointing at. 'You're going to make *him* captain? Of the A-team?'

She replies as if it was the most natural thing in the world, 'No. You're going to. Because you're good with people.'

Then she hands him another piece of paper. On it is the name 'Vidar.' Peter takes one look at it, then exclaims, 'NOT A CHANCE!'

'So you know Vidar?'

'Know him?! He . . . he . . .'

Peter starts shaking and actually turns right around, like a crazy egg timer. Sune is standing in the doorway with coffee. Zackell turns down the proffered cup but is given it anyway. Sune grins at the note. 'Vidar? That boy, yes. He probably can't play in your team. For . . . geographic reasons.'

Zackell's voice is matter-of-fact rather than smug when she replies, 'I've been assured that he's being released soon.'

'From the clinic? How's that happening?' Sune splutters.

Zackell doesn't say 'Richard Theo.' She just says, 'That's not my problem. My problem is that I need a goalie, and he seems to be Beartown's best goalie.'

Peter is literally hugging himself with anger. 'Vidar is a criminal and . . . and a *psychopath*! He's not playing on *my* team!'

Zackell shrugs her shoulders. 'This isn't your team. It's mine. You asked me what I want? I want to win. And I can't do that with a few old A-team players no one else wants. You have to give me more than that.'

'What?' Peter grunts, leaning disconsolately against the wall of the house.

Zackell blows out a cloud of cigar smoke. 'A gang of bandits.'

Teemu Rinnius walks into the Bearskin. Ramona leans over the bar and pats him tenderly on the cheek. He's carrying two bags of groceries, one of them largely filled with cigarettes. When Holger left her, Ramona stopped going out. Teemu has never criticized her for that; he's just made sure she's never gone short of anything. So she very rarely criticizes his life choices. Morals can always be debated, but the two of them know that most people are only trying to get through the day. As Ramona usually says, 'Everyone's wading through their own shit.'

Teemu can look almost harmless, with his neatly combed hair and clean-shaven chin. And Ramona can look almost sober, if you get there early enough in the morning.

'How's your mother?' she asks.

'Okay, she's okay,' Teemu says.

His mother is always tired, Ramona knows that. She's rather too fond of sleeping pills and difficult men. Once Teemu got old enough, he was able to throw the men out, but he's never been able to do anything about the pills. In his blue eyes he carries all the lives he wishes his mother could have had, and perhaps that's why Ramona has allowed herself to care more about Teemu than all the other men who have wandered into and out of the Bearskin over the years. But today those blue eyes are lit up with something else as well: hope.

'Vidar just called! You know what he said?' he exclaims.

There are police investigations that claim that Teemu Rinnius is lethally dangerous. There are plenty of people who say he's criminal. But there's one pub in Beartown where he'll only ever be a little boy, uncertain and eager.

'What is this? Some sort of quiz? Just tell me, boy!' Ramona snaps impatiently.

Teemu laughs. 'They're letting him out! My little brother's coming home!'

Ramona doesn't know what to do with her feet and ends up dancing around in circles twice before she gasps, 'We need better whisky!'

Teemu has already put a bottle on the counter. Ramona hurries around the bar and hugs him. 'This time we're going to take better care of your brother. This time we're not going to let go!'

The old bartender and the young fighter laugh. Today the pair of them are too happy to ask themselves: Why is Vidar being released so early? Whose hand is turning the key?

Politics is an endless series of negotiations and compromises, and even if the processes are often complicated, the foundations are always simple: everyone wants to be paid, one way or another, so most parts of all bureaucratic systems work the same way: give me something, and I'll give you something. That's how we build civilizations.

Richard Theo is very fond of his car; he drives many thousands of miles each year. Technology may be good for a lot of things, but it leaves evidence. Emails, text messages, phone messages, they're all a politician's worst enemies. So he drives a long way to talk quietly about things no one will ever be able to prove.

Peter Andersson is right. Theo called Elisabeth Zackell because he recognized her PR value. A female coach in a club known for violent masculinity. Theo also understands the value of winning, so when Zackell had gone through the list of Beartown Hockey's A-team players, Theo asked what she needed. She replied, 'First and foremost? A goalie. There was a junior here a couple of years ago with good stats, Vidar Rinnius. He seems to have vanished. What happened to him?' Theo knows nothing about hockey, but he understands people.

It was simple to find out which treatment centre Vidar was in: over the years Theo has been a good friend to people working in various authorities and public bodies. So he called Zackell and asked her, 'How much do you really want Vidar?' Zackell replied, 'If you can promise me him and I can find three more good players in Beartown, I can win.'

Richard Theo had to cash in a few personal favours. It cost him some more promises and plenty more driving in the car. But Vidar Rinnius will soon be released, considerably earlier than expected. No laws have been broken, no rules have even been bent. The only thing that has happened is that Richard Theo has become friends with the chair of the right committee, and that the case happened to be given to a new adviser, who considered that Vidar's 'treatment requirements needed to be reevaluated.'

Vidar was only seventeen when he was arrested for assault and possession of narcotics, so he was sentenced to treatment in a secure clinic. Bureaucracies can be complicated things, mistakes can be made, and, hand on heart: Shouldn't treatment requirements be reevaluated from time to time? Considering the acute shortage of places in treatment centres, wouldn't it actually be politically irresponsible to leave a youngster in there any longer than necessary?

In his statement, the new adviser declared that Vidar Rinnius had been a promising hockey player before he was sent to the clinic and that his rehabilitation to a 'prosocial life' would be improved if 'the youth in question was given the opportunity to resume meaningful occupation in a more open setting.' Normally his release would have been handled more gradually, via other facilities and homes, but such things can be reconsidered if he has access to a 'secure, stable home.' So an apartment in the Hollow, owned by Beartown's communal housing association, was found to be vacant. Naturally, Richard Theo had nothing to do with that, because that would have been corruption. And obviously the adviser on Vidar Rinnius's case wasn't from Beartown, because that would have looked suspicious. But the adviser's mother-in-law, who passed away recently, was from there. The adviser's wife has inherited a small lakeside property, and in a few months' time an application may well, entirely coincidentally, be submitted to the council, requesting permission to build a number of small holiday cabins on the plot. Ordinarily applications of that sort are rejected out of hand, because construction so close to the water isn't permitted, but on this occasion the adviser will be fortunate enough to have his application granted.

One signature on a sheet of paper in return for a signature on another one. Bureaucracy in action. Elisabeth Zackell gets her goalie, Teemu Rinnius gets his little brother back, and Peter Andersson will get dangerous enemies. And, last of all, Richard Theo will get everything he wants. Everyone wants to get paid; the only difference is the preferred currency.

When Peter leaves the row house, Sune and Zackell walk the little girl, Alicia, home.

'Can I come back again tomorrow and do some more?' the four-and-a-half-year-old asks.

Sune promises that she can. Zackell's face is expressionless. Sune had to tell her not to smoke her cigar in front of the child. Zackell seemed to have difficulty understanding if that was because it was a bad thing in and of itself or if the child was trying to give up smoking and didn't want to be tempted.

Once Alicia runs into her house, Sune turns to Zackell with a frown. 'Are you serious about bringing Vidar onto the team?'

'He's a good goalie, isn't he? I saw the numbers from his last season. Were they wrong?'

'Vidar may be the best goalie this town has ever had. But he's also had . . . problems.'

'Is he available to play or not?'

'Availability isn't the same thing as suitability,' Sune notes.

Zackell's lack of understanding is almost touching. 'Hockey's hockey. If he's any good, then he's suitable. Why is Peter so angry with him?'

Sune does his best not to laugh. 'Peter isn't . . . angry.'

'He seems angry.'

'Vidar has problems with his . . . impulse control. He has difficulty restraining himself. And Peter doesn't like . . . mess.'

'Mess?'

'Vidar . . . well, where do I start? His brother is . . .'

'A hooligan. The leader of "the Pack." I've heard about that,' Zackell interrupts.

Sune clears his throat. 'Yes . . . well . . . there isn't necessarily any "Pack" here . . . it all got a bit exaggerated by the media.

But . . . yes, well, once a fight did break out outside the rink between the fans after an A-team game. Teemu was involved. The juniors were going to play a game straight afterward, but when it was supposed to start Beartown didn't have a goalie, because Vidar was sitting in a police car. He'd run outside and thrown himself into the fight, still wearing his skates. On another occasion he broke into the rink and drove his moped around the stands. He was . . . well, a bit drunk. Another time he heard that Peter Andersson had spoken out against "hooligans" during a board meeting, so he spent all night going around collecting all the pucks. And I mean *all* the pucks. From the rink, from the pro shop, from people's garages . . . we had to ask the spectators at a boys' cup game the next day to go home to see if they had any pucks hidden away somewhere so we could play the game. And another time Vidar hit a referee in . . . a sensitive part of his body. In the middle of a game. Peter banned him from the club, so Vidar broke into the rink and took a shit on Peter's desk.'

Zackell nods, unconcerned. 'And Peter doesn't like mess?'

Sune chuckles. 'Peter has a breakdown if anyone spills coffee on his desk. He's just having trouble forgiving the business with the shit. He won't let you put Vidar on the team.'

Zackell gives the distinct impression that she doesn't understand how any of this hangs together. 'Have you got a better goalie in Beartown than Vidar?'

'No.'

'I coach hockey teams. The only thing I know how to do is to treat everyone fairly, not treat them all the same. A good player is a good player.'

Sune nods. 'Bloody hell. Peter's going to kick up one hell of a fuss.'

'Is that bad?'

Sune smiles. 'No. A vibrant club needs to be full of people burning with passion, and you only get fire from friction.'

'And forest fires,' Zackell points out.

Sune sighs. 'You're spoiling my metaphor.'

'Was that a metaphor? Sorry. I'm not good at –'

'People? Feelings?' Sune guesses.

'Pussyfooting around. I need players who . . . go for it.'

'That's why you need Peter. He motivates them, you coach them.'

'Yes.'

'He won't even talk to Vidar. But I can talk to Vidar's brother.'

'His brother?'

'Yes.'

'And the other three? Benji, Bobo, and Amat? Will Peter talk to them?'

'No.'

'No?'

'If you want him to motivate Benji, Bobo, and Amat, you don't need him to talk to the boys. He needs to talk to their mothers and sisters.'

'This is a very odd town,' Zackell declares.

'So we've been told,' Sune says.

16

Beartown Against the Rest

The news on the local paper's website spreads quickly. Possibly because there isn't much other news to talk about. Possibly because hockey is more important here than in a lot of other places. Or perhaps because the wind happened to change at that moment, without most people even realizing.

'Beartown Ice Hockey Saved by New Sponsor: General Manager Peter Andersson Engaged in Secret Talks,' the paper trumpets. A couple of lines farther down comes the next revelation: 'Sources indicate that national women's team player Elisabeth Zackell will be the new A-team coach, the first female coach in the history of Beartown Hockey.'

The newspaper doesn't say where it got the information from, just that it was 'a reliable source close to the club.'

Politicians need conflict to win elections, but they also need allies. Richard Theo knows only two ways of getting someone who doesn't like you to fight on your side regardless: a shared enemy or a shared friend.

The same day Peter Andersson meets Elisabeth Zackell, a reporter from the local paper calls another politician in the council building. But Richard Theo answers the phone. 'I'm afraid the person you're trying to reach is on holiday, I was just passing in the corridor and heard the phone ringing,' he says amiably.

'Oh . . . I got an email from his assistant asking me to call . . . something about a "tipoff about Beartown Ice Hockey"?'

Theo has an exceptional ability to play stupid. The fact that the other politician's assistant has a password consisting of a swear word followed by '12345' as his email password is happy coincidence.

'A tipoff about Beartown Ice Hockey? It could be about the new sponsor or the new coach, maybe?' Theo suggests helpfully.

'What?' the reporter exclaims.

Theo fakes hesitancy. 'Sorry . . . I thought it was already common knowledge . . . silly of me . . . I've probably said more than I should have done. I'm really not the right person to be talking about this . . .'

The reporter clears her throat. 'Could you . . . say a little more?'

'Can I trust you not to give my name in whatever you write?' Theo asks.

The reporter promises, and Theo says magnanimously that he 'just doesn't want to steal Peter Andersson's thunder, because he's the one doing all the work!'

When the news appears on the website, Theo sets off to the supermarket, asks for the owner, and is directed to the storeroom.

Tails is shifting stock, an old hockey giant driving a forklift, but dressed in a suit the same as usual. When he was younger, he had trouble attracting girls' attention, so he started to dress up more than the other guys. When they wore T-shirts, he wore a smart jacket, and when they went to funerals in suits, he would show up wearing tails. Which is how he got his nickname.

'My name is Richard Theo,' the politician says, unnecessarily.

'I know who the hell you are, we were at school together,' Tails grunts and jumps down from the forklift.

The politician holds out a large box. The supermarket owner takes it warily.

'I want to help Beartown Ice Hockey,' Theo says.

'People around here don't want to give a politician any control of the club,' Tails replies.

'A politician . . . or *this* politician?' Theo wonders ironically.

Tails's voice is wary but not unfriendly. 'I daresay you know your own reputation. What do you want with me?'

'I want us to help each other. Because you and I have a friend in common, Tails, and I think that's more important than having enemies in common.'

Tails opens the box, looks down into it, tries not to look shocked, but fails. 'What . . . what am I supposed to do with these?'

'Everyone says you're the best salesman in Beartown. So sell them,' Theo says.

He puts his hands into the pockets of his expensive trousers. He's wearing a crisp white shirt beneath a grey waistcoat, a red silk tie, shiny, polished shoes. No one dresses like that in Beartown, apart from him and Tails. The supermarket owner looks down into the box again. He loves just two things apart from his family: his town and his hockey club. So as Richard Theo turns to walk away, he sees Tails smile.

The box is full of T-shirts. On them are the words BEARTOWN AGAINST THE REST. Tails sells all of them in less than an hour.

There's a loser in every relationship. We may not like to admit it, but one of us always gets a little more and one of us always gives up a little more readily.

Kira is sitting on the steps outside the house, breathing in through her nose, but her lungs never feel full. These forests can suffocate a person if she's longing for something else, but how do you hold a family together if you think only about your own breathing? She's been offered better jobs, far from Beartown. She's been offered a managerial role in the firm she works at now, but it would have meant longer working days and being available on weekends. And that would be impossible, because weekends mean guitar lessons and training and hockey games. She has to sell programmes and pour coffee and be a couple of kids' mum and someone's wife.

Naturally enough, her colleague, a fanatical antimonogamist, keeps telling her 'not to put up with that shit!' But what is a marriage if you take away the infatuation? A negotiation. Dear Lord, it's hard enough for two people to agree what TV programme to watch, let alone fashion an entire life together. Someone has to sacrifice something.

Peter gets out of the Volvo with a bunch of flowers in his hand. Kira has an extra wineglass on the steps beside her. White flags. In the end she smiles, mostly at the flowers.

'Where did you find those at this time of day?'

Peter blushes. 'I picked them from a garden. In Hed.'

He holds out his hand, touches her skin, and their fingertips touch tentatively.

It's only a hockey club. Only a game. Only pretend. There will always be people who try to tell Alicia that, and obviously she'll never listen to them, the little brat. She's four and a half years old, and tomorrow she will knock on Sune's door again. The old man will teach her to fire hockey pucks harder and harder at the wall of his house. The marks on the wall will be like the grandchildren's drawings other old men pin up on their fridges: tiny etchings in time to prove that someone we love grew up here.

'How are you getting on at preschool?' Sune asks.

'The boys are stupid,' the four-and-a-half-year-old says.

'Hit them in the face,' Sune advises.

The four-and-a-half-year-old says she will. You have to keep your promises. But when Sune walks home with her later, he adds, 'But you have to be a good friend to the kids who haven't got any friends. And you have to defend the ones who are weaker. Even when it's hard, even when you think it's a nuisance, even when you're scared. You always have to be a good friend.'

'Why?' the girl asks.

'Because one day you're going to be the best. And then the coach will make you team captain. And then you have to remember that a great deal is expected of anyone who's been given a lot.'

The girl doesn't know what that means yet, but she will

remember every word. Every night until then she dreams of the same sound. *Bang. Bang. Bang-bang-bang.* Her club lives on. She's blessed enough never to really understand what happened this summer, how close it came to dying, and how it came to survive. And at what cost.

If you live with the same person for long enough, you often discover that although you may have had a hundred conflicts at the start of the relationship, in the end you have only one. You keep slipping into the same argument, albeit in different guises.

'There's a new sponsor –' Peter begins.

'The paper's already written about it online, everyone's talking about it,' Kira says.

'I know what you want to say,' Peter says, standing at the bottom of the steps in front of their home.

'No. Because you haven't asked,' Kira replies, and drinks a sip of wine.

He doesn't ask now either. Instead he says, 'I can save the club. I promised Maya that I'd –'

Kira's grip on his fingers is gentle, but her voice is merciless. 'Don't drag our daughter into this. You're saving the club for your own sake. You want to prove to everyone in this town who doesn't believe in you that they're wrong. Again. You never get through having to prove that.'

Peter grinds his teeth. 'What am I supposed to do? Let the club die while people around here . . .'

'It doesn't matter what *people* think,' she snaps, but he cuts her off in turn: 'My death was announced in the paper! Someone threatened my life!'

'Someone threatened *our* lives, Peter! Why the hell do you always get to choose when this family is a team or not?'

His tears fall onto her hair. He squats down in front of her. 'Sorry. I know I have no right to ask any more from you. I love you. You and the kids. More than anything . . .'

She closes her eyes. 'We know, darling.'

'I know the sacrifices you've made for my hockey. I know.'

Kira hides her despair behind her eyelids. Every autumn, winter, and spring the whole family lives according to the dictates of hockey, raised up to the heavens when the team wins and tumbling headlong when it loses. Kira doesn't know if she can bear to put herself through yet another season. But she still stands up and says, 'What's love if we aren't prepared to make sacrifices?'

'Darling, I . . . ,' Peter says, but tails off.

Kira is wearing a green T-shirt. The words BEARTOWN AGAINST THE REST are printed on it. She bites her cheeks, broken by what she's giving up but proud of her choice. 'Tails called. He's selling them in the store. Our neighbours were each wearing one when they got home. Christ, Peter, they're both over ninety. What sort of ninety-year-olds wear T-shirts?'

She smiles. Peter's eyes dart about in embarrassment. 'I didn't know Tails . . .'

Kira touches his cheek. 'Tails loves you. Oh, how he loves you, darling. There may be people in this town who hate you, and you can't do anything about that. But there are far more who worship you, and you can't do anything about that, either. Sometimes I wish you weren't indispensable to them, that I didn't have to share you, but I knew when I married you that half your heart belongs to hockey.'

'That's not true . . . please . . . ask me to resign, and I'll do it!'

She doesn't ask him. She spares him from having to reveal that he's lying. You do that if you love someone. She says, 'I'm one of the people who worship you. And I'm on your team, no matter what. Go and save your club.'

His answer is barely audible. 'Next year, darling, just give me one more season . . . next year . . .'

Kira hands him the wineglass. It's either half full or half empty. She kisses her husband on the lips, and he whispers 'I love you,' his breath mingling with hers. She replies, 'Win, darling. If you're really going to do this . . . win!'

★

134

Then she goes into their house. Sends an email to her colleague: 'Can't take the premises. Not this year. Sorry.' Then she goes to bed. There are three women in the bed that night. Only three.

The reporter from the local paper calls Peter late that night and asks straight out, 'Can you confirm the rumours? Is there a new sponsor? Can you save the club? Have you appointed a female coach? Is Beartown still going to play Hed in the first game of the season?'

Peter gives the same response to each question; then he hangs up.

'Yes.'

17

Smells Blood and Catches Fire

On the wall of Richard Theo's office, beside the picture of the stork, is a printout from the website of the Ice Hockey Federation. It's the schedule for Beartown Ice Hockey's season. First game: Hed Hockey.

A fly makes its way in through the open window. Theo doesn't kill it, just lets it buzz about, more and more lost. He recently read a book about terrorism in which a historian drew an analogy with a china shop: a lone fly can't overturn a single teacup, but a fly buzzing in the ear of a bull until the bull panics and rushes into a china shop in a rage can accomplish any amount of devastation.

Richard Theo has no need of devastation; he's happy with conflict. So he's spent a long time listening to everyone. To people in the supermarket, in the DIY store, in the Bearskin pub, in the Hollow, in the Heights: he's looked everyone in the eye, and instead of expressing an opinion, he has asked questions. 'What should we politicians be doing for you?' 'Where do you see Beartown in ten years' time?' 'How much tax did you pay last year? Do you get value for money from it?' From that he has learned that people around here are worried about three things: jobs, health care, and hockey.

So he sat down at his computer and started to write. All summer the local paper has been publishing articles about the rumours that the hospital in Hed is going to be closed, and Theo has commented repeatedly and anonymously using half a dozen fake accounts. He never spreads hate, never draws attention to himself, just discreetly tosses more fuel onto the already smouldering fire. When one worried pregnant woman wondered what was going to happen to the hospital's maternity unit, one of Theo's anonymous pseudonyms wondered, 'Have you heard anything?' The woman replied, 'I know someone who works there she says its being shut down!!!' Theo's pseudonym replied, 'We'd better hope the government doesn't raise gasoline taxes, or we won't even be able to afford to give birth in our cars.' When an unemployed man, recently laid off from the factory in Beartown, replied, 'Exactly! Always us out in the sticks who have to suffer!,' another of Theo's identities wrote, 'Why should all our money go to the hospital in Hed instead of opening a new clinic in Beartown?'

The man and woman were joined by other angry voices, the tone quickly became more inflamed, and Theo merely nudged the general frustration in the right direction when he wrote, 'So the women around here will have to give birth in their cars, but the council always seems to have enough money to support Beartown Ice Hockey?'

Hospitals and hockey aren't funded from the same budget, those decisions aren't even made by the same politicians, but if you ask a difficult enough question, there will always be a receptive audience for the simplest answer. So day after day, in different comment sections, Richard Theo has been doing what he does best: creating conflict, setting one thing against another. Countryside against big city. Hospital against hockey. Hed against us.

Us against you.

And now more and more people, of all ages and from all parts of town, are wearing green T-shirts bearing the words BEARTOWN AGAINST THE REST.

Politics is never strictly linear, big changes don't come out of nowhere, there's always a series of smaller causes. Sometimes politics is finding a hockey coach for a hockey club, sometimes it's just answering a phone when all the other politicians are on holiday. The reporter who calls Richard Theo the second time is the same temp who called before. This time she's trying to fill the summer news drought with simple questionnaires, such as 'How did our local celebrities celebrate Midsummer?,' and of course Richard Theo is 'both a politician and something of a celebrity,' and of course he was so helpful the last time they spoke. Naturally, Theo doesn't pass up the opportunity:

'I was actually in Hed, watching the Midsummer celebrations – you know the council always pays for the festivities there? But of course I'd much rather have celebrated Midsummer here in Beartown!'

'You mean the council ought to organize Midsummer festivities in Beartown?' the reporter wonders.

'I think in times like these, taxpayers in Beartown may well be getting a little concerned that all the council's resources seem to be going to Hed,' Theo says.

'How . . . how do you mean?'

'You only have to look at the comment sections of your own website, really, don't you?' Theo suggests.

The reporter hangs up and soon finds the comment section below the articles about the hospital. By now Richard Theo has deleted all his own comments, but plenty of other people have already repeated, 'So Beartown has to find its own sponsors while the COUNCIL foots the bill in Hed? Why is there money for Hed Hockey but not for the HOSPITAL?'

The reporter calls Theo again. He says modestly that he 'hasn't been involved in any discussions concerning the hospital' and suggests that the reporter might do better to ask the leader of the largest party on the council instead. So the reporter calls him. He answers on his cell phone, on vacation in Spain. The reporter gets straight to the point: 'Why are you transferring all the council's funding from Beartown Ice Hockey directly to Hed Hockey? Can't Hed Hockey find their own sponsors so that the council can invest the money in the hospital instead?' Perhaps the politician is too relaxed, perhaps he's even had a glass of wine, but he replies, 'Listen, my dear, it's not the same money at all, surely you can see that? Completely different budgets! As far as hockey is concerned, we're focusing the council's resources where we believe they will do most good, and right now that's with Hed Hockey, not Beartown.' The reporter quotes him online but leaves out the word 'hockey.' So now it just says, 'right now that's with Hed, not Beartown.' The comments section soon fills up: 'Ha! As usual, Hed gets everything!! Do they think we don't pay taxes in Beartown or something?!' Then: 'Like someone said before, why is there money for Hed Hockey, but not for health centres in Beartown???' Then: 'What do politicians think is most important? Hockey or health care?'

The reporter calls the politician in Spain again, and asks, 'What do *you* think is most important? Hockey or the hospital?' The politician clears his throat and tries to explain. 'You can't make simple comparisons like that,' but the reporter keeps probing until the politician snaps, 'Surely to God you understand that I think hospitals are more important than hockey!' The reporter quotes him directly and provides a few extra words of context: 'He said, when we contacted him in his summer house in Spain.' The article also mentions in passing the fact that the Spanish-home-owning politician lives in Hed rather than in Beartown.

When the reporter calls Richard Theo again to request another interview, Theo asks if the reporter would mind conducting it in the council building, because Theo is at work all summer. 'Being a local councillor here isn't a job, it's a privilege,' he adds.

The next article in the local paper includes a photograph of him alone in the dining room of the council building, hard at work. In response to the question 'Hockey or health care?' he replies, 'I believe taxpayers deserve a society where we don't have to choose between health care and opportunities for exercise and leisure.'

Soon another article will appear on the website of the local paper. No one really knows how a summer temp could have dug up a piece of news like this, but suddenly there is documentation to prove that prominent councillors have been engaged in secret discussions about the Hed hospital all spring. It is claimed that jobs in one hospital department could be saved if another 'more cost-heavy' department was closed immediately. Somehow the paper has managed to find out, from a 'reliable source,' that the department that the 'leading elite of establishment politicians' would prefer to save has more employees who live in Hed, while the one threatened with closure has more staff living in Beartown.

This later turns out not to be the case, but by then it won't matter, because all summer the headline is 'More Unemployment for Beartown.'

The comment section does what the comment section always does: smells blood and catches fire.

At one point during the summer, a female politician arrives at Hog's garage to pick up her car, which had to be repaired when visibility through the windshield was slightly obscured by the unfortunate appearance of an axe in the hood. Bobo has repaired and repainted it, but when the woman goes to take out her wallet, the boy shakes his head and says, 'It's already been paid for.' The boy doesn't say who by, but the woman understands. She drives home, still terrified at the very thought of catching sight of any men in black jackets, but there is nothing threatening waiting outside her door. Just a magnificent bouquet of flowers. The card reads, 'Don't be scared; you've still got friends, we won't let the forces of darkness win! Richard Theo.'

The woman calls to thank him. Theo is humble, says he doesn't want anything in return, and she respects him for that. He smiles as he hangs up. He often has a plan, but not always; sometimes he's just like a good hockey player: he's got quick reflexes. That afternoon just before Midsummer, after the establishment politicians had their meeting with Peter about Beartown Hockey, the insecure female councillor was standing in the corridor, not daring to go outside. Richard Theo passed her at the coffee machine and asked, 'You look worried – what's the matter?'

The female councillor represented a party that had publicly

distanced itself 'in the strongest possible terms' from Richard Theo, but a few kind words can go a long way. She admitted, 'Oh, I don't know. Everyone's saying that Beartown Ice Hockey is going to go bankrupt, but I've got no interest in sports! What am I supposed to say if anyone asks me?'

Theo put his hand on her shoulder and said, 'It's not that serious. The council still has another hockey club, after all. Just say that everyone ought to start supporting Hed Hockey instead!'

And the woman walked out of the council building, and while a Hed fan was filming her she said exactly that. Then she got an axe embedded in the hood of her car. Her party colleagues weren't remotely sympathetic the next day and just snapped, 'How could you be stupid enough to say that everyone ought to support Hed? In *this* council district?' What was she supposed to say to that? That Richard Theo had told her to say it? She kept her mouth shut, her party colleagues yelled at her, and she burst into tears when they weren't looking.

That evening Theo came to her office, listened and commiserated, even apologized to her. She had new enemies, so she needed a friend. Theo offered to drive her car to a garage, promised to pay for the damage, told her not to worry. He drove her home and told her to call him if she felt even remotely threatened, no matter what time it was. 'You don't have to be afraid, you've good friends,' he reminded her. Then he said, 'I'll see to it that the club punishes the hooligans who attacked you. I'm going to get them to do away with the standing area in the rink!'

None of the woman's party colleagues asked how she was, none of them reached their hand out to her, so she took the only one on offer. Which belonged to someone with quick reflexes.

The Spanish-home-owning politician realizes his mistake the moment he sees the newspaper, quickly abandons his holiday, and returns home. He is met at the airport by Richard Theo.

'What are you doing here?' the Spanish-home-owning politician asks.

'I want to help you,' Theo says.

The Spanish-home-owning politician laughs. 'Really? We've never exactly been on the same . . . side.'

But he is curious, and the newspaper articles about the hospital have put him into a tight corner. So Theo offers to get him a cup of coffee, then explains good-naturedly that 'you and I both want what's best for the area' and that 'no one gains anything from anxiety and discord.' They talk a bit about the articles about the hospital, and Theo laments the fact that everything has been 'unfortunately expressed.' The Spanish-home-owning politician spends a while cursing 'bastard journalists,' after which Theo suddenly exclaims, 'Have you heard about Beartown Ice Hockey's new sponsor?'

The Spanish-home-owning politician nods, then grunts, 'Yes! Everyone seems to be talking about it, but no one seems to know who this mysterious "sponsor" actually is!'

Theo leans forward and reveals, 'It's a company that's going to buy the factory in Beartown. They've contacted me, I can let you hold the press conference when the deal becomes official. There'll be a lot of new jobs for the area.'

The Spanish-home-owning politician stammers, 'How do you . . .? I hadn't even heard . . .'

Without going into detail, Theo explains that he was tipped off by some old friends from his banking days in London. He also explains what the factory's new owners are hoping to get from the council: 'Obviously they need a degree of political goodwill. Investment in . . . infrastructure.' The Spanish-home-owning politician understands what that means: subsidized land, reduced rent, more or less public subsidies for the restructuring of the factory. But he also appreciates the value of being the politician who can promise new jobs at a press conference.

'Why are you telling me this?' he asks suspiciously.

'Because I don't want to be your enemy,' Theo replies gently.

The Spanish-home-owning politician laughs out loud at that. 'You're a horse trader, Richard. What do you want?'

Richard Theo replies calmly, 'A seat at future negotiation tables. You just have to mention me and my party during the press conference, open the door to future cooperation, and the other parties will follow your lead.'

'You want me to clean up your political reputation?'

'I'm offering you the chance to be the politician who saves jobs in Beartown.'

The Spanish-home-owning politician plays hard to get, but he's already sold. So he requests just one thing from Theo: 'All the new jobs at the factory have to go to people from Beartown! Under no circumstances must my party be seen to be favouring Hed right now!'

Richard Theo makes a solemn promise. It isn't worth much. He has nothing against the Spanish-home-owning politician; they're actually fairly similar, but that's the problem. The Spanish-home-owning politician knows everyone with money in the area, but he's also known to be a lover of sports who has always done his best to prop up the hockey clubs, and that's a dangerous combination. Richard Theo needs an opponent who's easier to beat. So when the Spanish-home-owning politician is driving home, Theo calls his friend in London at once. 'It's done. The new owners will get everything they need. There's just one thing that's cropped up . . .'

The factory's new owners naturally understand when Theo explains that, bearing in mind the heated local debate about the closure of the hospital, it would be greatly appreciated 'among local politicians' if the new owners could give an undertaking to recruit a large number of their new workers from Hed.

So that no one thinks that Beartown is being shown any favouritism.

One evening towards the end of the summer Richard Theo knocks on a front door. The female politician looks surprised when she opens it. She asks Theo in, but he smiles apologetically and says he 'doesn't want to disturb her.' He can see her husband and children inside the house.

'The factory's new owners are going public with the deal soon. They're going to announce new jobs and the fact that they'll be sponsoring Beartown Ice Hockey. They're going to hold a press conference with the politicians who have made the deal possible,' Theo says.

The woman isn't skilled enough at the game to understand how this affects her, so she says, 'Congratulations. That'll be a feather in your cap for the next election.'

Theo smiles modestly. 'I won't be there. But your party will be there, of course, seeing as you're still the biggest party on the council.'

'I'm not high enough up the hierarchy to take part in a press conference. Especially after . . . you know, the axe in my car,' the woman says.

Theo is gratified that there's a note of anger as well as fear in her voice. 'What if I could arrange for you to be there, next to the leader of your party?'

'You can't do that . . . can you?'

She falls silent, but Theo says nothing, so the woman goes on, 'What do you want from me?'

'I want to be your friend,' he says.

'What do I have to say at the press conference?' she asks, a little too eagerly.

'The truth: that it isn't just Beartown that needs jobs but Hed, too. A responsible politician always thinks about the whole district.'

The woman shakes her head, her eyelids flutter. 'I can't . . . you must see that I can't possibly . . .'

Theo's hand touches hers, calm and reassuring. 'You're scared. Don't be. No one's going to hurt you.'

She sees in his eyes that he's serious. She gasps, 'So you want me to demand that some of the jobs in the factory must go to people living in Hed?'

He nods. 'Half.'

'Do you have any idea how hated that will make me in Beartown?'

Richard Theo shrugs his shoulders pragmatically. 'Yes, but they'll love you in Hed. And Hed has a bigger population. If you're already hated in one place, you have to try even harder to be loved in the other. You don't win elections by having as few enemies as possible, only by having the most friends.'

'Is this even legal? Can you even . . . what happens if my party expels me?'

'You misunderstand me. You won't just have a place in your party after this, you'll be its leader.'

Richard Theo is serious when he says this, too.

18

A Woman

Summer in Beartown is capable of enchanting anyone: the way the scent of roses gets stronger in darkened rooms, the way the light in a place so used to darkness is emotionally overwhelming. Greenery suddenly froths around us, it's light almost all night through, warm breezes chase one another around the corners of buildings like calves let out to pasture. But we have learned never to trust the heat; it's fleeting and unreliable and always lets us down. The trees shed their clothing quickly in this part of the country, all at once, like a nightdress; the days soon grow shorter, the horizon comes closer. Sooner than we realize, winter falls, white, and erases all the colour of the other seasons, the world becomes a blank piece of paper again, a frozen, freshly ironed sheet when we look out of the window one morning. We've pulled our boats from the lake, leaving parts of ourselves in the bottom of them. The people we were in July, those summer people, will rest on a bed of wood deep below the snow for so many months that we will almost have forgotten them by next spring.

September is on its way. A time that belongs to those who love hockey. Our year starts now.

Fatima and Ann-Katrin are finishing their shifts at the hospital. Every doctor who passes wants only to talk about hockey; the local paper's revelation that there's a 'mysterious new sponsor' who's going to save Beartown Ice Hockey is the big topic of conversation in both Beartown and Hed. 'What a season this is going to be!' one nurse exclaims in the staff room and immediately falls out with a nurse who supports the other team: 'Hed should have gotten that new sponsor instead!' 'This district isn't big enough for two hockey teams,' one of them says. 'Ha! Why not close down Hed if you can't survive without council money?' the other suggests.

It starts off as friendly squabbling, but Fatima and Ann-Katrin have followed hockey in these towns long enough to know that it will soon lead to genuine conflict, not just in the hospital but everywhere. People's best and worst feelings about one another will explode when Beartown and Hed play each other. Sports is so much more than just sports around here. Especially this season.

When Fatima and Ann-Katrin emerge from the hospital at the end of their shifts, a man in a tracksuit top is waiting in the parking lot.

'Peter? What are you doing here?' Ann-Katrin asks in surprise when she catches sight of Beartown Ice Hockey's general manager in the distance.

'I need to ask you both for something,' Peter says.

'What?' Ann-Katrin wonders.

'Your sons.'

Fatima and Ann-Katrin start to laugh; then they realize he isn't joking.

'Are you feeling okay, Peter?' Fatima asks anxiously.

He nods sternly. 'We've got a new coach, as you may have heard. And she wants to build the club . . . around your boys.'

Ann-Katrin tries to read his tone of voice. Asks, 'And you don't think that's a good idea?'

The corners of Peter's mouth twitch, but he lowers his gaze. 'I've always tried to build a hockey club that was . . . more than just a hockey club. I wanted it to foster young men as much as it did hockey players. I didn't want winning to be the most important thing. But . . . we've got a new sponsor now. And if we don't win this season . . . if we don't manage to beat Hed and get promoted to a higher league . . . then I don't know if we'll still be here next year.'

'Just say what you came to say,' Ann-Katrin says impatiently.

Peter's chest rises and falls. 'I'm afraid the club might demand more from your sons than it can give back to them.'

'How?' Fatima asks.

Peter turns to her. 'Amat stopped me when I was driving awhile back. He asked if he was going to be able to play in the junior team and I . . . I wasn't very nice to him . . .'

'Everyone has their bad moments, you're no worse than anyone else.' Fatima smiles, but Peter cuts her off. 'He asked about the junior team, Fatima, but dear Lord . . . we don't want Amat on a junior team. We want him on the A-team!'

Fatima swallows. 'With . . . with all the grown men?'

Peter doesn't attempt to hide the truth from her. 'It's going to make huge demands of him. And all the older players will go for him extra hard. There have been plenty before him who've been broken by that. Being the youngest in the team, surrounded by adults . . . it won't be easy for him.'

The look in Fatima's eyes is implacable. 'No one's ever promised my son that it would be.'

Peter tugs his beard in embarrassment. 'I should have told Amat that my daughter and I still owe him a huge debt of gratitude for standing up at that meeting back in the spring and telling the truth . . .'

Fatima shakes her head. 'You can give him *your* thanks, but Maya doesn't owe anyone anything. We should be asking her forgiveness, the whole town. As far as my son is concerned, he just wants to play hockey. So he'll play if you can give him somewhere to do it.'

Peter nods gratefully. Then he turns to Ann-Katrin. 'I'm not going to lie to you . . .'

Ann-Katrin smiles. 'You wouldn't dare.' She's married to Hog, Peter's childhood friend, and has seen Peter get older almost as closely as she has her husband. So Peter tells it like it is: 'We need Bobo this season. We've got a shortage of defencemen. But to be completely honest, he's not good enough to play at a higher level . . . so if we win, if he helps us move up to a higher league . . .

he won't stand a chance of making the team next season. This season will be his last. I'll demand blood, sweat, and tears from him, he'll have to prioritize hockey ahead of everything else, school, girls . . . everything. But I can only offer him one year in return.'

Ann-Katrin breathes through her nose. Her body hurts; in hindsight Peter will think she looked thin and exhausted because she'd just worked a difficult late shift. Like almost everyone else, he doesn't know about her illness. That's as it should be; she doesn't want their sympathy. But she does want to watch her son play hockey one last time. So she smiles. 'One year? A year is an eternity.'

Her husband, Hog, had to stop playing hockey after suffering one too many concussions. The doctors forced him to give up, and he was quiet for weeks, grieving for himself as if he'd attended his own funeral. For months he couldn't bring himself to go near the rink because he felt he'd let his team down. Let them down! Because he wasn't immortal. Bobo has inherited his broad shoulders and brute strength from his dad, but he's also inherited his need to be part of a gang. They both hate being alone. They need a context in which they feel loved and accepted, so when Hog no longer had the locker room to go to, it was as if part of him had been amputated. What wouldn't he have given for one more year? One last game? One last moment where you can feel your whole life in your gut and the spectators are roaring and everything is at stake?

Ann-Katrin will hardly be able to stand when she gets home tonight, and Hog will fetch her from the car, that big, clumsy lump of a man will carry her into the house and when she's too tired to dance he'll spin her around slowly and tenderly in his arms across the kitchen floor. She'll fall asleep with his lips against her neck, his still infatuated hands beneath her top. Bobo will read Harry Potter to his brother and sister in another room. Early tomorrow morning, Ann-Katrin will go back to see her doctor again.

One year? What wouldn't we give for one more year? A year is an eternity.

*

Five old uncles are sitting at the counter in the Bearskin again. They've got something new to argue about.

'A woman, though? As a hockey coach? Is that really a good idea?' one of them asks.

'Can't help thinking this whole equality thing has gone a bit too far,' another says.

'Oh, shut up! That woman's probably forgotten more about hockey than the pair of you have ever known, you senile old fools,' a third protests.

'You think? You can't tell the difference between icing and ice cream, all last season I had to sit there like a guide dog telling you where the puck was!' the fourth chuckles.

'Can you get talking guide dogs these days, then? It's bad enough that you keep lying about watching the 1987 World Championships in Switzerland,' the fifth says.

'I *did*!' the fourth insists.

'Really? Pretty impressive, seeing as the 1987 World Championships were held in Austria!' the fifth points out.

They laugh, all five of them. Then the first, or possibly the second, says, 'But a woman as coach? Is that really a good idea?'

'She sleeps with women too, they say. Are we really going to have one of those in this town?' wonders the second, unless it's actually the first.

The fourth or fifth retorts, 'There are probably more here already. They're everywhere these days.'

The first snorts, 'It's all very well if they're discreet about it, but why does everyone have to make such a fuss about things? Does everything have to be political now?'

The third leans forward on his barstool, and it's hard to know if it's the chair or his body creaking when he asks Ramona for another beer. As she pours it, he says, 'I tell you, if this new coach beats Hed in the first game, she can sleep with *my* wife for all I care.'

They laugh again, all five of them, at one another as much as with them.

★

Ramona gets out some nibbles for them, the old bastards. Nuts for the nuts.

Peter rings on the door of the Ovich family's row house. Benji's mum opens it. 'Peter! Come in and eat!' she commands at once as if he were late, even though he hasn't seen the woman in he doesn't know how long.

Benji isn't home, which Peter is pleased about: he's not here to see him. All three of his sisters are sitting in the kitchen, Adri, Katia, and Gaby. Their mother cuffs each of them across the forehead in turn for not laying a place for their guest quickly enough.

'I won't stay long, I've already eaten,' Peter starts to say, but Adri grabs his arm. 'Shhh! If you turn down Mum's food, you're a braver man than I thought!'

Peter smiles, at first amused, then alarmed. You can joke about most things with the Ovich family, but not food. So Peter eats, three helpings more than he can manage, plus coffee and four different types of biscuits, and is given the rest to take home in plastic containers and aluminium foil. Adri walks him happily to the door. 'You've only got yourself to blame if you show up here at dinnertime.'

Peter puts a hand on his stomach. 'I wanted to talk about Benjamin.'

'We realized that. That's why we let Mum talk to you about everything else,' Adri says with an even broader grin.

She composes herself when she sees the serious look in Peter's eyes.

'We've got a new coach. Elisabeth Zackell.'

'So I've heard. Everyone's heard that. It's even been in the paper.'

Peter holds out a crumpled sheet of paper. Adri reads the names, sees her brother's, but it's as if she doesn't quite grasp the significance of the '(C)' beside it. Peter helps her out: 'She wants to make Benji team captain.'

'Of the A-team? Grown men? Benji's —'

'I know. But this Elisabeth Zackell doesn't seem . . . how can I put it? She doesn't do things the way other people do,' Peter says forlornly.

Adri smiles. 'No, and thank God for that. But *my* brother as captain? Does she have any idea what she's letting herself in for?'

'She says she doesn't want a team, she wants a gang of bandits. Can you think of anyone who'd make a better bandit than your brother?'

Adri tilts her head to one side. 'What do you want from me?'

'You have to help me control him.'

'No one can do that.'

Peter scratches his neck nervously. 'I've never been much good with people, Adri. But this Elisabeth Zackell, she's —'

'Even worse?' Adri suggests.

'Yes! How did you guess?'

'Sune called me. He said you'd be showing up.'

'So you let me sit through that whole meal completely unnecessarily?' Peter exclaims.

'Are you saying there's something wrong with my mum's cooking?' Adri snaps, so sharply that Peter backs away with his hands in the air, as if he were being robbed in an old cowboy film.

'Please, Adri, just help me. We need Benji if we're going to stand any chance of winning.'

Adri looks at the sheet of paper in her hand. 'But you need a Benji who's a leader. A bandit but not a lunatic.'

'We need a Benji who's not quite . . . not quite so Benji as usual.'

'I'll do what I can,' Adri promises.

Peter nods gratefully. 'And we need you as coach of the girls' team, if you're still up for that. I can't afford to pay you, and I know it's a thankless task . . .'

'It's not thankless,' Adri says.

Peter can see the fire inside her. You understand it only if you're a hockey person. They part with a firm handshake, the general manager and the sister, the father and the girls' team's coach. But before Peter leaves Adri asks, 'Who are you getting the money from? Who's this "mystery sponsor" the paper's been writing about, what do they want?'

'Who says they want anything?'

'Everyone with money wants something, Peter. Especially when it comes to money and hockey.'

'I can't say anything until it's official. You can understand that, can't you?' Peter pleads.

Adri's reply sounds almost threatening but is actually sympathetic. 'Just don't forget who stood up for the club when things were at their worst.'

Adri doesn't have to mention the Pack. Peter knows what she means by the people who stood up.

'I'll do my best,' he promises.

Even though they're both well aware that that's never enough in this town.

19

The Same Blue Polo Shirt

It's still warm when the autumn term starts at Beartown School. The sun is shining, the clouds are drifting light and high, the temperature is still lying treacherously about short sleeves and garden furniture, but if you've lived here all your life you can feel winter coming. The cold will soon freeze the lakes, snowflakes will fall, heavy as oven gloves, and darkness will land on the town as if it had been attacked from behind by an angry giant who tosses all the buildings into a black sack to use on the model railway in the secret room in his basement.

It feels as though in Beartown every year comes to an end in August, which may be why it's so easy to love a sport that starts in September. Outside the school building someone has hung green flags in the trees. This seems innocent enough to a lot of people, but to others it is a provocation.

It doesn't start here. But it gets worse from here.

Ana and Maya are standing two hundred feet from the entrance, taking deep breaths and holding each other by the hand. All summer they have been free, but a school is a different sort of island. It's not the sort where you can hide away with your best friend but one where you drift ashore unwillingly after some terrible accident. All the pupils are shipwrecked here, none of them has chosen the company of the others, they're all just trying to stay alive until the term is over and they can get out of here.

'Are you sure you don't want me to get my rifle?' Ana asks.

Maya laughs. 'Fairly sure.'

'I wouldn't shoot anyone. Not badly, anyway,' Ana promises.

'You can put laxative in the milk dispenser in the cafeteria if anyone's stupid,' Maya says.

'And take the lightbulbs out of all the bathrooms and stretch plastic wrap across all the toilets,' Ana nods.

Maya laughs. 'You're so sick.'

'Don't let the bastards see you cry,' Ana whispers.

'Never,' Maya replies.

They walk into the school side by side. The stares cut into their skin, the silence threatens to burst their temples, but they walk with their heads held high. The two of them against the world. The walk to Maya's locker is less than a hundred feet, but nothing in life will ever frighten them so much. Two young women striding straight through a school full of whispers, without lowering their eyes once. You can't show these women a damn thing after what they've already seen.

William Lyt is marching along the corridor surrounded by four of his teammates. Maybe they're not actively seeking out foes, maybe they just swing around the corner and bump into Bobo by accident. But the fight is instantaneous, almost instinctive in its clumsiness, and in the narrow corridor the young men flail around as if they'd stumbled into a swarm of bees. In the spring, when Amat stood up at that meeting in the rink and said he'd seen Kevin rape Maya, some of these guys set off towards the Hollow one night to punish him. Bobo was with them but changed sides at the last minute. If he hadn't taken such a severe beating for his new friend, they might well have killed Amat. That fight isn't over yet.

Someone pushes Bobo, and he falls backward along the corridor. Everyone is shouting, but Lyt and his allies quickly fall silent. Bobo is lying on the floor, and a couple of feet behind him stands Benji. He doesn't say anything, just stands there with his eyes half open and his hair a mess, as if they'd started the fight next to the bench he'd spent the night sleeping under. Hands in pockets, an arrogant look in his eye, so certain of his own effect that it isn't even meant to be threatening.

'Are we going to do this now, Lyt, or do you want to fetch more friends first?' Benji asks, as if he was wondering if Lyt wanted a medium or large drink with his burger.

Lyt's friends glance at him for guidance. Lyt meets Benji's gaze, but not for long. He manages to utter an insult, but it doesn't sound particularly convincing as he mumbles, 'Who cares, we'll do this on the ice instead. Good luck with your goddamn lesbian coach! She suits you! You've always played like pussies!'

Benji is standing on his toes, Lyt on his heels. When the teachers come hurrying through the corridor, Lyt raises his hands a little too quickly and pretends it's their fault, and he sets off in the other direction. But Benji doesn't move, doesn't look down, and everyone who sees that knows what it means for the balance of power in the school.

One of the pupils who pays extra attention is Leo Andersson.

Maya and Ana are standing at Maya's locker when they hear the commotion and shouting. It's as if school buildings are intentionally built with acoustics so that sounds will always reach you no matter where you are, so that the pupils will never be able to escape one another. Maya sees the staff hurry towards the disturbance, sees some final-year students swinging wildly at each other farther along one of the corridors. She realizes it's ridiculous the moment the words leave her mouth, but she asks out loud, 'What are they fighting about now?'

A girl the same age as her spins around a couple of feet away, her voice dripping with derision when she replies, 'Don't act stupid, you lying piece of –'

One of the girl's friends stops her before she says the last word. As if that makes any difference. Maya stares at her slightly too long. The girl's eyes are wide open, her fingernails digging into her palms as she shouts, 'Like *you* don't know what they're fighting about! You're enjoying this, aren't you? The fact that all the trouble in this whole damn town is about *you*! Maya Andersson, Beartown's very own little princess!'

She says Maya's name as if she were spitting on her grave. The girl's friends pull her away. She's got a red Hed Hockey badge on her backpack – her boyfriend and brother both play there. They used to be friends with Kevin Erdahl.

Maya and Ana stay where they are, leaning against the lockers so hard they can feel the metal doors shake in time with their heartbeats. This will never end. Never. Maya groans in resignation, 'How many things can they actually hate me for? I'm either a rape victim or a lying bitch or a . . . a *princess*?'

Ana stands beside her, staring at the floor, then clears her throat noisily and suggests, 'Look . . . if it's any consolation, I still think you're just a perfectly ordinary idiot!'

Maya's mouth struggles to remain solemn but can't resist breaking into a broad grin. 'You're so stu—'

'Says the idiot!' Ana snorts.

Maya bursts out laughing.

You must never let the bastards see you do the opposite.

Bobo is crawling about on the floor like an overweight deer. Amat runs over and holds out his hand and together with Benji pulls him to his feet, groaning.

Amat grins. 'How can you possibly be so heavy but so easy to knock over?'

Bobo, who isn't exactly known for his sharp wits, unexpectedly manages to fire back, 'My cock affects my centre of gravity.'

Amat and Benji's laughter echoes along the corridor. They're the only three members of last season's junior team who are still with Beartown Ice Hockey, and right now that feels as though it might just be enough.

'Have you heard I'm practicing with the A-team today?' Amat asks excitedly.

Bobo nods, then looks suddenly perplexed. 'What did Lyt mean, "lesbian coach"?'

Amat and Benji stare at him in surprise. 'You haven't heard that Beartown's A-team has got a new coach?'

Bobo's face radiates incomprehension. Rumours may spread quickly in Beartown, but not quickly enough to reach Bobo.

'Yeah, but a lesbian? We're going to have a *lesbian* coach?'

Benji says nothing. But Amat clears his throat. 'Bobo . . . we said the *A-team*.'

'Are you saying I don't belong on the A-team?' Bobo snaps.

Amat shrugs. 'If we need an extra obstacle in training, maybe. Your skates are actually faster when you're not wearing them . . .'

Benji bursts out laughing and Bobo tries to grab Amat, but Amat is far, far too quick for him.

They're joking, all three of them, but deep down none of them knows if he's really good enough. If there's any chance of their making the A-team. And where would that leave them? If they're no longer hockey players?

The school slowly fills with staff and students. A new term, equal measures of expectation and anxiety, bittersweet reunions with everyone you love and everyone you hate, and the knowledge that there's no way to avoid breathing the same air as both groups.

In the headmaster's office sits a young teacher, Jeanette, making a last attempt to persuade the man in the smart jacket who's massaging his temples in front of her.

'Just give me a chance! Let me turn it into part of PE!'

The headmaster sighs. 'Please, Jeanette. After everything that happened this spring, I just want to get this school through *one* term without any scandals and attention from the media – and you want to teach the students how to fight?'

'It's not . . . for heaven's sake . . . it's martial arts!' Jeanette snaps.

'What did you say it was called again?'

'MMA, mixed martial arts,' Jeanette repeats patiently.

The headmaster rolls his eyes. ' "Arts"? It always seems a bit odd to call it an "art," don't you think? It's not like you can put on an exhibition of broken noses, is it?'

Jeanette clasps her hands together in her lap, possibly to stop herself from throwing something at him. 'Martial arts teaches students discipline and respect for their own and other people's bodies. I've already got somewhere to do it, up at Adri Ovich's kennels, just let me ask the students if they're interested, and –'

The headmaster polishes his glasses more thoroughly than necessary. 'I'm sorry, Jeanette. The parents would go mad. They'd see it as you teaching their children to be violent. We can't afford any more controversy.'

He stands up to indicate that it's time for Jeanette to leave his office, but the moment he opens the door a hand very nearly hits him in the face. The man standing outside was just about to knock on the door.

'I've got a feeling this is going to be a very long year,' the headmaster mutters.

Jeanette is standing behind him, unable to conceal her curiosity. 'Hi!' she says.

The man in the doorway smiles. 'I'm . . . I'm starting work here today?' he says.

'Yes! Our new philosophy and history teacher!' the headmaster exclaims, grabbing some sheets of paper from a shelf before adding 'And maths and science and . . . French? Do you speak French?'

The male teacher in the doorway looks as though he's about to protest, but Jeanette gestures with a smile that he should go along with it. The headmaster heaves a pile of books and papers into his arms. 'Best get going, then! Your schedule's on top there!'

The teacher thanks him and sets off along the corridor. The headmaster watches him go and sighs, 'Freshly qualified. I know I should be happy that he's come here of his own volition, but dear Lord, Jeanette? How old do you think he is?'

'Twenty-five? Twenty-six?' Jeanette guesses.

'And you saw the way he looks.'

'I didn't notice a thing,' Jeanette deadpans.

'The school is raging with hormones, and we employ a teacher who looks like he's in a bloody boy band! We'll have to lock up half the female students,' the headmaster mutters.

Jeanette coughs under her breath. 'And probably some of the female teachers, too.'

'What?' the headmaster says.

'What?' Jeanette repeats innocently.

'Did you say something?'

'No! I've got a class now!'

The headmaster mutters unhappily, 'You can put up one poster about your martial arts training. *One* poster, Jeanette!'

Jeanette nods and goes out into the corridor. She pins up four posters and watches the new teacher's hips as she heads after him along the corridor.

The new teacher is standing in the classroom writing on the board as the students tumble into the room in little clusters. When the bell rings, it can barely be heard over the scrape of chairs and the sound of backpacks being dropped on the floor, as well as the enthusiastic chatter about everything that's happened during the summer and the fight that just broke out in the corridor.

Benji comes in last of all, and hardly anyone notices him. His hair is still a mess, his denim shirt is half tucked in, as if he'd just pulled on his trousers in a darkened room. He looks the way he did when he got out of the bed in a cabin in a campsite between Beartown and Hed not long ago, on the night that was full of Nietzsche and cold beer and warm hands.

All the other students in the room are too preoccupied with one another and themselves to see the new teacher turn towards the door and lose his breath. Benji's not an easy young man to surprise, but he stops, his chest pounding with shock.

The teacher is wearing the same blue polo shirt as he was that night.

20

Shaving Cream in Your Shoes

It's hard to care about people. Exhausting, in fact, because empathy is a complicated thing. It requires us to accept that everyone else's lives are also going on the whole time. We have no pause button for when everything gets too much for us to deal with, but then neither does anyone else.

When the class is over, the students rush out of the classroom as if it were on fire, as usual. Benji seems to be last by accident; he's good at giving the impression of nonchalance. The teacher is sweating with nerves, the collar of his blue polo shirt flecked with moisture.

'I . . . I didn't know you were still at school, Benjamin. If I'd known . . . I thought you were older. It was a . . . a mistake! I could lose my job, we shouldn't have slept together . . . I don't make a habit . . . you were just . . . just . . .'

Benji steps closer to him. The teacher's hands are shaking. 'Just a mistake. I was just a mistake,' Benji says, finishing his sentence for him.

The teacher nods helplessly with his eyes closed. Benji stares at his lips for a few moments. When the teacher opens his eyes again, Benji is already gone.

Bobo goes straight home after school as usual, throws his backpack into his room, gets changed, and goes out to help his dad, Hog, in the workshop. Just as he always does. But today Hog rather than Bobo is the one keeping an eye on the clock.

'That's enough, Bobo. Get going!' Hog says when it's time.

Bobo nods, relieved, and shrugs off his overalls. Hog notes that they're getting to be too small for him. While Bobo fetches his hockey gear Hog hesitates for a long time before saying anything, possibly because he doesn't want his son to see how full of anticipation he is. Fathers' hopes can so easily suffocate their sons. But in the end he can't help asking, 'Nervous?'

It's a stupid question, Bobo's as nervous as a long-tailed cat between two rocking chairs. This is his first training session with the A-team, he's eighteen years old, and hockey has a definitive way of letting children know when they've grown up. The son shakes his head, but his eyes are nodding. His dad grins. 'Keep your head down and your mouth shut. Do your best. And wear a pair of shoes you don't like.'

Bobo opens his mouth to make the noise he's made ever since he was little when he doesn't understand something: 'Huh?'

'The older A-team players will fill your shoes with shaving cream while you're in the shower. They'll make life hell to start with, but you just have to accept that. Remember, it's a sign that they respect you. It's when they're not messing with you that you need to be worried, because that means they know you're on your way out of the team.'

Bobo nods. Hog looks as though he's about to pat him on the shoulder but reaches for a tool from the bench behind him instead. Bobo turns to go change his shoes, but Hog clears his throat, 'Thanks for your help today.'

Bobo doesn't know what to say. He helps his dad in the workshop every day, but his dad never thanks him. But today he goes on: 'I wish your life could be less complicated. That you only had to worry about school and hockey and girls and whatever your friends worry about. I know it's been tough, having to help in the workshop, and now all this business with your mum not . . .'

He tails off. Bobo doesn't finish the sentence. He just says, 'No problem, Dad.'

'I'm so damn proud of you,' Hog says, looking down under the hood of a Ford.

Bobo goes and gets an old pair of shoes.

★

Amat is the smallest guy in the locker room. He's doing his best to make himself even smaller; he can feel the way the older players are looking at him and knows they don't want him there. Bobo's sitting beside him, and it's worse for him because he's big. The older players, the ones who didn't find other teams when the club was teetering close to bankruptcy in the summer and are damned if they're going to lose their places to a gang of juniors now, immediately start to target him. Just little things, someone hitting him with his shoulder, someone accidentally kicking his gear across the floor. As they start to joke about noisily, Bobo desperately tries to make funny comments. It's obvious that he's trying too hard to gain acceptance, and for that reason it only makes things worse. Amat tries to nudge him with his elbow to get him to shut up, but Bobo is on a roll. One of the older players grunts, 'So we're getting a female coach now, too? Can't the GM find some other way to drum up a bit of PR? Are we going to end up as some sort of political gesture?'

'There's no way she got the job on her own merits, this is to meet a quota!' another snaps.

'Have you heard she's a lesbian?' Bobo blurts out, a little too loudly.

The older players ignore him. But one of them says, 'Definitely a rug muncher. You can tell just by looking at her.'

'Huh? What's a rug muncher? Oh, hang on . . . I get it! Lesbian, right? I get it!' Bobo yelps.

No one reacts. The older players just go on, 'Can't a hockey team just be a hockey team? Does everything have to be political? It's only a matter of time before they replace the bear on our shirts with a goddamn rainbow!'

As if struck by lightning Bobo exclaims, 'And force us to play in, like, ballerinas' tutus!'

He stands up and does a clumsy pirouette, stumbles into a bench, loses his balance, and falls flat on his back on top of two hockey bags. Then something happens. A couple of the older players laugh. At him rather than with him, but as long as they're looking at him he devours their attention. He gets to his feet and does another pirouette, and one of the older guys pretends to be serious and says, 'Your name's Bobo, right?'

'Yes!' Bobo nods intently.

The other players grin expectantly, aware that the older man is teasing the boy.

'You ought to show her your cock,' he says.

'Huh?' Bobo says.

The older player points at him demonstratively. 'The new coach. She's a lesbian. Show her your cock! So she can see what she's missing!'

'Let the anaconda out of the cage, Bobo! You're not chicken, are you?' another player cries, and soon they're all shouting, as if he were getting ready to attempt the long jump.

'But she . . . won't she be . . . angry?' Bobo wonders in confusion.

'She'll just think you've got a decent sense of humour!' one of the older players replies eagerly.

In hindsight it's easy to say that Bobo's crazy, but when you're eighteen years old in a locker room full of grown men who are suddenly cheering you on, 'no' is the hardest word in the world.

So when Elisabeth Zackell walks past in the corridor, Bobo leaps out of the locker room as naked as the day he was born. He's expecting her to be shocked. Or at least jump. She doesn't even raise an eyebrow.

'Yes?' she asks.

Bobo squirms. 'I . . . well . . . we heard you were lesbian, so I . . .'

'BOBO WANTED TO SHOW YOU HIS COCK SO YOU KNOW WHAT YOU'RE MISSING!!!' someone shouts from the locker room, followed by two dozen men giggling hysterically.

Zackell puts her hands on her knees and leans forward in interest towards Bobo's crotch.

'That?' she wonders, pointing curiously.

'Huh?' Bobo says.

'Is that the cock you're talking about? Wow. I've seen women with bigger clitorises than that.'

Then she turns and walks towards the ice without another word. Bobo has turned bright red all over when he steps back inside the locker room.

'It's . . . okay, she said . . . a clitoris can't get this big, can it? I mean . . . how big can a clitoris get? Roughly?'

The locker room is rocking with mocking laughter. At him, not with him. But Bobo is still smiling sheepishly, because sometimes any attention at all can still feel like validation.

Amat is squirming inside his gear as he looks at Bobo, already thinking that this is going to end badly.

When the practice begins, the players gather around the centre circle at a very leisurely pace, demonstratively arrogant, to show Elisabeth Zackell that she's not welcome. She doesn't seem to pick up the hint at all, just comes out with six buckets under her arm.

'What are you good at in Beartown?'

When no one answers she shrugs her shoulders, 'I've watched all your games from last season, so I know you're completely useless at pretty much everything. It would really help me to know what you're good at.'

Someone tries to mumble a joke – 'drinking and fucking' – but not even that raises more than a stifled grunt from the rest of the group. Then someone suddenly starts to laugh, not at the remark but at something happening on the ice behind Zackell. Bobo is skating out from the bench, over two hundred pounds of him, wearing a skirt he's stolen from the figure skaters' storeroom. He performs three pirouettes in a row and is met by applause and cheering from the older players at the centre circle. Elisabeth Zackell lets him carry on, even though they're no longer laughing at Bobo but at her.

But when Bobo is halfway through his fourth pirouette the

cheering suddenly stops, and before Bobo knows what's hit him everything goes black. When he opens his eyes, he's lying on the ice, he can hardly breathe. Elisabeth Zackell is leaning over him expressionlessly and says, 'Why hasn't anyone taught you to skate properly?'

'Huh?'

'You roll like a ferry, but I've seen you pull an axe from the hood of a car. If you could skate properly, I'd never be able to knock you down that easily. And then you wouldn't be utterly worthless as a hockey player. So why hasn't anyone ever taught you?'

'I . . . I don't know,' Bobo gasps, still lying on his back with his chest aching as if he's been run over rather than tackled.

'What are you good at in Beartown?' Zackell asks seriously.

At first Bobo doesn't answer, so Zackell gives up and skates back to the centre circle. The young man slowly crawls up from the ice, pulls off the skirt, and says, in a voice that sounds both angry and humiliated, 'Hard work! We're good at hard work in Beartown. People can say a lot of shit about this town, but we know about HARD WORK!'

The older players squirm. But no one protests. So Elisabeth Zackell says, 'Okay! Then that's how we win. We work harder than all the others. If you need to be sick, do it in these. I've heard the GM doesn't like mess, so I daresay he doesn't want vomit on the ice. I take it you're familiar with how to skate lengths?'

The players groan loudly, which she interprets as 'yes.' She sets out the buckets she brought with her. The rest of the practice consists of excruciating fitness exercises. Skating at top speed between the boards, then darting sideways, wrestling, work, work, work. Not a single bucket is empty by the time they're done. And the only player still standing at the end is Amat.

At first the older players try to stop him, not obviously but by little tricks that look like accidents: a sharp elbow in the corner, pulling his jersey when he's about to take off, a discreet skate nudging his to make him lose his balance. Most of the players on the ice are fifty or sixty pounds heavier than Amat, so just leaning on him is enough. It isn't Amat's fault that they're doing this, he's not trying to show off or draw attention to himself, he's simply too good. He makes the others look slow, and they can't tolerate that. Time after time they trip him, and time after time he gets up. Skates faster, fights harder, digs deeper inside himself. The look in his eyes gets blacker and blacker.

No one knows what the time is; Elisabeth Zackell shows no sign of having finished with them. One after the other the older players crumple and collapse. As they stare down at the ice, Amat carries on skating. However many times Zackell orders him to skate from board to board, she can't exhaust him. His jersey is black with sweat, but he's still standing. Bobo is lying on the ice, almost unconscious, and is filled with both pride and envy as he watches his friend work, work, work.

Amat is the youngest on the team. As he stands in the shower after the practice, his thigh muscles are shaking so much that he can barely keep his balance. When he drags himself into the locker room with his towel around his waist, he sees that his shoes have been filled with shaving cream.

And then it's all worth it.

When Elisabeth Zackell walks through the rink long after the end of practice, one lone player is sitting in the locker room. Bobo is the size of a dairy cow, yet still as small as a frightened hedgehog. His eyes are moist, staring at a pair of shoes that no one has filled with shaving cream. The only thing the older players roared when he emerged from the shower was 'Thanks very much for the fitness training, you little shit! "We're good at hard work"! How the hell could you say something so completely stupid to a hockey coach?'

Amat tried to comfort him. Bobo laughed it off, and Amat was too exhausted to persist. After he and all the others have gone, Bobo is still sitting in the same place, smallest in the whole world.

'Turn the lights out when you leave,' Zackell says, because she's not one for this whole business of emotions.

Bobo sniffs. 'How do you get respect?' he asks, and Zackell looks extremely uncomfortable.

'You've . . . you've got snot everywhere,' she says, gesturing towards her face with her hand.

Bobo wipes himself, and Zackell looks as though she feels like curling up in the fetal position.

'I want them to respect me. I want them to put shaving cream in my shoes, too!' Bobo says.

Zackell groans. 'You don't have to be respected. It's not as important as people think.'

Bobo chews his lips. 'Sorry I showed you my cock,' he whispers.

Zackell stretches herself to smile.

'In your defence, it wasn't much of a cock,' she says, measuring a few measly inches between her thumb and forefinger.

Bobo starts to laugh. Zackell sticks her hands in her pockets and gives him some quiet advice: 'You need to be useful to the team, Bobo. Then they'll respect you.'

She walks off without waiting for him to ask any more questions. Bobo will lie awake at night wondering what she meant.

He stops off at the supermarket on the way home and buys shaving cream so his dad won't be sad. When Hog sees the ruined shoes in the hall, he gives his son a hug. That doesn't happen often.

21

He's Lying on the Ground

Sune is walking slowly through the rink, breathing hard through his nose. He misses his coaching job every second, but he can hardly get up the stands anymore. Hockey gets younger while everyone involved in it gets older, and when it's done with us it discards us without any sentimentality at all. That's how it develops and stays alive, for the sake of new generations.

'Zackell!' Sune calls out breathlessly when he catches sight of the woman who's taken his job.

'Yes?' she responds, heading for the locker room.

'How did today's practice feel?'

' "Feel"?' Zackell asks, as if it were a foreign word.

Sune leans against the wall and smiles weakly. 'I mean . . . it's not easy to be a hockey coach in this town. Especially not if you're . . . you know.'

He means 'if you're a woman.' So Zackell replies, 'It's not easy to be a hockey coach anywhere.'

Sune nods sadly. 'I heard that one of the players showed you his . . . genitals . . .'

'Hardly,' Zackell retorts.

Sune coughs awkwardly. 'He hardly showed you his genitals?'

'It hardly counted as genitals,' Zackell corrects.

'Oh, that's just . . . you know, guys, sometimes they . . .' Sune says, staring down at his knees.

Zackell looks annoyed. 'How did you know someone showed me his genitals?'

Sune misinterprets that to mean that she's upset about the

genitals. 'I can talk to the guys if you like, I can understand that you feel offended, but –'

'You're not to talk to my players. *I* talk to my players. And the only person who decides if I'm offended is me.'

Sune raises an eyebrow. 'I'm guessing you don't often feel offended?'

'Feeling offended is an emotion.'

Zackell looks as though she's talking about tools when she says the word. Sune sticks his hands in his pockets and mutters, 'It's not easy being coach in Beartown. Especially if things start to go badly. Believe me, I had my job a whole lifetime before you got here. And there are people in this town who won't be happy with a coach who . . . who looks like you do.'

The old man looks deep into the woman's eyes and sees a characteristic that he always lacked: she doesn't care. Sune always cared, deep down. He wanted the players to like him: the fans, the old men and women in the Bearskin. The whole town. But Elisabeth Zackell isn't afraid of opinions, because she knows what all successful coaches know: they'll like her when she wins.

'I'm going to get something to eat,' she says, managing to sound neither friendly nor unfriendly.

Sune nods. Smiles again. Leaves her with one last thought: 'Do you remember that little girl, Alicia, who was firing pucks in my garden? She came to the rink today, seven times. She ran away from her preschool to watch the A-team train. I took her back, but she ran away again. She's going to keep on doing that all autumn.'

'Is it possible to lock children up?' Zackell wonders, possibly not quite understanding the point Sune is trying to make, so Sune clarifies: 'Children take all the things they grow up with for granted. After watching you coach the A-team today, Alicia will take it for granted that women do that. When she's old enough to play on an A-team, there may not be female hockey coaches. Just . . . hockey coaches.'

That means something to Sune. Something important. He doesn't know if it means anything to Elisabeth Zackell, because it honestly doesn't look as though it does: she just looks as though she wants to go and get something to eat. But hunger is a feeling, too.

Just before Zackell walks out through the door, something flashes in her eyes, something she does actually care about, so she asks, 'How's it going with my goalie? That Vidar?'

'I'll talk to his brother,' Sune promises.

'Didn't you promise that Peter was going to talk to Benjamin Ovich's sisters, too?' Zackell wonders.

'Yes?' Sune says in surprise.

'So why didn't Benjamin come to training today?'

'He didn't?' Sune exclaims.

It hadn't even occurred to him that Benji might not have appeared for practice. Children aren't the only ones who take things for granted.

In a cabin on a campsite sits a man in a blue polo shirt. He has lessons to prepare, a teaching job he has spent several years training for, but can't get anything done. He sits in the little kitchen with a book about philosophy on the table in front of him, staring out through the window and hoping to see a young man with sad eyes and a wild soul. But Benji doesn't come. He's lost. Today the teacher looked him in the eye and told him he was a mistake, even though the mistake was the teacher's.

Everyone in this town knows that Benji is dangerous, because he strikes hardest. Yet few people seem to appreciate that everything about him does just that – strike hardest, beat hardest – the whole time. Including his heart.

Inside the Oviches' home one of the sisters, Gaby, walks into Benji's room. Gaby's two children are playing with Legos scattered across the whole floor. Gaby can say many harsh things about her little brother, but there's no better uncle in the world. Her children will grow up saying that this room in their grandmother's house, their uncle's room, was the safest place in the entire universe. Nothing bad could happen to them here, no one would dare do anything to them, because their uncle would protect them against everyone and everything. Once one of them said to Gaby, 'Mum! There are ghosts in Uncle Benji's wardrobe; they have to hide in there because they're scared of him!'

Gaby smiles and is just walking out of the room when the thought hits her. She spins around and asks the children, 'Where did you get the Legos?'

'It was in the presents,' the children reply, unconcerned.

'What presents?'

The children go into defence mode, as if they've been accused of theft: 'The presents on Uncle Benji's bed! They had our names on them, Mum! They were for us!'

The doorbell rings. Gaby doesn't walk to answer it. She runs.

Adri, the oldest sister, opens the door. Amat, Benji's teammate, is standing outside. The boy doesn't get worried until he sees how worried Adri gets, but she realizes everything all at once.

'Is Benji home?' Amat asks, although he already knows the answer.

'Shit!' Adri replies.

Gaby comes rushing out into the hall, yelling, 'Benji left presents for the children!'

Amat clears his throat nervously: 'He wasn't at practice. I just wanted to check that he was okay!'

He calls the last words after Adri. She's already run past him, heading towards the forest.

Benji occasionally skips practices, but never the first of the season. His feet are too desperate to get back onto the ice, his hands miss his stick, his brain the flight across the rink. He wouldn't miss the chance to play today, not when Beartown is playing Hed in the first round of games. Something's wrong.

★

Ramona is standing behind her counter, the way she always has, with as little emotional disturbance as possible. She's seen this town blossom, but in recent years she's also seen it take a beating. People in Beartown know how to work, but they need somewhere to do it. They know how to fight, but they need something to fight for.

The only thing you can rely on in all towns, big and small alike, is that there will be broken people. It's nothing to do with the place, just life; it can beat us up. And if that happens, it's easy to find your way to a pub; bars can quickly become sad places. Someone who has nowhere else to go can grasp a glass a little too tightly; someone who's tired of falling can take refuge in the bottom of a bottle, seeing as you can't fall much further from there.

Ramona has seen fragile souls come and go here; some have moved on, and some have gone under. Things have gone well for some of them, and some – like Alain Ovich – have gone off into the forest.

Ramona is old enough neither to jump with joy when things are going well nor to bury herself when things are going badly, and she knows how easy it is to have unrealistic expectations of a hockey team in an autumn like the one they're facing now. Because sports isn't reality, and when reality is hell we need stories, because they make us feel that if we can just be best at one thing, perhaps everything else will turn and start to go our way, too.

But Ramona really can't say. Can things ever turn around? Or do we just get used to them?

The last thing Alain Ovich did before he took his rifle and went out into the forest was to leave presents for his children on their beds. No one knows why someone would get it into his head to do a thing like that, but perhaps he was hoping that that was how they'd remember him. That he could go far enough into the forest for them to believe he had just abandoned them, so that they could fantasize that he was a secret agent who had been called away on a top secret mission or an astronaut who had gone up into space. Perhaps he hoped they would have a childhood, in spite of everything.

It didn't turn out that way. Adri, his eldest, will never be able to explain how she knew where he was. She just had a feeling about where he'd gone. Maybe that's why dogs like her, because she has a heightened sensitivity to things that normal people lack. She didn't shout 'Dad!' as she moved through the trees; the children of hunters don't do that, they learn that every man in the forest tends to be someone's dad, so if you want to get hold of yours you have to shout his name as if you were just anyone. Adri never became just anyone, not entirely; she was born with something of Alain in her. He could never go far enough into the forest for her not to be able to find him.

A pub can be a gloomy place, because, taken as a whole, life always gives us more opportunities for grief than celebration, more funeral drinks than wedding toasts. But Ramona knows that a pub can be other things, too, from time to time: small cracks in the blocks of stone you carry in your chest. It doesn't always have to be the best place on Earth, it just doesn't always need to be the worst.

The past few weeks have been full of rumours. It's said that the factory is going to be sold, and Beartown has been through enough setbacks to know that this could just as easily mean bankruptcy. It's easy to call that attitude cynical, but cynicism is simply a chemical reaction to too much disappointment. The young men in the Bearskin aren't the only people talking about unemployment; everyone is worried now. In a small community the loss of any employer is a natural disaster, everyone knows someone who's affected, until eventually it spreads to you.

And it might be easy to call the inhabitants paranoid when they keep saying that the politicians focus all their resources on Hed and don't give a damn if Beartown even survives another generation, but the worst thing about paranoia is that the only way to prove you're not paranoid is to be proved right.

*

Some children never quite manage to escape their parents; they're guided by their compass, see through their eyes. When terrible things happen, most people become waves, but some people become rocks. Waves are tossed back and forth when the wind comes, but the rocks just take a beating, immovable, waiting for the storm to blow over.

Adri was a child, but she took the rifle from her father and sat on a stump holding his hand in hers. Perhaps it was shock, unless she was consciously saying good-bye, both to him and to herself. She became someone different after that. When she stood up and walked back through the forest to Beartown, she didn't scream for help in panic; she walked purposefully to the homes of the best and strongest hunters, so that they could help her carry the body. When her mother collapsed screaming in the hall, Adri caught her, because the girl had already done her crying. She was ready to be the rock. Has been ever since.

Katia and Gaby were their mother's children, but Adri and Benji were their father's. Causes of conflict, finders of war. So every time Adri has set off into the forest to look for her little brother since then, she knows she's going to find him, as if he had magnets under his skin. That's not what she's scared of. She scared he's going to be dead, every time. Younger brothers never know what they put their big sisters through. Anxiety hidden behind eyes, words hidden behind other words, keys to gun cabinets hidden under pillows at night.

Benji isn't sitting in a tree. He's lying on the ground.

Elisabeth Zackell walks into the Bearskin. It's long past dinner-time, but she takes a seat in one corner and Ramona takes her a large plate of potatoes without her having to ask.

'Thanks,' the coach says.

'I don't know what vegetarables like you eat, apart from potatoes. But there are mushrooms in the forests around here. They'll soon be in season!' Ramona replies.

Zackell looks up. Ramona nods sternly. The bar owner isn't big on emotions, either, but this is her way of saying she hopes the hockey coach is going to stick around for a while.

Benji's body is still, his eyes open but his gaze far away. Adri can still remember how her dad's hand felt when she sat there on the stump as a child. How cold it was, how still without the pulse running through it.

Carefully, gently, without making any noise at all, the big sister lies down on the ground beside her little brother. Her hand on his, just to feel the heat and heartbeat within.

'You'll be the death of me. Don't you dare lie on the ground when I'm looking for you, you stupid pea brain!' she whispers.

'Sorry,' Benji whispers.

He is neither drunk nor high. He isn't running from his feelings today. That makes her more worried.

'What's happened?'

The last light of summer bounces off the tears clinging to Benji's eyelashes. 'Nothing. Just a . . . mistake.'

Adri doesn't reply. She isn't the sister who talks about broken hearts, she's just the sister who fetches her brother home from the forest. She waits until they're getting close to the edge of town before she says, 'The new coach is thinking of making you team captain.'

She sees something in Benji's eyes that she hasn't seen for many years.

He's scared.

Zackell has almost finished her meal when Ramona returns to the table and puts a beer down in front of her.

'From the regulars,' Ramona says.

Zackell looks over at the five old men at the bar. 'Them?'

Ramona shakes her head. 'Their wives.'

In the far corner sit five old women. Grey hair, handbags on the table, wrinkled hands tightly clutching glasses of beer. Several of them have children and grandchildren who work at the factory; some of them worked there themselves. The old women have old bodies but new T-shirts. All the same. Green, with four words written on them, like a war cry:

BEARTOWN
AGAINST
THE
REST

22

Team Captain

There's no real autumn in Beartown, just a quick blink before win-ter. The snow doesn't even have the manners to let the leaves decompose in peace. The darkness comes fast, but at least these months have been full of a lot of light: a club that fought and survived. A grown man who put a reassuring hand on a four-and-a-half-year-old's shoulder. Hockey that was more than a game. Beer on a stranger's table. Green T-shirts that said we fight together, no matter what. Boys with the biggest dreams. Friends who formed an army.

Unfortunately, that isn't what we're going to remember in a few years' time. Many of us will just look back on these months and remember . . . the hatred. Because that's how we function, for better or worse: we always define different periods by their worst moments. So we will remember two towns' loathing for each other. We will remember the violence, because it's only just started. Of course we won't talk about it; we don't do that here. We'll talk about hockey games that were played instead, so that we don't have to talk about the funerals that took place between them.

Darkness has settled comfortably upon Beartown and Hed as a thin figure makes its way through the forest. It's starting to get cold now; the days don't let on, but the nights are honest, not hiding temperatures below freezing behind rays of sunlight. The figure shivers and hurries on, as much from nerves as to keep warm.

The ice rink in Hed doesn't have an alarm, and the building is old and full of back doors that someone might forget to lock. The figure doesn't have a detailed plan of how the break-in is going to work, just a vague idea of padding around the building and feeling all the door handles. He has no luck there but does better with one of the bathroom windows. He manages to pry it open, even if it takes the full strength of the twelve-year-old's arms.

Leo climbs inside, runs through the gloom. He's played enough away games in Hed to know where the locker rooms are. The A-team has its own lockers. Most of them don't have the players' names on them, but some of the players are too infatuated with their own names to be able to resist the opportunity to write them on the labels at the top. Leo uses the flashlight on his cell phone to find William Lyt's. Then he does what he came to do.

Adri, Katia, and Gaby Ovich bang on the door of the Bearskin after closing time. Ramona yells, 'I'VE GOT MY SHOTGUN LOADED!' which is her way of saying 'I'm afraid we're closed,' but the Ovich sisters march inside all the same, and Ramona jumps when she sees all three of them.

'What have I done now?' she pants.

'Nothing, we just want to ask a favour of you,' Katia says.

'Nothing? When the three of you come through that door together, an old bag can't help but think she's going to get a beating, surely to God you can understand that?' Ramona whimpers, clutching her chest theatrically.

The sisters grin. As does Ramona. She puts beer and whisky on the bar, then pats each of them fondly on the cheek. 'It's been a long time since I saw you. You're still too beautiful for this town.'

'Flattery like that won't get you anywhere,' Adri says.

Ramona nods. 'That's why the good Lord gave us strong liquor.'

'How are you?' Gaby asks.

Ramona snorts. 'I'm starting to get old. And it's shit, let me tell you. Your back aches, and your eyesight starts to go. I don't give a damn about dying, but this ageing business, I can't see the point of it.'

The sisters smile. Ramona slams her empty glass down on the counter and goes on, 'So? What can I do for you?'

'We need a job,' Adri says.

When the Ovich sisters emerge from the Bearskin, their little brother, Benjamin, is leaning against the wall. Adri knocks the cigarette out of his hand, Katia folds his collar down roughly, and Gaby licks her fingers and combs his hair with them. They curse him and tell him they love him in the same sentence, the way only they can. Then they push him through the door. Ramona is standing behind the counter, waiting.

'Your sisters say you need a job.'

'Apparently so,' Benji mutters.

Ramona can clearly see Alain Ovich's eyes in his son's face. 'Your sisters say you're restless, that you need to be kept busy. They can't stop you from ending up at the counter in a bar, but they can at least try to make sure you end up on the right side of it. I told Adri that giving you work as a bartender could be like leaving a dog to guard a steak, but she's not the sort of person you can reason with, that one. And Katia swore you've got experience of being behind a bar, from her place in Hed. Is that the place the Reds call the Barn?'

Benji nods. 'The Reds' is what Ramona calls people from Hed.

'I'm not welcome there anymore because a degree of conflict about aesthetic matters arose between me and the . . . native population,' he explains.

Ramona doesn't have to roll up Benji's sleeve to know that there's a tattoo of a bear under it. She has a weakness for boys who love this town more than they should have the sense to.

'Can you pour a beer without spilling it?'

'Yes.'

'What do you get if you ask to run a tab?'

'A slap in the face?'

'You're hired!'

'Thanks.'

She snorts. 'Don't say that. I'm only doing this because I'm frightened of your sisters.'

Benji smiles. 'Everyone with any sense is.'

Ramona gestures towards the shelves on the walls. 'We have two types of beer, one type of whisky, and the rest is mostly for decoration. You wash the glasses and clean, and if there's a fight you *don't* get involved, you hear me?'

Benji doesn't disagree, which is a good start. He clears the backyard of a pile of wood and tin that's been lying there for months; he's strong as an ox and knows how to keep his mouth shut. Ramona's two favourite character traits.

When it's time to turn the lights out and lock up, he helps her up the stairs to her apartment. There are still photographs of Holger, her husband, everywhere. Him and Beartown Ice Hockey, her first and second loves, green flags and pennants on every wall.

'You can ask what you want to ask now,' Ramona says mildly, patting the young man on the cheek.

'I don't want to ask anything,' Benji lies.

'You're wondering if your dad used to come to the Bearskin. If he used to sit in the bar down there before he . . . went off into the forest.'

Benji's hands disappear into the pockets of his jeans, and the years are stripped away from his voice.

'What was he like?' the boy asks.

The old woman sighs. 'Not one of the best. Not one of the worst.'

Benji turns towards the stairs. 'I'll take the garbage out. See you tomorrow evening.'

Ramona takes hold of his hand and whispers, 'You don't have to become like him, Benjamin. You've got his eyes, but I think you can become someone else.'

Benji isn't ashamed of crying in front of her.

Early the next morning Elisabeth Zackell sticks her head into Peter Andersson's office. Peter is wrestling with an espresso machine. Zackell watches. Peter presses a button, and brown water dribbles out of the bottom of the machine. Peter panics and presses all the buttons at the same time while simultaneously reaching with an impressive display of acrobatics for a roll of paper towels while he balances in front of the leaking machine on one foot.

'And I'm supposed to be the weird one for not drinking coffee,' Zackell notes.

Peter looks up, still in the middle of some sort of modern dance interpretation of office cleaning, swearing in a way that Zackell has reason to believe is very unlike him. 'For f—I'm so bloo—Shi—'

'Shall I come back later?' Zackell wonders.

'No, no . . . I . . . this damn contraption is a complete nightmare, but it was a gift from my daughter!' Peter admits, embarrassed.

Zackell offers no reaction. 'I'll come back later,' she concludes.

'No! I . . . sorry, what can I do for you? Have your wages been paid okay?' Peter wonders.

'It's about rope,' Zackell says, but Peter has already launched into his defence. 'The new sponsor, our contract isn't quite in place. But everyone should have been paid by now.'

He wipes the sweat from his brow. Zackell repeats, 'I'm not here about my paycheck. I'm here about rope.'

'Rope?' Peter echoes.

'I need rope. And a paintball gun. Can you buy those around here?'

'A paintball gun?' Peter echoes again.

Zackell explains in a monotone, but not impatiently, 'Paintball is a war simulation game played on a specially designed course. Two teams shoot at each other with small pellets of paint fired from guns. I need one of those guns.'

'I know what paintball is,' Peter assures her.

'It didn't sound like it,' Zackell says in her own defence.

Peter scratches his hair, getting coffee on his forehead. He doesn't notice, and Zackell spares him the panic that telling him would probably trigger.

'They probably have rope in the hardware store opposite the Bearskin pub.'

'Thanks,' Zackell says, and is already out in the corridor before Peter has time to call out, 'What do you want rope for? You're not going to hang anyone, are you?'

Then he says it again, with genuine concern in his voice: 'ZACKELL! YOU'RE NOT GOING TO HANG ANYONE, ARE YOU? WE'VE GOT ENOUGH PROBLEMS AS IT IS!!!'

Benji's former coach, David, used to say that Benji would be late for his own funeral. If his teammates didn't check that number 16 was out on the ice, he could easily be lying asleep in the locker room when the game started. Sometimes he missed practices, sometimes he showed up high or drunk. But today he arrives at the rink on time, gets changed at once, and goes straight out onto the ice. Elisabeth Zackell turns towards him as if she's surprised that a hockey player has turned up for hockey practice. Benji takes a deep breath and apologizes, the way you learn to do if you've big sisters who hit hard: 'Sorry I didn't come to practice yesterday.'

Zackell shrugs. 'I don't care if you come to practice.'

Benji notices that there are five thick ropes lying on the ice, several yards long. Zackell is holding a paintball gun in her hand: the hardware store in Beartown didn't have any, but the one in Hed managed to find one in the storeroom. A scattering of small paint spatters on the plexiglass at one corner of the rink indicates that Zackell has already practiced firing the hard little pellets of paint.

'What are you doing?' Benji asks, baffled.

'What are you doing here so early?' Zackell counters.

Benji looks at the time. He's right on time for the practice, but the only other players on the ice are Amat and Bobo. He grunts, 'My sister says you're thinking of making me team captain. That's a bad idea.'

Zackell nods without blinking. 'Okay.'

Benji waits for her to go on. She doesn't. So he asks, 'Why me?'

'Because you're a coward,' Zackell says.

Benji has been called many things in his life, but never that.

'You're full of crap.'

She nods. 'Maybe. But I'm giving you the thing you're most terrified of: responsibility for other people.'

Benji's eyes darken. Hers are expressionless. Amat is standing behind them, his skates twitching with restlessness, until he eventually loses patience and blurts out, 'Practice is supposed to start now! Why don't you go and get the others from the locker room?'

Zackell shrugs her shoulders nonchalantly. 'Me? Why would I care about that?'

Benji squints at her, increasingly frustrated. He looks at the time again. Then he leaves the ice.

A lot of the older players in the Beartown locker room are only half changed when Benji walks in.

'Practice is starting,' he says.

Some people can make themselves heard without raising their voice. Even so, some of the older players misinterpret Benji at first and reply, 'She doesn't care if we're on time or not!'

Benji's reply is brief, but the silence that follows it is deafening: 'I care.'

Power is the ability to get other people to do what you want. Every adult man in that locker room could have rendered the eighteen-year-old powerless by remaining seated on the benches. But he gives them thirty seconds, and when he walks back to the ice, they get up and follow him.

That's not when he becomes their team captain. That's just when they all – including him – realize that he already is.

Benji doesn't want to lead his team, but he does so anyway. William Lyt is over in Hed, and he wants nothing more than to be told to lead his team, but he isn't. It isn't fair, but sports isn't fair. The player who spends the most hours practicing doesn't always end up being the best, and the player who deserves to be made team captain isn't always the most suitable. It's often said that hockey isn't a contemplative sport: 'We just count goals.' That isn't strictly true, of course. Hockey counts everything, it's full of statistics, yet it's impossible to predict. It's governed too much by things that aren't visible. One term that is often used to describe talented players, for instance, is 'leadership qualities,' even though this is an utterly immeasurable concept seeing that it is based on things that can't be taught: charisma, authority, love.

When William Lyt was younger and Kevin Erdahl was made team captain, William heard the coach say to Kevin, 'You can force people to obey you, but you can never force them to follow you. If you want them to play for you, they have to love you.'

Perhaps no one loved Kevin more than William did, and he did all he could to get that love reciprocated. He was unfailingly loyal, even after the rape; he followed Kevin to Hed Hockey when Kevin's best friend, Benji, stayed with Beartown. William gathered his guys and beat up both Amat, who had snitched on Kevin, and Bobo, who tried to defend Amat.

When Kevin suddenly disappeared, William stayed at Hed, disappointed but still faithful. He has the same coach he had in Beartown, David: it was he who persuaded William and almost all the other old players to switch clubs. Not by defending Kevin but by using the simplest argument that sports can offer: 'We're only interested in hockey. Not politics. What happens off the ice stays off the ice.'

William believed him, and deep down he hoped that now that Kevin and Benji were both off the team, maybe David would finally recognize William's loyalty. But there was no show of gratitude, not a single word of encouragement. He is still being ignored.

So when William comes into the locker room today and opens his locker and sees what someone has left in the bottom of it, things happen that no statistics can measure. There's a cigarette lighter lying there. The same sort that filled William's mailbox back in the summer, the same sort Leo had on the beach.

At the same time, one of his teammates comes through the door and says, 'Hey, Lyt, have you heard about Benji? Beartown's new coach has made him team captain!'

23

'All It Takes for the Only Thing That Matters'

People say that leadership is about making difficult decisions, unpalatable and unpopular decisions. 'Do your job,' leaders are constantly being told. The impossible part of the job is, of course, that a leader can carry on leading only as long as someone follows him, and people's reactions to leadership are always the same: if a decision of yours benefits me, you're fair, and if the same decision harms me, you're a tyrant. The truth about most people is as simple as it is unbearable: we rarely want what is best for everyone; we mostly want what's best for ourselves.

Peter is weighed down by thoughts as he switches his office computer off, puts his files back on their shelves, and walks down the steps towards the ice. He sits down in the standing area at the end of the rink. Fatima is cleaning some distance away. He waves, but she just nods back to him. She doesn't like to draw attention to herself; she has to finish cleaning before the A-team training session starts, and she doesn't want Amat to feel ashamed in front of his teammates. As if that boy has ever felt ashamed of his mother, Peter thinks.

Fatima is in many ways a more typical Beartown inhabitant than Peter: soft spoken, proud, hardworking, and with absolutely zero tolerance for bullshit. At the start of the summer, when the club's bank accounts were empty, Peter realized that Fatima hadn't been paid, but when he called her she just said, 'Don't worry, Amat and I will manage.' Peter knew that Amat went around collecting cans at the end of each month so he could collect the deposit, so he said, heavy with embarrassment, 'You can't not get paid, the club has a duty to –' But Fatima interrupted him: 'The club? It's my club, too. My boy's club. And we'll manage.' It takes a special person to say that, and a special club.

It's autumn now, and Fatima has been paid. Peter, too. This morning he tried to pay the bills, and because his computer was acting up he phoned the bank. The man at the other end was confused: 'Those bills have already been paid.' Not just one. All of them. Richard Theo wasn't making empty promises; the sponsor has paid some money in, even though the press conference hasn't taken place yet. Peter will be able to save his club. So why is he so racked with anxiety?

The A-team's practice starts. Everyone down on the ice takes it for granted that the lights will go on in the rink every day, that wages will be paid, that fans will flock to games. In hockey, money is always something that is just supposed to be there. We never really grow up in this sport; on the ice we remain the same kids who just want to play: a puck, a few friends, lights on! Let's play!

But Peter knows the cost. He's sitting on it. It's just wood and metal, chewing tobacco trodden into the floor, dented railings. But when the men in the black jackets leap into the air in this part of the stand, it bounces, and when they sing they raise the roof: 'We are the bears, we are the bears, we are the bears, the bears from Beartown! WE . . . ARE . . . THE . . . BEARS! WE ARE . . .'

That's a powerful wall to have behind you when things are going well and a terrible force to have against you when they aren't. Over the years no one in the club has ever criticized the Pack more than Peter. When they fought, he tried to introduce surveillance cameras in the rink; when highly paid players who were underperforming suddenly wanted to tear up their contracts, he tried to prove that they had been threatened by Teemu's boys. For years men in suits stood in the boardroom arguing with Peter because he was being 'needlessly provocative' when in fact they were frightened, too. They allowed the Pack to use violence to rule this town as long as it benefited the suits' own purposes. So what now? Now Peter has an opportunity to get rid of the Pack, but he's hesitating. Why? Because he feels he owes them for voting to keep him on in the club? Because he's a coward? Or is it about Richard Theo? Is Peter just afraid that he's exchanging the influence of the hooligans for that of politicians? Who are worse: the guys with tattoos on their necks or the suits and ties?

During his first years as general manager Kira used to remind him that 'we're not a family that runs from a fight.' She's always had thicker skin than he has; the hot-tempered lawyer had more of an appetite for victory than the diplomatic general manager. But now Peter is the one looking for a fight and Kira the one hesitating. Perhaps Richard Theo is right about Peter being naive. The world is complicated, but he wishes it were simple.

When he was playing in Canada, his coach said, 'Winning isn't everything. It's the only thing!' But Peter lacked the killer instinct. When his team had a big lead during practices he would ease up, because he didn't want to humiliate his opponents. The coach's philosophy was 'Never take your foot off the enemy's throat,' but Peter didn't have it in him. Winning was enough; you didn't have to crush anyone. Then came a practice when their opponents managed to turn around a 5–0 deficit. 'Sort your head out!' the coach yelled. But Peter never quite managed to.

Perhaps that was why he missed that shot in the final twenty years ago, and perhaps that's why he's scared of fulfilling his promise to Richard Theo now. There's a limit to the number of enemies a man can survive. Peter knows he needs to do his job – he's just not sure which job that is.

He sees Elisabeth Zackell on the ice. He wishes he were more like her. She doesn't take her foot off anyone's throat.

Elisabeth Zackell divides the players into two teams and ties the teammates together with the ropes. If one player falls, the whole team falls.

'WHAT SORT OF SHITTY WOMAN'S GAME IS THIS?' one of the older players bellows when he's brought down by an unsteady teammate and hits the ice hard, but Zackell doesn't care.

They're made to work until they learn to cooperate and move together, as a single unit. They're made to sweat and throw up, not for the last time. Only when Amat sinks to his knees does Zackell let them untie the ropes. Then she fetches her paintball gun. One of the older players mutters, 'The bloody woman's had some sort of stroke . . .'

Perhaps Zackell reads his lips – who knows? – but she says, 'I understand that there's a lot of talk of "women." I can only assume that you're worried you might start playing like women if you're coached by one.'

The players squirm. Some of them are still being sick in the buckets. Zackell fires a paint pellet at the crossbar of one of the nets, making the metal sing and the hard little ball explode in a splat of yellow. 'I coached a girls' team once. They were no good at dealing with rebounds in front of the net and didn't want to block shots; they were frightened it was going to hurt. So I got them to strip off and try to skate from the centre line to the net and touch the post while I tried to hit them with a paintball gun. Every time they got there, they earned themselves a beer. You know what they said to me?'

No response, so she answers her own question: 'They told me to screw myself. But obviously they were women. So what are you?'

The men on the ice stare, but Zackell waits them out. A minute passes. Some of the men giggle nervously, but she stands motionless with the paintball gun.

'You're . . . you're kidding, right?' someone eventually asks.

'I don't think so. I've been told I'm no good at humour,' Zackell informs them.

Then another player stands up. He puts his helmet down on the ice, then pulls off his jersey and pads until his top half is naked.

'Will this do, or do I have to get my cock out as well?' Benji asks.

'That'll have to do,' Zackell replies, and fires a pellet of paint that just misses his neck.

All the other players hunch up, but Benji doesn't hesitate; he just takes off and skates straight at the net. The first time he touches the bar, Zackell manages to hit him twice; the second and third times, she manages to fire twice as many pellets. According to the man in the shop, the pellets move at a speed of three hundred feet per second, so Zackell is strongly advised to fire only at people wearing protective clothing from at least thirty feet away. Benji's skin is bare. Zackell manages to land one shot on his back, and he jerks with pain as the paint dribbles down his shoulder blade.

The older players look on, at first as if they can't quite believe their eyes, then with increasing fascination. In the end someone yells out a number; no one remembers if it was 'eight' or 'nine,' but after that the whole team counts each time Benji touches the bar. Eventually they are roaring the number of beers he's won. FOURTEEN. FIFTEEN. SIXTEEN. Zackell reloads the gun, and Benji sets off again. No normal person would behave like that. That's the point. Zackell doesn't want a normal team captain.

At one point Zackell hits Benji right on his collarbone and sees in his eyes what he's capable of. 'I can win anything with this one,' she thinks to herself. He doesn't stop skating, and she doesn't stop firing until he's earned a whole crate of beer. She fetches it from the bench. As she gives it to him she says, 'Anyone who feels responsibility isn't free, Benjamin. That's why you're scared.'

For someone who's bad with feelings, the woman's not so bad with feelings after all. Benji walks to the locker room, bruised, stinging, and spattered with paint. There he shares the beer with all of his teammates. Even Amat drinks; he wouldn't dare turn it down.

Benji goes and showers on his own. For a long time. When he comes back, the beer is all gone and his shoes are full of shaving cream.

Peter Andersson stands behind the boards while Zackell picks up her ropes.

'You have very . . . interesting coaching methods. Do they

really make the players better?' Peter asks as diplomatically as he can while he tries his very best not to hyperventilate at the sight of the splats of paint all over the ice.

'Better? How should I know?' Zackell replies, unconcerned.

'You must have some reason for using these methods?' Peter says.

He has a migraine. Richard Theo promised him 'complete control' over this club, but it really doesn't feel like it.

'Hockey coaches don't know as much about what we're doing as we pretend; most of it's guesswork. I assumed you knew that,' Zackell replies.

Peter feels the muscles in his back tighten. 'You have an . . . unusual view of leadership.'

Zackell shrugs. 'If the players think I'm an idiot, they've got someone to talk to each other about. Sometimes a team needs an enemy to unite them.'

Peter watches her as she walks off. He could almost swear she was smiling slightly when she made that last remark. Then he goes and fetches cleaning materials and spends several hours scrubbing and wiping the paint off the ice.

Perhaps he should have gone home instead, to drink wine with his wife and fall asleep in their bed. But he and Kira haven't quite made up yet; they've just stopped arguing, and that's not the same thing. They're not yelling at each other, but they're not really talking, either. The whole family is getting quieter and quieter, like a room that's become such a mess that it feels less bother to brick up the door than get to grips with the problem. Peter realizes he's trying to make work for himself, so he goes home, getting there after everyone has gone to bed.

Then he lies awake half the night reading the instruction manual of a coffee machine instead of calling the daughter who gave it to him and confessing that he doesn't have a clue what he's doing anymore. Or for whose sake he's fighting.

★

The A-team coach in Hed is named David. His red hair hasn't been cut in months, and his face is chalk white because even on a fine summer's day the sun doesn't reach into the video room inside the rink. He's giving the job everything he's got; he has to. His girlfriend is pregnant, and Hed Hockey is his career trampoline to a higher league, if he wins.

He never wanted to coach this A-team, he wanted to coach Beartown's. He fashioned a group of small boys all the way until they were juniors, when they were lined up to win the national championship and become the core of the A-team: Kevin and Benji on the ice, David on the bench. That almost happened. But only almost.

David didn't leave Beartown because he wanted to defend rape. At least that's not how he sees it. He doesn't even know if Kevin is guilty. The boy was never convicted of any crime, and David is neither a lawyer nor a police officer; he's a hockey coach. If hockey clubs start to punish players for things that not even a court would punish them for, where would that end? Hockey needs to be allowed to be hockey. Life outside the arena needs to remain separate from life inside.

So David didn't leave Beartown because of what Kevin was accused of but because Peter saw to it that the boy was arrested on the day of the final. Which meant that the whole team was punished, not just Kevin. David couldn't accept that. So he switched clubs and took almost all of Beartown's best players with him.

He doesn't regret his decision. The only thing he regrets is Benjamin Ovich. That boy symbolized everything David wanted from a team, but when it really mattered, David wasn't able to get through to him. Benji stayed in Beartown when all the others switched to Hed, and back in the spring David saw him kissing another boy. Benji doesn't know that David knows, and evidently no one else knows either. If David is honest, he can't help hoping that no one else ever finds out, either. This isn't the sort of place where he'd wish a revelation of that sort on any hockey player, not even if he's coming here as an opponent this autumn.

Is David proud of himself? Definitely not. So why doesn't he just go see Benji and tell him the truth: that he is ashamed of having been such a poor leader that the boy didn't feel safe enough to tell the truth about himself. Why doesn't David just apologize? Probably for the same reason that all of us commit all our stupidest mistakes: it's hard to admit that we've been wrong. And the bigger the mistake, the harder it is.

David never imagines that he's a good person, but he does believe he does all he can for the good of hockey. He puts the team, the club, the sport first. He's never going to let it get political. Not even now.

There's a knock on the door of his office. William Lyt is standing in the doorway. 'Have you heard that Benji's been made team captain of Beartown?' the huge forward roars.

The coach nods. 'This is Hed. Not Beartown. Don't worry about what they're doing.'

William is quivering on the threshold of the room, unable to bring himself to leave even though the look on his coach's face indicates that that's the end of the discussion.

'Is anyone in our team going to wear number sixteen this year?' William asks. He doesn't mean it as an accusation; he's just asking his coach to love him. And that's the problem: love is like leadership. Asking for it doesn't help.

'That's not your concern,' David says coldly.

Sixteen was Benji's number in Beartown. David is refusing to give it to anyone in Hed.

'Who's going to be our captain?' William asks jealously.

David answers the question he really wants to ask: 'You're too young, William.'

It's a very particular way of breaking someone's heart, when a hockey player sees in the eyes of his coach that he really wants someone else.

'Would you have said the same thing if I was Benji?'

David is honest. He shakes his head.

William Lyt goes out onto the ice with a greater need for violent affirmation than ever. David pretends not to understand, but of course he does, all too well. He didn't become a hockey coach by accident; he knows what his words can accomplish. All while the boys were growing up, he has watched William compete against Benji for everything, without winning a single time. David knows that jealousy is a terrible feeling, but it can also be a motivating force. So he distributes it in small doses, on purpose, because leadership is a matter of manipulating emotions to achieve results. David knows that what he's doing is dangerous; he knows that William may well hate Benji so much that he'll hurt him in the game. But all the best hockey teams have someone who plays on the edge and sometimes goes over it. William is at his best when he's full of hate.

David still loves Benji, more than any other player he's coached, and he's ashamed that the boy didn't dare confide in him. One day David may be able to make up for that, as a human being. But those feelings belong to life outside the rink, and this is life inside. Here Benji is an opponent. If William crosses the line in the game, then so be it. If Benji gets injured, then Benji gets injured. David's a hockey coach; he's doing his job. He's doing all it takes for the only thing that matters.

Winning.

Benji is lifting weights on his own in the outhouse at the kennels when darkness falls. Before he raises the bar he takes off his wristwatch. It's old and worn, heavy and clunky, and doesn't really suit him. But it was given to him by David. They haven't spoken a word to each other since the coach switched clubs, but Benji still doesn't go anywhere without it.

William Lyt is doing push-ups until his arms hurt as much as everything else. He falls asleep holding the cigarette lighter that was left in his locker. He knows who put it there. William might not be thinking of hurting Benji, not yet, but that doesn't mean he can't hurt someone else.

24

But the Bear Inside Her Has Just Woken Up

Ramona stomps down the stairs from her apartment in a cloud of invective to see who's banging on the door of the Bearskin after closing time. She's expecting to see a drunk but finds something else.

'What are you doing here, you silly old fool? It must be at least forty years since you last showed up at my door trying to get a drink in the middle of the night! It didn't work then, and it's not going to work now!' she snaps at Sune as she buttons her dressing gown.

Sune laughs so loudly that he frightens the puppy beside him. 'I need a piece of advice, Ramona. Two, maybe.'

Ramona lets him in and gives the dog a bowl of water. The dog empties it and starts to chew the furnishings.

'Well?' she grunts.

'I want you to talk to Teemu Rinnius for me,' Sune says.

If anyone else had asked, Ramona would have said 'Teemu who?' But not Sune. The old man has spent all his life dealing with difficult boys with a talent for hockey, while Ramona has spent hers dealing with the ones without any talent.

'About what?'

'The club.'

'I thought you'd stopped being coach. What have you got to do with the club?'

'They're keeping me for the women. Eye candy.'

Ramona laughs up a whole decade of cigarette smoke. Then she gets serious. 'There are rumours, Sune. The paper's talking about a "new sponsor" and the GM taking part in "secret meetings." That sort of thing makes Teemu and his boys nervous. It's their club.'

'It's not only their club,' Sune corrects her.

He can't help thinking what a colossal nightmare of a town this is in which to try to make anyone happy. If the club had gone bankrupt, Peter would have gotten the blame, and now that he's managed to save it financially, he's still getting shit. Ramona puts three whisky glasses on the counter. One for Sune, two for her.

'So what do you think about the new coach? She comes here and eats potatoes from time to time,' she says.

'Zackell? I don't know. She's mad. She doesn't seem to give a damn about what Peter Andersson thinks –'

Ramona grins. 'Good start.'

'– but I have a suspicion Teemu and his guys aren't quite so enthusiastic about having a female coach.'

Ramona snorts. 'They love their club. You know that. They're worried she's been appointed as some sort of PR stunt. They don't want to be made fools of, and they don't want to see a load of political agendas dragged into hockey.'

Sune rolls his eyes. '"Agendas." Is that what we're calling it now? Can't women be allowed to sleep with whoever they like?'

'Ha! There's no one who has more sympathy for lesbians than me, because as far as I can see they've drawn the winning ticket! There's no reasoning with men, so you might as well get rid of them!'

'So what's the problem with Zackell, then?'

'The problem is that the boys think she's steered by Peter Andersson and the sponsors and the politicians, and they don't want another coach who's –'

She stops herself. Sune takes over. 'Who's like me? Weak?'

He knows what people say about him. That he let the sponsors and politicians take over the club in recent years and let them run the club into the ground without a fight. People are right. Sune got older, too tired to argue. He always hoped that the hockey would be good enough to keep the club on an even keel, both financially and morally, but he was proven wrong on both counts.

'I didn't mean any criticism,' Ramona mutters.

'Oh, they're right. I wish I'd given this town more to be happy about. But Zackell isn't me.'

'In what way?'

'She's the sort who wins.'

'You're here for my advice? The boys need proof.'

Sune sighs. 'Then tell Teemu that as soon as his little brother gets let out of custody, he should go straight to the rink.'

Ramona is left speechless. That takes a lot of doing.

Peter gets home late again. Kira is sitting at the kitchen table with her laptop; she came home from work early today to cook for the children and do the washing and cleaning. Now she's working again, but without her bosses seeing: she puts in more hours than any of her colleagues but will soon be known in the office as the woman who always goes home early. Being a mother can be like drying out the foundations of a house or mending a roof: it takes time, sweat, and money, and once it's done everything looks exactly the same as it did before. It's not the sort of thing anyone gives you praise for. But spending an extra hour in the office is like hanging up a beautiful painting or a new lamp: everyone notices.

Peter talks to her, she talks to him, but without making eye contact. How was your day? Fine, how was yours? Fine. Have the kids eaten? Yes, there's leftovers in the fridge. Can you drive them to school tomorrow? I need to get to the rink early. She says 'Of course' even though she feels like yelling 'And what about my job?' He says 'Thanks' even though he feels like whispering 'I feel like I'm drowning.' She says 'No problem' when she feels like shouting 'Help!' Neither of them says anything else, even though they're both thinking 'I miss us.' Peter leaves the kitchen without running his fingertips through her hair. She sits there without breathing against the back of his neck.

Ramona is staring at Sune. 'Is this some kind of joke?'

'No. Elisabeth Zackell has no sense of humour.'

'Is she going to let Vidar play hockey again? What does Peter say about that?'

'She doesn't care what Peter thinks.'

Ramona chuckles. She's always been a bit fonder of the Rinnius brothers than all of the Bearskin's other boys. Teemu gets her groceries for her every week; Vidar used to do his homework here. Many years ago, just after Holger died, the boys heard someone say that Ramona had 'started to forget things, could be Alzheimer's.' It wasn't, it was just a perfectly ordinary broken heart, but the boys read online that you can delay the ageing process in the brain, so they started forcing her to do crosswords. Every morning they would bring her a new one. She swore loudly and loved them unconditionally for that. So now she says, 'So Vidar shits on a desk and Zackell doesn't give a shit about Peter? That's not going to end well.'

'No,' Sune agrees.

Ramona scratches under her chin with one of the whisky glasses. 'It's not like you to go against Peter.'

'No,' Sune concedes.

'Why? Is she that special, this coach?'

Sune sighs deeply, making the hairs in his nostrils sway wildly. 'Either we win or we go under, Ramona. Vidar used to be one hell of a goalie, and if he still is, then I'm prepared to take a chance on his . . . personality.'

Ramona smiles. 'When the Devil gets old, he gets religious.'

'Can you see to it that Teemu takes Vidar to practice?' Sune wonders.

Ramona raises an eyebrow. 'Listen, you old fool, do you remember how Vidar used to play hockey? You had to drag him off the ice when practice was over! And now he's been locked up for . . . hell, you won't be able to keep him away from that rink, no matter how well armed you are!'

Ramona doesn't say what she's thinking: that she'll drag Vidar to the rink herself if need be. She was never quite able to save Teemu; he was too angry to change. But perhaps Vidar can still have a different life, and Ramona isn't about to let that opportunity go, even if it's the death of her.

Sune nods and sips his whisky. It makes his eyes water. 'Well, then.'

He falls silent. Ramona snorts. 'Anything else?'

Sune is embarrassed at being so transparent. 'I want to ask for something else. Not for the club, just for me. There's a little girl named Alicia. She's four and a half, lives over in —'

'I know who the little lass is,' Ramona says gloomily, not because she knows the girl but because all the local bar owners know the adults who live in the same house.

'Can you help me keep an eye on her?'

Ramona pours more whisky. 'Are you sure you're not here to charm me into bed? You're doing better now than you ever used to.'

Sune smiles. 'I'd have a heart attack before you had time to undo your bra, but thanks for the offer.'

Ramona drinks. Then she says unhappily, 'I don't speak for anyone in this town, Sune. But Peter's my boy, too. So tell him to remember who stood up for Beartown, for his own sake. No matter what this new sponsor demands.'

Sune nods. He knows she means the Pack's standing area in the rink. This is a hard town to keep secrets in.

'I'll do my best,' he says.

It won't be enough.

Peter stops outside Leo's room. The boy is twelve years old, almost a teenager. Peter thinks back to when he was born, that shattering moment when he heard his son cry for the first time. When he was allowed to pick up that fragile naked body, support the little head, with its scrunched-up eyes and plaintive cries . . . and when the wailing stopped. The first time Peter realized that the tiny person was sleeping soundly in his arms. What are we prepared to do for our children at that moment? What aren't we prepared to do?

But the years whistle past. Fathers need to live in the moment; general managers are never allowed to. Fathers need to seize the day, because childhoods are like soap bubbles; you get only a few seconds to enjoy them. But general managers need to think about the next game, the next season, onward, forward, upward.

Peter is standing with two sticks in one hand and a tennis ball in the other. Leo used to drive him crazy asking him to go and play in the driveway. 'Dad, can you move the car? Dad, can we play? Dad? Just a little while! First to five goals!' Peter would be sitting with the remote in his hand, watching a recording of a game or struggling with a stack of files and a pocket calculator, working on the budget, and would reply, 'You need to do your homework first.' After his homework was done, it was too late. 'Tomorrow,' the father would promise. 'Okay,' the son would reply. Men are busy, but boys don't stop growing. Sons want their fathers' attention until the precise moment when fathers want their sons'. From then on we're all doomed to wish that we'd fallen asleep beside them more often, while their head could still fit on our chest. That we'd spent more time sitting on the floor while they were playing. Hugged them while they still let us.

Peter knocks on Leo's door now, and the twelve-year-old replies without opening it. 'Mmm?'

'I've . . . moved the car out of the driveway,' the father says hopefully.

'Oh?'

'Yes . . . I thought maybe you might like . . . might like a game?'

He's clutching the tennis ball so hard that the sweat from his hand is leaving marks in the green fabric covering. Leo's reply is merciless: 'I have to do my homework, Dad. Tomorrow, maybe!'

Peter almost opens the door and asks him again. But instead he puts the sticks back into the cupboard. Then he sits down on the sofa on his own with the ball in his hand and falls asleep there.

Kira closes the lid of her laptop. Looks into Leo's room. He pretends to be asleep; she pretends to believe him. She walks past the living room, puts a blanket over Peter, then stops as if to brush some hair from his forehead. But doesn't.

She sits on her own on the steps in front of the house, looking at the same stars she could have looked at from anywhere in the world. At work today her colleague gave her an envelope, sent by an older woman whom both Kira and her colleague had idolized for several years, a director and investment genius who had changed direction and set up a big charitable foundation fronted by artists and actors and backed by multiple millions. Kira and her colleague met the woman at a conference last year, they managed to attract her attention, and when they parted the woman gave Kira her business card and said, 'I'm always looking for smart people with a bit of fire inside them. Get in touch if you ever need a job.' Kira didn't really take the offer seriously, perhaps didn't dare to, and let it remain a vague little dream. But the envelope today contained an invitation to a large conference that the woman's foundation is organizing in a couple weeks' time, in Canada.

'Why is she inviting us to go? Does she want to use the firm?' Kira asked breathlessly.

Only then did she see the jealousy in her colleague's eyes. Kira looked at the invitation again and realized that it mentioned only her name. Her colleague did her best to be proud but still sounded like a little girl who was about to lose her more talented friend to the big wide world: 'She's only asked you, Kira. She doesn't want to use the firm. She wants to give you a job.'

Kira sits on the steps outside the house with the envelope in her hand, looking at the stars. They're the same stars you can see from Canada. She moved there once so that Peter could play in the NHL, with the best in the world. She knows what he'd say if she says she wants to go to the conference. 'Do you really have to go right now? There's so much going on with the club, darling. Maybe next year?'

Kira will never be able to explain. Peter will never understand that she has her own NHL.

★

Ramona phones Teemu. They have a brief conversation because neither of them wants the other to hear their weakness. Ramona doesn't say she wants Vidar to have a better life than Teemu's, and Teemu doesn't say he wants the same thing. Then Ramona asks Teemu for a favour, and she waits up until he phones her back to say that it's done.

Teemu stands outside a small house in a different part of town until the lights go off in the children's room. When he knows that only the adults are awake, he doesn't ring the doorbell, he doesn't knock on the door; they'll never know how he got in. He just stands there in the kitchen while they reach for the kitchen counters to cling on to and try to catch the glasses their shaking hands have just knocked over. He sees that they know who he is, so all he has to do is pick up a hockey bag, drop it onto the table, then ask, 'Does Alicia live here?'

The adults nod, terrified.

'From now on the kitty at the Bearskin pub will pay for all her hockey equipment each year for as long as she wants to play. I don't know if she has any siblings in the house, but she's got brothers now. And the next adult who hurts her will have to explain why to each and every one of us.'

He doesn't need to wait for an answer. When he leaves the house, none of the people left behind dares to move for several minutes, but eventually the bag is carried up to Alicia's room. The four-and-a-half-year-old is dreaming deeply about the sound of pucks hitting a wall, and for a long time she won't have any bruises she doesn't get on the ice. She will play hockey every day, and one day she will be the best.

The girl may be fast asleep tonight. But the bear inside her has just woken up.

25

'Mother's Song'

William Lyt is like all other teenagers: permanently on the boundary between hubris and the abyss. There's a girl he likes, she's in the same class, back in the spring they were at a party and she kissed him on the cheek when she was drunk and he's still dreaming about it. So when he's standing by her locker today his facade crumbles and he asks, 'Hi . . . look . . . would you . . . I mean . . . would you like to do something sometime? After school? You and . . . me?'

She looks at him with distaste. 'Do something? With you?'

He clears his throat. 'Yes?'

She snorts. 'Ha! I'm from Beartown, and that means something to some of us! I hope Benji *crushes* you in the game!'

It isn't until she's walking off that Lyt sees she's wearing a green T-shirt bearing the text BEARTOWN AGAINST THE REST. Her friends are wearing similar shirts. When they pass Lyt, one of them snarls, 'Kevin Erdahl's a rapist, and you're no better!'

Lyt stands there, comprehensively flamed. All his life he's tried to do the right thing. He's attended every practice, loved his captain, obeyed his coach. He's followed all the rules, done as he's been told, swallowed his pride. Benji has done the exact opposite, always. And who's the one everyone loves, in spite of all that?

How can William Lyt feel anything but hatred about this?

When he turns around, he sees Leo standing at the other end of the corridor. The twelve-year-old has just seen William Lyt's weakest point, and the little bastard's grin pierces the eighteen-year-old's skin all over. William goes into a bathroom and punches his own thighs until tears spring to his eyes.

When school is over for the day, Maya and Ana change into tracksuits and run into the forest. It's Ana's idea, and a weird one, because Maya has always hated running, and even if Ana has spent almost all her life running through the forest, she's never done it specifically as exercise. Never in circles. Even so, Ana forces Maya out this autumn, because she knows that even if Kevin is no longer in Beartown, they still have to reclaim the things he stole. Twilight. Solitude. The courage to wear earbuds when it's dark, the freedom to not look over your shoulder the whole time.

They run only where there are lights. They don't say anything but are both thinking the same thing: guys never think about light, it just isn't a problem in their lives. When guys are scared of the dark, they're scared of ghosts and monsters, but when girls are scared of the dark, they're scared of guys.

They run a long way. Farther than either of them thought they could. But they stop abruptly some way from Ana's house, beside the running track that coils around the Heights. It's the best-lit patch of track in the whole of Beartown, but that's irrelevant. That was where Maya held the shotgun to Kevin's head.

She's hyperventilating. Can't bring herself to take another step. Ana puts a comforting hand on hers.

'We'll try again tomorrow.'

Maya nods. They walk back to Ana's. Outside the door Maya lies and tells her friend that she's fine, that she can go home on her own, because Ana is fighting hard to make everything normal again and Maya can't bear to disappoint her.

But when she's alone she sits down on a stump and cries. Sends a text to her mum: 'Can you pick me up? Please?'

*

At a time like that, there's no mother in this forest or any other who drives faster through the trees.

No one knows exactly where violence comes from; that's why someone who fights can always find a reasonable justification. 'You shouldn't have provoked me.' 'You know how I get.' 'It's your own fault, you deserved it, you were asking for it!'

Leo Andersson is twelve years old and has never had a girlfriend. When a girl two years older comes up to him at his locker in school, he feels a rush of intoxication that he will never experience so strongly again.

She smiles. 'I saw you on the beach when you stood up to William Lyt. Pretty brave!'

Leo has to hold on to the locker door as she walks off. When he has lunch, she sits down at the same table. That afternoon, after his last class, she appears in the corridor and asks if he wants to walk her home.

Leo is usually picked up by one of his parents so he has time to get to hockey practice. But his parents have been in their own little worlds recently, and Leo isn't planning to play hockey this autumn. He wants to be something else now, he doesn't know what, but when this girl looks at him he thinks, 'I want to be the sort of person she thinks is brave.' So he texts his parents to say he's going over to a friend's. They'll just be relieved they don't have to pick him up.

The girl and Leo take the path that runs through the tunnel under the main road between the school and the residential area on the other side. He takes a deep breath and summons up the courage to reach out his hand and take hold of hers. The tunnel is dark, and she slips from his fingers and runs. He stares in surprise as he hears her shoes patter on the concrete. Then there are other sounds, from other shoes. They're walking into the darkness from both directions. One of them is the girl's older brother. Leo didn't notice the red top under her jacket.

The council installed this tunnel many years ago after years of campaigning by parents saying that children shouldn't have to cross the busy road. The tunnel was supposed to keep children safe. But now it's a trap instead.

When Kira picks Maya up, her daughter pretends that everything is fine again. She's starting to get good at that. She says she twisted her ankle while she and Ana were jogging, and Kira is happy. Happy! Because a twisted ankle is so normal. It's part of normal sixteen-year-old life.

'Do you feel like doing something? We could drive to Hed and go for a coffee,' Kira suggests, with all the training in rejection of a mother of teenagers, so her heart skips a beat when her daughter unexpectedly replies, 'Okay.'

They drink coffee. They talk. They even laugh, as if this were all normal, and of course Kira is the one who spoils it. Because she can't help asking 'How are you getting on with . . . counselling? Or with the psychologist? I don't know the difference, but . . . I know you don't want to talk to your dad and me, but I just want you to know that you . . . that you can if you want.'

Maya stirs her coffee. Clockwise, anticlockwise, in turn. 'It's okay, Mum. I'm feeling good.'

Kira dearly wants to believe that. She tries to keep her voice steady. 'Your dad and I have been talking. I'm going to cut my hours for a while, so I can be home a bit more . . .'

'What for?' Maya blurts out.

Kira looks confused. 'I thought you'd be pleased! If I'm . . . home more?'

'Why would I be pleased?' Maya wonders.

Kira squirms. 'I haven't been a good mother, darling. I've been so focused on my career. I should have spent more time with you and Leo. Now your dad has to focus all his effort on the club for a while, so –'

'Dad's always focused all his effort on the club!' Maya interrupts.

Kira blinks. 'I don't want you to remember me as an absentee mum. Especially not now. I want you to feel that you've got a . . . normal mum.'

Maya puts her spoon down at that. Leans across the table. 'Stop it, Mum. You know, I'm so damn proud of your career! Everyone else had a normal mum, but I had a role model. All the other moms have to say to their kids that they can be whatever they want when they're older, but you don't have to say that, because you're demonstrating it every day.'

'Darling, I —' Kira begins, but her voice breaks.

Maya wipes her tears and whispers, 'Mum. You taught me that I don't have to have dreams. I can have goals.'

Perhaps William Lyt doesn't want to hurt anyone. There's a particular type of person who enjoys harming other people, but it isn't clear if he's one of them. One day he might wonder about that himself, how we end up the way we do. Unless he becomes the kind of person who goes through his whole life surrounded by excuses for violence: 'You shouldn't have provoked him.' 'You know how he gets.' 'You were asking for it.'

His friends are with him, but he doesn't have their unconditional support. They're not with him out of love or admiration, the way they followed Kevin and Benji; they're just going along with him because he's strong. So he needs to crush everyone who challenges him, because a lack of respect is like sparks in a summer forest: if you don't trample them out at once, the fire spreads until you find yourself surrounded.

His guys stand at the ends of the tunnel. William goes in. It didn't need to get out of hand, because William starts by saying 'Not so tough now, are you?'

If Leo had looked frightened, it could have stopped there. If the twelve-year-old had just had the sense to tremble and sink to his knees and beg William for mercy. But it isn't William who sees fear in Leo's eyes, it's Leo who sees it in William's. So the twelve-year-old says mockingly, 'How tough are you, little Willie? You wouldn't even dare fight Benji! Are you going to wear a diaper when you play Beartown or what?'

Leo may not really know why he says this. Unless he doesn't care. The girl tricked him; he's going to carry a lump of black fury in his gut forever to remind him of how he felt when she ran and he realized that they'd planned this and how they must have laughed when they did. And there's something about violence, about adrenaline, about the different frequencies in some people's hearts.

Leo takes something out of his pocket and throws it onto the ground in front of William Lyt. A cigarette lighter. William lashes out instantly, and his fist hits Leo's face as hard as a block of wood. Leo collapses and rolls around on all fours to keep the blood out of his eyes. He knows there's no way he can fight William and win. But there are many ways to avoid defeat. He sees that William has tears of rage in his eyes as he gets ready to kick him. He manages to dart out of the way in time, and in the same movement he kicks out as hard as he can and hits William in the crotch. Then he gets to his feet and hits as hard as he can.

That might have been enough if he'd been bigger and heavier and William smaller and lighter. But Leo's punches are weak, half of them miss, and William merely sways. The boys at the ends of the tunnel stand motionless. William's fingers grab hold of Leo's top and close like a claw. Then the eighteen-year-old head butts the twelve-year-old in the nose. Blinded, Leo falls to the ground. And then? Dear God.

Then William Lyt doesn't stop stamping.

Mother's Song

You asked 'Am I a good mother?,' always the same, the same . . .
. . . answer that you were seeking, when you should have known that
You were the strength inside
You were all that I could become

*You taught me the value of 'sorry,' but the only time you retreated was when
you were taking aim
You taught me the humility of tears but never let me apologize for existing
You didn't dress me up in fragile garments, you gave me armour
You taught me that daughters don't have to have dreams — we can have goals.*

The boys at the ends of the tunnel stand silent. Perhaps some
of them feel they should intervene, call out that that's enough, that
the kid's only twelve, for God's sake. But it's easy to become desen-
sitized; you can see something happen right in front of you
without it having any greater effect than if you were seeing it in a
film. Perhaps you have time to feel scared, think, 'Good thing it
isn't me,' unless you're so shocked that you feel paralysed.

Could William have killed Leo in that tunnel? No one knows.
Because someone stops him.

Jeanette, the teacher, has lots of little bad habits that she does her
best to hide from both the pupils and the other staff in the school.
She cracks her knuckles when she's nervous; she started doing that
when she played on Hed Hockey's girls' team. When she got older,
she took up boxing, then martial arts, and she has plenty of strange
habits left from those days. She stretches when she feels restless,
warms up before classes each morning as if she were preparing for a
game. For a while she was good, really good. Maybe she could even
have become the best. For a single wonderful year she was a professional fighter, but hardly anyone in this town knows that because
she got injured and things went the way they always do: either
you're the best, or you're everyone else. She studied to become a
teacher, lost the fire in her heart, the killer instinct. She had a coach
who told her, 'Jeanette, you have to want to go into the ring and
crush another girl's dream, because if you don't, you've no business
being here.' That may have been true, she wishes it weren't, but
perhaps sport really is precisely that merciless.

She doesn't miss the pressure and stress, just the adrenaline. There's nothing in normal life that can replace it, that life-affirming fear when she climbed into the ring and there was just her and her opponent. You against me. Right here, right now.

She tries to find other ways of getting kicks. Working as a teacher often feels hopeless, but every now and then there are tiny, shimmering moments that make the long hours and humiliating wages worthwhile, when she manages to get through to someone. Maybe even save something. There aren't many jobs that give you the chance to do that.

In the afternoons, after the end of the school day, she goes up the hidden access ladder onto the roof. And up there, behind a ventilation drum above the dining room, a teacher can stand and look out across almost the whole of Beartown and have a cigarette without anyone seeing. That's the worst habit of all.

She can see the tunnel from there, the one built under the main road to keep the children safe. She sees Leo and the girl go in. Only the girl runs out. Jeanette sees William and his guys approach from both directions. She drops her cigarette and runs for the ladder. This is a small school in a small town, but the building feels endless when you're running through it in panic.

Kira and Maya arrive home. When Maya goes into her room, Kira sees the concert tickets on her wall. She can still remember the very first one, possibly more clearly than her daughter, and how Maya and Ana carried the tickets in their pockets for weeks. They secretly bought eye shadow and put far too much on, then cut off their denim shorts until they were way too revealing. Kira dropped them off outside the concert and made them promise to come straight out the moment it was over, and they promised and laughed, and they were only children but Kira knew she'd lost them, ever so slightly, at that moment. They ran off towards the stage hand in hand, along with hundreds of other screaming girls, and that first taste of freedom is something you can never take away from someone. Music transformed Maya and Ana, and even if they chose completely different styles of music later in life and did nothing but argue about what was 'junkie music' and what was 'bleep-bleep music,' they still had that in common: music saved something inside them that might otherwise have been lost. Imagination, power, a glowing spark in their chests that always reminded them: 'Don't let the bastards tell you what to be, go your own way, dance badly and sing loudly and become the best!'

Now Maya is sixteen years old and she kisses her mum on the cheek and goes into her room. Her mum sits in the kitchen thinking about all the stories about girls being trampled and crushed at concerts in recent years, about terrorists bombing arenas. What if she had known all that back then? Would she have let the girls go? Not a chance. How can you ever do that again when you know that the whole world wants to hurt your child?

Jeanette will always wonder what would have happened if she'd gotten there faster. Would William have found it easier to back down then? Would Leo have been less full of hate? Would the guys at the ends of the tunnel have been able to admit to themselves that things had gone too far?

She yanks William's heavy body out of the way. He's lucky; he recognizes her quickly enough to stop himself taking a swing at her, too. There's a wild look in her eyes; they're a fighter's eyes, not a teacher's. William gasps for breath and doesn't even look at Leo when he splutters, 'It was him who started it! He was asking for it!'

Jeanette will always feel ashamed of what she does next. She has no excuse. But everything that happened in the spring, the rape and silence towards one of the girls in Jeanette's own school and the vile behaviour that this community demonstrated afterward filled Jeanette with shame and anger. She's not alone; the whole town is angry. She sees the same thing in William Lyt; he's just angry at different things than she is. We rarely take out our anger on those who deserve it; we just take it out on whoever is standing closest.

'What did you say?' Jeanette hisses.

'He was asking for it!' William Lyt repeats.

Her kick hits him so hard in the side of his knee that his body disappears; he falls as if he's been shot. Her balance is so perfect that she's already standing on both feet by the time he hits the ground, so relaxed that she could have started whistling.

But when she realizes what she's just done, her lungs tighten. Her martial arts coach always used to stress, 'Never lose control! Never let your feeling grab the wheel, Jeanette. Because that's when you do really stupid things!'

Kira is sobbing helplessly in the kitchen, hiding her face in her sweater so her daughter won't hear her. On the other side of the door her daughter is lying on her bed beneath walls covered with concert tickets, crying hard under the covers so her mum won't hear her. She's grateful that it's so easy to fool your parents. That they're so desperate for you to be happy that they believe you even when you're lying.

Maya knows that her mum and dad need to be allowed to regain control of their lives, in their own ways. And take back what Kevin took from them, too. Her mum needs to feel that she's good enough, her dad needs to rescue his hockey club, because they need to feel they can succeed at something. Stand up, hit back, win. They mustn't end up afraid of the dark, because it won't be possible to survive together then. Their daughter can hear them arguing, even when they aren't saying a word. Where there used to be two wineglasses in the kitchen she now sees only one. She knows her dad is getting home later and later, sees him stand outside the door for longer and longer before coming inside. She notices the envelopes containing invitations to conferences that her mum never asks if she can attend. Maya knows that if her parents split up they'll say it wasn't her fault. And she'll know that they're lying.

She was the one Kevin broke. But they were the ones who snapped.

★

212

William Lyt gets hesitantly to his feet. 'Lucky for you I don't hit women,' he pants.

'I'd advise you not to try!' Jeanette replies even though all the voices of reason in her head are yelling '*Keep quiet, Jeanette!*'

'I'm going to report you, you —' Lyt begins, but Jeanette snaps back, 'And say what?'

She's an idiot, she knows that, but she's an angry woman in an angry town, and normal rules no longer seem to apply around here. The youths at the ends of the tunnel have backed away. They're not fighters, just bullies, tough only when they've got the upper hand. William is different, Jeanette can see that, he's got something inside him that makes him worse. He spits on the ground but doesn't say anything else. Perhaps he's worried that he's killed Leo when he turns and walks away, unless perhaps his brain is suppressing it, finding excuses: 'He shouldn't have provoked me. He knew what would happen.'

When the tunnel is empty, Jeanette bends over Leo. His face is bloody but his breathing is regular, and to Jeanette's surprise his eyes are open. Calm and alert. William stamped and kicked him, but something must have restrained him, because Leo's face hasn't been smashed in. Nothing is broken. His body is covered in bruises, but those can be concealed by clothing, just like the scratch marks, and the swelling around his eyes and nose is no worse than for him to be able to lie to his mother and say he was hit in the face by a ball during a gym class.

'You shouldn't have done that,' the boy tells the teacher.

'No,' she agrees.

She interprets it as a mark of consideration, but that's not what Leo means.

'Don't you ever watch wildlife documentaries? Wild animals are always at their most dangerous when they've been wounded,' Leo gurgles, tasting blood in his mouth.

As soon as the blows stopped raining down on the twelve-year-old, he started to think about how he could get his revenge. He could feel William choosing to stamp on his thighs instead of his kneecaps, aiming for the softer parts of his body instead of knocking his teeth out, giving him bruises on his shoulder instead of trying to break his arm. Leo won't regard William's display of mercy as goodness, merely as weakness. He's going to get his own back.

When the twelve-year-old crawls to his feet, Jeanette says dutifully, 'We have to report this to –'

Leo shakes his head. 'I fell. William was trying to help me up. And if you say any different, I'll say I saw you kick a pupil!'

The teacher should protest; it will be easy to condemn her in hindsight for not doing so. But you learn to keep your mouth shut in this forest, for better and for worse. She knows who Leo's big sister is, knows all his reasons for being angry. If Jeanette reports this to the school or the police, he will never trust her again. She will never have a chance to get through to him then. So she says instead, 'Let's make a deal. I don't report this to anyone, and you come up to Adri Ovich's kennels. You know where that is?'

The boy nods, not cockily, and wipes blood from his nose on his sleeve. 'Why?'

'I'm running a martial arts class there.'

'You want to teach me to fight?'

'I want to teach you *not* to fight.'

'I don't want to be unkind, but you seem pretty bad at not fighting,' Leo points out.

Jeanette's face cracks into an embarrassed smile. Leo starts to move away, slowly and painfully, but when she tries to help him, he brushes her hand away. Not aggressively, but definitely not as the start of any negotiations. Leo knows what the teacher is trying to do. She's trying to rescue him.

She won't succeed.

26

Whose Town Will It Be?

You try to be a good parent, in every way, but you never know how. It's not a difficult job. Just impossible. Peter is standing outside his daughter's room with a pair of drumsticks in his hand. She used to be his little girl, it was his job to protect her, but now he can't even look her in the eye because he feels so ashamed.

When she was little, they lay together on a bed that was too narrow on one of those nights when it felt as though they were the last two people on Earth. The little child lay asleep against his neck, and he hardly dared breathe. Her heart was beating like a rabbit's, and his kept pace; he was so happy that he was terrified, so complete that he could think only of the fragments if life shattered again. Children make us vulnerable. That's the problem with dreams: you can get to the top of the mountain and discover that you're scared of heights.

She's sixteen now. Her dad stands outside her room, too much of a coward to knock. He always used to call her 'Pumpkin' when she was little. She never liked hockey, so when she fell in love with playing the guitar, Peter learned to play the drums, just so he could play with her in the garage. That happened less and less as the years passed, of course, because he was always so busy. Work, the house, life. You start to say 'Tomorrow' more often. When his daughter brought him the drumsticks he would ask, 'Have you done your homework?'

But now he's the one standing there with the drumsticks in his hand. He knocks tentatively on Maya's door. As if he almost hopes she won't hear.

'Mmm?' she grunts.

'I just thought I'd see if you've . . . got your guitar? Do you feel like . . . having a jam in the garage?'

She opens the door. Her sympathy crushes him. 'I'm studying, Dad. Tomorrow, maybe?'

He nods. 'Sure. Sure, Pumpkin. Tomorrow . . .'

She kisses his cheek and closes the door. He can barely look her in the eye. He's trying to find a way to be her dad again, but he doesn't know how. You never know how.

That evening the Andersson family are as far from each other as it's possible to get in a small house. Maya is lying on her bed with headphones on at high volume. Kira is sitting in the kitchen dealing with emails. Peter is sitting in the bathroom with the door locked, staring at his phone.

Leo hides the bruises on his body under a thick tracksuit and blames his swollen face on the fact that he got hit by a ball in gym class. Perhaps they believe him. Unless they just want to believe him. Everyone is caught up in his or her own anxiety this evening, so no one hears when Leo opens his window and sneaks out.

Peter calls Richard Theo. He answers on the third ring.

'Yes?' the politician says.

Peter gulps, even though his mouth is dry, and the only thing he seems to swallow is his pride. 'I want to ask something about our . . . agreement,' he says. He's whispering, sitting in the bathroom because he doesn't want his family to overhear.

'What agreement?' the politician asks, wiser than anyone who talks about that sort of thing on the phone.

Peter takes a deep breath. 'It might be difficult to . . . get hold of a carpenter in Beartown. At this time of year.'

It's his way of asking the politician not to force him to rip out the standing area in the rink. Not to force him to confront the Pack. Not right now. But the politician replies, 'I don't know what you're talking about. But . . . *if* we had an agreement, you and I, then I would have expected you to keep your side of it. Without exception. Because that's what friends do!'

'You're asking me to do something . . . dangerous. You know a local politician around here has had an axe embedded in her car, and I . . . I've got a family.'

'I'm not asking you to do anything. But you're a sportsman, and I didn't think sportsmen defended violent hooligans,' Richard Theo replies scornfully.

Peter holds the phone to his ear long after the politician has hung up. He can still see the announcement of his death in front of him if he closes his eyes. He's going to be able to save his club, but what dangers is he exposing his family to? He'll be able to give this town a hockey team. But whose town will it be?

They say 'Small leaks sink big ships.' But sometimes not fast enough for some men. Richard Theo makes a call to London. Then an email is sent from the factory's new owner to the general manager of Beartown Ice Hockey. Its content is simple: as the new sponsor, he demands a guarantee that Peter Andersson 'really does intend to keep his promise to create a more family-friendly, fully seated arena.' No one mentions anything about the Pack or any 'hooligans.' The email never reaches Peter; it's obviously just a harmless mistake – the sender spelled his surname with one *s* instead of two.

If anyone were to ask later, everyone will be confused: Peter will say he never received the email, the sponsor will say that it negotiated through a go-between, and the harder it is to get a clear idea of what actually happened, the more convinced people will be that everyone involved is hiding something.

No one will ever need to explain exactly how a copy of the email suddenly ended up in the hands of the local paper. The reporter will refer to a 'trusted source.' Once the news is out, it won't matter where it came from.

In the end no one will be able to prove whose idea it was to get rid of the standing area at the rink.

★

The members of the Pack always embrace when they meet and before they part, with their fists clenched against each other's backs. Some people see this as a sign of violence. But to them it isn't.

Teemu Rinnius still lives at home with his mother. Police investigations have suggested that this is because he can't get a home of his own using the illegal earnings he lives off of, and he lets everyone believe that. The truth is that he can't leave his mother alone. Someone needs to do the counting at home. There are lots of jokes about the Rinnius brothers' criminality, such as 'What's a triathlon for the Rinnius brothers? Walking to the swimming pool and cycling home!' and 'The Rinnius brothers are sitting in a car; who's driving? The police!' When Vidar became the goalie on the boys' hockey team, someone in the stands joked, 'Of course that family make good goalies, they can't keep their hands off anything!' That joke was told only once. You can say what you like about the Rinnius brothers, but math was their best subject at school. They've been counting all their lives: How many pills are left in the bottles in the bathroom, how many hours has Mum been asleep? When Vidar got caught and was sent away, that responsibility fell to Teemu alone. It was worse then because all their mum wanted to do was sleep longer and deeper once her youngest son was taken off to the treatment centre. Vidar was always her little baby, no matter what he got up to.

Teemu is sitting at her kitchen table now. She's clattering with frying pans and saucepans, and he's not used to it; she laughs out loud, and it's been a long time since she last did that. When Teemu told her that Vidar was being released early, she cleaned the whole house in a rush of happiness. The next morning was the first time in years that Teemu counted the same number of pills in the bottles two days in a row.

'My baby, my baby,' his mum sings happily to herself over at the stove.

She never asked why Vidar is being released or who arranged it, but that anxiety is gnawing away at Teemu. He tells himself that he just wants the same as all simple men do: to have his little brother home, make his mum happy, live a simple life. But that isn't true: he has to protect them, too, that's always been his responsibility, his obsession.

'My baby, my baby, coming home to Mama!' his mum sings.

Teemu's mind wanders off. The Pack was never as coordinated or as militarily organized as people thought. Everyone says 'What pack?' or 'Teemu who?' if strangers ask, but that isn't entirely put on. He isn't a dictator; the black jackets are basically just a group of friends who stick together because of two simple loves: hockey and each other. The politicians and board members and journalists talk an awful lot of bullshit about 'hooligans' when it suits their purposes, but those greedy bastards don't love the club or the town the way the members of the Pack do.

Teemu's two best friends, Spider and Woody, can fight like wild animals. But they never attack innocent people, and when the worst storm in a century hit the forest a few years ago, those two were the guys who went from house to house clearing trees from gardens and mending roofs and windows without asking for any form of payment. Where were the journalists and board members then? Police investigations describe Woody and Spider as gang members, but to this day they can't walk past any of those houses without being invited in for coffee. Teemu isn't a child, he knows his guys haven't got hearts of gold. But they have honour. Their own sort.

Spider was bullied as a child, never wanted to shower after PE, so a gang of boys in his class thought that meant he was gay. They threw him into the shower and beat the crap out of him with twisted wet towels. 'Gay' was the worst insult they could think of, the weakest thing a boy could be. So Spider has hated two things ever since: gays and bullies.

After an away game six or seven years ago, the Pack got stopped by the cops. Teemu's little brother, Vidar, who was only twelve at the time, was sitting alone in a branch of McDonald's, and a gang of opposing fans were on their way there. When Spider realized that, he tore free from the police. Dogs, horses, and a rapid response unit were unable to stop him. He and Vidar held off ten of their opponents inside McDonald's for twenty minutes. Spider landed four people in hospital, and twelve-year-old Vidar smashed a chair and used the legs as weapons. A warrior even then.

Woody is different. He comes from a nuclear family, lives on the edge of the Heights, works in his dad's business. But he has the same things inside him as Spider. When Woody was a teenager, his cousin was raped by some lowlife when she was on holiday. When Teemu found out, he stole a car, drove through the night, and got to the airport just in time to stop Woody from getting onto a plane, because Woody was planning to go and take on the whole country. He sobbed with rage in Teemu's arms, his fists clenched behind his back.

Woody has a girlfriend now, she has a good job in administration at the council's housing association, and they've just had a daughter. It was Woody who persuaded Teemu that the Pack should take Maya Andersson's side in the spring rather than Kevin Erdahl's. 'I don't care if we end up in the lowest league on the planet, I'll stand in that rink anyway, but I'm not standing up for a rapist!' he said. The Pack made a decision then, and now they're dealing with the consequences.

They voted to keep Peter Andersson in the club, and now they've heard that the rat has brought in sponsors who want to get rid of the standing area. Teemu's phone hasn't stopped ringing. The guys want war.

'But I don't understand why my *baby* can't live at home with his own *mother*!' Teemu's mother suddenly repeats, and he is wrenched from his daydreams.

'What?' Teemu mutters.

His mum tosses an envelope from the council's housing association on the table. 'It says in that letter that Vidar's got an apartment of his own! What's the point of that? He's got a *mother*!'

Only then do the pieces of the puzzle fall into place for Teemu.

★

When the man in a suit comes out of the council building and opens the door of his car, the figure is suddenly standing behind him. Richard Theo is alarmed but not surprised. He collects himself quickly and asks, 'Who are you?'

Teemu Rinnius takes two steps forward. He doesn't lay a finger on him, but he's close enough for them to feel each other's breath, meaning that the politician feels physical fear. That afflicts all of us, those of us who can't fight, it doesn't matter if we have money or power or know that a courtroom could give us justice. No one can protect us in a dark parking lot for the few seconds it takes a man like Teemu to assault us and knock us out. We know that. As does he. So he says, 'You know who I am. My little brother, Vidar, has been locked up, but now he's suddenly being released. I didn't understand why, but then I heard that Beartown Ice Hockey's new coach wants him on the team. No hockey club could get my brother out of that clinic. But perhaps a politician could?'

Richard Theo's pulse rate speeds up, but he manages to keep his voice steady. 'I'm afraid I don't know what you're talking about.'

Teemu looks at him ominously, but eventually he backs away and gives the politician some air. He raises a warning finger, to let the politician know that he isn't the only person in Beartown who's good at gathering information.

'My mum got a letter from the council's housing association. My brother's been given an apartment. We checked to see who filed the application. It was you.'

Theo nods. 'It's my job to help the town's inhabitants. All of them . . .'

The fact that Theo's address appeared in the housing association's register could, of course, have been a mistake. Unless it was a message that he assumed Teemu would eventually find. After all, his friend Woody does have a girlfriend who works in the offices of the housing association.

Teemu snarls, 'I'm the wrong person to play games with! What do you want with my family?'

Richard Theo plays dumb. Which is brave of him. 'I'm not the sort of man who asks people for things. Especially not people who belong to . . . what are you called again? The Pack?'

'What pack?' Teemu asks.

His face doesn't even harden; he's had years to practice that fake nonchalance, and it impresses the politician. So Theo raises his hands and says, 'Okay, I confess. I know who you are. And I think you and I can be friends, Teemu.'

'Why?'

'Because we have a lot in common. We don't always do what we should, but we do what we have to. I get portrayed in the media as dangerous and wicked, simply because I don't follow all the rules that the establishment has created to stop men like us. I daresay you can recognize yourself in that.'

Teemu spits on the ground. 'Your suit cost a month's wages for a normal person.'

Theo considers this. 'You're not a bad man, Teemu. You take care of your friends, your family, and you want a better life for your brother. Don't you?'

Teemu doesn't even blink. 'Get to the point.'

'The thing is, I have no illusions about what society is, and neither do you. We belong to different groups, we're different people, but we look after our interests the same way.'

'You don't know anything about me,' Teemu says.

The politician ventures a smile at this. 'Perhaps not. But I watched a lot of horror films when I was younger, so I know that the monster is always at its worst right before you set eyes on it. Our imaginations are always much more terrifying than we're actually aware of. I think you've constructed this Pack of yours the same way. There probably aren't as many of you as people think. You let people's imaginations make you more terrible than you actually are.'

Teemu's eyebrows sink. The only movement he allows himself. 'There is no pack.'

The politician says confidently, 'No, of course not. But everyone needs friends, Teemu. Because friends help one another.'

222

'With what?'

Richard Theo replies softly, 'Your standing area in the rink.'

Leo is walking through Beartown without really knowing where he's going. The swelling and bruises from the assault in the tunnel are slowing him down, but he needs to move about, needs to get out into the night air and prove to himself that he's not afraid.

At first he walks towards the Heights, towards William Lyt's house, like a child who's burned himself on a stove but can't help touching it again. But all the houses there are silent and dark, so Leo heads towards the town centre instead. There are men standing outside the Bearskin smoking. Two of them are Woody and Spider. Leo stands in the shadows and mimics their body language, lights a cigarette of his own and tries to smoke it the way they do. Perhaps the twelve-year-old hopes that if he can look like them, he can become like them, too: the sort of person no one messes with.

Richard Theo shows no sign of smugness when he says 'standing area.' Even though that gets Teemu's full attention in an instant.

'What about the standing area?' Teemu asks, as if he didn't already know.

Richard Theo takes his time replying. 'There are rumours that the new sponsors want it demolished.'

Teemu's mask cracks, and the hatred shines through. 'If Peter Andersson so much as *touches* our stand, he'll –'

He stops himself abruptly. The politician repeats in a conciliatory tone, 'Like I said: I want to be your friend.'

'Why?'

The politician gets straight to the point at last: 'Because this spring the membership of Beartown Ice Hockey voted on whether to let Peter Andersson continue as general manager, and you saw to it that he won. I'm a politician. I understand the value of a man who can get other people to vote the way he wants.'

Teemu peers at him skeptically. 'So you're going to persuade Peter not to touch the stand?'

The politician's lie comes effortlessly. 'No. Peter refuses to listen to politicians. He refuses to listen to anyone. He wants to control the club single-handedly. But I can talk to the new sponsors. They're reasonable people, and they'll appreciate the value of a . . . group of ardent fans. Isn't that what you are?'

Teemu chews the inside of his cheek thoughtfully. 'What happens to Peter?'

'I don't know anything about hockey, but general managers get fired from time to time, don't they? The wind can change direction quickly.'

'You'd better hope the wind never changes direction against my brother,' Teemu snarls.

Richard Theo bows politely. 'I can give you what you want. Your stand, your club, and a Beartown team containing guys from Beartown. Can we be friends?'

Teemu nods slowly. The politician gets into his car.

'Then I won't detain you any longer, Teemu, because I believe you have business in Hed this evening.'

Teemu's eyelids twitch. Richard Theo enjoys the moment. If you want something from a person, you need to understand what motivates him, and Teemu is a protector. As a child he fought grown men in his kitchen to protect his mother, as a teenager he founded the Pack to protect his younger brother, but that's not all. It's easy to believe that he doesn't even like sports, that it's just an excuse for the violence and a pretext for criminal behaviour. But if you look into his eyes when he talks about Beartown Ice Hockey, you'll see that this town is his home. That standing area in the arena is the only place where he isn't worried, isn't weighed down by a feeling of responsibility for everyone around him. Hockey is his fantasy world, just as it is for the general managers and coaches and players. And people like Teemu will always protect their happiest places with their most dangerous weapons. So he snaps, 'What are you talking about? Why would I have business in Hed?'

Richard Theo smiles. 'I thought you'd already seen the video clip?'

*

At that moment Teemu's phone vibrates in his pocket as a text message arrives. Then another. Then another.

Leo is still standing in the shadows on the other side of the street when the men outside the Bearskin get so many text messages in succession that their phones sound like pinball machines. They're all looking at the same video. Leo can't see what it is but can hear them talking about it: 'Those cocksuckers in Hed deserve to die!' Another one looks at his own phone and replies in a harsh voice, 'Teemu's just texted me. He's seen the video. He wants us to fetch the guys.' It doesn't take Leo a minute to find the clip on his own phone; everyone in his school has started to circulate it, and Leo figures out what's going to happen now. He runs straight into the forest. If he hurries, he might actually get to Hed before the Pack does.

There's going to be a fight.

Teemu Rinnius walks to the kennels in the darkness. Adri sees him through the window; he hasn't got any bottles with him, and he's alone.

'Is your brother here?' Teemu asks.

Adri recognizes the look in his eye. 'He's up on the roof,' she says.

Teemu smiles delightedly. 'I was thinking of buying him a beer. Do you want to come?'

Adri shakes her head slowly. 'If he gets hurt, I'll kill you.'

Teemu pretends not to understand. 'Hurt? From drinking beer?'

Adri raises her hand and reaches for his chin. 'You heard me.'

Teemu smiles. Adri goes into the house. She knows what's going to happen tonight. She wishes Benji wasn't going to be involved in the fight, but sooner that than him lying on his back in the forest whispering about 'mistakes.' She checks that the key to the gun cabinet is under her pillow. Then she goes to bed.

Benji is sitting on the roof of the outhouse smoking beneath the stars. Teemu climbs up the ladder and peers over the edge. 'Do you want a beer, Ovich?'

There's something about the way he says it, a hint of stifled laughter.

'What? Now?' Benji asks, immediately more sober.

Teemu holds up his phone and plays the clip that's gone viral online. 'Someone's burning a Beartown jersey in the square in Hed.'

'Why should I be bothered?' Benji wonders.

Teemu has already started to climb back down when he replies, he's so confident that Benji will climb down after him, 'It's my bear on the front of the jersey, Ovich. And it's your name on the back.'

His voice isn't angry. More playful. If anyone had seen Benji climb down from the roof, they'd have understood why: Teemu understands him, they're the same sort.

Benji smiles. 'What do you have in mind?'

'I was thinking of buying you a beer. I've heard they have good beer in Hed.'

27

Hatred and Chaos

Teemu and Benji walk past the town sign, calmly and sensibly, in no hurry. They stop in the main square in Hed. The remains of the burned jersey are lying on the ground. It's dark, but they don't need any light to know that there are eyes watching them from all the windows. The two walk up and down the main street in Hed, each clutching a beer bottle. Bare-chested, their bear tattoos shining like beacons in the night. They wait until they're sure phone calls have been made, bodies roused, metal pipes tossed into the back of cars. Then the two walk calmly out of Hed again, a couple of hundred feet into the forest, until they reach a clearing. There, six men in black jackets are waiting. A quarter of an hour later, twice as many men show up from Hed. That doesn't matter, because not all twenty from Hed can fight, and Teemu has only men who can. He's brought Spider and Woody and all his best guys.

Above all, he's brought Benji.

A fight in a dark forest isn't organized or choreographed. Nothing but hatred and chaos. It's no place for practiced footwork and elegant moves; just stay on your feet, survive, and make sure that as many of them as possible end up on the ground before you do. Never retreat, keep moving forward, there are no rules and no white flags. You might kill someone without meaning to, you might land one too many kicks or hit them somewhere you shouldn't. You knew what you were letting yourself in for when you came, and so did they. It's a terrifying experience for everyone; if you're not afraid, then you've never fought against an equal before. You have to dig deep within yourself and find something there, something terrible, something out of control. Your truest self.

Violence is the easiest and the hardest thing in the world to understand. Some of us are prepared to use it to get power, others only in self-defence, some all the time, others not at all. But then there's another type, unlike all the others, who seems to fight entirely without purpose. Ask anyone who has looked into a pair of those eyes when they turn dark, and you'll realize that we belong to different species. No one can really know if those people lack something that other people possess or if it's the other way around. If something goes out inside them when they clench their fists or if something switches on.

Almost all fights are won or lost long before they start; the brain needs to be working, the heart needs to be pounding before your hands can do the same. And you will be scared – if not just of being hit, then of being vanquished; if not of being injured, then of injuring someone else. That's why adrenaline appears, the body's biological defence: claws out, horns lowered, hooves raised, canine teeth bared.

The first blow? That doesn't decide anything, doesn't say anything about you. The rest, on the other hand, reveal everything. Anyone can throw one punch out of anger or fear or out of pure instinct. But punching an adult's jaw as hard as you can is like slamming your fist into a brick wall, and when you hear the crunch of bone giving way beneath your fingers, something happens. When the enemy slumps, stumbles backward, and you see the fear in his eyes. Perhaps he even raises a trembling hand to plead for mercy . . . What do you do then? Do you punch again? In the same place, even harder? That makes you a different sort of person. Because most people can't do that.

No one who has seen you throw that second punch will ever fight with you again.

★

Teemu and Benji go first, side by side. Bodies crouch low around them. The first man who rushes at Benji seems to have picked him out, but it's a bad decision; the man is taller and larger and heavier, but none of that matters here. Once Benji has landed his first punch, he holds the man up with his other hand so he can punch him again in exactly the same place even harder.

Benji feels nothing when he lets go and the man's head hits the ground with a dull thud, like a child dropping a cinnamon bun on a beach. Benji used to really feel it, the adrenaline, the rush, sometimes even a sort of joy. But something's broken; he's passed some sort of boundary.

He stops midmovement. He has time to think a thought, and you're not supposed to do that. Not in the forest, not in the darkness, not when they're armed. Someone creeps up on him from behind with a metal pipe, swings it at his knees, and Benji realizes too late that the men from Hed might lose a fight tonight, but they're going to win a hockey game.

We don't know people until we know their greatest fears. Benji hears the scream, how loud it is; he hears the scream before he feels the pain. He waits for his body to give way, for his knee to buckle under the impact of the pipe. He has time to wonder if he isn't only going to lose out on the game against Hed but on an entire career. After spending his whole life on the ice without serious injury, his knee will never be completely whole again, no chance, and he has time to think that the weirdest thing is that he isn't afraid. He isn't distraught. He doesn't care. How many years of training, how many hours? He doesn't give a damn about the game. He stands still, breathless at the realization of how little it means. But he's still standing. It takes him several seconds to realize that he's uninjured. That the pipe missed him.

From the corner of his eye he sees a boy, no more than twelve years old, swinging something wildly and indiscriminately around him in terror. The man who was swinging the pipe at Benji falls to the ground. It was his scream Benji heard, not his own. The boy is holding a thick branch. Tears are running down his cheeks.

Benji recognizes him. Leo Andersson, Maya Andersson's younger brother. Someone lands a glancing blow on the boy's eye. He stumbles backward, and Benji finds himself thinking that that isn't okay. He doesn't turn around and fight; instead he grabs the boy by the arm and runs. Up the slope, into the forest, away through the trees. He can hear the cries behind him, he knows the men from Hed will spread the story of how Benji Ovich ran from a fight. Coward. He doesn't care. Leo struggles against him for the first few steps, but soon he, too, is running, out into the darkness.

Leo gets to know Benji that night. Gets to know his fears. Benji isn't afraid of fighting, he's not afraid of getting beaten up, not even afraid of dying. But he's terrified of this: turning around and seeing a twelve-year-old get hurt and feeling responsible. Anyone who feels responsibility isn't free.

They run all the way back to Beartown. Leo, gasping for breath, doesn't stop until Benji does. The twelve-year-old's foot is hurting, and he wonders if he's got a stone in his shoe, then looks down and realizes that his shoe isn't there. He must have lost it during the fight and has run the whole way without noticing thanks to the adrenaline. His toes are bleeding.

'My name is Leo, and –'

Benji's breathing is measured, as if he's just had an afternoon nap beside a sun-drenched window. 'You're Maya Andersson's brother. I know.'

Leo's voice changes quickly. 'Don't give me some sermon about how I shouldn't fight because I –'

Benji holds one of his hands up abruptly. 'You're her brother. Apart from her, there probably isn't anyone around here with a greater right to want to punch someone in the face.'

Leo's breathing starts to calm down, and he nods gratefully. 'I didn't think . . . I was hiding in the forest, I just wanted to watch the fight . . . but you didn't see the guy with the pipe, he was about to –'

Benji smiles. 'If he'd been aiming at my head, it wouldn't have been a problem, there's not much left up there to damage. But if he was planning to hit my kneecap, I owe you a serious debt of thanks for making sure he couldn't do it. How's your eye?'

'Nothing to worry about . . .'

Benji pats him on the shoulder. 'You're a tough kid, Leo. When you get older, you'll realize that that's both a good thing and a bad thing.'

Leo spits on the ground and repeats the words he heard the men outside the Bearskin say, and they feel good in his mouth: 'Those cocksucking motherfuckers! William Lyt and his fucking cocksucker friends and all their fag fans in Hed. I hate them!'

Benji blinks sadly at each word, but not so that the boy notices. 'It's getting late. You should go home.'

'Can you teach me to fight like you?' Leo asks admiringly.

'No,' Benji replies.

'Why not?'

Benji's chin drops, and a knot in his chest tightens. He can see that Leo is awestruck by his ability to hurt other people. Benji doesn't know who he hates most for that.

'You haven't got it in you, Leo,' he says quietly.

The boy snaps. Not just his voice, his whole being. 'Kevin raped my sister! What sort of man am I if I don't —'

Benji hugs the boy and whispers in his ear, 'I've got sisters, too, and if anyone did to one of them what Kevin did to Maya, I'd be full of hate, too.'

Leo splutters in despair, 'If Kevin raped one of your sisters, you'd have killed him!'

Benji knows he's right. So he tells the truth: 'So don't end up like me, then. Because once you do, it's too late to change.'

28

'Goddamn homo!'

The next morning Ana and Maya stop a hundred feet from the school. They've started to do that every day. It's become an energy-gathering ritual that armour-plates them. Ana clears her throat and asks, very seriously, 'Okay . . . have diarrhoea every day for the rest of your life or *always* have to go to the toilet with the door open?'

Maya roars with laughter. 'What is it with you and shit these days? Is that all you think about?'

'Answer the question!' Ana commands.

'It's an idiotic question,' Maya points out.

'You're idiotic! Diarrhoea or an open door . . . *always* open. No matter where you go to the toilet. For the rest of your *life*!'

Maya giggles. 'I've got a class now.'

Ana shudders. 'How can we possibly have played this game our whole lives without you understanding the rules! You have to answer! That's, like, the whole *point*!'

Maya shakes her head teasingly, Ana gives her a shove, Maya laughs and shoves back, but Ana jumps out of the way so nimbly that Maya falls over. Ana sits on top of her, grabs hold of her hands, and yells, 'Answer before I mess up your makeup!'

'Diarrhoea! *Diarrhoea*,' Maya half laughs, half shouts.

Ana helps her up. They hug each other.

'I love you, you nutter,' Maya whispers.

'Us against the world,' Ana whispers back.

Then they get ready for yet another day.

There's a flutter somewhere between your stomach and your rib cage, like a flag flapping in a storm, those first moments when you fall in love with someone. When someone looks at you, those days after the first kiss, when it's still your incomprehensible little secret. That you want me. It's a vulnerability; there's nothing more dangerous.

By the time school starts for the day, someone has written three words on Benji's locker with a red pen: 'Run, Benji, run!' Because they know that's what he did last night. He's been untouchable for so long in this town that the slightest crack in his armour will be exploited mercilessly by his enemies. He ran from a fight. He fled. He isn't the person everyone thought he was. He's a coward.

They watch him when he arrives, waiting for a reaction when he reads the words, but it's as if he doesn't even see them. Maybe that's why they start to worry if he's understood. So when an entire school day passes without Benji showing the slightest sign of regret or shame, someone yells, 'GO ON, RUN, BENJI! RUN!' when he walks past the cafeteria. William Lyt and his guys are sitting at a table in the far corner. It's impossible to know who shouted, but Benji turns around and does as they suggested.

He runs. Straight at them. At top speed, with his fists clenched. Other pupils throw themselves out of the way; tables topple, chairs go flying. When Benji stops dead a foot from William Lyt, one of Lyt's friends has leaped under the table, two more are practically sitting in each other's laps, and one moves backward so hard that he hits his head against the wall.

But William Lyt hasn't moved a muscle. He sits still, eyes open, meeting Benji's stare. And Benji sees himself in him. He, too, has crossed a boundary. The cafeteria is silent, but the two eighteen-year-olds can hear each other's heartbeats. Calm, watchful.

'Sore feet, Ovich? We heard you ran all the way from the forest,' Lyt snarls.

At first Benji looks thoughtful. Then he takes off his shoes, then both his socks, and drops them into Lyt's lap. 'Here you go, William. Your only chance of a three-way.'

Lyt's jaw tightens, and his reply is more clenched than he would have liked. 'They're sweaty. Like a coward's.'

He's trying not to let his eyes land on Benji's watch but fails. He knows who Benji got it from, and Benji knows he knows, so jealousy eats away at William when Benji grins. 'I was actually looking for *you* in the forest, William. But you never dare take part in fights when the numbers are even, do you? You're only tough on video. That's why your team never trusts you.'

Small dots of shame burn on William's cheeks. 'I didn't know there was going to be a fight, I was at home, it wasn't *me* who burned the jersey,' he snaps.

'No, you're not man enough to do that,' Benji replies.

He turns and leaves the cafeteria, and only then does William Lyt shout something. Benji doesn't hear what, the only words he hears are 'GODDAMN HOMO!'

Benji stops so that no one sees him tumbling into the abyss that's just opened up in front of him. He sticks his hands into his pockets so no one will see them shaking. He doesn't turn around so that Lyt can't see what's happened as he asks, 'What did you say?'

Lyt repeats what he said, encouraged by the unexpected advantage. 'I said your coach is a disgusting goddamn homo! Are you proud of that? Playing on a bullshit rainbow team?'

Benji fastens his jacket so his pulse isn't visible through his shirt. Lyt shouts something else, and all his guys laugh. Benji walks out into the corridor, and through the crowd he sees a polo shirt. Green today. The teacher's eyes are pleading, as if he wants to say 'Sorry' but knows that the word is too small.

There's a flutter inside Benji then. A flag coming loose in a storm. He can't let anyone make him that weak, not this season. He leaves the school, walking slowly on purpose, but as soon as he's out of sight he runs. Right into the forest. Slamming his fist into every tree he passes.

A younger boy stops at a different locker in the same school. Twelve years old. Covered in bruises. Yesterday he grabbed a branch and threw himself into a fight without hesitation in order to smash the legs of someone who was trying to hurt Benjamin Ovich. That sort of thing doesn't go unnoticed in this town.

Today there's something hanging from his locker. At first he thinks it's a trash bag. He couldn't be more wrong. It's a black jacket. No logos or emblems or symbols, just a perfectly ordinary black jacket. It doesn't mean anything. It means everything. It's far too big for Leo, because they want him to know that he can't become one of them until he's much older. But they've hung it on his locker so that everyone in his school will get the message.

He's got brothers now. You don't touch him again.

It takes a huge amount of trust to fight at someone's side. That's why violent people prize loyalty so highly and are so sensitive about the slightest sign of treachery: if you retreat and run, you're exposing me to danger, making me look weak. So Benji knows he's let Teemu and the Pack down. And that isn't tolerated.

Even so, he pulls himself together after a few hours in the forest and walks back into town. He wipes the tears from his cheeks and the blood from his knuckles. He can't let anyone think there's anything wrong with him; everything has to carry on as normal. Even when blue polo shirts have torn him apart, even when he knows that the Pack might want to punish him for running from the fight in the forest. Because where would he go if he didn't have Beartown?

So he goes to work, stands behind the bar in the Bearskin, pours beer. The more crowded the bar gets, the more he avoids eye contact with other people. Several of the guys from the forest are there: Spider, about whose intelligence Ramona usually says, 'He's about as smart as mashed potato, that one.' But he's loyal; in the forest Benji saw him stick just behind Teemu the whole time, not because he was scared but because he was guarding his leader's flank. Spider was bullied all through childhood for being so lanky and crazy, but he found a place in the Pack. You can't buy that sort of devotion.

Beside Spider sits his physical opposite, a short, neckless man, as wide as a brick shithouse with a beard as thick as an otter's pelt.

He's called Woody because he works as a carpenter, because that's what his father did. Once someone asked Woody if he'd rather have a more imaginative nickname, but Woody just snorted, 'Are you gay or something?' If he's any smarter than Spider, he keeps it well hidden, but he was in the same class in school as Benji's sister Gaby and she says, 'He's no genius, but he's not a bad guy.' Woody's first love is having fun: beer, hockey, friends, girls. Drinking, dancing, and fighting. If there's any kind of trouble going on, he'll be there without a thought for the consequences, and if there's an offer of a scrap in the forest he never hesitates.

But he and Spider have other friends, too, hardly hardened warriors, who seem almost to consider fighting a shared hobby. Like golf. One of the guys who works with Woody is so sweet that if he sees you on a Tuesday he wishes you a good weekend, just in case he doesn't see you again before Friday. Another has four cats. How can anyone with four cats be dangerous? But he is.

The men who make up the Pack aren't extremists; what makes them dangerous is simply the fact that they stick together. Against everything, through everything, for one another. Benji remembers a book he read by some journalist who said on the subject of sport and violence that 'every large group you don't yourself belong to is a threat.'

There are men in Beartown who grew up with Teemu but who now work in offices; they wear white shirts rather than black jackets, but if Teemu calls them they still come. One became a father and started studying at college to give his kid a better life, and he got a monthly grant from the kitty at the Bearskin when his student loan wasn't enough. Another has a sister in the big city who got beaten up by her boyfriend and the police said they couldn't do anything. A third has an uncle whose printing business was threatened by a gang running a protection racket. The sister is happily married to a better man now, and the uncle never got any more visits from the gang. If Teemu ever calls in those men, they come. That's why they prize loyalty and are so sensitive to betrayal.

Neither Spider nor Woody is looking at him now, but Benji is well aware that if they want to hurt him this evening, they're not going to warn him first.

Maya and Ana go their separate ways after school. Ana lies and says she has to check on the dogs, even though it's actually her dad she's going to check on. She feels ashamed. Maya lies and says she's going out for a run, even though she's planning to go home and curl up under the covers. She feels ashamed for different reasons. They're like sisters, they've never had secrets from each other. But Kevin broke something between them, too.

It's almost closing time in the Bearskin when the crowd at one end of the bar parts discreetly. The bar gets a little quieter, not enough to have been noticed by strangers but enough for Benji to notice.

'Two beers,' Teemu says, looking him hard in the eye.

Benji nods and pours them. Teemu watches his hands; they're not shaking. Benji respects the situation he's in, and he isn't afraid. Teemu takes one of the beers and leaves the other on the counter. It takes a long time for Benji to realize what that means. So he slowly picks it up, and Teemu leans across the counter and touches his glass to his in a toast. So that everyone sees.

'You're one of us, Ovich. But we can't take you out into the forest anymore. I got it wrong yesterday. You could have been hurt, and we need you on the ice.'

'A little kid showed up in the forest . . . Leo . . .'

Teemu grins. 'We know. Tough kid. If you hadn't taken him off, he'd have kept fighting until he got killed.'

'He's only a boy,' Benji says.

Teemu stretches his neck, and something inside creaks. 'Boys become men. If the cops start asking Leo questions –'

'– he won't say a thing!' Benji promises.

'We're counting on that,' Teemu says.

Benji can see that Teemu finds the idea that the general manager's son dreams of rushing through the forest in a black jacket amusing. That Peter has tried for years to curb the Pack's influence over the club but now can't even stop their influence over his own child. He leans over the counter and touches his glass to Benji's again.

'Have you heard my little brother's coming home? And your coach is going to let him play! You and my little brother! And that Amat, the one who's as quick as a weasel after a chili enema. And Bobo, the big meathead! You're not like the older players, those greedy mercenaries, most of them don't even want to live in Beartown! They just want to get out of here. But you lot, you're a Beartown team made up of Beartown guys!'

Before the evening is over, Spider, Woody, and a dozen other black jackets have drunk toasts with Benji. He's one of them again now. You might think that would make things easier when his secrets are revealed, but the exact opposite is what happens.

29

She Kills Him There

Anxiety is a truly remarkable thing.

Maya walks home alone, like iron on the outside but a house of cards inside. The slightest little breeze is all takes. Today it was the line in the cafeteria. The crowd. Someone backed into her accidentally; she doesn't know the boy's name, and he didn't even notice. They hardly touched each other. It wasn't his fault. But Maya was plunged back into hell again in an instant.

When she and Ana were younger, they used to count butterflies all summer. It's different now, Maya counts them in a different way. She knows they die when the leaves fall.

Anxiety. It's such a peculiar thing. Almost everyone knows what it feels like, yet none of us can describe it. Maya looks at herself in the mirror, wonders why it can't be seen on the outside. Not even on X-rays – how does that work? How can something that bangs away at us so horribly hard on the inside not show up on the pictures as black scars, scorched into our skeletons? How can the pain she feels not be visible in the mirror? She's become so good at pretending. Goes to school, sits in classes, does her homework. She plays her guitar, perhaps that helps, unless she's just imagining that. Perhaps her fingers just need to be kept busy. She's looked into the books her dad reads about 'mental coaching,' and they talk about the brain having to steer the body but that sometimes the reverse is the only way to survive. She's seen depressed adults do the same thing: keep moving, exercising, and cleaning and renovating their summer cottages, finding things that force them to get up in the morning: plants to be watered, errands to be run, anything so they don't have time to think about how they feel. As if we hope that physical activity, tiny everyday rituals, might lull the anxiety to sleep.

Maya has learned to master her own skin, not let it burst with the fire that's burning inside her. She imagines that if she can just fool everyone else, she might eventually be able to fool herself. But the slightest little thing can set her back: a lamp that looks like the one Kevin had in the corner of his bedroom or the brief creak of a floorboard that sounds like someone finally coming up the stairs in his parents' house after she had spent a lifetime screaming. She can go for weeks where everything is okay, then suddenly there's a noise or a smell and she's back there again. On his bed. With his hand around her neck and his overwhelming force pressing against her mouth.

The boy in the cafeteria line just brushed against her; it meant nothing to him but flared like fire for her. She held the panic attack inside her like a bomb.

When people talk about rape, they always do so in the past tense. She 'was.' She 'suffered.' She 'went through.'

But she didn't go through it, she's still going through it. She wasn't raped, she's still being raped. For Kevin it lasted a matter of minutes, but for her it never ends. It feels as though she's going to dream about that running track every night of her life. And she kills him there, every time. And wakes up with her nails dug into her hands and a scream in her mouth.

Anxiety. It's an invisible ruler.

The police station in Hed is overloaded and understaffed, like every other small-town police station. It's easy to make fun of delayed response times and never-ending investigations, as if the staff were doing it on purpose. But the police officers aren't all that dissimilar to any other professional group around here: if you give them the time and opportunity to do their job, they'll do it. Give them a group of hockey fans dressed in red who show up battered and bruised at the hospital, and they'll ask the right questions. Give them a forest they know, and eventually they'll find something in it.

'Over here!' one of them calls after they've spent over an hour fine-combing the clearing where they've figured out that the fight took place.

He tosses something to one of his colleagues.

A shoe. Just the right size to fit a twelve-year-old.

Leo is sitting on the steps in front of the house. Maya looks surprised. 'Why are you sitting here?'

'I've lost my keys,' he mumbles.

Maya peers at him suspiciously. Notices that he's wearing a tatty old pair of shoes. 'Where are your new shoes?'

'I've gone off them,' her brother lies.

'You nagged Mum for *months* to get them for you!'

Maya is expecting her brother to give as good as he gets, but he just sits there staring down at the ground. His face is swollen, he's got a black eye, he has been telling everyone he got hit in the face by a ball in PE, but no one saw it happen. And Maya heard whispering at school today about a black jacket hanging on his locker.

'Are you . . . okay?' she asks cautiously.

He nods. 'Don't tell Mum I've lost my keys,' he begs.

'I'm not going to tell on you,' she whispers.

They've done a lot of mean things to each other, but they've never told on each other. She was the one who taught him that, one night when she was twelve and had been to her first big party and came home later than she'd said she would but didn't get found out by her parents because she knocked on Leo's window and climbed into the house that way. 'We don't tell on each other,' she told her sleepy little brother back then, and he was smart enough to realize that one day he'd benefit from the agreement.

★

Late that evening, a policeman is standing at the door. Peter knows him, his son used to play hockey in the same group as Leo. Perhaps that's why the policeman's words are tinged with regret when he says, 'Sorry to bother you this late, Peter, but we've had some trouble in the forest outside Hed, a fight. Several people seriously injured. The Pack was involved.'

Peter leaps to the wrong conclusion. 'You know very well that the club has nothing to do with the Pack, if you're –'

The policeman cuts him off by handing over a shoe. 'We found this at the site of the fight.'

Peter takes his son's shoe and holds it in his trembling hand. When did he last hold a shoe his son had lost? When Leo was two years old? Three? How did his feet get this big?

The policeman says regretfully, 'I wouldn't have known whose they were if my son hadn't been nagging me for weeks about wanting a pair exactly like that. I told him they were too expensive for a twelve-year-old, and he yelled at me and told me I was stupid because apparently "*everyone*'s got them!" I asked him to name one person, and he said Leo.'

Peter tries to keep his voice steady. They really were far too expensive for a twelve-year-old. Kira and Peter got them for Leo back in the summer only because they felt guilty about . . . everything.

'I . . . they're just ordinary shoes . . . there must be loads of twelve-year-olds who –'

The policeman holds out something else. A small key ring. 'We found these as well. If you were to close the door in my face, I have a feeling I'd be able to open it again.'

Peter doesn't make any more objections. He takes the keys. Nods silently.

'Leo will have to come to the station for questioning,' the policeman says.

'He's only twelve . . .' Peter manages to say.

The policeman feels for him but doesn't back down. 'Peter, this is serious. The guys from Hed had fought the Pack before, but this was different. Three of them are still in hospital with serious injuries. They're going to get revenge, and then the Pack will get revenge. This isn't a game. Sooner or later someone's going to get killed.'

Peter clutches the shoe and keys unconsciously to his chest. 'I . . . Leo's only . . . can I at least drive him to the police station myself?'

The policeman nods. 'Your wife's a lawyer, isn't she?'

Peter understands what he means. It frightens the life out of him. Once the patrol car has driven off, Peter doesn't open the door to his son's room. He kicks it open.

A moment later father and son are standing face-to-face shouting at each other, but they've never been farther apart.

Maya locks herself in the bathroom. She hears her dad shouting at Leo, then her mum shouts at her dad to stop shouting, then they shout at each other about who has more right to shout. They're frightened, angry, powerless. Parents always are.

Maya's seen photographs of them before they had children. They were young and happy then; they don't laugh like that anymore, not even in photographs. They used to be so in love that they hungered for each other, her dad's fingertips brushing her mum's bangs, her mum who could raise the hairs on her dad's arms with a single glance. Children have a purely biological reaction against their parents' love for each other, but when it disappears, they hate themselves.

Maya is sitting on the bathroom floor, opening and closing the dryer door, *click, click, click*. The sound feels almost meditative, until she sees the T-shirt inside it. It's Leo's. Only he would be stupid enough to tumble dry a cotton T-shirt, because he never does the laundry, he doesn't know how to do it. Maya pulls the shirt out; the bloodstains are still visible. She knows what he's done; she burned her own clothes after that night at Kevin's because no one at home would have understood. Leo has been fighting, and Maya knows who for.

She hears her dad shout louder, 'You want to play gangsters in the forest with *hooligans*? Have you lost your *mind*?' Leo shouts back, 'At least they're *doing* something! What the hell are *you* doing? You're just letting all the goddamn cocksuckers in Hed *trample all over our town*!' Then her mum yells, loudest of all, 'YOU DON'T USE THAT KIND OF LANGUAGE IN MY HOUSE!'

Click, click, click. Maya opens and closes the tumble dryer. She knows her family aren't arguing about words or about the fight or about anyone's town. They're arguing about her. Everyone is.

She used to count butterflies with Ana, talking about 'the butterfly effect,' that the beat of a butterfly's wings can have such a devastating effect on the universe that the tiny air current it creates can cause a hurricane on the other side of the earth. Maya sees a whole town failing in the wake of her decision now. She's the cause, and all the fighting and violence are the effect. If she hadn't been here, if she'd never met Kevin, never gone into his room at that party, not been drunk, not been infatuated, if she'd just said yes and not put up a fight. That's what she's thinking, that's how guilt works. If only she hadn't existed, none of this would have happened. Her dad is shouting 'We haven't raised you to be a *fighter*!' Leo yells back, 'SOMEONE IN THIS FAMILY HAS TO FIGHT, AND YOU'RE TOO MUCH OF A COWARD!'

Maya hears a door slam. Realizes that it's her dad who's stormed out. Blinded by grief.

That night Maya writes a song she'll never perform. It is called 'Hear Me.'

> *Every man I know, every father and brother and son,*
> *Always these clenched hands. Where did you get that idea from?*
> *Always this violence, always round holes and a square block,*
> *The absurd idea you were sold, that we want you to fight for us.*
>
> *If you want to do something for us,*
> *Put a weapon down for me,*

Close the maw of hell for me,
Be a friend to me,
Try to be good men for me.

You boast about all you're going to do for me.
So when are you going to stop ruining things for me?
Do you want to know what you can do for me?
Start by hearing me.

Her mum is standing outside the bathroom door, asking Maya in a whisper if she's okay. Maya lies: 'Yes.' Her mum says, 'We have to go to Hed. To . . . sort something out.' As if Maya doesn't understand. So Maya lies, 'Don't worry, I need to study, see you later.'

When Leo's mum fetches him tersely from his room, he doesn't protest. He's already got his coat on and puts on his new shoes. They set off for the police station, the door closes behind them, and Maya sits on the bathroom floor, unable to breathe. She gets up, feeling a desperate, panicky need for air. She suddenly has to get out of the house, away from the town. She knows only one place for that, and only one friend. So she texts Ana a single word: 'Island?'

She starts to pack a backpack and puts her phone into her back pocket. She doesn't wait for an answer, she knows Ana will come. Ana would never let her down.

30

They Aren't the Kind of People Who Get Happy Endings

Of course Ana will be there. You can't set out to grow a friendship like theirs. But there are other things you can't grow either: parents are a sort of plant you can't choose, with roots that go deep and catch your feet in a way that only the child of an addict can understand.

Ana is already in the forest on her way when her phone rings. It's Ramona. The old woman is hard but never cruel; she has made many such phone calls over the years and always speaks the same way: sympathetic but not patronizing. She says Ana's dad has 'drunk his way out through the door,' which means that someone had to throw him out of the Bearskin and he isn't in a fit state to get home on his own. 'It's starting to get cold,' Ramona says, because she doesn't want to have to embarrass Ana by saying that her dad has been sick all over himself and needs fresh clothes. She knows the girl understands. Ramona has watched people drink themselves into the gutter for half a century, and she has learned that some children need to see the worst aspects of alcohol so that they leave it the hell alone.

So she says, 'Your dad needs company on the way home, Ana,' and Ana stops in the forest, nods, and whispers, 'I'm on my way.' She always goes. She'd never leave him.

Anxiety. It owns us but leaves no trace.

Ana doesn't call Maya, because Maya has perfect parents. A mum who never abandons her family and a dad who's never been sick all over himself when drunk. They're like sisters, she and Maya, but the only thing they haven't had in common is that shame. Ana can't bear the thought of Maya seeing her dad like that.

*

Maya sits alone on the island all night. Looking at her phone. Eventually she gets a text message, but not from Ana. Another anonymous number, again. She's still getting messages, but she's stopped telling Ana about them, she doesn't want to go on making her friend sad. It's Maya's secret now: 'Do you suck cock for 300 kronor?' this one asks. She doesn't even know if the people writing them know why they're doing it anymore. It could just as easily be someone in Hed who wants to break her as some girl at school who hates her or a gang of kids who are daring one another to 'text that girl who got raped by Kevin Erdahl.' That's all Maya will ever be for those people. Victim, whore, liar, princess.

Back in the summer Ana buried an expensive bottle of wine out here; her dad had been given it by an elderly neighbour in the Heights because he'd given him some meat after a hunt. Ana didn't have the heart to throw it away, but she didn't dare leave it in the kitchen among all the fragments of her dad's heart, either. So she hid it out here. Maya digs it up and drinks it. She doesn't care if she's being selfish; being drunk doesn't bring relief or peace, just bitterness. 'I always rely on you to come,' she thinks about her best friend. 'I was relying on you when Kevin pushed me down on the bed, too. My best friend will come, I thought, because my best friend would never leave me!' She throws the empty wine bottle at a tree. It smashes, and one of the pieces flies back and cuts her arm. Blood drips from the wound. She doesn't feel it.

Every night recently Ana has dreamed that she's being suffocated in a coffin, someone is sitting on the lid so she can't open it, and no matter how hard she bangs, no one hears her. She hasn't told her best friend, because Maya seems to be getting a bit better and Ana doesn't want to upset her. She doesn't say anything about the text messages, either, because Maya doesn't seem to be getting them anymore and Ana doesn't want to remind her of how horrible they are. *Ping, ping.* Pictures of boys' dicks. Sometimes worse. She can't imagine what kind of sick satisfaction they get from doing it or if they even think of her as human. Maybe she's just an animal. A product to consume.

This isn't what Ana thought life as a teenager would be like. Adults say you should enjoy being sixteen, that it's the best time of your life. Not for Ana. She loved her childhood, when her best friend was happy and her dad was an untouchable hero she could worship. When Ana was little, four or five years old, two men on snowmobiles disappeared in a winter storm north of the town. The emergency services called the best local hunters, people who knew the terrain, and Ana's dad packed his things and set off in the middle of the night. Ana stood in the doorway, begging him to stay. She'd heard about the storm on the radio, and she was old enough to know that dads didn't always come home from things like that. But her dad crouched down, took her head in his hands, and whispered, 'We're not the type who let other people down, you and me.'

One of the lost men froze to death, but the other one survived. It was Ana's dad who found him. A couple of winters later, when Ana had just turned six, she was playing down by the lake just after dusk when she heard a cry. A child the same age as her was in the water, already chilled through. All the children of Beartown know how to move across the ice to help someone who's fallen through, but that doesn't mean all the children would dare to do it alone in the dark. Ana didn't hesitate for an instant.

Her dad has done a lot of stupid shit in his time, but he raised a daughter who saved the life of someone else's daughter. When she got home, she was wet through and chilled and her lips were blue, but when her mum cried in horror, 'What on earth's happened?' the little girl just beamed and said, 'I've found a best friend!'

Her mum left them a few years later. She couldn't bear the forest and darkness and silence. Ana stayed. She and her dad played cards and told each other jokes, and sometimes when he was in a really good mood, he used to make her jump. He was brilliant at that; he could stand behind a door in a darkened room hiding just so he could jump out with a yell, making Ana shriek and laugh until she was breathless.

She always loved him, even when he was sad. Perhaps he always was, deep down. Ana doesn't know if he got sad when her mum

248

left or if her mum left because he was already sad. Some people just have a core of sadness. He would sit alone in the kitchen, drinking and crying, and Ana felt sorry for him because it must be a terrible thing: being able to cry only when you're drunk.

She tends to think that she's got two dads, one good and one bad, and she made up her mind that it was her job to make sure that when her bad dad took himself out in the evening, he wouldn't damage his body so much that her good dad couldn't use it the next morning.

She finds him around the back of the Bearskin now; he's leaning against a wall, asleep. For a few terrible moments Ana can't find his pulse and is overwhelmed by panic. She slaps his cheeks with the palm of her hand until he suddenly splutters and opens his eyes. When he catches sight of her, he slurs, 'Ana?'

'Yes,' she whispers.

'Di . . . did . . . did I scare you?'

She tries to smile. He falls asleep again. It takes all the sixteen-year-old daughter's strength to lift his top half so she can pull off the vomit-covered shirt and put a clean one on him. Most people probably wouldn't have bothered, but Ana knows her good dad is in there somewhere. The dad who read her stories after her mum left them and knows there are other lullabies than whisky. She wants that dad to wake up in a clean shirt tomorrow morning. She puts her arm around his shoulder and pleads with him to stand up.

'We're going home now, Dad.'

'Ana . . .?' he slurs.

'Yes. It's okay, Dad. You're just having a bad evening. Things will be better tomorrow.'

He sniffs. 'Sorry.'

That's the worst thing. Daughters have no defence against that word. He stumbles, and she stumbles, too.

But someone catches her.

Kira's voice echoes through the whole police station. How can you draw a dividing line between the lawyer and the mother when the boy is twelve years old? She didn't yell at Leo in the car on the way here, because Peter has already done enough yelling for both of them. For everyone. So she's yelling now instead, venting all her anger and powerlessness on the police officers.

Peter is sitting slumped in a room next to Leo. His son is sitting straight-backed, confrontational, while his dad is shrunken, drained of life and energy. When did he last yell at Leo? Several years ago? Peter's dad used to fight, and Ramona at the Bearskin once told Peter that 'fathers and violence are like fathers and drink – either the sons fight and drink even worse, or you don't do it at all.' Once Peter tried to explain something similar to Leo: 'I don't believe in violence, Leo, because my dad used to hit me if I so much as spilled a bit of milk. That didn't teach me not to spill milk, it just made me afraid of milk.' He doesn't know if Leo understood. He doesn't know what to say anymore. He's called his son some terrible things this evening, but Leo doesn't seem remotely bothered. He soaked up his parents' scolding without blinking, and when the police ask the boy their questions his father shudders, shivering as if the windows were open. That's the moment he realizes he's losing his twelve-year-old son.

Leo used to play hockey because his dad loved hockey. He never fell in love with it, but he joined the team because he liked the sense of belonging, the solidarity. Peter can see that he's found the same things now, in a terrible place. When the police ask Leo what happened in the forest during the fight, Leo replies, 'I don't know what you're talking about.' When the police ask how his shoe and keys ended up there, the boy replies, 'I was climbing trees, I might have dropped them.' The police ask if he saw anyone from the Pack fighting. 'What pack?' the boy asks. The police show him a picture of Teemu Rinnius. Leo says, 'I don't know who that is. What did you say his name was?'

The boy is lost, Peter knows it. Because Peter is afraid of milk, and Leo isn't afraid of anything.

★

Benji walks out of the back door of the Bearskin with the garbage, and it's his hands that catch Ana. As he picks up both her and her father, she starts to cry. She breaks in all directions at the same time. Benji hugs her, she buries her face against his chest, and he pats her hair.

She says nothing about how used she is to carrying her dad. Benji says nothing about never having the chance to carry his.

'Why does everyone drink so much?' Ana sobs instead.

'Because it makes everything quiet,' Benji replies honestly.

'What?'

'All the crap you can't stop thinking about.'

Ana slowly lets go of Benji and runs her fingers through her dad's hair as his head bobs in time with his snoring. She says, so quietly that it's almost a song, 'It must be terrible to only be able to bear to feel things when you're drunk.'

Benji picks the stocky hunter up from the ground, draping one of his arms around his own neck. 'Better than nothing, I suppose . . .'

Then he half carries, half drags Ana's dad home, while she walks alongside and eventually plucks up the courage to ask, 'Do you hate Maya?'

'No,' Benji replies.

He doesn't play stupid, he understands the question, and Ana falls in love with him for that. She clarifies: 'I don't mean, do you hate her for being raped. I mean . . . do you hate her for existing? If she hadn't been there that night . . . you'd still have everything, your best friend, your team . . . your life was perfect. You had everything. And now –'

Benji replies in a neutral tone of voice, 'I ought to hate Kevin if I was going to hate anyone.'

'So do you?'

'No.'

'Who do you hate, then?' Ana asks, but she knows.

Benji hates his own reflection. So does Ana. Because they should have been there. They should have stopped it. Things shouldn't have gone completely to hell for their friends. It should always have been Ana and Benji. Because they aren't the kind of people who get happy endings.

It's hard to blame Ana, precisely for that reason. Everyone has moments when her skin's longing for someone else's touch becomes unbearable.

They're at her home. Benji has just laid her dad on his bed and has helped her empty the kitchen of bottles, and it's impossible to get angry with a sixteen-year-old girl for the fact that her feelings get too much for her brain to be able to deal with.

Benji touches her shoulder, very briefly, and says, almost inaudibly, 'We mustn't end up like our dads.'

He walks towards the door, and Ana runs after him, grabs his arms, and presses her body against his. Her tongue touches his lips, she takes his hand and leads it under her shirt. She doesn't know what she'll hate him for most afterward: the fact that he didn't want her or that he was so gentle when he let her know.

Benji doesn't push her away; he could have thrown a grown man across the kitchen, but he barely touches her as he slips away. The look in his eyes isn't angry, it's sympathetic, and, oh, how she's going to hate him for that. That he didn't even let her feel that she was being rejected, only that he felt sorry for her.

'Sorry. But you don't want . . . this isn't what you want, Ana . . .,' Benji whispers.

He closes the front door silently behind him when he leaves. Ana sits on the floor, racked with tears. She calls Maya. Her friend answers on the tenth ring.

'Aaaaana? What the hell? Go to hell your stupid wine is finished just so you know! You didn't *come*! You said you were coming to the island, and you didn't *come*!'

Ana drops everything when she realizes that Maya is drunk. She ends the call and rushes out of the house.

★

It's incredibly hard to blame her for what is about to happen. But also very, very easy.

Politics is difficult to understand. Perhaps no one does, not completely. We rarely know why a society's bureaucracy works the way it does, because it's impossible to charge anyone with corruption when everything could just as easily be blamed on incompetence. A telephone call is made to a police station, a police officer and a woman from an official body go into another room. Kira is furious and up for a fight, but when the police officer comes back, she is informed that Leo is free to go home. 'Considering the boy's age.' Kira yells that that's precisely what she's been shouting for more than an hour, but then she realizes that that's exactly what they want. They're going to make out that it was her, the lawyer, who managed to persuade them. But she can hear that it isn't true. Someone made a phone call.

When Kira, Peter, and Leo leave the police station, Peter sees a car he recognizes. He tells Kira to go on ahead of him with Leo. Kira tries to understand what that means but plays dumb. Peter waits until his wife and son are out of sight before he walks over to the black car. He taps on the window, and the man dressed in a black suit opens the door.

'Hello, Peter. What a surprise to bump into you,' the politician says.

Peter is taken aback that someone could lie so naturally. 'My son has been questioned by the police about a load of hooligans fighting, but suddenly they ran out of questions. You wouldn't happen to know anything about that, I suppose?' Peter snaps.

He can't hide his feelings, not the anger or the worry or his shortcomings as a parent. Richard Theo silently despises him for that. 'Of course not,' he says amiably.

'Let me guess: you've got a lot of friends?' Peter demands angrily.

Richard Theo wipes his saliva from the sleeve of his jacket. 'You've got friends, too, Peter. You'll soon be told the time and location of the press conference at which the factory's new owner will be presented. There'll be politicians there, representatives of the local business community, important people from around the district. As your friend, I'd appreciate it if you were there, too.'

'And that's where I have to speak out against the Pack?'

Richard Theo pretends to be horrified. 'You're going to speak out against *violence*, Peter. Violence that your own *son* seems to be getting dragged into!'

Peter feels as though he's suffocating. 'Why are you so keen to take on the Pack?'

Theo replies, 'Because they rule with the help of violence. A democracy can't allow that. Anyone who becomes powerful because they've physically fought their way to the top needs to be opposed. You can always be absolutely certain of one thing when it comes to power, Peter: no one who gets their hands on it ever lets go of it voluntarily.'

Peter hates the sound of his own voice when he asks, 'And what do I gain from that?'

'You? You get control of the club. You get to spend the sponsor's money how you like. They'll even let you handpick a board member!'

'A board member?'

'Whoever you like.'

Peter glances down at his shoes. Then after a while he whispers, 'Okay.'

He will soon be standing there at that press conference. Saying everything that needs to be said. No way back. It's him against the Pack now.

Richard Theo drives away without feeling evil, merely pragmatic. A man like Teemu Rinnius can affect the way people vote in elections. Theo needs to give him something in exchange. The only thing Teemu cares about is his standing area in the rink. Richard Theo can't give that back to him unless it's been taken away from him first.

★

Ana doesn't set out through the door with the intention of hurting anyone, she just can't bear to stay in the house. She doesn't even mean to follow Benji through the forest, she just happens to catch sight of his white top ahead of her through the trees; he's walking slowly, as if his feet hadn't quite reached agreement with the rest of his body. Ana is good at tracking animals, it's an instinct, so she follows him. Perhaps she just wants to know where Benji's going, if he's on his way to see a girlfriend. She manages to tell herself that it might feel easier then, if she sees him with someone ten times more attractive than her. The forest soon becomes dark, but she follows the red glow of his cigarette and the sweet smoke he leaves behind him.

Halfway between Beartown and Hed he turns off and follows a track down to the campsite. He stops at one of the cabins, knocks on the door. Ana recognizes the man who opens it. He's a teacher at school. Afterward Ana won't remember what she thought or felt when she watches Benji wrap his body around the man's and kiss him.

It's easy to blame Ana for everything she does now. She's in pain, but perhaps everyone is. She's never felt more alone, and loneliness drives everyone to make bad decisions, but perhaps none more than sixteen-year-olds. She pulls out her phone and takes pictures of Benji and the teacher. Then she posts the photographs online.

And all hell breaks loose.

BANG!

We always speak of secrets as if they're personal possessions. 'My' secret. But they're that only for as long as they remain out of other people's reach. We can't *almost* lose them – just altogether or not at all. As soon as they slip out into the world, they become an earthquake, an avalanche, a tsunami. It may take only a single rash comment, a fleeting thought, or some photographs posted online by someone with a wounded heart, but that sets the stones rolling and the snow loses its grip and the wall of water becomes insurmountable before we realize how it happened, and from then on it's impossible to hold everything back. Like capturing the scent of July and trying to hold it in your cupped hands. Everyone knows now. Everyone knows what no one was supposed to know.

Benji is woken up by it.

BANG! One single bang, but so hard that the walls of the cabin shake. Then silence. The teacher rolls over sleepily in bed, but Benji is already out of the bedroom, crouching down as he heads towards the door. He doesn't know why, but afterward he will remember that he was already filled with dread. He knew this was idiotic when he first arrived, when they kissed in the doorway.

One day he'll figure out that it was because he was in love. That's why he wasn't more cautious. He opens the door of the cabin, peers out, but whoever is waiting in the darkness doesn't make him or herself known. He's on the point of turning and going back inside when he sees where the noise came from.

Bang.

Like the sound of a puck hitting a wall or a heart thudding against a rib cage or a knife being embedded in the wood of a cabin door on a campsite. A plain piece of paper; three letters; the one in the middle is 'A,' and the triangle at the top of the letter is where the knife has been driven through into the wood.

FAG

Ana wanders around in the forest as if she were in a fever. The snow is falling fast, early, and deep this year even for this part of the country: an autumn storm is on its way in. It's so easy to underestimate the power of the cold, how quickly it can kill you. It's a soft-spoken murderer whispering that you can sit down and rest for a while if you're tired. Tricking you into thinking you're sweating, encouraging you to take your clothes off. Snow and freezing temperatures can summon up the same hallucinations as blazing sun in a desert.

Ana knows all that because she's more at home in the forest than the town. More squirrel than human, as Maya usually teases her. When Ana is among trees, she leaves reality behind, time stops, and what happens here could never affect life in town. That's what she's always liked to imagine, and that's why the full impact of what the hell she's just done doesn't hit her until she's almost home. Only when she reaches the door of her dad's house does the panic hit her, hard and brutal, and her chest hurts so much that she's left short of breath. It's so easy to think that what we post online is like raising your voice in a living room when it's actually more like shouting from the rooftops. Our fantasy worlds always have consequences for other people's realities.

Ana pulls out her phone and deletes the pictures of Benji and the teacher, but it's too late. She's already spread their secret like ash across the sea, and it can never be taken back.

Our spontaneous reactions are rarely our proudest moments. It's said that a person's first thought is the most honest, but that often isn't true. It's often just the most stupid. Why else would we have afterthoughts?

Peter bangs on the door of the Bearskin early in the morning. Ramona opens a window in the apartment upstairs, wrapped in a dressing gown and a lot of anger.

'You'd better hope the bar's on fire, lad! Waking decent folk at this time of day!'

But she relents because Peter was a boy, too, once upon a time. She called him so many times to come and take his drunk father home that Peter himself has hardly touched a drop since. His whole life has been shaped by the fact that he tries to mend everything. Make everyone happy. Hide other people's mistakes. Take responsibility. He confesses, 'There's going to be a press conference, Ramona. The factory's getting new owners, foreigners, they're the club's "mysterious sponsor" that everyone's been talking about. And I'm going to have to stand there and tell the reporters I'm going to get rid of the standing area and . . . get rid of the hooligans.'

It's possible that Ramona is shocked, but if she is she doesn't let it show. She lights a cigarette. 'What's that got to do with me?'

Peter clears his throat. 'They're going to let me handpick one board member. Anyone I like.'

'I'm sure Tails will be excellent,' Ramona snorts.

'Tails would rather it was you. So would I,' Peter replies.

A little puff of smoke emerges from one of Ramona's nostrils, the only indication that she's surprised.

'Have you been hit in the head, lad? You know I . . . given what you want to do to Teemu and the boys? They're *my* boys! That standing area is – it's *their* damn club, too!'

Peter stands there straight-backed, even if his voice gives up. 'I'm doing everything I can for the good of the club. But I've been told that no one surrenders power voluntarily. So if I'm really going to try to convince myself that I'm doing this for unselfish motives, I need to put someone on the board who won't always agree with me. Someone who'll fight me.'

Ramona goes on smoking quietly. 'If we both fight for what we believe in, then one of us will be out of a job at the end of it.'

Peter nods. 'But if we both fight for the club's best, the club will win.'

Ramona ties her dressing gown tighter. Thinks for a long time. Then she frowns. 'Are you having breakfast?'

'What sort?' Peter asks.

Ramona grunts. 'I've probably got some coffee somewhere. Or whatever it is you teetotal types drink.'

That's how Ramona gets a seat on the board of Beartown Ice Hockey, but the two are interrupted before they have time to finish the discussion. Peter's phone rings first. It's Tails, asking 'Have you heard about Benjamin?' That's how Ramona finds out. She will bear the shame of her reaction for the rest of her life, as will Peter, because their very first thought is, 'Not this, too!'

Our spontaneous reaction is often our most stupid.

Finding out the truth about people is like a fire, destructive and indiscriminate. The truth about Benji burns through Beartown and Hed, and everyone who has ever had the slightest reason to be jealous of him or dislike him can see a crack in his armour now. They stick their knives in as hard as they can, every last one of them.

Few people would have dared to say anything to Benji face-to-face, so they do what people always do: talk about him, not with him. He needs to be dehumanized, turned into an object. There are a thousand ways of doing that, but there's none simpler than the one we almost always use: taking his name away from him.

So when 'the truth' spreads, people don't write 'Benjamin' or 'Benji' on their phones or computers. They write 'the hockey player.' Or 'the school pupil.' Or 'the young man.' Or 'the queer.'

Some will later claim that they don't hate homosexuals, they just hate Benji. Many of them will claim that 'We were just surprised that he, of all people . . .' Some will suggest that, 'If there'd been any sort of . . . sign . . . it might have been handled better.'

Some will offer complex cultural analysis suggesting that the world of sports, and the hockey world in particular, symbolizes such deeply engrained masculine ideals that the shock is greater there. Others will claim that the reactions were nowhere near as strong as 'the media' would like to think. That it's all been exaggerated.

One voice might say, 'Obviously, no one has anything against them'; another will add, 'You just don't want the town to . . . be full of them.' A few more will mutter, 'Maybe it would be best if he moved, for his own sake, because there isn't much for him here, is there? Better for him to go to a big city. For his sake, obviously. Not that I've got anything against them. Not at all. But . . . you know.'

Some of the jokes online are probably just that, jokes – that will be the excuse. 'I always knew, my mum made me a meringue birthday cake when I was at primary school, and Benji only ate the bananas!' Others are more insinuating: 'Wonder what he and Kevin got up to in the locker room when the others had all gone home?'

Everything that pours in after that is just more in the same vein. Text messages from pay-as-you-go cell phones and anonymous comments online: 'Fag.' 'Queer.' 'Homo.' 'Poof.' 'Disgusting!' 'Its not natural your sick!' 'We always knew!' 'No homos in Beartown!' 'We're going to find you and slice off your tattoo! The bear isn't some gay symbol!' 'No rapists or queers in Beartown!' 'You're sick, just like Kevin!' 'Hope you get AIDS!' 'Hope you die!' 'Move away from here if you want to live!' 'Next time the knife will end up in you, not the door!'

*

Maya is sitting at home in front of her computer. She's reading everything the bastards are writing about Benji and remembers everything they've written about her. Nothing changes, everything just starts again. Maya's dad used to listen to an old record where a guy sang about everything having cracks in it, because that's how the light gets in. Maya looks at the pictures of Benji and the teacher over and over again, but it's not Benji and the teacher she's looking at. Back in the summer, when she was on the island with Ana, Maya played music on Ana's phone, something with guitars and sad singing, and Ana yelled, 'No junkie music on my island!' and Maya giggled as she held the phone out of reach and yelled, 'No bleep-bleep music in the forest, it's environmental pollution!' Ana tried to snatch her phone back. Maya jumped out of the way but ended up dropping it and it hit a rock. The glass of the camera lens cracked, not much but just enough so that all of Ana's pictures from then on have a little line up in one corner.

Maya expected Ana to be angry, but she just laughed and said, 'Now I'm going to see that crack in every photo I take, so you're going to be in all my pictures from now on, you idiot!'

Maya loved her best friend for that, but now she sits alone in front of her computer, looking at the pictures of Benji and the teacher over and over again, and all she can see is that little line up in the top corner. The same line in every picture.

A tiny, almost invisible crack. Where all the darkness gets out.

Long afterward none of us will be able to prove exactly who said what or where the different photographs that ended up online actually came from. But everyone has the chance to see the pictures of Benji kissing the teacher. A lot of people don't care, but they're silent, so only the others are heard. And that will be their excuse: they *care*, that's all. About the town, about the hockey team, about Benjamin himself. They care about the school. They care about *the children*.

A group of parents phone the headmaster, demanding a

meeting. Maggan Lyt, William's mother, is one of them. She's on the parent-teacher association, she's just doing her job, it's 'nothing personal.' As she points out at the meeting, 'We don't harbour any ill will to anyone, we're just concerned parents.' But she demands that obviously the teacher must be dismissed. Not because he's . . . different, of course not! But we can't tolerate the fact that he's had sexual relations with a pupil! Not after everything that's happened! First the rape, and now this? It doesn't really make any difference if it's a boy or a girl, surely everyone should be treated equally?

Things are always connected – when it suits us.

'How will we be able to feel safe with this teacher educating our children now that we are aware of his . . . agenda?' one parent wonders.

When the headmaster asks exactly what the parent means by 'agenda,' Maggan Lyt snaps, 'You know exactly what we mean!'

'What about *this*, then?' another parent cries, tossing a sheet of paper onto the headmaster's desk.

'It was on a noticeboard in the corridor! So that teacher, Jeanette, is going to teach pupils how to *fight*?' Maggan Lyt adds.

'It's . . . martial arts . . . she's offering the pupils training in –' the headmaster says but is predictably interrupted: 'Violence! Training in *violence*! So one teacher has sexual relationships with his pupils, and another wants to fight with them! What sort of school are you running here, exactly?'

Then Maggan Lyt says, 'I'm going to call the council!'

And she does. The first councillor who answers is Richard Theo.

Maya bangs on the door of Ana's house so hard that the dogs start barking, as if she wants to tear the building apart. Ana opens the door, pale and lifeless, crushed and full of self-loathing. But Maya is too angry to stop her fury, she just yells, 'YOU TOOK THOSE PICTURES! HOW COULD YOU DO THAT?'

Ana is panting hysterically, sobbing and sniffing so hard she can barely get her words out. 'I wasn't . . . I kissed him, Maya! I *kissed* him! He could have said he was . . . he could have *said* something, because I just . . . I just thought he had a girlfriend, but he . . . I kissed him! I . . . if he'd only said he was . . .'

Maya doesn't let her finish; she just shakes her head and spits on the ground between herself and her best friend, and then she isn't that anymore. 'You're just like everyone else in this town, Ana. As soon as you don't get what you want, you think you have the right to hurt other people.'

Ana is crying so hard that she can't stand up. She collapses in the doorway. Maya doesn't catch her; she's already walking away.

Perhaps what everyone says is true; perhaps it isn't personal. Perhaps it's just the last straw for a few people who have long felt that they're living with their backs against the wall. Jobs are disappearing, the politicians are corrupt, the hospital is going to be closed down, and the factory is changing owners. Reporters show up here only when something negative happens, and all they ever want is to be able to depict the inhabitants as backward and prejudiced. But perhaps some people around here feel that there's just too much politics all at the same time. Too much change forced upon hardworking people who have already been through enough. Maybe it's nothing to do with Benji or the teacher or Elisabeth Zackell or anyone else. Perhaps the people posting online are just 'isolated malcontents.' Perhaps no one meant any harm. 'In the heat of the action people have a tendency to overreact, that's all.' Perhaps we'll explain it by saying that there were too many things going on at once, it was a complex issue, and people have to be allowed to respond emotionally.

It's always the aggressors' feelings we have to defend. As if they're the ones who need our understanding.

The news that a teacher at the school has had 'a long-term relationship with a pupil' and 'is now suspended while the matter is investigated' quickly reaches the local paper. At first the comments section is cautious, but soon the questions start: 'Do you think this is a coincidence, then?? First that coach, and now a teacher??' No one says 'woman,' no one says 'homosexual.' Everyone says 'people like that,' 'like them.' Someone writes, 'And you're not allowed to complain either, because then you're made out to be the bad guy! But surely we have to be allowed to react, for the sake of the *children*? What sort of town do we want to live in? Why do we have to be some sort of experiment for everything?'

Most of them don't even mention Benji. That makes it easier. But a picture appears. The first time it is published is from an anonymous online account, no one remembers where, and as soon as it starts to spread, the account is deleted. No one asks where the picture came from; rumours spread out in all directions, but it doesn't matter. The only thing that matters is what the picture shows.

It's a hockey helmet. It looks as though it's been photographed on a bench in a locker room, and on the side is a picture of the bear, the logo of Beartown Hockey. A rainbow has been painted around it. Someone writes, anonymously, 'I think it looks great! I don't even like hockey, but I think we should take the opportunity to do something symbolic with the whole club to show our support! Like a political gesture, hand in hand with hockey!'

Then the picture spreads beyond Beartown, and a newspaper in a big city posts it on its website with the caption, 'Hockey player comes out as gay – this is his club's admirable response!'

By the time the reactions start to appear, Richard Theo has already closed his laptop. He's closed the window after letting out the last of the flies; it's cold out there, and they'll soon freeze to death. But they've had their summer, served their purpose.

As Richard Theo is leaving his office, someone is already writing online, 'Beartown isn't going to become some bullshit rainbow town, and Beartown Ice Hockey isn't going to become some bullshit rainbow team! The Pack will never allow that to happen!'

★

When the image turns out to be a fake, manipulated using a common computer programme, reporters from all over the country start calling the general manager of Beartown Ice Hockey, asking, 'Why don't you want to show support for homosexual players? Why have you distanced yourselves from those helmets with the rainbow flag on them?'

Peter Andersson tries to explain, without knowing what he really wants to say. Everything is going so fast. In the end he doesn't dare answer his phone anymore.

But when the reporter from the local paper calls Richard Theo and asks what he thinks of all the 'turbulence' surrounding Beartown Ice Hockey, naturally Theo has a very simple answer: 'I don't think we should mix hockey and politics. Just let the guys play.'

That will be heard more and more often in coming days. 'Just let the guys play!' It will mean different things to different people.

Maya gets home to a house where the only sound is the gentle tapping of a computer mouse and keyboard. Leo is sitting in his room, so close to the screen that the world disappears, as usual. Maya is envious of his escape route.

'What are you doing?' she asks, ridiculously.

'Playing a game,' he replies.

She stands in the doorway for a few moments, opens her mouth as if to ask something, but nothing comes out. So she shuts the door and walks towards the kitchen. Perhaps he can hear from her footsteps that something's wrong, unless little brothers just know things that other people miss, because without taking his eyes from the computer he calls, 'Do you want to play?'

32

Then He Takes the Shotgun and Goes Out into the Forest

Hockey is the simplest sport in the world, if you're sitting in the stands. It's always so easy to say what everyone should have done when you know that what they actually did didn't work.

Peter heads to the rink with tunnel vision. His phone is still ringing, but he's stopped answering. He tries calling Benji, but Benji doesn't answer. He opens his email. It's an avalanche.

He slumps forward, blinded by a migraine, unable to breathe. For a few minutes he worries that he's having a stroke. He can still remember the terrible emails and text messages that appeared after Maya reported Kevin to the police. It's starting again. It's all happening again.

Most of them don't use the word itself, they use words such as 'distraction' and 'politics' instead. 'We just don't want any distractions or politics in the club so close to the game against Hed, Peter!' Everyone means well, obviously. No one has anything against Benji, of course. 'But for the boy's own sake, perhaps it's best if he has . . . a little break? You know how sensitive . . . some people . . . not *us*, but there are *others* who might react negatively, Peter! We're only thinking of the *boy's* best!' Naturally. 'Just let the guys play!' several correspondents urge.

Just not all the guys.

But one of the emails is different. It comes from one of the parents of the little league players, and there's a picture attached, taken in the

A-team's locker room, but it's not of Benji. It shows Elisabeth Zackell, who appears to be leaning forward and examining Bobo's genitals. It may have been a harmless joke when it happened, but someone on the A-team took a photograph. No one knows how the picture spread, but there's another email containing the same picture. Then another one appears. 'First teachers sleeping with their pupils, then teachers training their pupils to fight, and now THIS??!!!'

The emails that follow stick to the usual progression: First worried emails. Then hate-filled emails. Then threatening emails. Finally an anonymous email: 'If that bitch and that queer take part in one more Beartown training session, you're going to be in serious trouble!!!'

It's so easy to be wise in hindsight; hockey is so simple from the stands. If Peter hadn't had a daughter who had been depicted as the enemy of the entire hockey club back in the spring, he might have reacted better now. Or perhaps worse. But his instincts are heading in all different directions, so in the end he prints out the picture of Zackell and Bobo, finds the coach down on the ice, and shouts, 'Zackell! What the h—what's *this*?'

Zackell is standing on her own, shooting pucks, and she skates calmly over to the boards and looks at the picture. 'That's me. And that's Bobo. And that little thing is a penis.'

'But you . . . it's . . . what's . . .?'

Zackell taps her stick on the ice. Shrugs. 'You know how it is. Hockey teams test the boundaries when they get a new coach. It's between them and me.'

Peter is clutching his head as if it's cracked and he's glued it back together and is waiting for it to dry. 'But, Zackell . . . it isn't between you and them anymore. Someone's posted the picture online! The whole town is going –'

Zackell examines the tape on her stick. 'I'm a hockey coach. I'm not the mayor. The town's problems are the town's problems. In here we just play hockey.'

Peter groans. 'Society doesn't work like that, Zackell. People will interpret this as . . . they're not used to . . . first this business with Benji, and now this, with you and this . . .'

'Penis?' Zackell suggests helpfully.

Peter glares at her. 'We've received a threat! We have to cancel today's practice!'

Zackell doesn't seem to hear him, and asks instead, 'What's happening with Vidar? Our new goalie? Are you going to let him play?'

'Did you hear what I said? We've received a threat! Never mind about Vidar! We have to cancel practice!'

Zackell shrugs again. 'I heard. I'm not deaf.'

She goes back out onto the ice, as if he's finished. Then she calmly carries on firing pucks. Peter storms up to the office and calls the A-team players. They all answer apart from Benji. Peter explains the threat in the email. All the players understand. Not one of them stays at home.

When the practice begins, the team gathers on the ice in front of Zackell. She taps her stick on the ice and says, 'Have you heard that the club's received a threat?'

They nod. She clarifies, 'If I coach you and if Benjamin plays with us, apparently we're "going to be in serious trouble." So if you don't want to train today, I won't hold it against you.'

No one moves. A lot of shit has been said about this team, but they don't scare easily. Zackell nods. 'Well, then. I understand that there are a lot of . . . emotions right now. But we're a hockey team. We play hockey.'

The older players wait for her to demand to know who posted the picture of her and Bobo on the Internet. She doesn't even mention it. Perhaps that wins her some respect, because eventually one of them calls out, 'We mostly turned up for the beer!'

The laughter that follows is liberating. Even Bobo looks a little less embarrassed.

★

It's only words. Combinations of letters. How can they possibly hurt anyone?

Benji is standing in Adri's kennels; the dogs are playing in the snow around his feet. They don't care, and he wishes no one else did either. He doesn't want to change the world, doesn't want anyone to have to adapt themselves to him, he just wants to play hockey. Go into the locker room without it falling silent because nobody dares to mess around anymore. He just wants all the usual things: sticks and ice, a puck and two nets, the desire to win, to struggle. You against us, with everything we've got. But that's over now. Benji is no longer one of them.

Perhaps one day he'll find words for that feeling of being different. How physical it is. Exclusion is a form of exhaustion that eats its way into your skeleton. People who are like everyone else, who belong to the norm, the majority, can't possibly understand it. How can they?

Benji has heard all the arguments, he's sat next to adults in the stands and in buses on the way to tournaments, people who say, 'There are no homosexuals in ice hockey.' There were jokes, all the usual stuff, but that never really affected Benji. It was the little choices of vocabulary that everyone seemed to find obvious that cut deepest, when 'fag' was used as an insult. 'You play like fags!' 'Fag referee!' 'Damn fag coffee machine doesn't work!' Three little letters used to describe weakness, stupidity, anything that didn't function properly. Anything that was defective.

Naturally there were adults who never said the word. Some of them said other things instead. They didn't even think about it, but Benji stored up tiny splinters of conversations for years. 'They don't bother with hockey. How would that even work? With the locker room and everything? Are we going to have three different locker rooms, just in case?' The people saying these things were ordinary parents, kind and generous people who did all they could for their children's hockey team. They didn't vote for extremist parties, they didn't wish anyone dead, they'd never dream of being violent. They just said obvious, self-evident things such as, 'People like that probably don't feel at home in hockey, they probably like other things. You have to bear in mind that hockey's a tough sport!' Sometimes they said it straight out: 'Hockey's a sport for men!' They said 'men,' but even as a small boy Benji would stand alongside in silence, knowing that what they actually meant was 'real men.'

It's only words. Only letters. Only a human being.

Benji doesn't train with his team today, because he knows he's no longer one of them. He doesn't know who he ought to be instead. And he doesn't know if he wants that.

When the practice starts, Sune is sitting in the stands. Peter sinks down beside him.

'Have you reported the threat to the police?' Sune asks.

'They don't know if it's serious or not. Could just be some kid.'

'Try not to worry.'

'I don't know what to do,' Peter admits impotently.

Sune doesn't offer any comfort, he never does. He demands that people take responsibility. 'You don't know *what* to do, or what you *ought* to do?'

Peter sighs. 'You know what I mean. It's a messy situation to try to handle . . . Zackell and the team . . .'

Sune nods towards the ice. 'They chose to come. Let the guys play.'

'What about Benjamin, then? How am I going to help him?'

Sune adjusts the fold of his T-shirt over his stomach. 'You can start by giving up the idea that he needs help. It's everyone else who needs help.'

Peter snaps back, hurt: 'Don't come here and try to tell me that I'm prej—'

Sune snorts. 'Why are you still involved in this sport, Peter?'

Peter takes a deep breath. 'I don't know how to stop.'

Sune nods.

'I tell myself that I'm still here because the ice is the only place I know where everyone is equal. Out there it doesn't matter who you are. All that matters is if you can play.'

'There may be equality on the ice. But the same thing doesn't apply to the sport in general, Peter.'

'No. And that's our fault. Yours and mine and everyone else's.' Peter throws his arms out. 'But what are we supposed to do?'

Sune raises an eyebrow. 'We see to it that the next kid who says he's different in some way is met with a shrug of the shoulders. We need to say, "So what? That doesn't matter, does it?" And one day perhaps there won't be homosexual hockey players and female coaches. Just hockey players and coaches.'

'The community isn't that simple,' Peter says.

'The community? We are the community!' Sune replies.

Peter rubs his eyes. 'Please, Sune . . . I've had reporters calling me for hours now . . . I . . . hell, maybe they're right. Maybe we ought to do something symbolic for Benjamin. If we painted our helmets . . . would that help?'

Sune leans back in his seat. 'Do you think that's what Benjamin wants? He chose not to tell anyone. Some lowlife gave it away. I'm sure loads of journalists would like to make him into some sort of figurehead now, and loads of nutters on the other side will want to vent all their hatred on him. And neither side knows a damn thing about hockey. They'll turn every game he plays in into a battle between their conflicting agendas, a political circus, and that may be what he's most frightened of: becoming a burden to the team. A distraction.'

Peter snaps back in frustration, 'So what do you think Benjamin wants us to do, then?'

'Nothing.'

'We have to do something!'

'Do you care about his sexuality? Does it change the way you look at him?'

'Of course not!'

271

Sune pats Peter on the shoulder. 'I'm a silly old man, Peter. I don't always know what's right and what's wrong. But Benjamin has been the cause of a lot of crap outside this ice rink over the years, fighting and smoking dope and God knows what else. But he's a damn good player, so you and everyone else has said, every time, "That has nothing to do with hockey." So why should *this* have anything to do with hockey? Let the boy live his life. Don't force him to become a figurehead. If we're uncomfortable with his sexuality, then he's not the one with the damn problem – we are!'

Peter flushes and swallows. 'I . . . I didn't mean . . .'

Sune scratches his remaining hair. 'Secrets weigh a person down. Can you imagine what it must have been like to carry around that secret about yourself your whole life? Hockey was his refuge. The ice may have been the only place where he felt just the same as everyone else. Don't take that away from him.'

'So what do I do?'

'Let him earn his place in the team on the strength of his hockey alone, just like everyone else. He's going to be treated differently everywhere else now. Don't let that happen to him here.'

Peter says nothing for a long time. Then he says, 'You've always said we should be "more than just a hockey club," Sune. Isn't that exactly what we should be now?'

Sune considers this. Eventually he whispers sadly, 'Maybe. Like I said, Peter, I'm an old man. I don't know what the hell I'm saying half the time.'

Benji isn't his father. He doesn't do what Alain Ovich did. He doesn't leave any gifts, doesn't give any signs or symbols.

His mum and sisters call him; they've read the same things online as everyone else, and they're worried. So he says everything's okay. He's good at that. He goes to Adri's kennels, because one of the dogs was ill last night; Adri got home late from the vet's and is still asleep.

Benji closes the door downstairs just hard enough to wake his sister from her slumber, and she falls asleep again straight away.

Adri only ever sleeps really deeply if she knows her little brother is home, otherwise it's just anxious dozing. Benji takes the garbage out, folds his bedsheets, and puts them neatly into a cupboard the way she's always nagging at him to do. Then he goes out to see the dogs. They're also asleep when he goes silently upstairs, knowing exactly which floorboards creak and which ones don't, like a boy taking part in the world's slowest game of hopscotch.

He very carefully slides his hand under Adri's pillow and takes the key. He kisses his sister's forehead for the last time.

Then he takes the shotgun and goes out into the forest.

After practice, Zackell stands in the parking lot smoking a cigar. Peter comes outside, stops beside her, and asks, 'Do you really want Vidar on the team?'

She lets the smoke out through her nose. 'Yes.'

Peter groans. 'Hold an open tryout, then. Say that anyone who hasn't got a contract with another club can attend. If Vidar is good enough, he can play. But he only gets his place if his hockey's good enough, like everyone else!'

Peter opens the door to go back inside, but Zackell asks, 'Why are you so angry with Vidar? Is it normal to be that angry if someone shits on your desk?'

Peter suppresses his gag reflex at the thought of Vidar's visiting card. He ended up with shit between the keys on his computer keyboard, and that's not the sort of thing you get rid of easily, either from the keyboard or from your memory. But he shakes his head.

'Vidar's unreliable. A team has to be able to rely on its goalie, but Vidar is completely unpredictable. Egotistical. You can't build a team made up of egoists.'

'So why have you changed your mind?' Zackell asks.

Peter doesn't know what to say. So he replies honestly, 'I want this to be a club where we make people better. Maybe we can make Vidar a better person. Maybe ourselves, too.'

The snowflakes turn somersaults in the wind, and Peter is horrified that he has realized this too late. Benji might never come back. You can say a lot of things about Benjamin Ovich, but he was never an egoist.

It will be claimed that this happened to one person. It will be a lie. We will say, 'Things like this are no one's fault,' but of course they are. Deep down we will know the truth. It's plenty of people's fault. Ours.

33

Not Waking Up

Benji is deeper in the forest than ever when he finally stops. The snow is still falling, its flakes tentatively brushing his skin before melting with his body heat and trickling angrily through the hairs on his lower arms. The freezing temperature colours his cheeks, his fingers stiffen around the rifle, the breath from his mouth forms smaller and smaller clouds. In the end he isn't breathing at all.

There's a long period of silence. Then a single shot echoes between the trees.

In Beartown we bury those we love beneath our most beautiful trees. It's a child who finds the body, but the child doesn't walk calmly through Beartown the way Adri did when she found her father, Alain Ovich, all those years ago. This child is running.

Amat and Bobo are sitting in the locker room. They'll remember this as their last conversation, their last raucous laughter, before they found out that someone had died. It will feel as if they'll never really be able to laugh as loud ever again.

'What do girls find sexy?' Bobo asks.

He says it the way he says everything: as if his brain is a coffee machine that someone has forgotten to put a coffeepot under, so his thoughts drip straight onto the hot plate beneath and spray everywhere.

'How should I know?' Amat says helplessly.

It's not long since Bobo asked if it was true that contact lenses are made out of jellyfish. Another time he wondered, 'You know how it's supposed to be unlucky to leave your keys on the table? Okay, but what if someone borrows my keys and leaves them on a table when I'm not even there, do I still get the bad luck?' Back in the spring he wanted to know: 'How do you know if you've got a nice-looking dick?' At school the other day he asked Amat, 'How long should shorts be?' then almost immediately afterward, 'You know, in a vacuum, like in space, if you cry there . . . what happens to your tears?'

'I heard some girls in school say an actor was sexy because he had "a defined chin and high cheekbones." How do you know if you've got those?'

'I'm sure you have,' Amat says.

'You think?' Bobo says hopefully.

His face is as shapeless as an overboiled potato, but Amat still nods kindly.

'I'm sure you're sexy, Bobo.'

'Thanks,' Bobo says, clearly relieved, as if he can tick that off his list of things to worry about. Then he asks, 'Have you ever been anyone's best friend?'

Amat groans. 'Please, Bobo . . . yes . . . of course I've had a best friend.'

Bobo shakes his big head. 'No, I mean have you *been* someone's best friend? I've had lots of best friends, but I don't think I've ever been anyone else's best friend. Do you understand what I mean?'

Amat scratches his ear. 'Can I be honest? I hardly ever understand what the hell you're going on about.'

Bobo starts to laugh. So does Amat. The loudest, most uproarious laughter for a long time.

'You're never alone in the forest.' All the children around here learn that. Benji stops dead when he sees the animal appear, thirty feet away. Benji looks it right in the eye. He's hunted in these forests all his life, but this is the first time he's seen such a large bear.

Benji has been walking into the wind, it hasn't caught his scent. The bear is close enough to feel threatened, and Benji has no chance of running. All the children around here learn the same things when they're small: 'Don't run, don't scream, if the bear runs towards you, curl up on the ground and play dead, and cover your head with your backpack! Don't fight until you're sure you have no other choice!'

The rifle is shaking in Benji's hands; he shouldn't fire. The animal's heart and lungs are shielded by its powerful shoulders; only extremely skilled hunters stand any chance of shooting a bear and staying alive long enough to talk about it afterward. Benji ought to know better. But his heart is pounding, he hears his own voice roar from the depths, and then he fires into the air. Or directly at the bear, he doesn't remember. And it vanishes. It doesn't run away, it doesn't slope off into the forest, it just . . . vanishes. Benji stands in the snow, and the forest eats up the echo of the shot until nothing remains but the wind, and he isn't at all sure if he's dreaming. If there really was a bear, or if he imagined it, a genuine threat or an imaginary one. He goes over to where the bear ought to have been standing, but there are no tracks in the snow. Even so, he can still feel its stare, like when you wake up early in the morning and don't have to open your eyes to know that the person next to you is looking at you.

Benji is breathing hard. There's a sense of invincibility about deciding to die and then not going through with it. A sense of power over yourself. He walks home with a feeling that his body doesn't belong to him, without knowing who's going to inhabit it now.

But at least he goes home.

Amat and Bobo are still laughing. But Bobo stops abruptly, before Amat has time to realize what's happened. Bobo has always been told that he's a bit slow on the uptake, he knows all the jokes by heart: 'That boy couldn't pour water out of a boot if it had holes in the toes and the instructions under the heel' and 'Bobo's so stupid he can't piss his own name in the snow.' But that doesn't mean

277

his brain isn't busy; his mum always says that it just works in a different way from other people's.

So Bobo has been expecting this. Outside he may appear unfocused, but inside he has been preparing for this moment ever since his mum took him out into the forest and told him she was ill.

The child runs through Beartown, in through the door of the ice rink, gesticulating wildly at the people who ask where she's going. Some of them recognize her, it's Bobo's little sister. One of them may even have realized and whispered, 'Oh, no . . .'

When his little sister stands in the doorway of the locker room sobbing, 'She's not waking up, Bobo! Dad's gone to get a car, and Mum won't wake up even though I've tried shouting at her!' Bobo has already dealt with his own grief. His tears trickle into his little sister's hair, but mostly for her sake. She was brave enough to run through the whole town, but she's in pieces now, and there's no one she trusts as much as her big brother.

Only then does the girl feel safe enough in his arms to dare to shatter into a billion pieces. She will always run to Bobo when she feels sad, all her life, and he stands with his arms around her and knows that he has to be strong enough to bear that responsibility now.

Amat hugs them both, but Bobo doesn't feel it. He's already wondering about how he's going to find a tree beautiful enough for his mum to sleep under. That's when he becomes an adult.

Adri Ovich wakes up from a terrible dream. She fumbles in a daze under her pillow and feels her pulse throb in her temples when her fingers finally close around the key. She's breathing so hard that it hurts. She goes downstairs and finds her little brother sleeping on the sofa. The rifle is standing in the gun cabinet, as if nothing had ever happened.

She kisses him on the forehead. Sits on the floor beside him for hours. Can't quite seem to get beyond just waking up.

34

Violence Against a Horse on Official Service

In many years' time we may not know what to call this story. We will say it was a story about violence. About hate. About conflict and difference and communities that tore themselves apart. But that won't be true, at least not entirely.

It's also a different sort of story.

Vidar Rinnius is in his last year as a teenager. His psychologist's report suggests that he has 'a lack of impulse control,' but most people would probably expand that to say 'a complete lack.' He's always gotten into fights; sometimes he and his big brother Teemu tried to defend their mother, and sometimes they defended each other. And if there wasn't anyone to defend, they would fight with each other. The bit about impulse control is true, Vidar has never been able to stop himself. About the time that other people get an idea into their heads along the lines of 'I wonder what would happen if . . .' Vidar would already have done it. When Vidar was a boy, his coach once said that was what made him such a good goalie. 'You just don't know how to *not* stop those pucks!' Everyone says that Vidar's problem is that he 'doesn't think,' but the opposite is actually the case. He can't stop thinking.

He was twelve years old when he realized that he was alone. He went to another town with his brother and his brother's friends when the Beartown A-team was playing an away game there. After the game, Teemu told Vidar to go to McDonald's and wait there, because he had a feeling there was going to be trouble. Vidar was sitting there eating when a group of opposing fans burst in through the doors. Teemu and the Pack had been stopped by the police, and Vidar was sitting alone in a corner dressed in the wrong colours, and the opposing fans knew who he was. During the game they had seen the twelve-year-old yelling insults about their club and giving them the finger. 'You're not so tough without your brother, are you?' they cried as they attacked him.

That was when Vidar realized he was on his own. Everyone is. We are born alone, die alone, and fight alone. So Vidar fought. He thought he was going to die, he watched adults leave the fast-food restaurant, he might have been a child but no one tried to help him. The staff ran to the kitchen, he didn't know how many enemies there were, all he knew was that he didn't stand a chance. He lashed out anyway. Then Spider appeared out of nowhere, Vidar's memory has him jumping through a window, but who knows? Spider defended him as if they were family, and after that they were. That was when Vidar realized that you don't have to be alone. Not all the time. Not if you have a pack.

When Vidar was sixteen, they were at another away game. Spider had been found guilty of a number of minor offences and was on probation. He and Vidar waited in a park while the rest of the Pack moved on, because Spider also had a head that was never quiet, and just like Vidar he had realized that everything slowed down sometimes if you took the right drugs. The police came around the corner on horseback, saw the two suspected hooligans, and Spider panicked and ran. He had drugs on him, as did Vidar. Vidar could have outrun Spider, but Spider was on probation and Vidar lacked impulse control. He couldn't help himself from protecting someone he loved.

So while Spider ran off in one direction, Vidar ran in the other – towards the police. The charges filed against him afterward were numerous and varied, Vidar can't even remember them all. Possession of narcotics was one, he knows that much. Violently resisting a public official was another, he thinks. Then there was something about his hitting a police horse. Vidar has never really liked horses.

Violence against a horse on official service? How long do they lock you up for that?

That was how he ended up in the clinic, and that was where he met Baloo. He worked there and was called that because he was the same size and had the same posture as the bear in *The Jungle Book*. When they became friends, it was fairly natural that the sinewy, dark-haired Vidar would be given the nickname Mowgli. Perhaps that helped him, getting a different name. Perhaps he was able to pretend to be a different person then.

Baloo didn't say much, but he realized that Vidar had a lot of energy that needed a positive outlet if it wasn't to explode in a negative way. When he found out that the boy played hockey, he borrowed some goalie's gear, and every time the fuses in Vidar's head were threatening to explode in impulsive outbursts of rage about anything at all, Baloo would suggest calmly, 'Okay, Mowgli, let's go to the basement.' There was a storeroom in the basement, large enough for Baloo to stand by one wall throwing tennis balls as hard as he could towards Vidar at the other end. After a month or so Baloo laid a new floor, smooth enough to feel like ice, so he could fire real hockey pucks.

They played as often as they could; sometimes Baloo even broke the rules and played with Vidar at night. He did it because he hoped it would help Vidar to learn not to break all the other rules. Definitions of 'care' and 'punishment' are always changing, and Baloo did what he could to give them a defined shape. He rarely said much, but he was the one who protested loudest when Vidar was released. 'He's not ready!' Baloo declared. No one cared. Vidar had a powerful friend somewhere, someone who had made sure that all the documentation that was required suddenly materialized. So when Vidar left the unit Baloo just whispered sadly to him, 'Stay on the ice, Mowgli. Concentrate on hockey.'

Maya and Leo are sitting at the computer, and in her memory it will feel as though they spent several days playing. She holds the words inside her for as long as she can, but in the end she can't help saying,

'Don't fight for my sake again. I know you love me, but don't fight for my sake. Fight for other things if you must. But not for me.'

'Okay,' her little brother promises.

They don't say much after that. But sometimes Leo gets something wrong and is so angry that he hits himself in the thigh and yells *'Idiot!'* and then Maya laughs so loudly that her throat starts to hurt. A bit like old times for a short while. Simple.

But then Maya gets something right in the game and even Leo is impressed, so he turns to give her a high five. She doesn't react in time, and his hand hits her shoulder instead.

Maya jumps so hard that she knocks her chair over, as if he'd burned her. She stands there gasping, eyes wide open, and curses herself and tries to pretend it was nothing. But Leo has already understood. Sometimes little brothers do that. Hardly anyone has touched Maya since the rape. It doesn't matter that Leo is her brother; fear isn't logical, the body reacts independently of the brain.

Leo switches the computer off. 'Get your jacket,' he says sternly.

'Why?' Maya wonders sheepishly.

'I'm going to show you something.'

When Vidar walks out from the unit, Teemu, Woody, and Spider are waiting outside in a car. Teemu has to give Spider a shove to get him to stop hugging Vidar. But he will never set foot in the apartment he has been given by the council's housing association.

'I have to live at home. I have to help you count,' he tells his brother.

Teemu kisses him on the head.

The first thing Vidar wants to talk about? Beartown Ice Hockey! What does the team look like? What players have we got this year? Are we going to beat Hed? He's the team's keenest fan and — after his mum's kitchen — the place he's missed most is the standing area in the rink. Teemu can't stop patting his younger brother on the shoulder and doesn't even tell Vidar that he won't need his place in the stand this year, that he's going to get a chance to play instead. Teemu doesn't say anything because he doesn't want to make his brother nervous, and for a few short minutes his own happiness is pure and uncomplicated. He doesn't want to spoil that.

Then Vidar asks about Benji Ovich. The last time the guys talked to Vidar, they told him that the new coach had made Ovich team captain, and they had been ecstatic at the time, because they regarded Benji as one of them. A Beartown kid who stood tall, took one hit, and meted out three in response. But when Vidar mentions his name both Spider and Woody fall silent. Their eyes harden, their words are worse.

'We've found out something about him . . .'

Vidar listens. The guys can't bring themselves to use Benji's name; they talk as if he'd died. Perhaps he has, at least in part, the person they thought he was. He's no longer one of them.

Vidar may be unlike most of the members of the Pack because he doesn't care who the hell anyone sleeps with, he never has. But the men in the black jackets aren't talking about sexuality, Vidar knows that, they're talking about trust and loyalty. Benji has pretended to be something he isn't. He's a fake, he can't be trusted, and Spider and Woody think he's shamed the Pack.

'We had his back, and all the time he wanted to screw us up the ass!' Spider snaps.

Vidar says nothing. When he was twelve or thirteen, just after Spider had fought for him in McDonald's, Vidar asked, 'Are we hooligans?' Spider shook his head seriously and replied, 'No. We're soldiers. I stand up for you, and you stand up for me. We haven't got anything if we can't trust each other a thousand percent. Get it?' Vidar got it. The members of the Pack have held together all their lives, and you don't build up that sort of friendship without complex sacrifices.

They have different reasons to hate Benji. Some are disgusted, and some feel betrayed; some are just worried about what opposing fans are going to sing about them now. Some have the bear tattooed on their necks, and how much do you have to love something to do that? So Vidar says nothing. He's just glad to be going home, that everything will be going back to normal.

And when Teemu leans forward and whispers, 'The new coach is holding an open A-team tryout for you. If you're good enough, you'll be allowed to play!' Vidar's joy sings so loudly inside his head that there's no room for him to think about anything else.

It's only sports.

The dogs at the kennels start to bark in the distance as the siblings approach, but Adri comes out blearily and quiets them down. Leo and Maya stop, alarmed.

'Is Jeanette here? Our teacher at school . . . she's supposed to have a martial arts club . . . is it here?' Leo asks.

' "Club" might be a bit optimistic. But she's in the barn.' Adri chuckles and yawns as she scratches her wire-wool hair.

Leo nods but doesn't move, hands in pockets but staring with interest at the dogs. 'What breed are they?'

Adri frowns, looks from Leo to Maya, tries to figure out what they're doing here. Perhaps she realizes, because she, too, has sisters. So she asks, 'Do you like dogs?'

Leo nods. 'Yes. But Mum and Dad won't let me have one.'

'Do you want to help me feed them?' Adri asks.

'*Yes!*' Leo exclaims, looking happier than a puppy with two tails.

Adri looks warmly at Maya. 'Jeanette's in the barn, you'll find her there.'

So Maya walks into the barn alone. Jeanette is practicing with a sandbag and stops midmovement, trying not to look surprised. Maya looks as though she's already regretting her decision to come. Jeanette wipes the sweat from her brow and asks, 'So you want to try martial arts?'

Maya rubs her palms together. 'I don't really know what's involved. My brother kind of dragged me here.'

'Why?' Jeanette wonders.

'Because he's worried I might hurt someone.'

'Who?'

Maya cracks as she admits, 'Me.'

So where do you start? Jeanette looks at the girl and eventually chooses the easiest option: she sits down on the mat. After an eternity Maya sits down opposite her, a foot away. Jeanette moves closer, the girl flinches, so she stops. She explains gently, 'You'll hear people say that martial arts is violent. But to me it's about love. Trust. Because if you and I are going to practice together, we have to trust each other. Because we borrow each other's bodies.'

When Jeanette reaches out her hand and touches her, it's the first time since Kevin that Maya has been touched by anyone except Ana without flinching. When Jeanette shows her how to wrestle, how to take a grip and how to get out of it, Maya has to learn to be held without panicking. On one occasion she does panic, throws her head back, and hits Jeanette in the face.

'It's okay,' Jeanette says, not bothered by the blood on her lip and chin.

Maya looks at the clock on the wall. They've been wrestling for an hour, free from thought, and she's sweating so much that if her eyes are streaming she doesn't even know it herself.

'I'm just . . . I'm so fucking terrified sometimes that it's never going to be okay,' she pants.

Jeanette doesn't know how to reply, either as a teacher or as a human being, so she says the only thing she can think to say as a coach: 'Are you tired?'

'No.'

'Then let's go again!'

Maya doesn't heal inside that barn. She doesn't build a time machine, she doesn't change the past, she isn't blessed with memory loss. But she will come back here every day and learn martial arts, and one day soon she will be standing in the line at the supermarket when a stranger accidentally brushes past her. And she won't flinch. It's the greatest of all small events, and no one understands. But she will walk home from the store that day as if she were on her way somewhere. That evening she will come back to train some more. And the next day.

It's only sports.

Ana is sitting high up in a tree, not far from the kennels. She sees Maya and Leo walk home through the forest. She's been following them, she doesn't know why, just wants to be close to Maya somehow. Everything feels far too cold without her.

They're only a few feet apart when Maya passes beneath her on the ground. Ana could have called something, climbed down and begged and pleaded with her best friend to forgive her. But this isn't that sort of story. So Ana sits where she is, high above, and watches her friend walk off.

The next day Vidar takes the bus to school. Plenty of people know who he is, so no one dares to sit next to him. Not until a girl a few years younger gets on at a stop on the outskirts of the Heights. She has scruffy hair and sad eyes, and her name is Ana.

The first thing Vidar notices is how beautiful her ankles are, as if they weren't meant for floors but for running through forests and over rocks. The first thing Ana notices is Vidar's black hair, so thin that it hangs over the skin of his face like raindrops on a windowpane.

In many years' time we might say this was a story about violence. But that won't be true, at least not entirely.

It's also a love story.

35

But Only if You're the Best

There's going to be a press conference in Beartown. It's the worst possible timing for some people, when the whole town feels like it's on its way towards imploding from a hundred different conflicts, but of course it's the best possible timing for other people. Richard Theo, for instance.

The representatives of the factory's new owners fly in from London; the local paper photographs them cheerfully shaking hands with the Spanish-home-owning politician in front of the factory. Peter Andersson stands dutifully alongside; his voice is unsteady and his eyes are fixed on the tarmac, but he promises to 'get to grips with hooliganism.'

The Spanish-home-owning politician is so proud that his shirt is practically bursting. He starts the press conference by mentioning his esteemed and modest colleague, Richard Theo: 'He deserves our thanks for his great service to the district. Without Richard's contacts and hard work over the course of several months, this deal couldn't have been concluded!' The Spanish-home-owning politician goes on to describe, rather less modestly, his own involvement in the deal. Taxpayers will benefit enormously, he explains, and the most important thing: 'Jobs in Beartown have been saved!'

When the female politician at his side suddenly opens her mouth, the Spanish-home-owning politician is so taken aback that he doesn't have time to react at first. She says, 'And not just in Beartown, of course. In collaboration with the factory's new owners we have reached an agreement in which the workforce in Hed will also be prioritized! That's one of the conditions: if the council is to support the factory financially, the *entire* council district needs to benefit!'

The journalists take notes and photographs, film the press conference. The Spanish-home-owning politician stares at the woman, and she meets his gaze. He's powerless, because what can he say? That he's not thinking of giving Hed any jobs? He'll be facing elections soon. He's shaking with rage, and his smile for the cameras is strained, but when he's asked about the jobs, he is forced to say, 'Any responsible policy obviously has to involve . . . the whole district.' He is standing slightly hunched as he says this, whereas the female politician feels herself grow several inches taller.

Early one morning in a few months' time, an envelope will be lying on the step outside her front door, and the documents inside will show how the Spanish-home-owning politician has been involved in undeclared property speculation in Spain. It will, admittedly, turn out that the Spanish-home-owning politician is entirely innocent, but Richard Theo doesn't need evidence, just doubt. The headlines about 'dodgy deals' will be big; the notification of his innocence will be confined to a few modest lines on the back pages of the local paper. The Spanish-home-owning politician's political career will already be over by then, after his party colleagues agree unanimously that 'the party can't afford any scandals.' He will be replaced by a female colleague who appears to have plenty of enemies in Beartown but even more friends in Hed.

Benji doesn't turn up for practices with the team. He doesn't call, he doesn't answer when anyone calls him. But late one evening when most of the lights in the rink are out and the locker rooms are empty, he is standing alone on the ice wearing jeans and skates, with a stick in his hand. He's come here to shoot some pucks, the way he's done a million times before, and to see if it still feels the same. If it can be the way it used to be. But his gaze has been caught by the image of the bear in the centre circle. Someone glides out onto the ice and stops beside him. Elisabeth Zackell.

'Are you going to play in the game against Hed?' she asks with a complete lack of sentiment.

Benji swallows hesitantly, still staring at the bear. 'I don't want to be a . . . problem. For the team. I don't want them to feel that –'

'That's not what I asked. Are you playing or not?' Zackell asks.

Benji closes his eyes quickly, opens them slowly. 'I don't want to be a burden to the club.'

'Are you planning to have sex with anyone in the locker room?'

'What the . . .? What?'

Zackell shrugs. 'That's what people think, isn't it? That gays have a problem with discipline? If everyone starts having sex with each other in the locker room?'

Benji frowns. 'Where the hell have you heard that?'

'Are you planning to have sex with anyone in the locker room or not?'

'Like hell!'

Zackell shrugs again. 'So you're not a burden. Hockey is hockey. People can say what they like about you outside the rink, but in here it doesn't matter. If you're good, you're good. If you score goals, you score goals.'

Benji doesn't look convinced. 'People hate me. You as well. Maybe it's just too much for them, that you and I are both . . . you know. Maybe they could live with *one*, but two in the same team, that's . . . too much for people.'

Zackell sounds taken aback. 'What do you mean?'

Benji's eyebrows twitch. 'That you're . . . gay.'

'I'm not gay,' Zackell replies.

Benji stares at her. 'Everyone thinks you are.'

'People think a lot of things. They're far too obsessed with their emotions.'

Benji just gawps at her for a long time. Then he starts to laugh. He can't help it. 'Seriously, Zackell, you must see that everything would have been a hell of a lot easier for you in this town if you'd just told everyone that you're not –'

'Like you?'

'Yes.'

Zackell snorts. 'I don't think you have any obligation to tell everyone who you want to have sex with, Benjamin. I don't think I have, either.'

Benji scrapes the side of his skate against the ice. He thinks for a while before he asks, 'Do you ever wish you were a man?'

'Why would I?' Zackell wonders.

Benji looks at the bear on the ice. Tries to find the right words. 'So you didn't have to be a female hockey coach.'

Zackell shakes her head slowly, but for once she doesn't look entirely unmoved. 'My dad probably wished I was a boy sometimes.'

'Why?'

'Because he knew I'd always have to be twice as good as the men to be accepted. The same thing applies to you now. You'll be judged differently. The people who hate me might let me coach a team, but only if we win. And they'll let you play, but only if you're the best. Just being good isn't enough for you anymore.'

'It's fucking unfair,' Benji whispers.

'Unfairness is a far more natural state in the world than fairness,' Zackell says.

'Did your dad tell you that?'

'My mum.'

Benji swallows hard. 'I don't know if I can be captain.'

'Okay,' Zackell replies.

Then she turns and leaves him without any more words. As if any more were needed.

Benji is left standing alone at the centre circle. Eventually he fetches a stack of pucks from the boards, drops them onto the ice one after the other, for possibly the last time. This sport is never happy being just part of you, you have to sacrifice too much, there are too many things you know only if you've spent your whole life in here. How much your feet hurt when you skate for the first time after the summer. How unbelievably bad your gloves smell at the end of the season. The sound when you slam into the boards or fire a puck into the glass. How every rink has its own unique echo. How every stride sings when the stands are empty. How it feels to just play. How your heart beats.

Bang bang bang bang bang.

The first morning Ana sits next to Vidar, neither of them says anything. Ana is too weighed down by guilt and loss to speak. For the entirety of her childhood she has always gone to school with Maya, and the loneliness is a shock. She's sleeping a lot, because she's hoping she might wake up and realize that the mistake of her life was a dream. It never happens.

But the second morning she sits next to Vidar again, and just as the bus is approaching the school she glances at him. He pretends to be busy with his phone, but she sees him looking. He's the sort who can't help it.

'What are you playing?' she asks.

'What?' he mumbles, as if he's only just noticed her.

She's not that easily fooled. 'You heard.'

He starts to laugh; he does that when he's nervous. He will soon discover that when Ana gets nervous, she makes sarcastic jokes instead. If they spend their whole lives together, they might become the least suitable couple to encounter at a funeral: one who can't stop making jokes and one who can't stop giggling.

'*Minecraft*. I'm playing *Minecraft*,' he says.

'Are you seven or something?' Ana wonders.

He laughs. 'It helps me to not . . . I have trouble with my impulse control. My psychologist says *Minecraft* is good. I can concentrate better when I just play.'

The bus stops. The students spill out. Ana doesn't look away from him. 'You're Teemu Rinnius's little brother, aren't you? You were the one who was in prison?'

Vidar shrugs. 'It was more like a holiday camp.'

'What do you mean, about not being able to concentrate? Have you got some sort of syndrome or something?'

'I don't know.'

Ana smiles. 'You're just an ordinary nutter, then?'

Vidar laughs. 'Some people say I'm a psychopath! You shouldn't be talking to me!'

Ana looks him carefully up and down. His black hair is draped around his eyes. 'You look too kind to be a psychopath,' she says.

He frowns. 'Watch out! I might have a knife!'

She giggles. 'If you had a knife I wouldn't be scared of you, even if I was a loaf of bread.'

Vidar falls head over heels for her, because he's the type who doesn't know how to stop himself.

36

'Don't psychopaths go for walks, then?'

Elisabeth Zackell holds her open tryout early one morning. A handful of players show up, a few juniors who haven't got anywhere else to play because Beartown didn't manage to put together a team for them this year and some older players who have been let go by other clubs and are out of a contract. None of them is anywhere near good enough to get onto Zackell's team, but that doesn't matter; they're only there as extras so that the club can say it was an open session. Vidar is the only player of interest, but Zackell has to go and look for him when he doesn't appear on the ice. She finds him in the equipment storage room.

'Can I help you?' she asks.

'Have you got a saw?' Vidar asks.

'What for?' Zackell wonders.

Vidar holds up his goalie stick. 'This is too long!'

During all those nights he was locked in the unit and played with Baloo, Vidar needed to be able to fire the balls and pucks back to the other side of the basement after he'd saved Baloo's shots. He couldn't wear skates in the basement, so he sawed the top off his stick to make it the right length. He accidentally sawed off too much and it ended up too short, but he discovered that that meant he could make harder passes and more accurately, too. The only thing you have an excess of when you're locked up is time, so Vidar started to experiment with different lengths and types of tape on his stick. He ended up taping it without leaving a lump at the end, the way most goalies do, which made his grip better.

Zackell finds him a saw, without understanding what he's doing. But when Vidar is happy with his stick and goes out onto the ice, he stops a puck and fires it without any effort, sending it from one end of the ice to the other.

'Can you do that again?' Zackell asks.

Vidar nods. Zackell puts him in front of one net and goes and stands by the other one. 'Pass to me!' she calls.

So he does. Right across the whole rink, right to the blade of her stick. It might not sound like a big thing if you're not bothered about hockey, but Zackell knows that most goalies in Beartown's league couldn't get a puck to hit water even if they fell out of a boat. 'This guy will be our goalie when we haven't got the puck but an extra player when we have,' she thinks. And she can win that way.

'Get in goal,' she commands.

He obeys. She starts firing puck after puck, and she's a good shot, but he saves everything. She lets the other players in the open session have a go, but not one of them manages to score. She gets two of them to shoot at the same time, then three, from different angles. Vidar pretty much doesn't let anything past. His reflexes are remarkable.

Zackell looks around the stands. At the top, over in one corner, sits Peter Andersson. As far away as it's possible to get on the other side, in the standing area, is Teemu Rinnius. Spider and Woody are standing next to him. Teemu tries to hide how proud he is but fails. Spider and Woody don't even try.

Zackell turns to Vidar and calls, 'Take a break and have a drink!'

The other players stop shooting. Vidar takes off his helmet; his sweaty black hair is stuck to his face. He turns his back on Zackell and lifts his water bottle. So she takes aim and fires a slap shot that hits him hard right in the back. Vidar jumps and turns around, and Zackell immediately fires another shot that whistles past his unprotected head just a foot away.

Teemu yells '*No!*' from the stands, but Vidar doesn't hesitate, he's already set off towards Zackell at full speed. No one on the ice has time to realize what's happening, so if Teemu hadn't known his brother so well, Zackell might not have got out of the rink alive. Vidar throws himself at her, taking wild swings with his gloved hands, and Teemu sets off from the stands, wrenches open the door to the bench, and leaps over the boards. His boots slip on the ice, but he manages to grab hold of his brother and uses all his strength to wrestle him onto the ice and pin him down. Spider and Woody are a few steps behind, and it takes all three of them to stop Vidar from getting up and beating Zackell to death.

'ARE YOU COMPLETELY INSANE???!!!' Teemu yells at her, but the female coach isn't remotely frightened and is grinning from ear to ear.

'Can you promise that he'll show up for practices on time and he'll play every game?'

Vidar is still struggling frantically to pull free of his friends' iron grip. Teemu glares at Zackell. 'You could have killed him! He . . . *You* could have died! He could have killed *you*.'

Zackell nods delightedly. 'Exactly! Vidar doesn't give a damn about me being a woman, he was going to kill me anyway, wasn't he? To him I'm just a hockey coach. Can you promise that he'll show up on time to each practice?'

Teemu peers at her. She's obviously crazy. 'You mean he's got a place on the team?'

Zackell snorts. 'A place on the team? I'm building the whole team around him! I'm going to make him a professional!'

Teemu swallows hard and replies tersely, 'Okay. I promise he'll show up on time for practice.'

Zackell nods and leaves the ice at once. She's done here. The other players at the open session will merely receive a short message telling them that they're not good enough for her team. She's honest, fair, and unsparing. Just like the sport.

Out on the ice Vidar eventually calms down. He lies on his back, sweaty and exhausted. Teemu sits down next to him. Vidar turns to him skeptically and mutters, 'What the hell, bro, are you crying?'

'I'm not fucking crying,' Teemu snarls, and turns his face away.

'You look like you're —'

'BACK OFF!' Teemu yells, and hits Vidar's arm so hard that

his little brother curls up whimpering on the ice while Teemu gets to his feet and walks out of the rink.

Elisabeth Zackell bounces into Peter Andersson's office. 'Did you see the tryout?' she blurts out.

'Yes,' Peter says.

'Can he play?' Zackell asks.

'Can you control him?' Peter asks.

'No! That's the whole point!' Zackell says jubilantly.

She looks happy. It gives Peter a headache.

Outside in the parking lot there's an old Saab. Teemu comes out of the rink, lights a cigarette, walks alone towards the car, gets into the passenger seat, and closes the door behind him. When he's sure no one is watching, he leans his head on the dashboard and closes his eyes.

He's not crying.

Back off.

The next morning Ana sits next to Vidar on the bus again. He's playing *Minecraft*, because he has to concentrate so he doesn't get too nervous to dare to ask her, 'I'm going to be playing on the Beartown A-team. Do you want to come and watch?'

Ana sounds suspicious. 'I didn't know you played hockey. I thought you were a hooligan, like the others in the Pack.'

She says 'the Pack' without fear. No one else in this town does. Vidar's counterquestion is shy, almost hurt: 'Don't you like hooligans?'

She snorts. 'I don't like hockey players.'

He laughs. She's pretty good at making him laugh. But before the bus stops at the school he says seriously, 'The Pack aren't hooligans.'

'What are they, then?' Ana asks.

'Brothers. Every one of them is my brother. They stand up for me, and I stand up for them.'

She doesn't judge him for that. Who wouldn't want to have brothers?

Maya is driven to school by her mum. Kira doesn't ask why Ana doesn't go with her anymore, she's too happy that Maya lets her drive her all the way to school without feeling embarrassed. Just six months ago her daughter always asked to be let out a few hundred yards away so she could walk the last bit herself. But now Kira is allowed to drive all the way to the bus stop and her daughter leans over the seat, kisses her on the cheek, and says: 'Thanks! See you later!'

Those words are far too insignificant to topple a grown woman, but they mean the world if you're someone's mum. Kira drives away on a cloud.

Maya, on the other hand, walks into school alone. She fetches her books alone, sits in classes alone, eats lunch alone. It's her choice, because if she can't trust her best friend, who can she trust?

Ana walks into the school not far behind Maya. It causes a very particular sort of chill to have to see your best friend every day and know that she's no longer that. They used to part with a secret handshake that they came up with when they were children: fist up, fist down, palm, palm, butterfly, bent fingers, pistols, jazz hands, minirocket, explosion, ass to ass, 'outbitches.' Ana came up with the descriptions. At the end, after they banged their backsides together, she always threw her hands into the air and yelled, 'And Ana is *out*, bitches!'

Now Maya walks into school without even noticing that Ana is behind her. Ana hates herself, perhaps more for what she has done to Maya than for what she did to Benji, so this is her final act of love. To make herself invisible.

Maya disappears into the corridor. Ana stands motionless, broken. But Vidar reaches out his hand. 'Are you okay?'

Ana looks at him. There's something about him that makes her answer honestly, so she replies, 'No.'

He runs his fingers manically through his hair and mumbles, 'Do you want to get out of here?'

Ana smiles sadly. 'Where?'

Vidar shrugs. 'Don't know.'

Ana looks around in the corridor. She hates it. Hates herself here. So she asks, 'Do you want to go for a walk?'

'A walk?' Vidar repeats, as though it's a foreign word.

'Don't psychopaths go for walks, then?' Ana wonders.

He laughs. They leave the school and walk side by side through the forest for hours, and that's where Ana falls for him. For all his clumsy, jerky, nervous gestures. He falls for her because she's invincible and brittle at the same time, as if she were made of both eggshell and iron. He tries to kiss her, because he can't stop himself, and she kisses him back.

If they had lived their whole lives with each other, they would have become something remarkable together.

The headline in the local paper after the press conference reads 'New Jobs – But Half Earmarked for Workers from Hed!'

The article includes numerous quotes from politicians. Most are shocked when the reporter demands a response and try to give neutral answers, to avoid provoking either side. The only one who deviates from that line is of course Richard Theo. He manages to make his statement sound spontaneous, even though he's prepared it in minute detail. 'What do I think about the factory's quotas? I don't like any form of quota. I think that Beartown jobs should go to Beartown workers.' It's hardly soaring oratory, but it travels fast.

Within hours the slogan 'Beartown jobs for Beartown workers!' is being repeated not only online but in bars and around dinner tables. The next morning there is a note on the hood of the Spanish-home-owning politician's car.

To stop the note blowing away, the person delivering it has pinned it down with an axe. Notes can blow away so easily otherwise, when the wind changes direction.

Immediately after the press conference, Peter starts calling builders. They all answer, they are all available for work, until he tells them what the job is: demolishing the standing area in the arena. Suddenly some of them have no time after all, while others say they're 'not qualified to do that.' Some just hang up. Some spell it out in plain language: 'We've got families, for God's sake, Peter!' At one of the firms Peter calls, the phone is answered by a voice identifying itself as Woody. When Peter explains why he's calling, Woody laughs loudly. And derisively.

Later that day Kira finds a cardboard moving box outside the Andersson family home. Most people who opened it would have thought it was empty, but she knows better. She tips it slowly onto its side and hears the little metal cylinder roll across the bottom. She sees it glint in the light reflected from her children's bedroom windows.

A rifle cartridge.

37

What We're Capable Of

Most of us don't know what terrible things we're capable of. How can we, until someone pushes us far enough? Who has any idea how dangerous we can be until someone threatens our family?

Kira is standing hidden in the shadows. She's followed Teemu from the supermarket; he's carrying a bag of groceries in each hand, one mostly full of cigarettes. He goes into the Bearskin. When he comes out again, he's alone and the street is empty. Kira doesn't know what sort of demons take possession of her, but she suddenly finds the nerve to march forward.

'Teemu Rinnius!' she snarls, sounding more threatening than she feels.

He turns around. 'Yes?'

Kira walks up to him so close that she can feel his breath. She's holding a folded moving box. A window opens above the Bearskin, and an old woman peers out, but Kira is too agitated to notice.

'Do you know who I am?' Kira asks.

Teemu nods, his face five inches from hers. 'You're Peter Andersson's wife.'

Her head moves back, just a fraction, but her voice grows louder. 'I'm Leo Andersson and Maya Andersson's mother! And I'm a lawyer! So maybe I am afraid of you, just like everyone else, but you need to get one thing very clear. If you come after my family again, I'll come after *your* family!'

She throws the box on the ground between them. Teemu raises an eyebrow. 'Are you threatening me?'

Kira nods. 'You can be damn sure I am, Teemu Rinnius! And you can tell all the cowardly little lowlifes in your little "pack" that next time they leave a rifle cartridge on my drive, I'll put it in your head!'

Teemu doesn't answer, and his eyes aren't giving a thing away. Perhaps Kira should have been satisfied with that, but she's past the point where that's even possible. So she takes something out of her bag. Empty pill bottles. She holds them up mockingly in front of him.

'You lot came to my family's home, so I went over to yours, Teemu. This was in your mum's garbage bin. Classified medication. Does your mum have a prescription for drugs like this? Because if not, she's breaking the law. And above all, her supplier is breaking the law. And that's you, isn't it, Teemu? What do you think will happen when I come after you?'

Teemu blinks slowly, evidently fascinated. But when he takes a step towards Kira, she backs away. Because everyone does. His words are an order: 'Go away. Now.'

Kira lowers her head involuntarily. She'll end up cursing herself many times for doing this, but we don't know what we're capable of until someone pushes us far enough. She leaves the street, trying not to break into a run as she heads back to her car, and almost succeeds.

Up at the kennels Adri is feeding her dogs. There are no cars with their trunks full of liquor coming today. There won't be any hunters calling in for coffee, either. She doesn't know if it's because they don't want to or because they don't dare. It's never easy around here to know if people want to say something and are just not saying it or if they're not saying anything because they don't know what to say.

So Adri calls her friend Jeanette, who's still at school catching up on her grading. Throughout their childhood it was always Jeanette who called Adri and asked if she wanted to play, never the other way around. But now Adri asks, 'Do you want to come over and train?'

Jeanette goes at once. They lift weights and beat the punching bag until they can no longer lift their arms. Jeanette doesn't tell Adri that everything is going to be all right, because she doesn't

301

have a little brother and doesn't know if it ever will be all right. But she trains and trains for as long as Adri wants to continue, and when the road remains empty, with no sign of cars or hunters, Jeanette can't help thinking that may be just as well – she can see in Adri's eyes that if anyone shows up here and says the wrong thing about her brother, that person will have to be carried out.

Teemu is still standing outside the Bearskin, and the window on the first floor is still open. Ramona's voice carries down to him. 'Rumour has it that you left a black jacket for Leo Andersson in school, Teemu. But you gave Leo's dad a rifle cartridge. Where's the logic in that?'

Teemu sounds sure of himself, because he has a little brother he shares only the same mother with. 'Maybe we recognize that men don't have to become the bastards their fathers were.'

It's an excuse, Ramona is well aware of that as she stubs her cigarette out on the window ledge. 'If it was you who left that cartridge, then I don't actually know what to think about you.'

Teemu interrupts her in a tone that he never uses with anyone else, apologetic and shamefaced: 'It wasn't me. But I can't control every –'

Ramona interrupts him in turn, and her voice is anything but affectionate. 'Don't try that on me! You may not control everything your boys do, but you know damn well that *none* of them would do anything if you'd expressly forbidden it!'

'I –' Teemu begins, but Ramona cuts him off. 'You and I don't judge each other, Teemu. We never have. But children are the only people who don't have to take responsibility for anyone but themselves. The rest of us have to take responsibility for the things we cause to happen. You're a leader. People follow you. So frankly, if you can't take responsibility for the actions of your followers, that makes you nothing but a monster.'

Kira never mentions the rifle cartridge to Peter or the children, or anyone else for that matter. But when she gets back to the house

302

two of the neighbours, an old woman and an even older man, are sitting on tatty folding chairs in their driveway, wearing green T-shirts. Their front door is open, the light is on in the hall, Kira can see the old man's hunting rifle leaning against the wall inside. He's old and slow, and perhaps the rifle isn't even loaded, but it doesn't matter. The old woman nods to Kira and says, 'Go in and get some sleep, Kira. We thought we'd just sit here and watch the cars go by for a bit.'

The old man opens a thermos flask and mutters, 'There are rumours that a few moving companies have been given the wrong information and have been going to wrong addresses recently. That's not going to happen around here again.'

Small words. A small gesture. But that's all it takes to say that we live here, too. And nobody messes with us.

Teemu is standing thoughtfully outside the ice rink. Beartown is dark, and the only window still lit up is in Peter's office. What will a person do for his club? For his town? Who does it belong to? Who do you allow to live in it? Eventually Teemu calls Spider and asks, 'Who left the moving box outside Peter's house?'

Spider clears his throat in surprise. 'You don't usually want to know who does what. You usually . . . what is it you always say? "I'll let you know when you've gone too far"?'

It's true. That's the Pack's way of protecting Teemu. No one can ever hold him responsible for something he knows nothing about in any court case. He says, 'You went too far. Don't do it again.'

Spider's stubble scrapes against the phone. 'It wasn't . . . us. It was some youngsters, the kids in the standing area. Dammit, Teemu, you know how everyone feels! The kids hear their dads talking about all the jobs going to Hed, and then they hear us talking about Peter ripping out the standing area. They're just trying to impress you! They thought you'd be pleased!'

Teemu covers his eyes with his hand and lets out a deep sigh. 'Don't be too hard on them. Just make sure it doesn't happen again.'

Spider clears his throat again. 'The business with the moving box or . . . anything aimed at the family . . .?'

Teemu's voice gets sharper: 'We don't attack people in the club. We'll stand tall once those bastards have gone, and we're standing tall now, but we don't attack people in the club.'

'What about the standing area, then?'

Teemu admits, for the first time, 'I've had a meeting with a . . . politician. A friend. He's going to give us back our standing area. And we're going to be standing long after Peter Andersson has left this town.'

When darkness falls, Benji is sitting on the outhouse roof out at the kennels. He stubs out his cigarette and makes a decision, at last. Then he walks alone through Beartown. He doesn't hide in the shadows, he walks in the middle of the glow from the street-lamps. He hasn't been going to school, hardly anyone has seen him since they found out that he was gay. But now here he is, walking along out in the open.

Perhaps it's stupid. But sooner or later he has to confront every-one. This is too small a town to have many hiding places, and where would he go? What do you do when you just want every-thing to be the same as normal? You go to work. You hope for the best.

When he walks into the Bearskin, the bar falls silent. A stranger might not have noticed, might have thought the chat and argu-ments and clink of glasses were the same as usual. But every cell in Benji's body hears the oxygen being sucked out of the room. He stands still. The very fact that he's come here might seem crazy, but he was never the sort of child who lay in bed afraid of ghosts and monsters. He'd rather open all the doors, upturn all the mat-tresses, tell them to come and get him straight away if they were going to do it anyway.

Sooner that than just waiting.

★

A group of men at a table towards the back of the Bearskin stand up. First one, then all of them. Black jackets. None of them finishes his beer, their glasses are left demonstratively half full. Everyone moves out of the way as they walk towards the door, but none of the men touches Benji. They just stalk past, out, away. Within two minutes a dozen more, old and young, some in black jackets, someone without, some in hunting jackets, some in white shirts, have done the same thing.

Feelings are complicated. Actions are simple.

Vidar is one of the people sitting at the table at the back of the bar. When he was younger, he asked Spider why he hated queers so much. Spider replied without a trace of hesitation, 'Because it's disgusting! Men are men and women are women, and that's just some bullshit made-up sex in between! There's research, you know? They're missing something in their brains, some substance, and you know who else hasn't got it? Pedophiles and people who screw animals and that sort of shit. It's a disease, Vidar, they're not like us!'

Vidar didn't believe that at the time. He doesn't believe it now. But when Spider and Teemu and the others stand up and walk out, Vidar does the same. Because since he was little he's learned that soldiers stick together. He doesn't have to hate Benji, he just needs to love his brothers. Which is both complicated and not complicated at all.

Long after closing time, Ramona and Benji are still sitting in the bar. Just the two of them.

'It's . . . people have so much crap in their heads . . . it might not even be about you,' Ramona says tentatively, but she knows the boy knows she's lying.

'They left their beer. They don't want to drink with people like me,' Benji whispers.

His words are dry twigs, snapping under the slightest weight. Ramona sighs. 'It's a lot all to take in at once, Benjamin. A female coach, those damn politicians, sponsors getting involved in how the club's run . . . it's making people nervous. Everything's changing. They don't hate *you* . . . they're just . . . people just need a bit of time to digest things.'

'They do hate me,' Benji corrects.

Ramona scratches her chin with the whisky glass. 'Teemu and the boys saw you as one of them, Benjamin. That's what's making it worse. Some of them may have thought . . . I don't know . . . they might have thought stuff like this only happened on television. That men like that . . . well, that they only lived in the big cities and . . . you know . . . dressed in a particular way. They've lived their whole lives assuming it was something you could tell about a person at first glance. But you were . . . like them. They drank with you, you fought together, they yelled your name in the rink. You were a symbol, you proved that one of them could lead this team, this town . . . when they felt that every other bastard was out to get them. You were the middle finger they stuck up at the world. You were the bandit who proved they didn't have to adapt, that they could win anyway, that those of us out here in the forest could take on anyone who wanted to have a go at us.'

'I don't want . . . I never asked anyone to give a damn . . . I just want everything to be the same as normal.'

Ramona grabs hold of Benji's head, hard, with both hands. Until his ears feel like they're going to fall off. Then she yells, 'You've got nothing to apologize for, boy. You hear me? *Nothing!* I'm not defending *any* of the men who walked out of that door tonight, I'm just saying . . . the world turns quickly. Don't judge us too hard when we . . . well . . . just don't judge us too damn hard. Everything's changing at such a speed that some of us can't always keep up. We sit here and hear about "quotas" for all sorts of things, and it's easy to wonder when it's going to be our turn. When do we get a turn? I'm not defending anyone, boy, I'm just saying that some people around here feel they're being attacked from all sides. That everyone's telling them their way of life is wrong. No one likes having change forced upon them.'

'I'm not forcing anyone to do a damn thing . . . I just want things to be normal!'

Ramona lets go of him. Sighs. Pours more whisky. 'I know, boy. It is what it is. We're just going to have to find a new normal, that's all. There are two types of people now. Some of them need more time, and some need more sense. There's no hope for the second group, but we might have to wait to see how many there are in the first group before we start beating it into their heads.'

Benji is avoiding eye contact. 'Are you disappointed in me, too?'

Ramona starts to laugh, coughing up smoke. 'Me? Because you want to sleep with men? You sweet boy, I've always been very fond of you. I wish you a happy life. So I can only lament the fact that you want to sleep with men, because one thing I can tell you here and now is that it's impossible to be happy with men. They're nothing but a load of damn trouble!'

38

The Game

There's going to be an ice hockey game. Beartown Ice Hockey against Hed Hockey. The rest of the country is barely aware that it's taking place; no one cares except for here. But here everyone cares.

Some people can't understand things unless they've experienced them for themselves. The overwhelming majority of the world's population will live their whole lives in the belief that a hockey game is just a hockey game. That it's just a silly game. That it doesn't mean anything.

They're in a fortunate position. They don't have to go through all this.

What would you do for your family? What wouldn't you do?

Hog has never had any business cards, but if he did, there would be four things on it: 'Hockey player. Car mechanic. Father of three. Ann-Katrin's husband.' She still sings in his head, she still dances on his feet, he's never going to let her stop. He finishes work in the garage, just like on a normal day, even though things will never be normal again. When he goes into the house, Bobo, his eldest, is washing the dishes. It was Bobo who went to the undertaker's and organized the funeral and cremation. Then he came to grips with everything else. There's food on the table, the younger kids are already eating, and Bobo has done the laundry. Everything his mum used to do. Hog gulps hard when he sits down at the table, so that the younger children won't see him shatter. Then he says to Bobo, 'You should go and play in the game.'

Bobo whispers, 'I'm needed here . . . I've still got washing and –'

'Harry Potter!' his little brother says, even though his sister hushes him.

'Yes, I'll read some Harry Potter tonight. Like I always do,' Bobo promises, blinking as he stares down at the sink.

Hog chews, directing his own blinking at his plate. 'This is good. Really good.'

'Thanks,' Bobo whispers.

They say no more until the younger children have gone to brush their teeth. Then Hog gets up, washes his plate, and hugs Bobo as he whispers an order in his ear: 'I can read that damn Barry Trotter tonight. It's about time I learned how to. You hear what I'm saying?'

Bobo nods silently. Hog holds his cheeks and says, 'You and I are going to get through this, because Mum will never forgive us otherwise. So go and play your game now, because Mum'll be watching from wherever she is. Not even God or the angels or whatever else there may be could stop her watching her eldest son's first game on the Beartown A-team!'

Bobo packs his bag. When he walks out of the door, Hog expects the other children to beg and plead to be allowed to go, too. But they don't. Instead they stand on the steps with their hockey sticks and a tennis ball and ask, 'Do you want to play, Dad?'

So Hog watches his eldest son go off to his first A-team game, and then he plays hockey with his two younger children in the garage. They struggle and sweat and chase the ball for hours. As if it were the only thing that mattered. Because it is, at that moment. And that's the whole point.

What would you do for your family?

Peter Andersson goes from room to room in the house before he sets out from home. Kira is sitting in the kitchen with her laptop and a glass of wine.

'Do you want to come to the game?' he asks without much hope.

'I need to work,' she replies, predictably.

They look into each other's eyes. At least they do that. He moves on and knocks on the door to Maya's room. 'Do you . . . I . . . I'm going to the game now,' he whispers.

'I have to study, Dad. Good luck!' she calls from the other side of the door.

Mother and daughter say that because it makes things easier for him. They're giving him a chance to pretend that everything's fine. He knocks on Leo's door, too, but Leo isn't home. He's already gone to Hed. He's planning to watch the game from the standing area.

Peter knows he should stop him. Punish his son. But how do you do that when all you've ever done is nag your son to go to hockey games with you?

Ana is standing in front of the mirror trying to choose an outfit. She has no idea how she ought to look. She's been to a thousand hockey games but never one where Vidar has been playing. It's a stupid fantasy, but she wants him to turn towards the stands and catch sight of her. And realize that she's there for his sake.

Her dad is stumbling about in the kitchen downstairs. He knocks something over, then something else. She hears him swear. It aches so deeply in her, all his drinking. She throws on some clothes without picking them as carefully as she planned, because she wants to be out of the house before her dad gets so drunk that he needs help. She doesn't want to let the bad version of him steal this game from her. Not today.

He calls out to her when she reaches the door, and her first thought is to pretend she hasn't heard him, but something in his voice brings her up short. It's too clear, too steady — it's unusual. She turns around. Her dad has showered and combed his hair and is wearing a clean shirt. The kitchen behind him has been tidied up. There are bottles in the recycling bin, and he's tipped their contents down the sink.

'Have a good time at the game. Do you need any money?' he asks tentatively.

She looks at her good dad for a long time. The bad one seems so far away right now. 'How are you feeling?' she whispers.

'I want to try again,' he whispers back.

He's said that before. It doesn't stop her believing him. She hesitates for just a moment, then says, 'Do you feel like going for a walk?'

'Aren't you going to the game?'

'I'd rather go for a walk with you, Dad.'

So that's what they do. While two whole towns head to a hockey game, a father and his daughter go for a walk in the forest that has always been theirs. Him, her, and the trees. A family.

Bobo cycles through Beartown carrying an invisible backpack of stone. He arrives late at the pickup spot, but no one seems to care, and Zackell hardly seems to notice that he's turned up. Amat sits next to Bobo on the team bus to Hed but doesn't know what to say. So they say nothing.

The parking lot in front of Hed's ice rink is full of people, and there are lines even though there's still a long time before the game starts. The rink is going to be full, the towns are in an uproar, the hate has had plenty of time to grow. This is going to be war. The bus is silent. All the players are wrestling with their own demons.

Only when the A-team members have gotten off the bus and gone into the hall, along the corridor, and into the locker room and are all sitting down does one of the older players get to his feet. He walks over to Bobo with a roll of tape in his hand.

'What was your mum's name?' the older player asks.

Bobo looks up in surprise. Swallows hard. 'My mum? Ann . . . Ann-Katrin. Her name is . . . her name was . . . Ann-Katrin.'

'With a "K" or a "C"?' the older player asks.

'"K,"' Bobo whispers.

The older player writes 'Ann-Katrin' on a strip of tape. He sticks it onto the sleeve of Bobo's jersey. Then he repeats the process and fastens the tape onto his own sleeve. The roll of tape passes silently around the locker room. Bobo's mum's name is on every arm.

Amat skates out onto the ice. As he's done throughout his childhood, he starts skating around, around, around, to warm up. Normally he doesn't hear anything, he's gotten good at that, no matter how many people are in the rink. Everything becomes background noise, and he disappears into a zone of concentration that makes whoever is at the other end of the boards irrelevant. But today is different. Something breaks through the noise and yelling: his name. A few people somewhere are chanting it. Louder and louder. Over and over again. Until Amat looks up. Then the cheering gets louder.

In one corner, right at the top, stands a group of idiots jumping on their seats. They're not there to cheer for either of the teams, they're there for one single player. Because he's from the Hollow. They're singing the simplest, most beautiful, most important thing: 'AMAT! ONE OF US! AMAT! ONE OF US! AAA-MAT! ONE OF US!'

Fatima arrives at the rink in Hed on her own, but she's holding two tickets. She watches the game with an empty seat beside her, Ann-Katrin's. When Amat comes out onto the ice, she stands up and cheers, and when Bobo comes out, she cheers twice as loudly. She'll do that at every game Bobo plays and every game his younger siblings play. No matter where their lives take them, there'll always be a crazy woman in the stands cheering loud enough for two.

Why does anyone love team sports? Because we want to be part of a group? For some people the answer is simply that a team is a family. For anyone who needs an extra one or never had one in the first place.

★

Vidar Rinnius loved playing hockey when he was a child, just like every other kid. But unlike all the other kids, he loved the stands even more. He always promised himself that if he ever had to choose, he'd never pick the ice over the standing area. He said that to Teemu when he was little, and Teemu smiled and said, 'It's our club, remember that. When all the players have switched clubs, when the general managers and coaches have moved on to clubs that pay more, when the sponsors let us down and the politicians have sold out, we'll still be here. And we'll be singing even louder. Because it was never their club anyway. It's always been ours.'

Vidar sat on the team bus today, his gear is in the locker room, but he isn't there. He puts on a black jacket and goes up to the standing area instead, takes his place beside his brother and yells, 'WE ARE THE BEARS! WE ARE THE BEARS! WE ARE THE BEARS! THE BEARS FROM BEARTOWN!'

Teemu looks at him. Perhaps he wants to tell his little brother to go back to the locker room, that a better life awaits him on the ice. But the Pack is their family, and the club belongs to them. So he kisses his brother's hair. Woody and Spider hug Vidar, their fists clenched behind his back. And they sing, louder, more insistently:

'WE ARE THE BEARS! WE ARE THE BEARS!'

Love and hate. Joy and sorrow. Anger and forgiveness. Sports carry the promise that we can have everything tonight. Only sports can do that.

At one end of the rink, the Hed fans' standing area, the volume rises until nothing can penetrate the wall of noise. Their chanting is laced with *schadenfreude*. If you ask most people in the stand afterward, several years from now, they'll just give an embarrassed cough and mumble, 'It's just hockey . . . no harm intended . . . just something you sing in the heat of battle. You know what it's like! It's just hockey!' Of course it is. We support our team, you support yours, and we exploit every little weakness we can find. If we get a chance to hit below the belt, we grab it, anything to hurt you, get you off balance. Because we only want the same thing you do: to win. So the fans in Hed's stands chant the simplest, cruellest, and vilest things they can think of.

Beartown Ice Hockey's best player used to be Kevin Erdahl. He raped Maya Andersson, the daughter of the club's general manager. Kevin's best friend, Benjamin Ovich, is homosexual. What did we expect? That they weren't going to chant about all that? Those people who hate us?

Their voices don't number in the thousands, but in a small arena with a low roof, the silence of many can make the chanting of some of them sound as though everyone is shouting the same thing. The red fans turn towards the Beartown section of the stand, towards the Pack, and roar, 'Queers! Sluts! Rapists!'

It's easy to say you should just ignore it. Not let it get to you. It's only hockey. Only words. Doesn't mean anything. But chant it enough times, shout it loud enough, repeat, repeat, repeat. Until it eats its way in. One hundred red arms pointing across the ice, directly at the green fans. Their words thundering against the roof and echoing off the walls. Again. Again.

QUEERS!

SLUTS!

RAPISTS!

39

Violence

Over in the seated part of the rink Peter Andersson can't help hearing the chanting. He does his best to ignore it, but it's impossible. He leans forward towards the next row, taps Sune on the shoulder, and asks, 'Where's Benji?'

'He hasn't turned up,' Sune replies.

Peter leans back. The Hed fans' words hit the roof and bounce back, hitting him like burning oil. He feels like standing up and shouting, too, shouting anything at all. It's only a damn hockey game, and what's it worth now? How much has Peter sacrificed for this? How much has he put his family through? His daughter? How many bad decisions must a man have taken when his wife stays at home and his son would rather be with the hooligans than his father? If Beartown Hockey doesn't win this game after everything Peter's done, what does that make him worth? He's sold out his ideals, he's gambled everything he loves. If the club loses against Hed now, everything is lost. There's no other way of looking at it.

'Queers! Sluts! Rapists!'

Peter looks in silence at the people shrieking in Hed's standing area and wishes them ill, every last one of them. If Beartown takes the lead tonight, if the team gets the chance to crush those people and destroy every ounce of their desire to get out of bed tomorrow, Peter fervently hopes that his team won't ease up on them. He wants to see them suffer.

★

At some point almost everyone makes a choice. Some of us don't even notice it happening, most don't get to plan it in advance, but there's always a moment when we take one path instead of another that has consequences for the rest of our lives. It determines the people we will become, in other people's eyes as well as our own. Elisabeth Zackell may have been right when she said that anyone who feels responsibility isn't free. Because responsibility is a burden. Freedom is a pleasure.

Benji is sitting on the roof of one of the outhouses at the kennels, watching the snowflakes make their way to the ground. He knows the game is about to start, but he isn't there. He can't explain why; he's never been good at justifying or rationalizing his actions. Sometimes he does stupid things on instinct, sometimes he doesn't for the same reason. Sometimes he cares too little about things, sometimes too much.

Beside him on the roof sit his three sisters, Adri, Katia, and Gaby. Down on the ground, on a chair next to an unsteady table that's been pushed down into the snow, sits their mum. She'd do – and has done – almost anything for her children, but climbing a ladder to sit on an icy outhouse roof and ending up with a wet backside is somewhere beyond her limit.

The Ovich family has always loved hockey, even if its members haven't always loved the same things about it. Adri loved playing and watching games, Katia loved playing but not watching, Gaby never played but watches when Benji plays. Their mum always asks irritably, 'Why do there have to be three periods? Wouldn't two be enough? Don't any of these people eat proper meals?' But if you give her a date and a game ten years ago, she can tell you if her son scored or not. If he fought hard. If she was proud or angry. Often both. The sisters shuffle uncomfortably beside their brother. It's cold, not only because of the freezing temperature.

'If you don't want us to go to the game, we won't go,' Gaby says quietly.

'If you really, really, really don't want us to . . . ,' Katia clarifies.

Benji doesn't know what to say. Most of all, after everything that's happened, he hates himself for having put his family into this position. He doesn't want to be a burden to them, doesn't want them to have to fight on his behalf. He was once told by another boy's mother, 'You may not be an angel, Benjamin. But, dear God, you haven't suffered for the lack of a male role model. All your best qualities come from the fact that you've been raised in a house full of women.' Benji will always say she was wrong, because she made them sound like they were perfectly ordinary women. They aren't, not to him. His sisters did their best to replace their father, they taught their little brother to hunt, drink, and fight. But they also taught him never to mistake friendliness for weakness or love for shame. And it's for their sake that he hates himself now. Because if not for him, they wouldn't even consider not going to Hed.

In the end it's Adri who looks at her watch and says, 'I love you, little brother, but I'm going to the game.'

'I'm going too!' their mum shouts from down on the ground.

Because she and Adri are old enough to remember life before Beartown. The other children were too young, but Adri remembers what the family was fleeing from, and what they found here. A safe place to build a home. This is their town. Benji pats Adri's hand gently and whispers, 'I know.'

Adri kisses him on the cheek and whispers that she loves him in two different languages. When she climbs down, Katia and Gaby hesitate, but in the end they follow her. They go to the game for the same reason that they could have stayed at home: for their brother's sake and for their town's. They wish Benji was going to play, but they know that nothing they say will change his mind. Because he is after all a member of this family, and there are probably mules that accuse other mules of being 'as stubborn as an Ovich.'

Benji stays on the roof until his mum and sisters have driven off in the car. He smokes all alone. Then he climbs down, fetches his bicycle, and sets off through the forest. But not towards Hed.

★

When children first start to play hockey, they are told that all they have to do is try their best. That that's enough. Everyone knows it's a lie. Everyone knows that this sport isn't about having fun; it's not measured in terms of effort, only by results.

The Beartown Ice Hockey players enter the rink with a mother's name on their arms, and even though it's an away game large parts of the arena are filled with green shirts with the words BEARTOWN AGAINST THE REST on them. Men in black jackets unfurl a banner above one of the standing areas, similar to the one that's going to be demolished in their own rink, and the words are aimed as much at Peter Andersson as Hed's fans: 'Come and have a go if you think you're hard enough!'

The game starts down on the ice. The volume is unbearable, people's ears start to pop, and Beartown Ice Hockey's players do all they can. They fight for their lives. Give everything they've got. Their very, very, very best. But Vidar is in the stands, and no one knows where Benji is. The goalie and the captain. Maybe Beartown deserves to win, maybe it would have been fair for them to have a fairy-tale ending, but hockey isn't measured like that. Hockey only counts goals.

Hed scores. Then again. Then again, and again.

The singing from the red stand is deafening. Peter Andersson doesn't hear it, though. The ringing in his ears is the sound of his heart breaking.

At the campsite the teacher has already packed. His bags are in the car. Yet he's still sitting at the table in the kitchen of the little cabin, looking out of the window as he waits, hoping that someone with sad eyes and a wild heart is going to appear from between the trees. When he finally sees Benji, he's been waiting so long that at first he thinks he's imagining it. The teacher stands up and tries to gather all the words inside him when his heart leaps at the sound of the door opening and he finds himself staring at Benji's lips.

'I . . . was trying to write something . . . ,' he says apologetically, gesturing clumsily towards the pen and blank sheet of paper on the table.

Benji says nothing. The cabin is cold, but the teacher is wearing a thin white linen shirt. It's hanging loose outside his trousers, crumpled like Sunday-morning hair; he smells of warm skin and fresh coffee. Benji opens his mouth, but nothing comes out. He looks around the cabin; all the clothes are gone, all personal belongings removed. Perhaps the teacher detects a note of criticism in Benji's gaze, because he mumbles embarrassedly, 'I'm not as brave as you, Benjamin. I'm not the sort of person who stays and fights.'

There's still a deep mark in the front door made by the knife. Benji reaches out his hand, touches his skin one last time. Whispers, 'I know.'

The teacher holds his hand to his cheek, very briefly, closes his eyes, and says, 'Call if you ever want . . . ever want to be somewhere else. Maybe things could have been different for us . . . somewhere else.'

Benji nods. Perhaps they could have been, somewhere else. Something more.

When the teacher gets into his car, he finds himself thinking of a quote by some philosopher: 'Man is the only creature who refuses to be what he is.' He tries to remember who wrote it. Albert Camus, perhaps? He occupies his mind with this as he drives through Beartown, along the road, and out of the forest, because if he concentrates hard enough on those words, all the other feelings can't overwhelm him and stop him from seeing the road ahead of him.

Far behind the car Benjamin Ovich gets onto his bicycle and sets off in a different direction. Perhaps he'll be free one day. But not today.

Just as Hed Hockey makes it 4–0 towards the end of the second period, four boys from Hed sneak across the stand. They're just

319

schoolkids, that's why they were given the job, because no one would suspect them. They're not even wearing red jerseys, so they don't attract attention. They're carrying garbage bags, specially smuggled in during a practice of the boys' team late yesterday evening. They're going to throw the contents of the bags at the enemy. When the time is right, when the souls of the Beartown fans are at the breaking point, to push them over the edge.

A lot of people in the red part of the rink will say that this is just part of the game, purely symbolic, just hockey. Maybe even 'just a joke.' Just the sort of thing you do to hurt your opponents and get under their skin. Conquer. Destroy. Annihilate.

The boys have managed to sneak along the side of the rink, far too close to the Beartown fans' standing area, before someone finally notices them. But it's too late by then. The boys pull dildos and other sex toys from the bags, one after the other, hundreds of them. Vibrators rain down on the men in black jackets, hitting their hunched forms like missiles. And from the red stand at the other end of the rink the chanting rings out again, more hateful, more threatening:

'QUEERS! SLUTS! RAPISTS! QUEERS! SLUTS! RAPISTS!'

We can say what we like about Teemu Rinnius, because he says whatever he likes about us. In his experience every discussion of violence reveals how hypocritical almost everyone is. If you were to ask him, he'd say that most men and women aren't violent and that they believe this is because their 'morals' stop them. Teemu has one word for them: 'Liars.' Would they really not be violent if they could? When other drivers mess around with them? When people mess around with them at work? When people mess around with their wives in the pub or their kids at school or their parents in nursing homes? How many thousands of times does the average mortgage-paying Labrador owner dream of being the sort of person who really doesn't give a damn? Teemu is convinced that ordinary people's lack of violence has nothing to do with morals and that they would be only too happy to hurt people if they thought they could get away with it. The only reason they're not violent is that violence isn't an option for them.

They can't fight, they don't know anyone with the strength or the weight of numbers or the influence. If they did, they'd get out of their cars and lay into the idiot blowing his horn, beat up the dad at the parents' meeting who insulted their family, push that cocky waiter up against the wall and force him to eat the bill. Teemu is sure of that.

When he and Vidar were young, the brothers learned to hate one phrase more than all the others. They got called plenty of things: 'Skint bastards!' 'Thieves!' But it was 'Whore's kids' that hit them hardest. And it showed, so all the kids at school used that one more than the others. Teemu and Vidar had the same mother but different fathers, and when one brother is blond and the other dark, it's an open invitation in every schoolyard. They fought until everyone shut up, but some words never stop echoing inside. Whore's kids. Whore's kids. Whore's kids. Whore. Whore. Whore.

Now Teemu and Vidar are standing in the rink next to Spider and Woody. Spider, who got whipped in the shower with wet towels and called a 'queer' when he was little. Woody, who was prepared to get onto a plane as a teenager to fight anyone he could find in the country where his cousin had been raped, before Teemu dragged him back home.

They're no saints, they haven't got hearts of gold, and most of the worst things said about them are true. But when Woody went to Teemu back in the spring to say the Pack should stand up against Kevin Erdahl, the best player their cherished club has ever seen, Teemu agreed with him, because he knew what people were calling Maya Andersson at school.

And now the red fans at the other end of the rink are chanting 'QUEERS! SLUTS! RAPISTS!'

*

The Hed fans don't know any of this. They're just trying to shout the worst insults they can think of, anything they think will hurt, that will get under the skin of anyone with a bear on his or her chest. They succeed. As soon as the shower of dildos starts to hit the men in black jackets, eight of them set off down the stands. They take their jackets off, and eight other men in white shirts pull the jackets on and take their places. The security guards never notice Teemu, Vidar, Spider, Woody, and four others disappearing into a corridor, through a door, down into the basement.

Violence isn't an option for most people. But the Pack aren't most people.

Leo Andersson is twelve years old, and he'll never forget when he heard Teemu Rinnius turn to Spider and say, 'Get the guys. Just the hard core.' And how Teemu gave an almost invisible signal with a short nod, and seven men immediately set off behind him. The hard core, the central unit within the Pack, the most dangerous of them all.

Leo saw other men put their black jackets on and block the guards' view as the hard core left the stand and ran towards a door in a dark corridor beside the janitor's storeroom. There is a basement beneath the rink in Hed, most people don't even know it exists, but a couple of weeks ago there was trouble with the lights and a group of electricians was brought in. One of them had to go down into the basement because he said there was a circuit breaker down there. The janitor didn't think for a moment that there was anything suspicious about that. The electrician was careful not to show his bear tattoo.

Leo Andersson will never forget how much he wished he could have gone into that basement with them. Some boys dream of becoming professional hockey players. They stand and watch and wish they could be out on the ice. But some boys have other dreams. Other idols.

★

They head through the corridor in the basement of the arena. Eight of them. The very toughest of them. Nothing should be able to stop them, but one man does. He's standing on his own in the middle of their path. He has no friends with him, no weapons, and he's jammed a broom through the handles of the doors behind him to stop anyone opening them from the other side. Benji has locked himself into a corridor with them of his own volition.

He didn't want to come here. There was just nowhere else he'd rather be.

He cycled from the campsite to the rink in Hed, through the snow with the wind in his eyes. When he crept inside, the game had reached the final minutes of the second period, and all eyes were on the ice. Benji looked up at the scoreboard. 4–0 for Hed. He heard the chanting, saw the red sea of hate on one side and the black jackets on the other. He saw the shower of dildos. While everyone else looked on in shock, Benji just looked around for a way to get down through the stands. As soon as Teemu and Vidar and six others took their jackets off, Benji already knew where they were going.

He had been in that basement before. He played hundreds of away games and tournaments in the Hed arena while he was growing up, and no one is better than Benji at finding quiet corners in rinks where you can smoke a bit of dope in peace.

So he knows you can use the basement to get all the way from one standing area to the other. To appear in the midst of the enemy. Like a bomb.

Teemu stops halfway through the basement. The men around him stop, too. Woody and Spider are ahead of the others on one side of Teemu, and his younger brother, Vidar, is on the other. Teemu stares at the eighteen-year-old blocking the narrow corridor and gives him a single chance. 'Get out of the way, Benji.'

Benji slowly shakes his head. He's wearing battered shoes, grey tracksuit pants, and a white T-shirt. He looks small. 'No.'

Teemu's voice is implacable: 'I'm not going to tell you again . . .'

Benji's voice is trembling; they've never heard it do that before. 'I'm the one you want to beat the crap out of. No one else. So get going. Here I am. Some of you will get past me, I know that. But some of you won't.'

The silence that follows has sharp claws. Teemu's voice sounds momentarily muffled, then he snarls, 'We treated you like one of us, Benji. You're a fucking . . . liar . . .'

Benji replies, moist-eyed, 'I'm a fucking *fag*! Say it like it is! If you want to beat someone up, here I am! If you go up into the Hed stands, the ref will call off the game and Hed will win. Don't you see that's what they want? If you want to beat the crap out of a fag, here I am! Hit *me*!'

Teemu's knuckles are white when he replies, 'Get out of the way. Don't force me to –'

Benji's voice breaks. 'What? Fight if you want to fight! There are eight of you, so the odds are pretty much even! But if you go up into the Hed stand, the game is over, and we can't beat these bastards. Don't you get it? *But I can beat them!*'

Benji isn't staring at Teemu now. He's staring at Vidar. They played together a few years ago, but Kevin was Benji's best friend back then, and Kevin never liked Vidar, because Vidar was unreliable. Kevin demanded a goalie who obeyed orders, and Vidar never did that, and even if Benji was probably more like Vidar than anyone else on the team, his first loyalty was always to Kevin. Vidar in turn was always loyal to his brother and the Pack. They never spoke about it, never became friends, but perhaps they respected each other. So now Benji says, 'You hear me, Vidar? If the two of us play the third period, we can beat these bastards. Go up and fight in the stands if you want to, but we can take these bastards if we go out and play. Knock my teeth out if it feels better, I can play without my damn teeth. But I want . . . I really want . . . I just want to win! Screw you, screw the lot of you, I'll leave town tomorrow if that's what you want. I'll leave the club now if you . . .'

Benji tails off. But the other men don't reply. None of them so much as moves. So Benji beats his chest with his fists and yells in desperation, 'I'm standing right here! The doors are locked, so if you want to do something, just get it over with so I can go out there and play! Because I can beat these bastards!'

People talk about silences where you can hear a pin drop. You could have heard a blade of grass land on cotton in that corridor. This story will hardly ever be retold by anyone in either Beartown or Hed. But the men who were there will always know that there were eight of them and Benji was alone, and he was the one who had locked the doors.

A minute passes. Unless perhaps it was ten. God knows.

'Okay,' Teemu says slowly.

But he doesn't say it to Benji. He says it to his brother.

'Okay?' Vidar whispers.

Teemu roars, 'What are you standing here for? The third period's about to start, run and get changed, you idiot!'

Vidar's face cracks into a smile. He casts a last glance at Benji and nods, and Benji nods back. Then Vidar walks along the corridor towards the Beartown locker room. A few seconds later two members of the Pack turn and walk slowly after him. Then two more.

Only Spider and Woody are left standing with Teemu. Benji doesn't move. Teemu takes a long, furious breath through his nostrils and whispers, 'For fuck's sake. You went drinking with me. You fought alongside me . . .'

Benji doesn't try to wipe his tears. 'Go to hell, Teemu.'

And the leader of the Pack lowers his head. Just for a fleeting second. 'You're a hard bastard, Benji, no one can deny that. But we're not going to let this town go all . . . you know . . . rainbow flags and shit . . .'

Benji sniffs. 'I've never asked for that.'

Teemu sticks his hands into his pockets. Nods. That's enough to make Spider and Woody turn and walk away. Benji doesn't know if they still hate him, but at least they leave him alone with Teemu.

Teemu's fists are clenched. So are Benji's.

It's only a hockey game. An ice rink packed with people, two locker rooms full of players, two teams facing each other. Two men in a basement. Why do we care about that sort of thing?

Perhaps because it clarifies all of our most difficult questions. What makes us shout out loud with joy? What makes us cry? What are our happiest memories, our worst days, our deepest disappointments? Who did we stand alongside? What's a family? What's a team?

How many times in life are we completely happy?

How many chances do we get to love something that's almost pointless entirely unconditionally?

The corridor is deserted, yet the two men still feel as if they're standing with their backs to the wall. Teemu is still shaking with rage, and Benji is just shaking, for a thousand different reasons. Teemu stares down at the floor, breathing hard, and says, 'The papers are writing about you. Reporters are calling people in town, asking about you. Goddamn media assholes with their stupid politics, you know what they want, don't you? They want to get one of us to say something stupid so they can show that we're just stupid, bigoted rednecks. So they can go back to the big city on their high horse and feel so morally superior —'

Benji's cheeks are bleeding on the inside where he's bitten them. He whispers, 'I'm sorry . . .'

Teemu's knuckles turn slowly red again as the blood courses back into them. He replies, 'It's our club.'

'I know,' Benji replies.

Teemu's fists slowly unfurl. He rubs his cheeks with the palms of his hands. 'You say you can beat these bastards . . . right now we're 4–0 down. So . . . if you win this game, I'll buy you a beer afterward.'

Benji's face is wet, but his eyes are blazing when he replies, 'I didn't think you drank with people like me.'

The sigh that emerges from Teemu's lungs fills the whole corridor, bounces off the locked doors, and echoes off the low ceiling. 'For fuck's sake, Benji. Do I have to drink with *all* the damn queers now? Can't I start with just one?'

40

Always Fair. Always Unfair.

Speaking in front of other people isn't easy. The best hockey coaches don't always have a talent for it. Public speaking is an extrovert activity, but tactical understanding and a willingness to submit to nights watching video recordings of old games might appear to require an introverted personality. Of course it's possible to compensate for this by showing your feelings. But if you're no good at feelings, either, what the hell do you say?

Right before the third period starts, Peter gets to his feet. He can't sit still in the stands, he doesn't know where he's going or why, but he makes his way to the only place he really understands: the locker room. Naturally he stops himself in the corridor; he's the general manager, it isn't his place to storm in to see the players. That's the coach's job. He's sure Zackell is in there right now, giving an impassioned speech to the players about how they can turn this around. That they've got it in them, that they need to tell themselves that it's still 0–0, that they just need a quick goal to make a game of it again!

But when Peter turns the corner, he sees Zackell standing by the door to the parking lot. She's on her own, smoking a cigar. The whole team is sitting in the locker room, waiting.

'What do you think you're doing?' he snaps.

'What do you mean? I'm not allowed to smoke inside!' Zackell says defensively.

'You're 4–0 down! Aren't you going to say anything to the team?' Peter demands.

'Do you think they don't know they're down 4–0?' Zackell wonders.

'For God's sake . . . they need . . . you're a coach! Go in and say something inspirational!' Peter commands.

Zackell finishes her cigar. Shrugs her shoulders. Mutters resignedly, 'Okay. Right. Fine.'

Just as she reaches the locker room, a young man runs towards her from the other direction. Vidar Rinnius.

'Can I play?' he pants.

Zackell shrugs. 'Sure. Why not? It can hardly get any worse.'

A minute or so after Vidar bounces happily into the locker room to get his goalie gear on, another young man appears in the corridor. He's walking calmly, not running, and stops in front of Zackell. He asks politely, the way you do if you have sisters, 'Do you need another player?'

Zackell frowns. 'Are you thinking of having sex with anyone in the locker room?'

Benji tries to figure out if she's joking. It's impossible to tell. 'No,' he says.

'Okay,' she says.

Any normal coach would have scrubbed Benji from the lineup when he failed to show up for the first period. But Zackell isn't normal. She made the judgement that even if Benji wasn't here, he was still better than anyone else. Some people understand that, most don't. She steps aside, he goes inside the locker room. It was quiet before he arrived, and it's even quieter now.

His teammates are sitting there, two dozen pairs of eyes staring at the floor, and for the first time Benji doesn't know what to do in there – where he should sit, how he should start to get changed, not because he's uncomfortable but because he's worried someone else might be. He's different now.

He takes his shoes off, but that's as far as he gets. He rushes into the toilet and slams the door shut behind him, but everyone can still hear him being sick. His eyes are streaming, and he clutches the edge of the toilet so hard that the fixtures start to creak. If he'd had a means of escape right then, he might well have taken it, but there's only one way out of there. So who does he want to be? Everyone has moments when that's decided. When we choose.

He wipes his face, unlocks the door, and steps back into the locker room. It's the smallest of gestures, and all his teammates are still silent when he emerges, but when he gets back to his place, his shoes are full of shaving cream. Not just his. Everyone's. Every pair of shoes under every bench. Because the men around him want him to know that he's no different from anyone else. Not in here.

Benji sits down on the bench. Hesitantly pulls his shirt off. Suddenly a voice rises above the silence, from an unexpected direction opposite Benji, 'How do you know if you're sexy?' Amat asks.

Benji sits there bare-chested, his head tilted to one side. 'What?'

Amat's face is red. Everyone is staring at him, he's never felt more embarrassed, but he persists, 'I mean . . . how do you know what girls think is sexy about guys? Or what guys think is sexy about . . . guys?'

Benji's eyebrows sink. 'What the hell are you actually asking, Amat?'

Amat clears his throat. 'You've showered with me, so you should be an expert. Am I sexy?'

Before Benji has time to answer, Amat grins. 'I'm not asking for myself. I'm asking for my best friend.'

Beside him Bobo jerks as if someone had given him an electric shock. It's a small thing for one young man to do for another one, but you can handle a lot of things in life if you have a best friend. Even more if you're allowed to be someone else's. So Bobo coughs and manages to say, 'I, erm . . . Benji . . . I was just wondering how . . . you know. How you know if you know if you're . . . hot?'

Benji looks at Bobo, then at Amat, then back at Bobo again. Then he shakes his head. 'I've never once looked at either of *you* in the shower!'

The locker room erupts in laughter, but one of the older players remains serious and asks brusquely, 'What about the rest of us,

330

then? Are you seriously suggesting you haven't checked out any of us in the shower?'

Benji frowns. 'Christ, I'd rather look at girls than you guys.'

The older player's shoulders sink slightly. 'I can't help feeling a bit hurt by that.'

'I've been doing to my best to stay in shape,' another one mutters disappointedly.

Bobo and Amat grin. It's almost the same as usual. But Benji is more serious, and he points at Bobo's arm. 'I want one of those, too. If that's okay.'

Bobo writes 'Ann-Katrin' on a strip of tape and fastens it around Benji's arm. The letters are uneven because Bobo's hand was shaking.

Elisabeth Zackell is standing outside the locker room with Peter. She grunts unhappily, but Peter gestures firmly that she has to say something to the team. So she groans, walks in, and whistles loudly to get the men to be quiet.

'Okay. I've been informed that coaches are expected to give inspirational speeches in situations like this. So . . . well . . . you're 4–0 down.'

The men stare at her, and she stares back. Then she goes on, 'I'm just checking that you know. Four-zip! More than that, you're not just behind, you've also been playing really badly. So only a bunch of complete idiots would think you stand any chance of winning this game!'

The men remain silent. Zackell clears her throat. Then she adds, 'Anyway. I just want to say that I've been involved with hockey my whole life. And I've never met such a bunch of idiots as you lot.'

Then she leaves them. Peter stands in the corridor and watches her as she walks towards the ice. He's never heard a better locker room speech.

Inside the locker room they're all sitting motionless. Benji looks at the clock on the wall; they ought to be out on the ice by now, but no one's moving. In the end Amat kicks Benji's skate and says, 'They're waiting.'

'What for?' Benji asks.

'You.'

Benji stands up. The others do the same.

Then the members of the Beartown hockey team follow their captain through the door. Benjamin Ovich doesn't walk out onto the ice. He takes it by storm.

The three Ovich sisters arrive at the Hed arena with their mum. They walk in with the body language of women who have seen far worse things in even colder places. They're not scared.

The hall is full, every seat taken, everyone knows who they are but most people pretend not to. People whisper and point, but no one looks them in the eye. Perhaps some of them are ashamed, while others just don't know what to say. Perhaps a number of them would like to, but it's hard to be the first people to stand up.

But then five people do.

The uncles. They're wearing green BEARTOWN AGAINST THE REST T-shirts, and as they walk up the steps they tease each other about how damn old they've gotten. One of them takes Benjamin Ovich's mother by the arm and leads her to his seat. The other uncles give up their seats to the sisters. When Adri passes one of them, the old man squeezes her hand and says, 'Tell your brother that the people who shout the loudest may be the most noticeable. But they're not the majority. We are.'

The five uncles' wives are sitting in the next seats along. One of them has a cooler by her feet. Obviously you're not allowed to take things like that to a hockey game, but when the security guard on the door asked what she had in it, she said with deadly seriousness, 'My cat.' When the guard started to protest, one of the other women leaned forward and whispered, 'It's dead, but don't tell her, poor old thing.' The guard opened his mouth, but the third of the women grabbed his arm and asked, 'Do you have fresh tomatoes? I don't want those Belgian ones you usually have, I want proper ones! I have a coupon!' The fourth exclaimed cheerily, 'What a lot of people there are tonight! What film are you showing, again? Is Sean Connery in it?' And before the fifth one could embark on her practiced 'There's going to be snow tonight, I can feel it in my knees!' routine, the guard had sighed, given up, and let them in, cooler and all. Now the women take some beers from it and share them with Benji's mum and sisters, and then nine women from three generations drink a toast with each other. Five uncles stand on the steps alongside, like a guard of honour.

A cup of coffee is no big thing. Not really.

Everyone will remember the chanting from the Hed fans' standing area: 'Queers! Sluts! Rapists!' A lot of people will believe that that whole part of the stand was chanting, because it felt like it, and from a distance it's hard to differentiate among people. So everyone in the standing area will be criticized, even though by no means all of them were chanting, because we'll want scapegoats, and it'll be easy for anyone wanting to moralize to say that 'culture isn't just what we encourage but what we allow to happen.'

But when everyone is shouting, it can be hard to hear the opposition, and once an avalanche of hate has started to roll, it can be hard to tell who is responsible for stopping it.

So when a young woman in a red shirt bearing a picture of a bull on the front leaves her place in the standing area, no one notices at first. But the woman loves Hed Hockey as much as the people shouting, she's supported the team all her life, this part of the rink belongs to her, too. Going to stand among the seated fans, the hot dog brigade she's always mocked, is her silent protest.

A man in a green shirt sitting a short distance away sees her and stands up. He goes to the cafeteria, buys two paper cups of coffee, then walks down and gives one of them to her. They stand there next to each other, one red, one green, and drink in silence. A cup of coffee is no big thing. But sometimes it actually is.

Within a few minutes, more red shirts have walked out of the standing area. Soon the steps of the seated part of the rink are full. The chant of 'Queers! Sluts! Rapists!' is still echoing loudly, but the people chanting are exposed now. So everyone can see that there aren't as many of them as we think. There never are.

One of Hed Hockey's players is named Filip. He's the youngest on the team, but he's on his way to becoming the best. This story isn't about him; in fact, his involvement is so brief that we could easily have forgotten to mention him at all.

Just before the start of the third period, he leaves the ice. William Lyt and a few of the other players shout at him to stay, but Filip walks through the players' tunnel, up the steps to the stands, and all the way over to the standing area. He's still wearing his skates and clutching his stick. He marches straight up to the biggest, strongest, most tattooed Hed fan he can find, interrupts him in the middle of 'QU—' grabs him by his top, and says, 'If you shout that one more time, I'm not going to play.'

Filip is only seventeen years old, but anyone who knows anything about hockey can see how good he's going to be. The Hed fan stares at him wildly, but Filip doesn't back down. He points to the red-clad fans standing on the steps of the seated area and says, 'If you shout that one more time, I'm going to stand over there for the rest of the game.'

He walks back to the ice, leaving a heavy silence behind him. Filip isn't naive, the world hasn't changed, he knows they'll chant the same thing at other games. But not today. When he reaches the bench, someone yells, 'Hed! Hed! Hed!'

'WIN! WIN! WIN!' the rest of the stand shouts.

That's all they chant for the rest of the game. By the end the standing area is full again, singing loud enough to raise the roof.

★

Hockey is simple. It's both the fairest and the most unfair sport in the world.

Beartown scores a goal. Then another. When they reduce the deficit to 4–3 and are just one goal behind with twenty seconds left on the clock, everyone already knows what's going to happen. They can feel it in the air. This can only end one way. Like a fairy tale.

Benji gets the puck, rushes into the Hed zone, fakes a shot, and passes to Amat instead. All of Hed's players think Benji's going to take the shot himself, only one of the men in red knows that he isn't that selfish.

William Lyt knows Benji.

Amat storms towards Hed's net; his wrists feel supple, his balance is perfect when he fires the shot. It looks so simple, he should have been the hero, that would have been the perfect ending. But William has already read the situation. He throws himself down on the ice; the puck hits his helmet, then the post, before rebounding towards the boards. Filip retrieves the puck and lifts it out of the zone; it glides mockingly past the outstretched sticks of the Beartown players, and then it's all over.

The final buzzer blares mercilessly. The red fans explode in a roar of delight, and William Lyt is buried under a heap of happy teammates. The green-clad players slump in despair, and in the stands people with bears on their chest sit numb with incomprehension.

Hed wins. Beartown loses.

Hockey is simple. Always fair. Always unfair.

The Beartown Ice Hockey locker room is quiet. There are only two ways for losing teams to get changed: at once or not at all. Either it takes them five minutes to leave the rink, or it takes them several hours. This time no one can summon up the energy even to have a shower.

Peter Andersson walks in. He looks at them and knows exactly how they feel. He desperately wishes he had something inspirational to say, so he mutters, 'Well, guys . . . that was a tough game. But you lost, and I want you to –'

One of the older players snorts and interrupts him: 'With all due respect, Peter, don't try telling us to "forget about it" or some other tired cliché. If you haven't got anything useful to say, it would be better if you did what you always do: keep quiet and go and hide in your office!'

It's a direct challenge. They don't respect him. Peter stands in the door with his hands in his pockets. At most times in his life he would have done as he's been told: gone and hidden in his office. He would have told himself that he's the general manager, not the coach, and that it's not his job to be respected by the players. But today isn't like those other days. So he clenches his fists in his pockets and blurts out, 'Forget about it? *Forget?* Do you think I want you to *forget* this? I want you to *remember this!*'

He gets their astonished attention with that. He usually never so much as raises his voice, but now he points at each of the players, from the oldest all the way down to Benji, Bobo, Vidar, and

Amat, and roars, 'Today you're losers. Today you *almost* made it. Remember exactly how this feels. So that you and I never have to feel like this again! *Never!*'

Perhaps he would have gone on to say more, but a monotonous banging sound is echoing through the walls of the arena, and everyone in the locker room looks up. At first it sounds like a drum, then like someone kicking a door, but soon it grows to a roar and only Peter knows where it's coming from. He's heard it before, but that was twenty years ago, during a magical season when an entire town lived and died with the victories and losses of a hockey team. Back then Peter heard that sound in every rink.

'Go back out onto the ice,' he tells the team.

They obey. Peter doesn't go with them; he knows he's not welcome.

The Beartown Ice Hockey players go back onto the ice. Almost all the stands are empty now, and the lights have been switched off. But at one end of the rink a group of men in black jackets are still standing, refusing to be quiet. They're jumping up and down, their feet drumming on the wood beneath them. There aren't even a hundred of them, but they're singing like ten thousand. 'We'll stand tall if you stand tall! We'll stand tall if you stand tall! We'll stand tall if you stand tall!' they chant over and over again.

To let everyone know that they're still there. To remind them what the club means. That it's a privilege, not a right.

In the end the whole of the Beartown A-team is standing on the ice joining in. 'WE'LL STAND TALL IF YOU STAND TALL! WE'LL STAND TALL IF YOU STAND TALL!' The rest of the rink is deserted and dark, but no one else would have been welcome anyway. This is between the team and their closest supporters: family.

Peter stands alone in the locker room with his hands in his pockets. Then he leaves the rink and walks the whole way home to

Beartown through the forest, taking deep breaths of the winter that's on its way and feeling more of a loser than ever. Everything is slipping away from him: his children, his marriage, his club.

Was it worth it? How are we supposed to know that in advance?

The coaches of the Beartown and Hed teams meet after the game in the referee's room. They talk the way coaches do – politely, but not friendly.

'Good game,' says David, dressed in red.

'You won. So only you had a good game,' replies Zackell, dressed in green.

David smiles. They're the same type, he and she.

'How are your guys getting on?' he asks.

'My guys in general or one in particular?' she counters.

David tries to find something to do with his hands. 'Benjamin. I was wondering how Benjamin is getting on.'

'We're playing you again in December. He'll play the whole game then,' she replies.

David grins. That's not an answer to his question, but it's her way of saying she's not planning to lose next time they meet. She's a hockey coach, first and foremost, just like David.

'Good game!' David repeats.

He holds out his hand, but she gives no indication at all that she's thinking of shaking it.

'That Filip of yours, your defenceman, he could be very good indeed,' she says instead.

David feels himself standing tall with pride. Filip was the smallest, worst player throughout his childhood, but David continued to give him opportunities, and now he's grown into a star.

'Yes. He just needs –' David begins, but Zackell interrupts, 'Don't let him go up into the stands again. Don't let him get dragged into the politics.'

David nods in agreement. He and Zackell really are the same sort. They know that Filip has the potential to become the best but also that he has nothing to gain by picking fights with the supporters. Elite sports doesn't tolerate that sort of distraction. Players should just play. Hockey should just be hockey.

'He was a bit slower than normal tonight, but he's probably a bit stiff after the preseason training,' David says.

'He's got a pain in his hip,' Zackell says without any trace of doubt.

'Sorry?'

'His right hip. He's overcompensating; look at his back when he's standing, and you'll see it's not straight. He hasn't mentioned it to you because he's worried about letting you down.'

'How do you know that?' David wonders.

'I did the same thing when I was his age.'

David hesitates for a long time before asking 'Who was your coach?'

'My dad.'

Zackell's expression doesn't change at all as she says this. Taken aback, David scratches his neck. 'Thanks. I'll talk to Filip . . .'

Zackell pulls a piece of paper from her pocket and scribbles down a phone number.

'This is the number of a physiotherapist. He's the best when it comes to this sort of injury. Take Filip to see him, say hi from me.'

Then she walks out of the room. David calls after her, 'I'll call you when I get a job at one of the elite teams! You can be my assistant coach!'

The woman's response from the corridor is as obvious as it is confident: 'You can be *my* assistant coach!'

The following morning, David takes Filip to see the physiotherapist. Driving there and back takes all day, and in a few years' time Filip will talk in interviews about how David used to drive him there once a week for the rest of the season. 'Best coach I've ever had! Saved my career!' The physiotherapist works for one of the biggest hockey teams in the country, and the following year it recruits Filip. David gets a coaching job there at the same time.

★

339

Elisabeth Zackell will apply for the same job but won't get it.

Always fair. Always unfair.

It's late when David's doorbell rings. His pregnant girlfriend answers. Benji is standing outside.

When David comes down the stairs, he loses his breath for a single moment, and the whole of the boy's childhood flickers past: Benji and Kevin, best friends, the wild boy and the genius. God, how David loved those two. Will he ever feel like he did as their coach again?

'Come in!' David says delightedly, but Benji shakes his head.

He's eighteen now. A man. When he and Kevin were children, David used a hundred different ways to motivate them, and perhaps none was more unusual than the fact that he used to let them borrow his watch. He had been given it by his father and the boys used to admire it, so when one of them had a particularly good game, he was allowed to borrow it. Benji holds the watch out to him now.

'Give it to your kid. It doesn't really suit me.'

Back in the spring, just after David left Beartown Ice Hockey, he saw Benji kiss another boy. There was so much the coach wanted to say at the time but no way he could think of saying it. So he left his dad's watch on Benji's dad's grave, along with a puck on which he had written, 'Still the bravest bastard I know.'

'I –' David whispers, but nothing else comes out.

Benji puts the watch into his hand, and David's fingers close tightly around the metal. His girlfriend is crying quietly for him.

'I'll keep the puck, that's enough,' Benji says.

David feels like hugging him. It's odd that you can forget how to do that. 'I'm sorry for everything you've had to go through,' he whispers honestly.

Benji bites his cheek. 'You're the best coach I've ever had,' he replies with equal honesty.

'Coach.' He doesn't say 'person' or 'friend.' Just 'coach.' That will never stop hurting David.

'There'll always be a jersey with the number sixteen on it, on all my teams,' David promises.

He knows what Benji's response will be before he says it: 'There's only one team for me.'

Then the boy disappears into the darkness. As usual.

A couple of days later, Beartown plays its next game. It's another away game, but the green jerseys and black jackets make the trip, and the same stubborn chant rings out throughout the game: 'We'll stand tall if you stand tall! We'll stand tall if you stand tall! We'll stand tall if you stand tall!'

Beartown wins the game 5–0. Amat is a whirlwind, Bobo fights as though it's the last game of his life, Benji is the best player on the ice. At one point towards the end of the game, Vidar comes close to fighting one of the opponents, but Benji skates across the ice as fast as he can to hold the goalie back, stopping him from throwing the punch.

'If you fight, you'll be suspended! We need you!' Benji yells.

'He's talking shit!' Vidar yells back, pointing to the other player.

'What's he saying?' Benji asks.

'That you're a fag!'

Benji gives him a long stare. 'I am a fag, Vidar.'

Vidar hits the bear on his chest. 'But you're *our* fag!'

Benji looks down at the ice and lets out a long sigh. That's the most dysfunctional compliment he's ever received. 'Can we just play hockey now?' he begs.

'Okay,' Vidar mutters.

So they play. Benji scores twice. Vidar doesn't let a single goal in. When Benji gets to the Bearskin that evening, there's a beer waiting for him on the bar. He drinks it, with Vidar and Teemu standing beside him. They manage to make it feel almost like normal. Perhaps it will be, one day.

42

They Take It by Storm

In Beartown we bury our dead under our most beautiful trees. We grieve silently, we talk quietly, and we often seem to find it easier to do something rather than say something. Perhaps because there are both good and bad people living here, and that makes us complicated, because it isn't always so damn easy to see the difference. Sometimes we're both at the same time.

Bobo is trying to knot his tie; he's never really managed to learn how to, it always seems to end up either too long or too short. One attempt fails so badly that his little brother and sister start to laugh. Today, of all days, he manages to make them laugh. Ann-Katrin would have been proud of him for that.

They're so different, her three children. Bobo has never really figured how three siblings can end up like that. The same genes, the same upbringing, the same home. Yet still utterly different people. He wonders if his mum thought the same or if she saw equal amounts of herself in each of the children. There are so many things Bobo ought to have asked her. Death does that to us, it's like a phone call, you always remember exactly what you should have said the moment you hang up. Now there's just an answering machine full of memories at the other end, fragments of a voice that are getting weaker and weaker.

Hog comes into the room and tries to help Bobo with his tie, but it doesn't end up much better. It was always Ann-Katrin who knotted their ties, both her husband's and her son's, whenever the family had to go to a funeral. So Bobo ties it around his head like a headband instead, and his brother and sister burst out laughing.

He wears it like that all the way to the funeral, just because it makes them laugh.

The priest talks; no one in the family really hears what's being said, even though they're sitting at the front, as close to one another as they can get. Ann-Katrin always liked that, the fact that her family was a little flock that sought warmth from each other. She used to say, 'A bigger house? Why would we want a bigger house? We're always all in the same room anyway!'

People come up to Hog afterward, trying to sum her up. It's impossible, she was too many things: a talented nurse at the hospital, a much-loved colleague who was always willing to help, a loyal and cherished friend. The great love of one man's life and the only mother three very different children will ever have.

There's only one person being buried, but she was many more women than that for those left behind.

All the people in the church wish they had asked her more questions. Death does that to us.

It's as if Peter and Kira are living in parallel now rather than together. After the funeral they walk out of the church side by side, but there's a distance between them, just enough to prevent their hands accidentally brushing against each other. They get into separate cars, but neither of them puts the key into the ignition. They're both falling apart, at opposite ends of the parking lot.

It's terrible being dependent on other people, the pair of them have always known that. One summer night a few years ago, they were sitting on the steps in front of the house; there'd been a news report of a road accident in which two young children had died, and it had brought their own grief back to them. You never stop losing a child. Kira whispered to Peter, 'God . . . it was so painful, darling . . . when Isak died, if I'd had to deal with that much pain alone . . . I'd have killed myself.' Perhaps she and Peter have managed to stick together through everything because they didn't trust themselves to cope alone. So they were constantly on the hunt for other things to live for: each other, the children, a job with a purpose, a hockey club, a town.

Peter looks through the windshield and sees Kira sitting in her car. So he gets out and walks over to her, opens the passenger door, and says tentatively, 'We should go back to their house, darling. To Hog and the children.'

Kira nods slowly and wipes eyeliner from the small lines in the skin around her eyes. When Isak died, Hog and Peter's other childhood friend, Tails, travelled all the way to Canada as soon as they could. They knew Peter and Kira would be in shock, so Tails helped with the practical arrangements, papers and documents and insurance. To start with, Hog mostly sat on the steps in front of the house, unsure of what to do. He'd never even been abroad before. But he noticed that the handrail of their living room stairs was broken, and handrails in Canada are much the same as they are in Beartown, so Hog fetched some tools and mended it. Then he went on mending things for the next few days.

'Your car or mine?' Peter whispers now.

'Mine,' Kira says, moving her purse from the passenger seat.

She drives to Hog and the children's house. Halfway there she cautiously reaches across. Peter takes her hand and holds it tight.

Fatima, Amat's mother, is already there. She's standing in the kitchen making food, and Kira helps her. Amat is there, too, he goes to get Bobo and his brother and sister and says the only thing a teenage boy can think of to say to a friend who's just lost his mother: 'Do you want to play hockey?'

They fetch sticks and a puck. Bobo wraps his tie around his head again, holds the younger children's hands, and sets off towards the lake. It's frozen over, the world is white, and they play as if nothing else matters.

Peter finds Hog in the garage, he's already gone back to work. His hands need to be busy to stop his heart from breaking even further.

'Is there anything I can do?' Peter asks.

Hog is sweaty and distracted when he replies, 'The roof got damaged in the storm, can you take a look at it?'

Grief can do that to a person – he's forgotten that his friend is all thumbs and couldn't even mend his own handrail in Canada. But Peter loves Hog, the way children love their best friends, so he fetches a ladder and clambers up onto the roof.

While he's sitting up there, without the faintest idea of where to start, he sees a cavalcade of cars approaching through the forest. At first Peter thinks it's Hog's family, but when the cars stop, a group of young men get out.

Teemu and Vidar are first, followed by Spider and Woody, then another dozen men in black jackets. They usually get their cars and snowmobiles fixed here, as do their parents. If a snowblower or piece of forestry machinery or even a kettle breaks around here, people bring them to Hog. So they're here now, now that he's broken. Teemu walks into the garage, shakes the mechanic's oil-smeared hand, and says, 'We're sorry for your loss, Hog. What do you need help with?'

Hog wipes the sweat and dirt from his face. 'What have you got?'

'A carpenter, an electrician, a few guys who are just strong, and some who aren't much use at all,' Teemu says.

Hog gives him a weak smile.

Peter is still sitting on the roof when Woody and Spider climb up. They look at each other, and Peter takes a deep breath and admits, 'I don't know anything about roofs. I don't even know where to start . . .'

Woody doesn't say anything. He just shows Peter what to do. Then the three of them spend several hours working together. When they finally climb back down, they may well be enemies again, but they've taken a breather up on the roof. Death can do that to us, too.

Teemu goes into the kitchen. He stops abruptly when he catches sight of Kira. Her jaw muscles tense and her fists clench, so quickly that Fatima instinctively stands between them without knowing who's in greater danger. But Teemu takes a step back, his shoulders sink, and he lowers his head, making himself as small as possible. 'I just want to help,' he says.

Because sometimes it's easier to do something rather than say something. So Fatima and Kira glance at each other. Kira gives a curt nod and Fatima asks, 'Can you cook?'

Teemu nods. Fatima knows who his mother is, she realizes that the boy had to learn to prepare meals at an early age. She asks him to chop vegetables, and he does it without protest. Kira washes up afterward. Teemu dries. They don't make peace, but they take a break. The complicated thing about good and bad people alike is that most of us can be both at the same time.

It's so easy to place your hope in people. To think that the world can change overnight. We demonstrate after an attack, we donate money after a disaster, we lay our hearts bare online. But for every step forward we take, we take an almost equally large step back. Seen over time, every change is so slow that it's barely visible when it's happening.

The bell rings in Beartown School. Classes start. But Benji is standing a hundred feet from the entrance with feet made of cement. He knows who he is in everyone's eyes now, one hockey game isn't going to change that. They may accept him on the ice, as long as he's the best, but he's always going to have to give them much more than everyone else now. He will always have to be grateful just for being allowed to take part. Because he isn't one of them. And never will be again.

He knows people are still writing shit about him, saying shit, making jokes. It doesn't matter who he is, how good he is at a particular sport, how much he fights, how hard he plays. In their eyes he will still only be one thing. A certain type of person will always take everything he ever achieves and boil it down to the same three letters. Like the note on the door of the cabin at the campsite, where the letter 'A' was drawn like a target, flanked by the letters 'F' and 'G,' with a knife stuck through the middle. That's all he's allowed to be now.

He turns around to walk off in the other direction. For the first time in his life he's scared of school. But there's a young woman standing a short distance away, waiting. She doesn't touch him, but her voice still stops him in his tracks.

'Don't let the bastards see you cry, Benji.'

Benji stops, his eyes wide open. 'I can't bear it . . . how do you do it?'

Maya's voice is weaker than her words. 'You just go in. With your head held high and your back straight, and you look every single bastard in the eye until they look away. We're not the ones there's something wrong with, Benji.'

Benji hears himself crack as he asks, 'How did you bear it? Back in the spring, after . . . everything . . . how did you cope?'

The look in her eyes is hard, her voice brittle. 'I refuse to be a victim. I'm a survivor.'

She walks towards the school. Benji hesitates for an eternity before following her. She waits for him. Walks by his side. Their steps are slow; perhaps it looks as though they're moving slowly, but they don't creep quietly into that corridor. They take it by storm.

43

We're Everywhere

The days blur together in Beartown this year; perhaps we can't bear to keep track of either time or our feelings. At some point the autumn comes to an end and winter arrives, but we barely notice. Time merely passes, most of us are preoccupied just trying to get out of bed each morning.

Kira keeps going to work, but it never really feels like it. She arrives later and later, leaves earlier and earlier, and she knows that her name won't be mentioned next time there's talk of promotion. She doesn't go to the conference she was invited to attend. She doesn't have the energy to think about the future, she's just trying to get through the day, fixed permanently in survival mode.

As usual it's her colleague who tells her a few hard truths. One afternoon Kira manages to go to the wrong room for a conference call and walks in on a planning meeting where her colleague is presenting a strategic plan to an important client. Kira stops in the doorway and looks at her colleague's notes on the board. They're brilliant, as always, but if Kira had been involved, they would have been even better. She waits outside after the meeting, and when her colleague comes out, Kira says, 'That's my specialty, you know that! I could have helped you with the presentation! Why didn't you ask me to help?'

Her colleague doesn't look angry. She's not trying to hurt Kira. She just replies honestly, 'Because you've given up, Kira.'

Deep down inside most of us would like all stories to be simple, because we want real life to be like that, too. But communities are like ice, not water. They don't suddenly flow in new directions because you ask them to, they change inch by inch, like glaciers. Sometimes they don't move at all.

No one confronts Benji at school. Who would dare? But every day his phone fills up with text messages from unidentifiable numbers, and every time he opens his locker, people have stuck notes in the gap around the door. All the usual words, the same old threats, he soon gets used to it. He becomes very good at pretending nothing's going on, and those who wish him ill take this to mean that he has it too easy. That he's not being punished hard enough, not suffering enough, so they need to think of something else.

William Lyt comes to school one day wearing a T-shirt with a target on the front. It's so small and discreet that only Benji notices it. The note that was pinned to the door of the cabin that morning when everyone had just found out the truth had the same target on it, drawn as the letter 'A' in the word 'FAG.' Benji tore the note off at once and destroyed it, it never appeared anywhere online, so he knows that the person who left it there is the only person who knows what it looked like.

William Lyt wants him to know who it was. He wants Benji to remember the knife. Winning a game of hockey isn't enough.

Benji looks him in the eye. They're standing a few feet apart in a corridor on an ordinary day in a long winter term, and all the other students are blithely milling past between classes, on their way to the cafeteria. It's a moment that exists only for the two boys: one from a red team, one from a green, a bull and a bear. Sooner or later one of them will end up crushing the other.

The teams in the league play each other twice per season, one home game, one away game. Beartown Ice Hockey will win the rest of its games up until then, and Hed Hockey will win all of its. The schedule is counting down inexorably to the return fixture, this time in Beartown's ice rink.

All sports are fairy tales, that's why we lose ourselves in them. So of course there's only one way for this one to end.

★

Maya is skipping school, but she has carefully picked a day when she has hardly any classes. Even when she breaks the rules, she does so responsibly. She gets onto the bus and travels for a long time, to a town beyond reasonable commuting distance. Then she goes into a large brick building with a letter in her hand and at the reception asks for a lawyer. When she walks into her mum's office, her mum knocks her coffee over in surprise.

'Darling! What are you doing here?'

Maya hasn't been to Kira's office since she was little, but she used to love going there. Other children would get bored with their parents' workplaces, but Maya liked seeing her mum concentrating on something. Seeing her passion. It taught the daughter that there are some adults who have jobs they really care about and aren't only doing for the money. That work can be a blessing.

She looks worried when she puts the letter down on her mum's desk, worried about making her parent feel abandoned. 'It's from a . . . music school. I applied . . . it was just . . . I just wanted to know if I was good enough. I sent them a video of me playing my own songs and . . .'

The mother looks at her daughter's letter. Just seeing the letterhead is enough to make her start to sniff. Kira studied hard when she was growing up so that she would be accepted into a highly academic school; she dreamed of studying law even though no one in her family had ever been to university. She wanted rules and frameworks, security and a career ladder. She wanted the same thing for her children: a life where you know what to expect, free from disappointment. But daughters are never the same as their mothers, so Maya has fallen in love with the freest, least regulated subject she can think of: music.

'You got in. Of course you got in.' Kira sniffs, so proud that she can't even stand up.

Maya sobs, 'I can start in January. I know it's a really long way away, and I'll have to borrow money, I understand if you don't want –'

Kira just stares at her. 'Don't want? Of course I . . . darling . . . I've never been happier for you!'

They embrace, and Maya says, 'I want to do this just for me, Mum. Something just for me. Do you understand?'

Kira understands. Better than anyone.

The next day she gets to the office earlier than everyone else. When her colleague arrives at work, she finds Kira sitting in her chair. Her colleague raises her eyebrows, and Kira lowers hers. 'Don't you ever tell me I've given up again! All I ever do is *not* give up!'

Her colleague grins and whispers, 'Shut up and send an invoice!' The two of them hand in their notice that morning. Then in the afternoon they sign a contract for the premises they've been dreaming about and set up their own company.

People in Beartown have never been the sort to demonstrate on the streets. They don't go on marches, their opinions are conveyed by other means. That can be hard for outsiders to understand, but very little happens by chance in this community. Even if something looks like a coincidence, it usually isn't.

Beartown Ice Hockey plays a few home games at the start of the season with the standing area of the rink intact, and Peter can't help hoping, possibly naively, that his excuse that there's no one prepared to demolish it has been accepted. But the factory's new owner eventually sends an unambiguous email: 'If the club doesn't take firm action to get rid of the hooligans known as "the Pack," we will have no option but to cancel our sponsorship contract.'

So when the crowd arrives for one home game at the start of the winter, there are security guards standing in front of double layers of tape cordoning off the standing area.

★

Everyone has to make difficult choices this year. Peter chooses one path, for the survival of the club. So the Pack chooses its response, for its own survival.

Peter is sitting at the back of the stands, waiting for them to start shouting at him. He's half expecting someone to rush up and punch him. But no one so much as looks in his direction. The rink is sold out, but there are no banners, no signs. Everyone behaves as if this were just a perfectly normal game.

The things that happen when this town chooses a side are so small that you could miss them even if you were standing right in front of them. The majority of the hockey crowd here are ordinary, decent people who would never condone violence; a lot of them moan about the Pack in the privacy of their own homes, about how 'thugs' are giving the club a bad name and scaring off players and investors alike. But choosing sides in a conflict is rarely about who you're standing alongside and almost always about who you're standing against. This community may have its own internal arguments, but it always stands united against outsiders.

If a rich company wants to buy the factory and gain power over our jobs, we can't stop it, but if they think they can buy our club and control our way of life, they've picked the wrong town to fight with. The Pack may symbolize violence to a lot of people, but to the neighbours who received help clearing fallen trees in their yards and were then offered a pint in the Bearskin afterward, they symbolize other things, too. To them the Pack is a small group of people who refuse to take any crap, who don't change to suit the demands of power and money and politics. They have their shortcomings, they make mistakes, but it's hard for anyone in Beartown not to sympathize with them, especially in times like these.

It isn't completely right. But it isn't completely wrong, either. It just is.

★

It takes Peter a long time to notice the black jackets; they're sitting spread out around the hall, in different parts of the seated area. Obviously he had been expecting that, but there are considerably more of them than ever before. Several hundred. Only when Peter looks at them carefully does he realize why: it isn't just the Pack. There are pensioners, factory workers, cashiers from the supermarket, employees of the housing association. It's not a march, it's not a noisy demonstration, and if Peter had asked, they would have pretended not to understand. 'What do you mean? No, no, it's just a coincidence!' Peter doesn't have any proof, of course, because the jackets are different makes, different fabrics. But they're all the same colour. And there are very few coincidences in Beartown.

No one was surprised when he cordoned off the stand today, because someone saw to it that the news reached the right people in advance. He knows who. The only people Peter was obliged to tell in advance were the club's board members. He needed their approval to bring in extra security. Peter made his choice, and Ramona responded. He gave her a place on the board so she would make decisions she believes to be in the best interests of the club. Now he has to take the consequences.

In the intermission between the first and second periods, a young man stands up among the seats on the far side. He's well dressed, neatly turned out, doesn't look like a violent person. If anyone nearby had been asked, naturally they would have replied, 'Him? No, I don't know him. What did you say his name was? Teemu Rinnius? Never heard of him!'

He walks calmly and collectedly down to the front of the stand, walks along behind the boards, then turns up towards the cordoned-off standing area. There are two security guards there, but they make no attempt to stop him. Teemu climbs through the cordon and walks casually across the stand, even stopping in the middle of it to tie his shoelace. He glances across the ice, seeking out Peter Andersson in the sea of people. Then he crosses the standing area, walks down the other side, and goes off to buy coffee, as if nothing has happened, even though everyone knows: Teemu has just told Peter that this is his stand and he can reclaim it whenever he likes.

A few minutes later the chanting begins, at first only in the seated area on the far side of the rink; then, as if on command, some men a few rows below Peter start to shout as well. Then it comes from the right and left of him, too. No one looks Peter in the eye, but the men in black jackets are chanting just for him: 'We're everywhere! We're everywhere! We're everywhere! Come and have a go if you think you're hard enough! Because we're everywhere, everywhere, everywhere, we're everywhere!'

They chant it ten times. Then they stand up and switch to, 'We'll stand tall if you stand tall!' Then they stand completely silent, disciplined, and focused to show how quiet the rink is then. And how much everyone would miss the Pack's support if it disappeared.

Then, as if at an inaudible signal, they start to chant again, and this time the whole rink joins in. Old and young, black jackets, white shirts, green T-shirts: 'We are the bears, we are the bears, we are the bears, THE BEARS FROM BEARTOWN!'

Beartown Ice Hockey win the game 7–1. The chanting from the stands is deafening, the crowd forms a green wall on both sides of the ice. There's a roaring sense of unity in the hall at that moment. Us against everyone. Beartown against the rest.

Peter has never felt more lonely.

The following morning, there's an interview in the newspaper with the local politician Richard Theo. The reporter asks him what he thinks about Beartown Ice Hockey's decision to get rid of the standing area, and Theo replies, 'Beartown Ice Hockey is the people's club. It doesn't belong to an elite, to the establishment, it belongs to the ordinary, decent, hardworking people of this town.

I'm going to do all I can to persuade the general manager that the standing area ought to be kept. Our supporters make a huge contribution to the atmosphere at games. It's the people's club!'

A couple of hours later, Peter receives another email from the factory's owners. They've changed their minds. Suddenly they have 'been persuaded of the great value of the standing area to the local community.' That's how Peter finds out that he was being deceived all along, the whole time.

That evening he sits alone in his kitchen at home, waiting for the sound of a key in the lock. It never comes. Kira stays at work late into the night. By the time she gets home, he's fallen asleep on the sofa. She covers him with a blanket. On the table stand a bottle of wine and two glasses.

44

Storm and Longing

It's far too late in the evening for there to be any lights on in the rink, but Elisabeth Zackell is still firing pucks when Bobo arrives. He didn't know she'd be there when he set off from home, but he was hoping. He read Harry Potter and got his brother and sister off to sleep, he did the washing and cleaning. Then he packed his things and came down here. It was instinctive. He can't sleep, his brain won't stop thinking, and he knows only one place where everything falls silent.

'Can you teach me to skate?' he calls to Zackell.

She turns towards him. She's never seen a young man in greater need of an escape from reality.

'What do you mean?' she asks.

'The first time we met, you asked why no one had ever taught me to skate!'

It's more of a plea than a statement. Zackell leans thoughtfully on her stick. 'Why do you like hockey?'

Bobo chews his bottom lip. 'Because it's . . . fun?'

'That's not a good enough answer,' she says.

He breathes heavily. Tries again. 'I . . . I know who I am when I'm playing hockey. I know what's expected of me. Everything else is just . . . so hard. But hockey is . . . it's just . . . I know who I *am* here . . .'

Zackell taps her stick on the ice, evidently not entirely dissatisfied. 'Okay. I suppose I'd better teach you to skate, then.'

Bobo steps onto the ice and skates towards her, then stops and asks, 'Why do you like hockey?'

She shrugs. 'My dad liked hockey. I liked my dad.'

Bobo frowns. 'So why did he like hockey?'

'He used to say hockey is a symphony orchestra. He liked classical music. *Sturm und Drang*.'

'Is that a band?' Bobo asks, and Zackell laughs out loud for once.

'It means "storm and longing." My dad used to play me the same pieces of music, over and over again, and he would say, "It's every emotion, all at the same time, Elisabeth, can you hear? *Sturm und Drang!*" He felt the same about hockey. *Sturm und Drang*. The whole time.'

Bobo considers this for a while. Then he asks, 'So why do you stand here at night firing pucks?'

She smiles. 'Because it's fun.'

Then she teaches him how to skate. After a few hours Bobo asks if she thinks he could be a properly good hockey player one day. She shakes her head and replies, 'No. But you could be a decent coach, if you can figure out how to be useful to the team.'

Bobo lies awake for the rest of the night thinking about this. At practice the next day he walks straight out of the locker room, skates across the ice as fast as he can, and bodychecks Benjamin Ovich as hard as he can. Confused, Benji gets up and stares at him. 'What the . . .?'

Bobo doesn't answer, he just hits Benji's legs with his stick. The rest of the team just look on in amazement, unable to figure out how to react. Bobo's lost his mum, that might make anyone a bit crazy, but they all know Benji won't tolerate being hit again.

'Bobo, stop it,' Amat says gently, but Bobo hits Benji again.

No one has time to stop Benji. Bobo is one of the heaviest players in the team, but Benji sends him flying into the boards, throws his gloves down, and flies at him with his fists clenched.

'WHAT DO YOU THINK EVERYONE ELSE IS GOING TO DO?' Bobo yells.

Benji stops in surprise. 'What?'

'What do you think everyone else is going to do? Every team

357

we meet is going to try to provoke you, they *want* you to fight! They want you to take a penalty!'

Benji stares at Bobo, along with the rest of the team. Amat mumbles, 'He's got a point, Benji. People are going to shout worse and worse things until they find something that works. You mustn't react. Not you and not Vidar. You're both too important to the team.'

Benji is breathing furiously through his nose. But in the end he calms down and helps Bobo up. 'Okay. Keep trying, then.'

At every practice from then on, Bobo tries to find more and more creative ways to provoke both Benji and Vidar. Sometimes he succeeds and comes home with black eyes even though they both know that's precisely what he's trying to make them do. It turns out that this is Bobo's unique talent in life: teasing people beyond their endurance.

When Benji opens his locker one morning, there are notes at the bottom, as usual. But one of them is different. Just one word: 'Thanks.' The next day there's another one, in different handwriting, saying 'I told my sister I'm bisexual yesterday.' A few days later there's a third note, again in different handwriting, which says, 'I haven't told anyone else, but when I do I'm not going to say I'm gay, I'm going to say I'm like you!' Then someone sends him an anonymous text: 'Everyones talking about u they c u as a symbol I hope u know how important u are to all of us who darent say anything!!!!'

Just a few small notes and messages. Just words. Just anonymous voices who want him to know what he means now.

Benji throws them into the same garbage can as all the other notes. Because he doesn't know which feels worst, the threats or the love. The loathing or the expectations. The hate or the responsibility.

He receives another sort of text message, too. They always start the same way: 'Hi! Don't know if I've got the right number, are you the homosexual hockey player? I'm a journalist, I'd like to interview . . .' One morning Benji and his sisters go down to the lake, drill a hole in the ice, and drop his phone through it. Then they drill some holes farther away and fish and drink beer and keep quiet for the rest of the day.

When Beartown Ice Hockey plays its next game on the road, the rumours about Benji have reached that town, too. In every town he plays in from now on, there will be people who shout the most disgusting things they can think of to get him off balance. But Benji doesn't give in, he just scores goals instead. The more they yell, the better he gets. After the game Bobo hugs him and exclaims happily, 'If they hate you, you're doing something right! You're the best! They'd never hate you this much if you weren't best!'

Benji tries to smile. Pretend it's nothing. But he can't quite stop himself from wondering how long he's going to have to be the best. How long it's going to take before anyone just lets him play.

Ana and Vidar are the sort of love story in which neither of them really knows how to behave. So they end up just going for walks, every day, in the forest. The snow gets deeper in tandem with their infatuation.

One afternoon he touches her and she starts to cry hysterically. When he doesn't understand why, she tells him about Benji. How everyone found out about it, about the photograph, and Maya's furious reaction.

'I don't deserve you, I'm a horrible person! I must be a psychopath!' she cries.

Vidar stands in front of her, and he might as well be naked when he replies, 'Me, too.'

How could anyone help falling even more in love with him then? Perhaps someone knows. Ana isn't one of them.

The next morning when they get to school, Ana waits until she catches sight of Benji. When he opens his locker, small paper notes fall out, and Ana realizes what's written on them, she knows how much of other people's hatred Benji is having to carry within him now.

'I have to . . . ,' she whispers to Vidar.

Vidar tries to stop her, but it's impossible. She's suddenly set off along the corridor. Benji looks up in surprise and tries to hide the notes.

'I know you hate me, but −' Ana begins, but doesn't manage to say more before the tears start to fall and her voice breaks.

'Why would I hate you?' Benji wonders, and only then does Ana realize that Maya hasn't told anyone, not even him.

'It was me . . . it was . . . took the picture of you and . . . it was me! Everything you're going through is my fault . . . it was *me*!'

Her face contracts into wrinkles of shame that will never quite smooth out. Her whole body is shaking. Then she runs off, out of the school, away, away, away. Benji stands there for a moment, and his eyes meet Vidar's. The goalie does something he never does: he hesitates.

'She −' Vidar begins, but Benji cuts him off. 'It's okay. Go after her.'

So Vidar does. He runs after her, doesn't catch up with her until they're half a mile away; she's so fast and strong that he doesn't stand a chance of getting her to slow down. So he runs alongside her. Straight out into the forest until neither of them can breathe or think anymore. Then they collapse into the snow and just lie there.

Vidar doesn't say a word. It's the finest thing anyone has ever done for Ana.

Maya is sitting alone in the cafeteria, as she does every day. But out of the blue someone sits down opposite her, as if he's been invited. She looks up. Benji points at her plate. 'Are you going to finish that, or can I have it?'

Maya smiles. 'I shouldn't sit with you. You've got a bad reputation.'

Benji looks impressed. 'Ouch.'

She laughs. 'Sorry.'

Sometimes you have to laugh at the crap, that's how you make it bearable. Benji grins. Then he says, 'You should forgive Ana.'

'What?'

'She told me she posted the pictures of me and . . . and . . . me and . . .'

He's invincibly strong and unbelievably fragile at one and the same time. He reminds Maya a lot of Ana sometimes.

'Why should I forgive her? What she did to you was horrible!' she snaps.

'But you're like sisters. And sisters forgive each other,' Benji manages to say.

Because he's got sisters. Maya tilts her head and asks, 'Have you forgiven Ana?'

'Yes.'

'Why?'

'Because people make mistakes, Maya.'

Maya eats her lunch without saying anything else. But after school she walks through Beartown, knocks on a door, and, when Ana opens it, says at once, 'Get your running gear on.'

Ana doesn't ask why.

That saves their friendship.

45

Cherry Tree

Whenever we get someone really good at sports in such a small town, this far into the forest, people in Beartown usually say it's like seeing a flowering cherry tree in the middle of a frozen garden.

Peter Andersson was our first, so when he made it all the way to the NHL it didn't matter to us that he played only a handful of games before his career was cut short by injury. He was there. One of us had made it to the best in the world. Peter transformed the whole town, he condemned us to a lifetime of never-ending, impossible dreams.

Zacharias is sixteen years old. People like him are easily forgotten in stories like this one. Most people know him only as 'Amat's friend.' They know who Amat is because he's good at hockey, and hockey is the only thing that counts here. Zacharias's life is the sort that just carries on in the background.

He and Amat grew up with Lifa, and there may never have been three such different boys around here who ended up being best friends anyway. Zacharias's parents never liked Lifa, especially when he started to be seen with the 'bandits,' as Zacharias's parents called anyone in the Hollow who didn't seem to have a job to go to. But Amat, dear Lord, Zacharias's parents worshipped him. When he started playing on the A-team, they were as proud as if he'd been their own son. As if they wished he were. And things like that are impossible for a boy like Zacharias not to notice.

Zacharias played hockey right up until this spring, even though he was the worst player on every team and didn't even enjoy it much. He went to practices for his parents' sake, put up with it for

Amat's sake. When he heard there wasn't going to be a junior team this year he felt relieved, because it gave him an excuse to stop. He really only wanted to sit at home in front of his computer anyway. So when his mum and dad came home one day, all excited about an 'open tryout' at Beartown Ice Hockey, he was overwhelmed with anxiety.

'You have to go!'

Zacharias has never been able to explain to his parents how badly bullied he has been throughout his childhood. For everything: his weight, his appearance, his address. They've never seen him that way. They're from the same generation as Peter Andersson, the generation of impossible dreams. Zacharias mumbled, 'It doesn't work like that, Mum, you can't just show up –'

But his dad interrupted, 'It's an open session! Anyone can turn up! And the factory is sponsoring Beartown Ice Hockey now! Just tell the coach that –'

'That what, Dad? That she should let me play because my dad works at the factory?' Zacharias snapped, and regretted it at once.

Beartown Ice Hockey was set up by factory workers, and the older workers still think of it as the factory's club. Now that the factory's new owners are promising more jobs for people who don't have one and more work for those who have, as well as sponsoring the club, Zacharias's dad has started to hope that everything is going to be like it used to be again. An affluent town, a club in the top division, permanent jobs, maybe even a chance for the family to move out of the apartment in the Hollow and buy a little row house. Nothing big, nothing flashy, just one more room and a slightly bigger kitchen. Heating that's more reliable in the winter.

'Sorry, Dad . . . I didn't mean . . . ,' Zacharias said quietly.

His dad's eyes were still glinting with happiness. It would mean a huge amount for both parents to see Zacharias play with the bear on his chest again. So Zacharias attended the open tryout. Of course he did.

He gave it all he had. It was nowhere near enough. Afterward he didn't even get a pat on the shoulder from the coach, she just said,

'Sorry, we've got everyone we need, but thanks for coming,' without so much as a second glance.

When he got home, his parents looked as though they were fighting to hold back tears. Many years from now he'll look back on that and realize what a sign of devotion that was: they were so incapable of seeing how bad he was at hockey that they were genuinely disappointed.

That evening his mum had another go at him about playing computer games. He tried to explain how good he'd gotten, playing online, that he can hold his own against the best in the world. That he's even been invited to take part in a competition in another town.

'A competition? In that? That's a computer game, Zacharias – that's not a sport!' his mum snorted.

Zacharias sat up playing all night, but her words tore at his chest.

Alicia isn't even five years old yet, and children of that age shouldn't be as good at escaping from preschool as she is. 'We can't be held responsible for that! This isn't a prison!' the staff protested when Sune took her back for something like the twentieth time. 'It feels like it to her,' Sune replied. Alicia was devoted to him, because he understood.

He kept trudging back from the rink to the preschool with her each day, and she kept running away again to go and watch the practices. Any practice. The A-team, little league, figure skating, it didn't matter. As soon as the ice was empty for as much as a minute, she pulled her skates on and started to play. How do you stop that?

On one of the days when Sune dragged her back to preschool, the staff took pity on him and invited him in for coffee. In the end everyone accepted that it was easier if Sune just picked Alicia up from preschool in the morning, took her to the rink, and brought her back to preschool in the afternoon in time to have coffee there.

One day in early winter, the staff mentioned that the preschool was riddled with mould, that they'd complained repeatedly to the council but had been told there were no suitable alternative premises. Sune looked at Alicia. Thought the matter through carefully. Then he walked back to the rink, went up to Peter Andersson's office and asked him, 'Do you really need this office?'

'Sorry?' Peter said.

Sune gestured towards the rest of the upper floor of the rink. 'Almost all these offices are empty! There's only you, me, and Zackell here! Who else? A couple of office temps? The janitor?'

'There isn't anyone else. We . . . we're the club . . .' Peter said.

Sune grabbed pen and paper and started to draw. 'We knock out these walls. Put in proper ventilation. It's perfectly feasible!'

'Sorry, but what are you talking about?' Peter asked.

'More than a club! We can build more than a club!' Sune thundered.

The next day he went to the politicians with his plan to build a preschool inside the ice rink. Most of them are dubious, some are openly scornful, but one of them sees the potential at once. When the other councillors say no, this one politician goes to a parents' meeting at the preschool and mobilizes an email campaign. Eventually that convinces the other politicians to restructure the budget. Sune is given money to build the first 'ice rink preschool' in the country. The children spend as much time playing on skates as they do in shoes that winter. A few years from now Alicia will say it was those extra hours of practice that made her so fast and technically proficient.

She will have forgotten that the politician who attended the parents' meeting was named Richard Theo. But at the next election there will be plenty of parents with young children who remember him.

'It's only sports.' That's what we try to tell ourselves.

Amat calls Zacharias late one evening.

'What are you doing?' Amat asks.

'Gaming,' Zacharias replies.

Amat used to make fun of him for using that word. 'Gaming' instead of 'playing games,' as if Zacharias were trying to make it sound like . . . a sport.

'Do you feel like coming out for a while?' he asks.

'Out? Now? It's as cold as a polar bear's asshole!'

Amat laughs. 'I bet polar bears' assholes aren't cold at all! Just come out!'

'What for?'

Amat swallows. 'Because I'm so nervous about the game against Hed that I can't sleep. Just come out.'

So Zacharias goes out. Of course he does. They walk around the Hollow, freezing and talking, the way they used to when they were younger and had nowhere else to go.

'How's the gaming going?' Amat asks.

'Just don't, okay?' Zacharias says, hurt.

'No, seriously! Tell me . . . I . . . look, I just need to talk about something apart from hockey.'

Zacharias sulks for a while. But eventually he says, 'It's going well. Really well, actually. I've been invited to take part in a competition.'

'Can I come and watch?' Amat asks immediately.

Zacharias can't possibly describe how proud he is to be asked. So he just grunts, 'Sure.' Then he adds crossly, 'But not if you're going to say the same shit as my parents! That it's not a real sport simply because it isn't hockey!'

Amat mutters guiltily, 'Is that what your parents say?'

Zacharias kicks at the snow. 'They dream of having a son like you, Amat. Hockey's the only thing that counts in this town.'

Amat doesn't say anything. There's nothing he can say.

Maya arrives at the barn up at the kennels. Jeanette is already training inside with the sandbag, but Ana stops warily in the doorway.

'Is it okay if she joins in?' Maya asks.

Jeanette lets out a breathless, surprised laugh. 'Of course! If there are three of us, we'll soon be a real club!'

She isn't prepared for what happens next, none of them is, not even Ana herself. But when Jeanette shows her a hold that she and Maya have been practicing and Maya tries to remember exactly how to contort her limbs in order to get out of the hold but fails, Ana asks, 'Can I try?'

Jeanette hesitates. 'This is – well – pretty advanced. Maybe we should start with something lighter?'

'Can't I just try?' Ana asks.

So Jeanette lets her try, because sometimes you have to let some people fail in order for them to learn. The only problem with that theory is that Ana doesn't fail. Jeanette shows her the movement, and Ana duplicates it on her first attempt. Jeanette shows her a more difficult move, then another, even harder, and Ana manages them all by her second or third attempt.

Jeanette is panting with her hands on her knees after twenty minutes, but Ana doesn't seem out of breath at all. Jeanette's old coach used to talk about 'physical intelligence' and how some martial arts practitioners seem to have an equivalent of a musician's perfect pitch: when they see something, their body knows instinctively how to do the same thing. Ana played hockey for a few years when she was younger, but she's never done any martial arts. Even so, her physique seems perfectly suited to it. She's grown up in the forest, running on uneven ground, jumping and climbing. Her dad's a hunter and fisherman, she's tracked and shot and dragged heavy animals with him since she was a child, she's shoveled snow and dug ditches and drilled holes in the ice on the lake. She's strong, supple, resilient, and tougher than one of the Bearskin's pork chops.

Jeanette holds her hands up and says, 'Hit me as hard as you can.'

'Seriously?' Ana asks.

Jeanette nods. 'As hard as you can!'

Maya is sitting on the floor, and she'll never forget seeing this

367

happen. Ana hits so quickly and so hard that Jeanette staggers backward. Ana just explodes. Jeanette and Maya start laughing. Ana doesn't even realize what's so special about what she's just done, but Jeanette is already planning her career.

The three women inside the barn are wet with sweat; the landscape outside is deep-frozen, covered in snow, sunk in darkness.

But the whole town smells of cherry blossom.

Early one morning Zacharias's parents' doorbell rings. Amat is standing outside. Zacharias's mother looks both happy and frustrated. First the happiness: 'Amat, how lovely to see you! Congratulations on getting onto the A-team, we're so proud of you. Just think, we've had you running about here for so many years, you can't imagine how much we boast about you to the neighbours! Your mum must be so proud of you!'

Before Amat has time to reply, she moves straight on to the frustration: 'I'm afraid Zacharias isn't home. He's gone to play computer games with some friends. Several hours away! Can you imagine? What on earth's the point of that?'

Amat takes a deep breath, because he's very fond of Zacharias's parents, but he says firmly, 'Zach isn't playing games with "some friends." It's a huge competition. He qualified ahead of thousands of other players. You should come and watch him with me.'

Zacharias's dad is standing further back in the hall. He doesn't want to insult Amat but can't help snorting, 'It's good of you to stand up for him, Amat, but playing computer games isn't a real spo—'

Amat fixes his eyes on him. 'All through our childhoods Zach and I have competed to see who could turn professional first. He's going to win. If you aren't there to see it happen, you'll regret it for the rest of your lives.'

He turns and walks down the stairs before they have time to answer.

★

When Zacharias walks into the vast hall where the competition is taking place, several hours away from Beartown, Amat is there to watch. Not a big army, but an army nonetheless.

The floor where the computers are lined up is surrounded by tall banks of seating, full of spectators; there are screens hanging from the roof and music thundering from the loudspeakers.

'It's . . . almost like hockey,' Zacharias's father concedes in amazement.

He and Zacharias's mother caught up with Amat at the railway station. They drove here together instead. The parents walked in reluctantly, not really understanding any of it, but before the competition is over the people around them will be cheering and applauding what Zacharias has done. When he wins, Amat will yell out loud, and his parents will follow his example. A stranger in the row in front will turn around and ask Zacharias's mum, 'Do you know him?'

'He's my son!' Zacharias's mum will exclaim.

The stranger will nod and look impressed and will say, 'You must be incredibly proud of him!'

It's not that important. It's only a sport. A different sport.

Kira Andersson's own mother once said to her, 'The hardest thing about having a family is that you're never finished.' Kira can't quite forget that as she and her colleague furnish their office, chase clients and try to recruit staff, negotiate with the bank, and worry about money. Kira's phone keeps ringing the whole time. She looks at the photograph of the children on her desk with the same silent questions as always: For whose sake do you have a career? Is it worth all the sacrifices? How are you supposed to know that in advance?

Peter Andersson comes home to an empty house. Kira is at work, the children are out with friends. Peter makes a meal for himself and eats it watching a hockey game on TV. His phone is silent.

When he accepted the job of general manager all those years ago, he used to hate the sound of it ringing, because it never stopped, not even when he was on vacation. Now he misses it.

Maya Andersson puts the key into the lock and walks into the hall. Her dad gets up from the couch and tries to hide how happy he is not to have to be home alone. Maya is exhausted after her martial arts training, but when she sees the look on her dad's face she goes to get her guitar. They play three songs together in the garage. Then the daughter asks, 'Has Mum told you? About . . . music school?'

Peter looks surprised. Then embarrassed. 'We . . . your mum and I . . . we haven't had much time to talk lately.'

Maya fetches the letter. 'I can start in January. It's a long way away, I'd have to move and I'd need to borrow money, but . . . Mum said it was okay.'

Peter doesn't succeed in his attempt not to fall apart. 'I just want you to be . . . to be happy, Pumpkin . . . just happy!' he manages to say.

'You know what, Dad? That's all I want for you, too,' his daughter whispers.

Leo Andersson is walking alone through Beartown. He isn't going anywhere particular, has no plan, he's just walking about. When he's grown up, he'll remember this as the winter when he was desperate for something to feel passionate about. Everyone else seems to have something they love unconditionally: his dad has his club, his mum her new business, and Maya her music. Leo wants something of his own. Perhaps he'll find it. Perhaps that's another story.

But this evening when he comes home, his mum is still at work and his big sister has gone to bed. His dad is sitting in the living room watching television. Leo hangs his coat up, considers going straight to his room, like anyone else who's only just become a teenager, but this evening he goes into the living room instead. He sits down next to his dad. They watch a hockey game together.

'You . . . I . . . I hope you know how much I love you,' his dad says during one of the breaks.

'I know, Dad. I know.' Leo grins and yawns as if he takes that for granted.

Peter can't help hoping that he might have done something right as a parent after all. They're both asleep on the sofa when Kira comes home. She covers the pair of them with blankets.

You're never finished with a family.

46

We'll Say It Was a Road Accident

Have you ever seen a town fall? Ours did. Because sometimes it's so easy to make people hate one another that it feels incomprehensible that we ever do anything else.

This has been a story about ice rinks and all the hearts that beat in and around them. About people and sports and how they sometimes take it in turns to carry each other. About us, dreaming and fighting. Some have fallen in love and some have been destroyed; we've had good days and some very bad ones. Beartown has cheered, but it has also started to smoulder. Things were heading towards a terrible explosion.

A few girls made us proud, a few boys made us great. A car drove too fast through the night. We'll say it was a road accident, but accidents are quirks of fate, and we will know that we could have prevented this one. This one will be someone's fault. Many people's fault. Our fault.

Hockey is hockey. A game. Make-believe.

When winter comes to Beartown and Hed, it's dark when you set out for work and dark when you come home. The staff in the emergency room of the hospital in Hed pass the time the way everyone else does: they talk hockey.

Everyone is looking forward to the next game. Some support the red team, some the green team: there are doctors and nurses who can barely talk to each other. As the season has progressed and both teams have won all their other games, the next encounter between Beartown Ice Hockey and Hed Hockey has become more and more important. The club that wins could get the chance of promotion to the next league. The one that loses may not even exist next season. Things can turn that quickly.

We try to tell ourselves that hockey is only hockey, but of course it never is. One doctor mutters that 'money is ruining the sport.' One nurse gives a long speech in the staffroom about how 'the fat cats in the association keep coming up with impossible financial demands on smaller clubs, agents are sucking the market dry, the sponsors are just playing around, and games are decided in boardrooms rather than on the ice!' Someone reads an article from a paper in which a sports commentator far from here predicts that teams such as Beartown and Hed will end up as feeder clubs for the bigger teams in a few years' time. 'Feeder clubs? As if we're going to be slaves to the big cities!' Someone else snarls, 'If only Beartown had shut down, we could have concentrated all our efforts on one club,' which prompts the reply 'Why should *we* shut down? Why don't *you* shut down?' The hospital staff start to argue and fall out, just like everyone else around here.

But then something happens, the way it always does where they work: an alarm comes in, there's been an accident, injured people are on their way. They forget about hockey games and club loyalties. Everyone in the emergency room works together, fights together, comes together as a team.

They'll do their utmost to save the lives of everyone brought in by the ambulances tonight. It won't be enough.

If Ana and Vidar had been an ordinary love story, perhaps they could have lived their whole lives together. Perhaps they would have gotten fed up with each other, broken up, or perhaps they would have kept on falling in love with the same person. An ordinary life is long if you live it together with someone else.

But the thing about being an unusual teenager is that sometimes you just want to be an ordinary teenager. Ana is lying in bed, Vidar is lying quietly beside her, she's like *Minecraft* to him: he can concentrate when she's with him.

'Do you want to go to a party with me?' she whispers.

'What?'

'You heard.'

'What sort of party?'

'There's a party in one of the cabins at the campsite tonight. I heard about it at school. You don't have to come. But I . . . I just want to go to a party and feel . . . normal. Just for a while.'

'Okay,' Vidar says.

'Okay?' Ana repeats.

He grins. 'Are you deaf or something? *Okay!*'

She laughs. They kiss. It feels perfectly normal. Perfectly normal and perfectly wonderful.

They go to the party. It feels normal, at least for a while. But then Vidar goes to the toilet, and the guy who comes up to Ana at the bar is from Hed, so he doesn't know who she is. Perhaps he doesn't even know who Vidar is.

Ana tries to be pleasant; she turns down the drink the guy offers her and moves the hand he puts on her hip. The guy from Hed proudly shows her the tattoo of a bull on his arm and says he might be playing on the A-team next season. Ana pushes him away when he starts whispering in her ear. She tries to move away. He grabs hold of her arm and laughs. 'Come on! Don't be such a stiff! Live a little!'

He wraps his arms around her waist. He doesn't even see Vidar walking across the room, he doesn't see the black look in his eyes, the lowered brow as he pushes through the crowd. Vidar doesn't notice who he pushes aside or shoves into the tables around him. But Ana sees. She knows how simple it ought to be to get out of the situation, let the guy from Hed know he's touched the wrong girl, picked an argument with the wrong guy. It would be so easy. But Ana has never done anything the easy way in her life.

So she twists out of the guy's grasp, leans her upper body back, and head butts him. She hears a crunch when her forehead hits his nose. He falls screaming to the floor. Ana feels blood drip down her face, doesn't know whose it is.

The guy's friends are standing a few feet away, they're as shocked as everyone else, so Ana knows she has only a couple of seconds to act. She sees Vidar storm through the crowd with a murderous look in his eyes, and Ana does the only thing she can do, given that she is who she is and loves someone like him: she takes aim and punches Vidar right in the face.

The room falls silent. Ana hits him again, harder, and Vidar stumbles backward. Then she grabs him by the arm and runs for the door. She drags him into the forest with her and runs until no one at the party will be able to find them.

'WHAT'S YOUR PROBLEM?' Vidar shouts when Ana finally stops among the trees.

She feels almost guilty when she sees the way his face is swelling up. But she snaps, 'You know what my *problem* is? Guys! Goddamn *guys*! You're my problem!'

'What have I done now, then?'

She's sobbing with rage now. 'You would have killed him! If I hadn't got you out of there, you'd have beaten him to death and been sent to prison and I –'

She's gasping with angry, pent-up tears. Vidar stands in front of her, with a split lip and an eye that's swelling up a bit more with each breath he takes.

'I was just trying to . . . help you . . .'

'What is it with guys? Why do you think we want you to fight over us the whole time? Why do you think you have to do everything violently? What the hell's wrong with you?'

'I don't know,' he admits.

Ana starts laughing. 'I love you.'

'Is that why you hit me?'

'Yes!'

Vidar scratches his ear. 'Do you have to love me quite so . . . hard?'

'I don't want to be on some crappy pedestal!' she snaps.

'A what?'

'I don't want you to fight for my sake! I don't want you to do things for my sake! I just want you to believe in me. I don't want you to take me places, I want you to back me up so I can get there myself!'

'Okay.'

'What do you mean, "okay"?'

'Okay . . . I . . . just okay. Okay. I . . . I love you too!'

'You're so stupid!'

Her hand hurts so badly that she feels like curling up and howling. He leads her over to a snowdrift and makes her stick her hand in it. She screams. He tries to explain. 'You shouldn't hit someone like that, you need –' he begins, but she snaps, 'Don't you dare tell me how to punch you!'

'Okay.'

It's just possible that there are more normal love stories.

The next day Vidar comes to Ana's martial arts training. He doesn't say anything, just drags six wooden pallets in from the yard and piles them on top of each other to form rough steps. Then he goes and stands on them.

'What's that?' Ana wonders irritably.

'A pedestal,' Vidar tells her.

'Who for?' she asks.

'Me,' he replies.

She starts to laugh, but he's serious.

'I'll stand tall if you stand tall,' he says.

She stops laughing then and kisses him. Normal love stories have never held any appeal for her anyway.

How it started? We're never going to stop arguing about that.

Perhaps it started with that guy from Hed who was trying it on at a party with a girl from Beartown and ended up with a broken nose. Perhaps he bore a grudge.

★

Or perhaps it began much earlier, at that first hockey game of the autumn where the Hed supporters chanted terrible things about Benjamin Ovich. Perhaps some people in Beartown were unable to let go of that, especially after Hed won the game.

Or perhaps it started one morning in early winter, when someone left a bloody bull's horn outside the doors of the arena in Hed. It wasn't even real blood, probably just a stupid joke by some drunk teenagers, but not everyone in Hed saw it that way.

One evening not long after that, a guy from Beartown was standing in line at a pizzeria in Hed – his girlfriend was from Hed and was waiting for him at home. Some guys from Hed were standing farther back in the line and started chanting those same words. One of them leaned forward and shouted them straight in his ear. Another yelled that he should 'fuck off home' and 'leave women from Hed the hell alone!' The guy from Beartown turned around and told them to go to hell, and the guys from Hed knocked the pizzas out of his hands. The staff managed to get between them before there was any serious trouble, but perhaps that was how it started.

Unless it started with all the rumours about the hospital and the factory, when everything became a fight over jobs. Once upon a time, people used to worry that the politicians would try to merge Hed and Beartown to form a single, larger town, but now they worry that there might not even be enough room for two small ones.

Soon after the incident with the bull's horn outside the arena and the tussle in the pizzeria, Hed Hockey and Beartown Hockey's nine-year-olds met at a tournament some distance away. The game was evenly matched, the boys were wound up, and when one of the nine-year-olds from Hed started to chant 'Queers! Sluts! Rapists!,' a fight broke out among so many of the kids that their parents had to jump onto the ice to help the referee break them up. One father from Hed and another from Beartown tried to separate their sons, and one of the fathers thought the other grabbed his son a bit too hard. The dads started shouting, then jostling each other, and soon it was the kids who were trying to stop the adults fighting rather than the other way around.

Around the same time two older men started to squabble in the waiting room at Hed Hospital, because one thought he was having to wait longer than the other. The second man muttered, 'Bloody Beartown bastards, build your own hospital and stop coming here to use up our health service.'

Perhaps none of this would have mattered if it hadn't all happened during the same autumn and winter. Perhaps it wouldn't have escalated if there hadn't been a natural opportunity for all those people to meet in the same ice rink again before the year was out. But of course there was: another hockey game between Hed and Beartown.

One morning not long before the game, two men drive from Hed to the factory in Beartown to apply for jobs. They've been unemployed for a long time, they both have children, and when the factory's new owners offered them interviews it was like a gift from the gods. They park the car outside the factory. When they get back to it after their interviews, they find it's been smashed to pieces. The doors have been kicked in, and a large tree branch has been shoved through the windshield. There aren't any witnesses, of course, even though some men in black jackets are standing nearby. Among the broken glass on the driver's seat is a note reading 'Beartown jobs for Beartown people.'

Perhaps that was how it started.

Unless it started when a small group of men from Hed meet up soon after that to discuss how to get revenge. They want to hurt the Pack. They want to take something the men in the black jackets love away from them. 'I want to set fire to their goddamn homes,' one of the men from Hed mutters at that meeting. Perhaps he doesn't mean it literally. But one of his friends replies, 'Then that's what we'll do.'

47

A Love Story We Will Never Forget

It's hard to keep a secret in the locker room. Any sort of secret.

In the arena in Hed, practices are getting more and more tense. Every-one in there has stopped referring to Beartown inhabitants as people, increasingly preferring to use terms such as 'the greens.' Or 'the baby bears are going to get slaughtered.' Or 'the bitches.' Or 'the bastard fags.' William Lyt might have been expected to be one of the loudest voices, but for some reason he's becoming quieter and quieter.

When his teammates ask why he's being so quiet, he says he's 'just trying to focus on hockey.' He has no better answer. Something odd has been happening to him this autumn and winter: the more every-one has started to hate each other, the more fed up he is with himself. He has been angry for so long, angry at hockey, angry at school, angry at home, that in the end perhaps he simply doesn't have the energy to carry on being so angry. 'Focus on your hockey,' his mum said, patting his head tenderly. So that's what he's done. He's dis-tancing himself more and more from the rest of the team, training harder on his own. He meets a girl from Hed and starts spending his evenings with her. One day David calls him into his office. He gives him a note with a phone number written on it, belonging to a scout for one of the elite clubs several divisions above Hed. 'They're inter-ested in you, they want you to call them.' As William stares at the note, David walks around the desk and puts his hands on his shoul-ders. 'I've seen you focusing more on your hockey recently, William. And noticed that you've let go of all that other nonsense outside, the fighting and so on . . . That's good! That's why this club is inter-ested. You can be something, William, you can go a long way! But you know I'm going to fight to keep you playing for me. I think you'll be ready to be captain next season!'

Then David says something terrible. Something that completely destroys a young man who's scared of showing his feelings: 'I'm proud of you, William.' William walks straight out of the office and calls his mother.

It's hard to keep a secret in the locker room, so everyone congratulates William when he comes back. He's proud, obviously, but he also notices that they stop talking when he's around. He realizes that they're talking about something they don't want him to hear.

After practice there are two cars parked outside the ice rink, containing young men with bull tattoos and hooded tops. A couple of William's teammates, the ones who are young enough to want to fight and not good enough at hockey to have anything to lose, walk straight to the cars.

'Where are you going?' William asks.

One of them turns around. 'The less you know, the better, William. You're too important for the team to be involved in this. We need you on the ice!'

'What the hell are you planning?' William asks, confused.

The men with the bull tattoos don't reply, but one of the guys from the team is too excited to stop himself. So he shouts, 'We're going to see how well bearskin burns!'

The cars drive off, leaving William standing there alone.

When the police question them afterward, the men from Hed will have a thousand excuses. Someone will say they didn't mean to set fire to the whole building, they just thought the door would burn and they'd have time to put it out before it was too late. One will say they just wanted to 'make a point,' and another will say it was only supposed to be 'a joke.' None of them knew there was an apartment above the Bearskin pub. Or that Ramona was asleep up there.

★

Maggan Lyt picks her son up from Hed ice rink, just as she does after every practice. She has sandwiches and protein smoothies with her; she puts his bag in the trunk, plays his favourite music all the way home. But he doesn't say a word.

'What is it?' his mum asks.

'Nothing . . . it's nothing. I'm just . . . nervous about the game,' William mumbles.

He pretends it's true, and Maggan pretends to believe him. They don't want to hurt each other's feelings. They have dinner and listen as William's father talks about his day at work, laugh when William's sister talks about her day: she unscrewed the lids of the salt cellars on the teachers' lunch table so they fell off when the teachers tried to season their lunch! William taught her that. Maggan tries to scold her, but the girl's laughter is so infectious that she doesn't have the heart.

Today, more than usual, William watches his parents as they eat and chat. He's well aware of what people in this town say about his family, that his dad is 'so cheap he cries when he takes a shit' and that his mother is a 'crazy hockey mum.' That might be true, but there are other things that can be said about them, too. They've never had anything handed to them on a plate, they've had to fight for everything, and they want to give their children all the things they themselves never had: power over their own lives without having to struggle every day. Maybe they go too far sometimes, but William is only too willing to forgive them. This world isn't built for kind people. Kind people get exploited and crushed. William just has to look around Beartown to see that.

After dinner he watches a cartoon in his sister's room. When she was born, the doctors said there was something wrong with her. There wasn't, she's just special. People keep wanting to describe her using the name of her condition, but William refuses. She is who she is. The kindest person he knows. When she falls asleep, he goes down to the basement to do some weight training on his own. But those words are gnawing away at him: 'We're going to see how well bearskin burns!' He can't let go of them. So he puts on his tracksuit and tells his mum he's going out for a run. Maggan Lyt hopes it's because her son is nervous.

After the door closes behind him, she goes straight to the kitchen. She always worries about her children; whenever William isn't home she channels her anxieties into making food. 'Say what you like about Maggan Lyt, but she's a good cook!' people say. The fact that they feel the need to preface the sentence with 'Say what you like' doesn't bother her. She knows who she is. She fights for everything she's got. She ends up making a pasta salad, then some potato salad. 'No one can make so many salads out of things that aren't supposed to be salads as you, Mum – you can make any vegetable unhealthy!' William usually says with a grin.

She stays awake until he gets home, worrying the whole time.

William runs through Beartown. Suddenly he realizes that he's wearing his red tracksuit with the bull on the chest. Even he appreciates what a stupid provocation that is around here right now. He turns to run home and get changed but stops when he notices the smell. It catches in his nostrils.

Something's burning.

The smoke doesn't wake Ramona, she wakes up to find someone tugging at her. Ramona may have drunk one or two late-night snacks, so she reacts the way she always does when someone wakes her: she flails her arms, yells obscenities, and tries to find a solid object to use as a weapon.

But when she sees the flames licking the walls and hears the shouting from the street, she opens her eyes and finds herself staring into Elisabeth Zackell's.

The hockey coach may be bad with feelings, but she's still capable of getting nervous. She couldn't sleep tonight, was thinking too much about the upcoming game against Hed, so she went out jogging. She saw some men running away from the Bearskin, saw the fire take hold. Most people would probably have called the fire department and waited out in the street. No one normal would have run into the burning building. But of course Zackell isn't normal.

When she sinks down onto the street outside, coughing and gasping for breath, Ramona stands beside her in her nightdress muttering, 'You'd do that for a few plates of potatoes, girl? What the hell would you have been prepared to do if I'd given you some meat?'

Zackell coughs and laughs. 'I have to admit I'm starting to get a taste for beer. Vitamins are important.'

People come running from all directions, no one faster than Teemu. He throws himself into the snow and wraps his arms around Ramona.

'There, now, lad, calm yourself down. Everyone's still alive. It's just a few flames,' Ramona whispers, but he can feel her shaking.

'All your pictures of Holger!' Teemu exclaims, getting to his feet.

Ramona has to hold him back. That's how much she loves the boy, that she's prepared to hold him back to stop him rushing into the fire to rescue the photographs of her dead husband.

But she can't hold Teemu hard enough to stop him from doing what happens next. No one can.

The whole of Beartown is awakened by the fire; cries spread through the town faster than drums, faster than sirens. Everyone's phone rings, everyone's door opens.

Benji and his sisters come racing down the street. His sisters run towards the Bearskin. People have started to form a chain to pass buckets, cars are bringing tanks of water and hoses.

But Benji stands still, because he realizes that this isn't a coincidence. It never is. So Benji tries to find a perpetrator, and all he can see is the red tracksuit. William Lyt is standing a short distance behind everyone else, closer to the forest, alone and shocked with his hand over his mouth.

Benji rushes straight at him. For a moment William thinks he's going to attack him, but Benji stops abruptly as if he's realized something. People are running back and forth across the road, there are sirens in the distance now, on their way through the forest. Benji turns to William and snarls, 'You and me. Now. For real. No friends, no weapons. Just you and me.'

William could have protested, could have tried to calm Benji down and explain that he had nothing to do with the fire. But Benji is too wound up now to believe that, and perhaps William still hates him too much to back down. So he merely whispers, 'Where?'

Benji thinks for a moment. 'The running track on the Heights. No people, even ground, lights.'

William nods stiffly. 'So I won't have any excuses afterward, you mean?'

Benji's actions have always been worse than his words. For that reason, his reply is particularly loaded. 'There won't be an "after-ward" for you, William.'

They run to the jogging track. Through the whole town. They've done it a thousand times before; when they played hockey on the same team, they used to compete in every training session. Benji could never let William be best at anything – he used to take things from William that he didn't even want. Now, as they run with snow up to their ankles, they're those same boys again. They even run a few feet apart, as if Kevin were still running between them.

When they reach the running track on the Heights, they stop and catch their breath for a few seconds; thick clouds billow from their mouths. Then, still wearing his red tracksuit, William rushes straight at Benji, who's standing there waiting in his green shirt with his fists clenched. No friends, no weapons, just the two of them. A bull against a bear.

★

Spider and Woody find Teemu outside the Bearskin. Their first instinct is to help put the fire out, to protect people. This pub is their home, more than their homes have ever been. But Spider whispers in Teemu's ear, 'We know who they are, those bastards from Hed. Woody's girlfriend saw them through her kitchen window. They left their cars down by the supermarket. If we set off now, we can catch up with them!'

When the men in black jackets pull away from the crowd outside the Bearskin and run towards Teemu's Saab to hunt the enemy through the forest, hardly anyone notices them. The only person watching is a teenage boy. Leo Andersson. He follows them.

William and Benji don't pull their punches. Their blows are frenzied, they're both so strong that their faces are bloody after just a few seconds. William lets out a yell every time he swings and lands a punch, from a mixture of exhaustion and fury. He's taller than Benji, the only advantage Benji has never been able to take from him, and can punch downward while Benji has to punch up. It's harder to punch upward. They swing wildly at each other for what seems an age, until lactic acid forces them both to back away, gasping for air, streaming with blood. Benji has lost a tooth, and William can hardly see with his right eye.

'Were you in love with him?' he suddenly snarls.

'WHAT?' Benji shouts, spitting blood onto the snow.

They're standing a few feet apart, their lungs heaving. William puts his hands on his knees. One of his fingers is broken, and his nose is bleeding like a tap. He lowers his voice, as pain and exhaustion hit him. 'Where you in love with Kevin?' he pants.

Benji says nothing for several minutes. He's got blood in his hair and on his hands; it's impossible to tell where he's bleeding from and where he's just wiped it off. 'Yes.'

It's the first time in his life that Benji has admitted that. William closes his eyes and feels his nose throb as he tries to breathe through it. 'If I'd known that, I wouldn't have hated you so much,' he whispers.

'I know,' Benji says.

William straightens up. Stands with his hands by his sides, his tracksuit top torn and stained with sweat. 'Do you remember that summer when we were little, when it rained nonstop for a whole month? When the ice rink flooded?'

Benji looks surprised but nods slowly. 'Yes.'

William wipes his nose with the back of his hand.

'You and Kevin were always out in the forest in the summer, but when it rained you both used to come to my place and ask if we could play hockey in the basement. I don't know why you didn't go back to Kevin's, but –'

'Kev's parents were having their house renovated that summer,' Benji reminds him.

William nods in acknowledgement. 'Oh, yeah. That was why. We played hockey in my basement every day that month. And we were friends then. You were okay. We didn't mess with each other.'

Benji spits more blood on the snow. 'We slept on mattresses on the floor so we could start playing the moment we woke up . . .'

William's smile is heavy with missed opportunities and lost years. 'When other people our age talk about their childhoods, they always seem to remember the sun shining the whole time. All I remember is constantly hoping for rain.'

Benji stands still. In the end he sits down in the snow. William doesn't know if he's crying. Doesn't know if it shows that he is.

Then the two men go their separate ways. Not as friends and not as enemies. They just go their separate ways.

It's late by the time Maya and Ana finally stop training at their martial arts club. Far too late, in Maya's mother's opinion, but she still picks her daughter up without protest. She offers Ana a lift, but Ana shakes her head secretively and Maya teases her: 'She's going over to see Viiiiiidar . . .'

It makes Maya so happy, because that's the kind of thing

ordinary sixteen-year-old best friends do. Tease each other about boys. Maya gets into the Volvo, waves to Ana through the rear window.

Vidar is waiting at the edge of the forest. He and Ana walk hand in hand through the night. He's humming and whistling, he can't stop drumming his fingers against his leg, and if they had lived a whole life together perhaps Ana would have started to get irritated by his lack of impulse control. But right now she loves it, the fact that all his emotions live inside him in the same way: instantly.

If they had lived their whole lives together, perhaps they would have gone walking in other places. Perhaps in sunshine in some other country. Perhaps they would have moved away from here and started again somewhere else, grown up and built a home together. Perhaps had children, aged, and grown old together. Ana stands on tiptoe to kiss him. His phone rings. She notices the smell of smoke.

When she sees the sudden look of horror on Vidar's face and he starts to run, she doesn't try to stop him. She runs alongside him.

A white car is driving along the road, far too fast. The men from Hed inside it are little more than boys. Can we forgive them for that? How old do we have to be to be held accountable for our actions, even when the consequences end up being so infinitely worse than we imagine?

When the Saab appears in the rearview mirror and the men in the white car realize that they're being pursued, they panic. They speed up, the Saab behind them does the same, the driver of the white car takes his eyes off the road, and a moment later the headlights of a third car shine through the windshield and dazzle him. It's a large Volvo heading the other way.

The white car skids on the snow; the men from Hed inside it scream. The tires lose their grip on the road. Thousands of pounds of metal take flight, just for a moment, hanging silently in the darkness. Then comes a collision so terrible that we will never really stop hearing it.

Kira and Maya are sitting in the Volvo; they've just left the kennels when Kira's phone rings. It's Peter. He's already run into town.
'THE BEARSKIN'S ON FIRE! I DON'T KNOW WHERE LEO IS!' he roars.

The kennel is located a fair way into the forest. There are only two routes back to Beartown: the ordinary winding road that all normal people use, but also a barely maintained track through the trees with no lighting that's occasionally used by hunters. The track leads directly to the main road that runs between Beartown and Hed.

Never have a mother and a sister driven that track faster than they do tonight.

A few minutes later the Volvo slides out of the forest with its engine roaring, down onto the main road. Some way down the road an old man is driving towards them from Hed and blows his horn angrily. Kira couldn't care less. She puts her foot down.

Then she sees the white car; it's coming towards them far too fast. Maya lets out a scream before Kira has time to react. The driver of the white car loses control, and the car skids across the road. Kira slams on the brakes, steers the Volvo towards the ditch, and throws herself across the seat to protect her daughter. The white car loses its grip on the road, takes off, and smashes into a tree.

Leo Andersson is running through the forest, darting between the trees to get there before the cars. He isn't fast enough. Thank God.

He isn't fast enough.

There's an old man who's a regular at the Bearskin; he usually sits with four other old men arguing about hockey. His eyesight isn't good, the other old men sometimes swap his spectacles for cheap reading glasses to make him think he's gone blind when he puts them on. As Ramona usually snaps, 'So if he does go blind, how the hell is he going to know about it?'

The old man is wearing his own glasses tonight but still can't see well in the dark. He tried saying that to the staff at the hospital. His wife isn't home tonight, and his children have long since moved to bigger cities in search of better jobs and sushi bars and whatever the hell else young people want from big cities, and the old man woke up with a pain in his chest. So he got into his car and drove from Beartown to Hed and sat for several hours in the hospital before finally being told that it was nothing to worry about. Probably just indigestion. 'Have you ever considered drinking less alcohol?' the doctor wondered. 'Have you ever considered a lobotomy?' the old man wondered, and told the doctor off for making him wait so long. He doesn't see well in the dark! He promised his wife he wouldn't drive tonight! 'We're understaffed,' the doctor says. The old man drove away, feeling aggrieved. 'What sort of crappy hospital is this, anyway?'

Then, when he's driving back from Hed to Beartown, some crazy woman in a Volvo suddenly appears out of the forest and pulls out right in front of him. She'd evidently decided to take a shortcut to town, and the old man brakes and blows his horn and flashes his headlights, but of course the stupid woman doesn't care. That's just how people drive these days.

The Volvo is driving so fast that soon the old man can only just see its rear lights. Snow is blowing hard against the windshield. It's dark. The old man curses and squints through his glasses. He doesn't even see exactly what happens next, he has no chance to react. The stupid woman in the Volvo suddenly brakes and lurches towards the side of the road. Two cars are approaching from the other direction: perhaps the old man has time to see that the first one is white. It leaves the ground, rolls over, and smashes into a tree with horrific force. The car behind it is a Saab, the old man might have time to notice. It was evidently pursuing the white car, because it brakes sharply and slides across the entire width of the road, and Teemu, Spider, and Woody throw the doors open and leap out. The old man probably recognizes them from the Bearskin.

The old man brakes. But it's snowing. It's dark. Even if the brakes do all they can, perhaps no one could have stopped at that distance, not in this weather. Perhaps it isn't anyone's fault. The old man isn't wearing a seat belt, he's driving an old car, has old eyes. He passes the Volvo and then wrenches the wheel as hard as he can as he swerves past the Saab.

He doesn't have time to see what he hits. Never hears the thud on the hood of his car. He's already hit his head on the steering wheel and lost consciousness.

Kira throws herself out of the Volvo, runs around the car, and pulls Maya from the passenger seat. That's the mother's first thought: to get her daughter away from the road, protect her. They're hugging each other tightly in the ditch when a third person embraces them, hard, as if he thinks they'll leave him forever if he lets go.

It's Leo.

Ana and Vidar are running through the forest, faster than either of them really has the energy for. If they had lived a whole life together, perhaps they might have enjoyed competing against each other. If they had had children, they would probably never have stopped arguing about which of them was fastest.

They hear the crashes from down on the road and change direction instinctively, running towards the noise. Vidar hears Teemu's voice, then Spider's and Woody's, yelling 'Call an ambulance!' and 'Watch out!'

Vidar and Ana's fingertips nudge each other one last time. Theirs is no ordinary love story. They may have loved each other for a shorter time than many of us, but they've loved harder than most.

'It's on fire!' Ana cries as they reach the road.

On the far side they can see that a car has smashed into a tree, its front end crumpled around the trunk. The people inside are unconscious. Smoke is seeping out of the gaps in the hood. Ana shouts again, 'IT'S ON FIRE! IT'S ON FIRE!'

Then she runs. Vidar tries to stop her, but she's already out of his reach. Because she's been raised by a dad who told her, 'We're not the type who let other people down, you and me.'

So she runs towards the burning white car, straight across the road. The old man driving back from hospital in Hed doesn't see what he's heading towards until it's too late. He passes the Volvo and swerves around the Saab, braking as hard as he can. Ana is in the middle of the road.

Vidar runs, shouts, but everything happens too quickly. So Vidar throws himself forward and shoves Ana out of the way. Because he's the sort of person who lacks any impulse control. He can't help himself saving the life of the person he loves.

Ana rolls into the ditch, gets to her feet in the snow, and lets out a howl, but the person she loves isn't there to hear it. The old man's car is skidding too fast, it hits with full force, and the body slams onto the hood. Vidar Rinnius dies the same way he lived. Instantly.

Theirs was a love we will always remember.

48

'Oh God! Oh God! Oh God! My baby!'

Have you ever seen a town fall? Ours did.

Have you ever seen a town rise? Ours did that, too.

Have you seen people who usually can't agree on a damn thing, be it politics, religion, sports, or anything else, come rushing from all directions to help one another put out a fire in an old pub? Have you seen them save one another's lives? We did. Perhaps you would have done the same thing. Perhaps you're not as unlike us as you think.

We did our very, very best. We gave all we had that night. But we still lost.

There are many beautiful trees in Beartown. We sometimes say that's because a new one grows every time we bury someone. That's why the births are listed alongside the deaths in the local paper, so we never run out of either trees or people.

It doesn't matter.

We don't want a new tree. Another person. We just want this one back.

'Oh God! Oh God! Oh God!' Vidar's mother screams when she collapses into the arms of the men standing in her kitchen, drowned in tears.

The men have no words. They're tumbling into the same

darkness as she is. Vidar's mother lies on the floor wailing inconsolably 'My baby! Where's my baby? Where's my baby where's my baby where's my baby?'

Bloody kids.

How often does a mother think that while her children are growing up? 'Bloody kids.' How much does she have to shout at them? How many times does she have to tell a young boy to do even the simplest little thing? Like tying his shoelaces. 'Tie your laces!' she says. Does the boy listen? Of course not. 'Tie your laces before you trip!' she says. 'You'll end up falling and hurting yourself!' You'll hurt yourself. Bloody kid.

Leo didn't tie his laces properly that night. If he had, he would have been a few seconds quicker through the trees, out of the forest, onto the road. He would have been there when the car arrived. Just a few seconds. Just one shoelace and a badly tied knot.

So Kira falls asleep on Leo's bed that night, and he doesn't make her go away, and what an incredible gift that is to a mother from a teenager. They both wake up when Maya creeps in and curls up beside them. Kira holds her children so hard that they can't breathe.

Bloody kids.

Bloody bloody bloody kids.

When Vidar was little, he didn't seem to be afraid of anything. All the other children had nightmares and wanted the light left on, but not him. When he and Teemu shared a room and had a bunk bed, Vidar insisted on sleeping on the bottom. It took Teemu several months to realize why. He woke up one night and heard Vidar crying, so he jumped down and forced him to explain why. Eventually the little boy, no more than five or six years old, said he was convinced that there were horrible monsters that came into the house at night. 'So why the hell do you want to sleep in the bottom bunk, then?' Teemu asked.

Vidar sniffed. 'So the monsters will get me first and you have time to escape!'

He couldn't help himself. Ever.

The path back to normal life is indescribably long once death has swept the feet out from under those of us who are left. Grief is a wild animal that drags us so far out into the darkness that we can't imagine ever getting home again. Ever laughing again. It hurts in such a way that you can never really figure out if it actually passes or if you just get used to it.

Ana sits on the floor outside Vidar's hospital room all night. Teemu and his mother sit on either side of her. They hold Ana's hands, unless she's holding theirs. Three people loved Vidar Rinnius so much that they wouldn't have hesitated to change places with him if they could. That's not a bad achievement for anyone. One day they might be able to think that thought without falling apart.

A boy has died tonight. An old man, too. A mother and a brother and a girlfriend sit in a hospital, an old woman goes home to a house that will never stop feeling empty. Two men from Hed will go to prison for arson, one of them will probably never walk again after the car crash in the forest, and some of us will never believe that's anywhere near enough of a punishment.

Some of us will say it was an accident. Some that it was murder. Some will think it was only those men's fault, others will say that more were responsible. That it was many people's fault. Ours.

It's so easy to get people to hate one another. That's what makes love so impossible to understand. Hate is so simple that it always ought to win. It's an uneven fight.

Spider and Woody and the men in black jackets sit in the waiting room at the hospital for almost twenty-four hours. They're surrounded by men and women, old and young, in white shirts, green T-shirts. They stay long after the doctors emerge with sombre faces to shake everyone's hand and convey their condolences, as if Vidar won't be properly dead until they leave the hospital.

No one in either town will know what to say. Sometimes it's easier to do something instead. When the cars leave the hospital in Hed, Teemu and his mother drive at the back of the convoy, so at first they don't understand why everyone is slowing down. Not until they look at the trees.

Someone has knocked the snow from the bare branches and hung thin strips of fabric all the way back. It's no big deal, just strips of fabric fluttering in a forest in the wind. But every second one is red, and every second one is green. So that the families in the cars will know that Beartown isn't grieving alone.

When Teemu and his mother get home, there's someone sitting on the steps waiting for them.

'Is that Kira Andersson?' Teemu's mother wonders.

Teemu gets out of the car without saying anything. Kira doesn't speak, either. She just stands up and goes inside with them, goes straight to the kitchen, and starts to clean and make food. Teemu takes his mother to the bedroom and sits with her until the pills grant her the respite of sleep.

He goes back out to the kitchen. Kira hands him the brush without a word. He washes, she dries.

49

Everyone Gets a Stick. Two Goals. Two Teams

Life is a weird thing. We spend all our time trying to manage different aspects of it, yet we are still largely shaped by things that happen beyond our control. We will never forget this year, not the best of it and not the worst. It will never stop influencing us.

Some of us will move to different places, but most of us will stay. This isn't an uncomplicated place, but when you grow up you realize that nowhere is. God knows, Beartown and Hed have plenty of faults, but they belong to us. This is our corner of the world.

Ana and Maya are training in the barn up at the kennels. Hour after hour. Things aren't good, things will never be all right for either of them again, but they will still find a way of getting up each morning. When Ana falls apart and just screams and cries, Maya holds her best friend tight and whispers in her ear, 'Survivors, Ana. Survivors. We're survivors.'

Early one morning, as soon as the sun has struggled above the horizon, there's a knock on the door of a mechanic's workshop. It's the middle of winter, towards the end of a childhood, and when Bobo opens the door he finds Benji, Amat, and Zacharias standing outside. They go down to the lake with sticks and a puck and play together, one last time. As if it were all just a game and nothing else mattered.

In ten years' time, Amat will be a professional player, playing in huge arenas. Zacharias will be a pro as well, but in front of a computer. Bobo will be a father.

*

By the time they finish playing down on the lake, it's almost dark again. Benji gives the others a brief wave and shouts good-bye. As if they're going to see each other tomorrow.

Hed Hockey plays Beartown Ice Hockey for the second time this season in a game that means absolutely everything and nothing at all.

In the kitchen of a house up on the Heights, Maggan Lyt is making pasta salad and potato salad. She places them in big bowls and covers them with plastic wrap. She doesn't know if she's a good or a bad person, she knows that most people assume that they're good, but she never has. She has always seen herself first and foremost as a fighter. For her family, for her children, and for her town. Even when this town wants nothing to do with her. Sometimes good people do bad things out of good intentions, and sometimes the reverse happens.

She takes her salads and drives through the town, past the ice rink, and out along the road. She stops outside the home of the Rinnius family and knocks on the door.

Say what you like about Maggan Lyt. But she's someone's mother as well.

It's nearing the time for the puck to drop in the rink, all the players should be in their own locker rooms, but despite this, William Lyt is heading the other way along the corridor. He stops in the doorway and waits until Amat and Bobo catch sight of him.

'Have you got any more of those?' he asks quietly.

Amat and Bobo look confused, but one of the older players understands what William means. He fetches a black armband, the sort all the Beartown players are already wearing, and hands it over. William pulls it on over his sleeve and nods his thanks. 'I'm – I'm truly sorry for your loss. Our whole team is.'

The Beartown players nod curtly in response. Tomorrow they'll hate each other again. Tomorrow.

★

Benji stands outside the ice rink for a long time. He's smoking in the shade of some trees, his feet deep in the snow. He's played ice hockey his whole life, for so many different reasons, for so many different people's sake. Some things demand our all, and choosing this sport is like choosing a classical instrument, it's too difficult just to be a hobby. No one wakes up one morning and just happens to be a world-class violinist or pianist, and the same applies to hockey players: it takes a lifetime of obsession. It's the sort of thing that can absorb your entire identity. In the end an eighteen-year-old man is left standing outside an ice rink thinking 'Who can I be, if I'm not this?'

Benji doesn't play this game. He's already far away when it starts.

The coach of Hed Hockey seeks out the coach of Beartown Hockey in a corridor. Elisabeth Zackell looks surprised, and David gestures towards a shy seventeen-year-old behind him who's carrying his bag over his shoulder. David has an entire speech prepared in his head, one that's supposed to sound grown-up and understanding and just right in light of all the terrible things that have happened. But his lips refuse to let it out. He wants to be sensitive, or at least to sound sensitive, but sometimes it's easier to do things than to say them. So he nods towards the young man.

'This is our backup goalie. I think he can become a damn fine player with the right coach, and . . . well . . . he doesn't get much time on the ice with us. So if you . . .'

'What?' Zackell wonders, not taking her eyes off the seventeen-year-old, who's refusing to look up from the floor.

David clears his throat. 'I've called the association. Considering the circumstances, they're prepared to allow a transfer.'

Zackell raises her eyebrows. 'You're giving me a goalie?'

David nods. 'Everyone says you're good with goalies. I think you can turn him into a fantastic player.'

'What's your name?' Zackell asks, but the goalie merely mutters something in the direction of the floor.

David coughs awkwardly.

'The guys in the team call him "Mumble," because that's all he ever does.'

He's right. The boy will become a damn fine goalie, and he'll never utter an unnecessary word. Elisabeth Zackell takes an immediate liking to him. He comes from Hed, but he will play for Beartown for almost twenty years, never for any other club, and one day he will be more of a bear than anyone else in the eyes of the fans. But he will never wear number 1, because that's Vidar's number. He will write the number 1 on his helmet instead, and the black jackets will always cheer extra loud for him because of that.

David shakes his hand, and the seventeen-year-old goes into the locker room. David shuffles his feet awkwardly, then plucks up the courage to ask Zackell, 'How's Benji?'

Zackell's lower lip quivers almost imperceptibly. Her voice trembles ever so slightly. 'Okay. I think he's going to be . . . okay.'

She too will save a jersey with the number 16 on it, on all her teams, for as long as she's a coach. She and David look each other in the eye, and Zackell says, 'Give us hell out there on the ice this evening.'

David smiles. 'You give *us* hell!'

It's one hell of a game. People will talk about it for years.

Teemu comes to the kennels on his own. He's carrying an envelope, and he climbs up to join Benji on the roof. Teemu hesitates, then sits down next to him.

'Are you going to the game?' Teemu wonders.

Benji's reply isn't contrary. It actually sounds almost happy. 'No. Are you?'

Teemu nods. He'll never stop going to watch hockey. Some people might think the sport would remind him too much of his little brother now, but in actual fact, for long periods of Teemu's life it will be one of the few places where he can bear to remember Vidar. Where it doesn't hurt.

'You're going away, aren't you?' he asks eventually.

Benji looks surprised. 'How do you know?'

Teemu's eyes flash for a moment. 'You look the way I hoped Vidar would one day. Like you're thinking of getting out.'

Teemu looks as though the slightest puff of wind could blow him to pieces. Benji passes him a cigarette.

'Where would you have liked Vidar to go?'

Teemu blows smoke through his nose. 'Anywhere he could have become something . . . more. What are you planning to do?'

Benji takes a deep drag on the cigarette. 'I don't know. I just want to find out who I am if I'm not a hockey player. I don't think I can do that if I stay here.'

Teemu nods seriously. 'You're one hell of a hockey player.'

'Thanks,' Benji says.

Teemu gets up quickly, as if he's worried the conversation might go in a direction he's not ready for. He drops the envelope into Benji's lap. 'Spider and Woody read something online about there being a "Rainbow Fund" that collects money for . . . you know . . . people who've been assaulted and imprisoned and shit in other countries because they're –'

He falls silent. Benji looks at the envelope and whispers, 'Like me?'

Teemu looks away. Stubs out the cigarette and coughs. 'Well . . . the guys decided they wanted the money we had in the kitty at the Bearskin to go to . . . that. So they wanted to give it to you.'

Benji swallows, feeling crushed. 'So you want me to give the money to that Rainbow Fund because I'm one of them?'

Teemu has already started to climb down the ladder, but he stops and looks Benji in the eye. 'No. We want you to give them the money because you're one of us.'

Ramona is stomping around inside the Bearskin, drinking her lunch and directing the workmen with plenty of ripe swearing.

Peter Andersson walks in, looking just like the boy he once was whenever he came to collect his drunken dad.

'How's it going?' he asks, looking around at the renovations.

Ramona shrugs. 'It smells better after the fire than it did before.'

Peter smiles weakly. So does she. They're not ready to laugh yet, but at least they've started to move in the right direction. Peter takes such a deep breath that his pupils quiver before he says, 'This is for you. In your capacity as a board member of Beartown Ice Hockey.'

Ramona looks at the sheet of paper he puts down on the bar without saying anything. She has a pretty good idea what it is, so she refuses to touch it.

'There's a whole heap of dreary old men in smart jackets on that board, give it to one of them!'

Peter shakes his head. 'I'm giving it to you. Because you're the only person on the board I trust.'

She pats his cheek. The door to the Bearskin opens, Peter turns around and sees Teemu in the doorway. The two men instinctively raise their hands towards each other, as if to indicate that neither of them wants any trouble.

'I can . . . come back later,' Teemu offers.

'No, no, I was just leaving anyway!' Peter insists.

Ramona snorts at the pair of them. 'Shut up, both of you. Sit down and have a beer. On the house.'

Peter clears his throat. 'I'd take a coffee.'

Teemu hangs his jacket up. 'Me, too.'

Peter raises his cup in a vain attempt at a toast. Teemu does the same.

'Honestly! Men!' Ramona mutters irritably.

Peter looks down at the bar when he says, 'I don't know if this makes it better or worse, but I think Vidar could have gone a long way as a hockey player. Maybe all the way. He was very good indeed.'

'He was an even better brother,' Teemu says.

Then he smiles. So does Ramona. Peter clears his throat.

'It's a terrible loss . . .'

Teemu turns his coffee cup, watching the small ripples on the surface. 'You and your wife lost your first child, didn't you?'

Peter takes a deep breath and closes his eyes. 'Yes. Isak.'

'Do you ever get over it?'

'No.'

Teemu turns his cup, around, around. 'So how the hell do you go on living?' he asks.

'You fight harder,' Peter whispers.

Teemu raises his cup in another toast. Peter hesitates for a while before finally saying 'I know you and your guys have always seen me as an enemy of the Pack. Maybe you were right to. I don't believe violence has any place around sports. But I . . . well . . . I'd like you to know that I understand that not everything in life is uncomplicated. I know it's your club too. I'm sorry about the times when I . . . went too far.'

Teemu's fingernails click sadly against the porcelain cup. 'Politics and hockey, Peter. They should never come anywhere near each other.'

Peter takes a deep breath through his nose. 'I don't know if it's any use to you, but . . . Richard Theo tricked me. He's just playing people like you and me off against each other to get power. And people like him don't just want control of the hockey club, they want control of the whole town.'

Teemu scratches his stubble absentmindedly, a man with nothing left to lose. 'If they want us, they're going to have to come and get us.'

Peter nods. He still doesn't know who he's most scared of: the hooligans with tattoos or the hooligans with ties and suits. He stands up and thanks Ramona for the coffee. She's holding the sheet of paper but waits until he's left before reading it.

It's Peter's resignation letter. He's no longer general manager of Beartown Ice Hockey. He no longer works there at all.

★

Ramona pushes the letter across the bar. Teemu reads it. Drinks his coffee and says, 'Peter's an ass. But he kept the club alive. We won't forget that.'

'There isn't an ass on the planet who doesn't have someone who loves them,' Ramona replies.

She raises her glass, Teemu raises his cup, and they drink a silent toast. Then he goes to the game. Later that evening he eats pasta salad and potato salad with his mum.

Richard Theo is working alone in his office in the council building. Outside the flags are flying at half-mast. Maybe he cares, maybe he doesn't. Maybe he regrets some of the things he's done, maybe he just tells himself that in the end he will have done more good than harm in the world. Because he is convinced that only someone with power can influence politics, so it isn't enough to have good intentions, you have to win first.

At the next council election, he will promise investment in better fire safety measures in the historic buildings in the heart of Beartown, in the vicinity of the Bearskin pub. He will also promise to lower the speed limit on the road between Beartown and Hed, so that the tragic road accident will never be repeated. He will canvass for law and order, more jobs, better health care. He will become known as the politician who built the preschool in the ice rink and the politician who saved both the financing of Beartown Ice Hockey and jobs in the factory. Perhaps he even saved the hospital in Hed.

Of course, one day people in this town will realize that the new owners never had any intention of keeping the factory here. They will move it somewhere where property prices are even cheaper and wages even lower, as soon as that becomes the more profitable option. It won't make any difference to Richard Theo. Because before the next election, documents will be leaked to the local paper showing how senior councillors have been misusing taxpayers' money for years; hidden subsidies and loans have found their way into the pockets of the 'fat cats' on the boards of the hockey clubs and 'illegal investments' made to support the construction of a conference hotel in conjunction with the council's application to host the World Skiing Championships. Within no time at all a scandal will blow up, in which 'influential local politicians' have been bribed by 'wealthy businessmen.'

It doesn't matter that the female politician who is the current leader of the largest party has never been involved in the misuse of funds, she'll still end up having to spend the entire election campaign answering questions about corruption. Her husband and brother just happen to work for one of the companies implicated in the bribery scandal. They later turn out to be completely innocent, but it will be too late by then, because once the word 'corruption' appears alongside the female politician's name in newspaper headlines enough times, most people will conclude, 'She's bound to be corrupt, too. She's just like all the others.'

On the other side stands Richard Theo, and he doesn't even have to be perfect; all it takes is for him to be different. So he will end up winning the next election, because that's what men like him do. But he won't win the next time around, because men like him don't do that either.

Today he leaves the council building earlier than usual. He has a long drive ahead of him this evening, all the way to his brother's home down in the capital. Richard Theo's nephew turns six tomorrow, and ever since the boy was little, Richard Theo has called him every night to read him a bedtime story over the phone. The stories are almost always about animals, because Richard Theo and the little boy both love animals.

Tomorrow, on the boy's birthday, they're going to go to the zoo. See the bears and bulls.

Kira Andersson and her colleague are in their new office. It's cramped and full of boxes, and they're stressed and exhausted. They've managed to take a few big clients with them, but they're having far more trouble recruiting good staff. No one is willing to take a chance on working for a start-up, especially not in this part of the country.

There's a knock on the door, and Kira's colleague hopes it's one of all the lawyers she's interviewed coming back to say that he or she has had a change of heart. She cheerily throws the door open but finds herself looking at Kira's husband.

'Peter? What are you doing here?' Kira blurts out farther inside the room.

Peter swallows and rubs his sweating hands on his jeans. He's wearing a white shirt and a tie. 'I . . . this will probably sound stupid, but I saw on the Internet . . . well . . . a lot of companies have an HR department these days, human resources. It's . . . they deal with recruitment, training, staff welfare. I —'

His tongue sticks to his palate. Kira's colleague is trying not to laugh, without much success, but she fetches him a glass of water. Kira asks, 'What are you trying to say, darling?'

Peter steadies himself. 'I think I could be good at that human resources thing. It's like building a team. Holding a club together. I know I haven't got the right experience for your company, but I've got . . . other experience.'

Kira's colleague scratches her hair. 'Sorry, but I don't get it, Peter. What are you doing here? Isn't Beartown playing a game right now?'

Peter rubs his hands on his jeans again. He looks Kira in the eye. 'I've resigned from Beartown Ice Hockey. I'm here looking for a job.'

Kira looks at him for a long time, blinking hard. She wraps her arms tightly around herself. 'Why do you want to work here, of all places?' she whispers.

He straightens up. 'Because I want us to have more than a marriage. I want us to help each other to become better people.'

When two teams, one red, one green, finally skate out onto the ice to play their game that evening, there are people missing, both on the ice and in the stands – people everyone has always taken for granted. But everyone else is there, from two towns with a thousand different stories. Even so, the Beartown ice rink is completely silent. The seated area is sold out, but no one's talking, no one's clapping or chanting. In one of the standing areas is a crowd of green-clad figures, and in their midst stands a motionless group of men in black jackets. They're not chanting. It's as if they want to but can't summon up the energy, their lungs are empty, their voices inadequate. Even so, a chant suddenly rises up towards the roof. Their chant.

'Wee aaare the beaaaars! We are the beaaaars! We are the beaaaaaaars . . .'

It's coming from the other end of the rink, from the other standing area. The red-clad fans are chanting it. All of Hed's fans have grown up hating Beartown Ice Hockey, and tomorrow they'll do so again. They're not going to stop fighting each other, the world isn't going to change, everything is going to carry on as usual.

But today, one single time, their sad voices rise up to chant their opponents' song as a mark of respect:

'THE BEARS FROM BEARTOWN!'

It's a single, brief token of respect. Just words. The ice rink is quieter than ever afterward, and then it feels as though it never will be again. At first there's no noise, and then it's impossible to hear anything but an explosion of pride and love as an entire town tries to tell everyone that it's still here, that it's still standing tall, that it's still Beartown against the rest. When the people in the green stands containing the black jackets start to sing, they sing loud enough for it to be heard all the way to Heaven. So that he knows how much they miss him.

And then we do what we always do around here. We play hockey.

★

Maya's mum gives her a lift to the train station. She waits by the entrance as her daughter goes up the steps and looks along the platform until she sees what she's looking for. He's sitting on a bench.

'Benji . . . ,' she says quietly from a distance, as if calling an animal she doesn't want to startle.

He looks up, surprised. 'What are you doing here?'

'Looking for you,' Maya says.

'How did you know I was here?'

'Your sisters told me.'

He smiles radiantly. 'They're very untrustworthy, my sisters.'

Maya laughs. 'Untrustworthy as hell!'

The sleeves of her jacket are slightly too short; she's gotten taller this year without her jacket realizing it. Two fresh tattoos are visible on her lower arms. One is of a guitar, the other a rifle.

Benji nods. 'I like them.'

'Thanks. Where are you going?' she asks.

He considers his reply for a long time. 'I don't know. Just . . . somewhere else.'

She nods. Hands him a piece of paper containing a brief handwritten text. 'I got into music school. I'll be moving in January. I don't know if you'll be back here before then, so I . . . I just wanted to give you this.'

While he reads it, she starts to walk back towards her mum's car. When he's finished, he calls after her, 'MAYA!'

'WHAT?' she shouts back.

'DON'T LET THE BASTARDS SEE YOU CRY!'

She laughs with tears in her eyes. 'NEVER, BENJI! NEVER!'

Perhaps they will never meet again, but she wrote all the biggest things she feels for him on that scrap of paper:

> *I wish you courage*
> *I wish you rushing blood*
> *A heart that beats too hard*

Feelings that make everything too hard
Love that gets out of control
The most intense adventures
I hope you find your way out
I hope you're the kind of person
Who gets a happy ending

The sun will make its way up over our town again tomorrow. Incredibly.

A young woman named Ana will dig deep enough within herself to find the strength to go on living. Because people like her always do, somehow. A few months from now, a long way away in a big city, she will compete for the first time in her sport. Jeanette kisses her forehead in the locker room. Maya stands beside her, punches Ana's gloved hands with her own clenched fists, and whispers, 'I love you, you idiot!' Ana smiles sadly and replies, 'I love you, you moron.' She has the same tattoos as Maya on her lower arms: a guitar and a rifle. Ana's father is standing outside the locker room. He's still trying.

When Ana steps into the ring to confront her opponent, a section of the audience stands up, as if on command. They don't shout out, but they're wearing black jackets, and they all put one hand very briefly on their hearts when she looks at them.

'Who are they?' the referee asks in surprise.

Ana blinks up at the roof. She imagines the sky beyond it. 'Those are my brothers and sisters. They stand tall if I stand tall.'

When the fight begins, Ana has just one opponent in the ring. It doesn't make any difference, she could have been facing a hundred of them. They wouldn't have stood a chance.

And the sun rises. Tomorrow, again.

A boy from the Hollow, a boy named Amat, a boy everyone thought was too small and weak to be really good at hockey, will run all the way along the main road to the NHL. He becomes a professional on the ice, and his childhood friend Zacharias from the next block becomes a professional in front of a computer screen. Some of the girls and boys they grew up with will take the wrong path, some will pass away too soon, but some will find their way to lives of their own. Big, proud lives. None of them ever forgets where they came from.

A dad named Hog goes on repairing cars in a garage, fighting for his children, taking each day as it comes. They visit Ann-Katrin's grave each morning. His eldest son, Bobo, who can pull axes from car hoods but has still never really learned to skate well, gradually becomes good friends with a hockey coach who's bad at emotions. Zackell makes him her assistant coach. He does a hell of a good job at it.

Ramona rebuilds her pub. When it reopens, everyone in Beartown and a fair few of the bastards from Hed line up for hours to go in and buy a beer and leave their change in an envelope with the words THE KITTY written on it. Beartown's hockey coach eats her potatoes free of charge for the whole of the next year. But she has to pay for her beer; this isn't a damn charity, you know.

In one corner sit five old women. At the bar sit four old men. It isn't always easy. But if you say that to them, they'll reply that it's not supposed to be.

Alicia, four and a half years old, will turn five. She's in the ice rink every day, but she will still stand in an old man's garden from time to time and slap pucks into the wall next to his terrace, and one day she will be the best.

When spring comes, three grown men meet one Sunday afternoon in the parking lot outside the supermarket. Peter, Tails, and Hog. They have slightly less hair and slightly larger stomachs now than when they last played together twenty years ago, but they have their hockey sticks and a tennis ball with them. Their wives and children carry out one net, laughing and shouting cheeky challenges to their dads as they carry the other. Then the families start to play, as if nothing else mattered.

★

Because it's a simple game if you strip away all the crap surrounding it and just keep the things that made us love it in the first place.

Everyone gets a stick. Two nets. Two teams.

Us against you.

READING GROUP QUESTIONS

1. Sports has the power to divide and the power to unite. On balance, do you think Beartown would be better off with or without its hockey club?

2. Backman describes the struggle between Beartown and Hed as one between the Bear and the Bull. What does this metaphor represent besides two fearsome animals fighting each other? What do these symbols say about the character of each town?

3. Kira makes sacrifices so that Peter can be manager of Beartown's hockey club. Does Peter make sacrifices for his family, too? Discuss the way their relationship changes over the course of the book.

4. Peter tells Ann-Katrin: 'I'm afraid the club might demand more from your sons than it can give back to them.' Bobo, Benji and Amat must take their place in the world of men when they join the A-team. How does this change force them to grow up? In what ways does it expose their immaturities? What are the different ways each boy tries to fit in with and be accepted by the older players? In the end, are Peter's fears of what the club will demand of the players justified?

5. People from Hed burn a Beartown jersey in their town square. This event doesn't hurt anyone physically, but would you still consider it an act of violence? How does this symbolic act become amplified and have the power to do so much relational damage?

6. What special challenges do Maya and Ana face as they near adulthood? Do you think two such different girls will be able to maintain their friendship as they head down separate paths?

7. 'When we describe how the violence between these two towns started, most of us will no longer remember what came first'. What do you think the tipping point was? What does the novel say about human beings' innate tendency towards violence?

8. A theme in *Us Against You* is tribalism versus community. Both dynamics are grounded in a sense of loyalty formed around a shared identity, but what makes them different? How does a strong community become insular and intolerant?

9. Two outsiders come to town: Elisabeth Zackell and Richard Theo. How does each person understand the culture in Beartown, and how do they use that understanding to their individual advantage?

10. 'People's reactions to leadership are always the same: if a decision of yours benefits me, you're fair, and if the same decision harms me, you're a tyrant'. Are there any characters in *Beartown* who act against their own self-interest? What do you think are their reasons for doing so?

11. When Ana breaks Benji's trust and reveals his secret, do you understand her actions? Is what she does to Benji made more forgivable because of the circumstances?

12. 'We will say "things like this are no one's fault", but of course they are. Deep down we will know the truth. It's plenty of people's fault. Ours.' Do you agree with this statement, or are there forces outside of the Beartown citizens' control that are, in part, responsible for the violence?

ENHANCE YOUR BOOK CLUB

1. Interview fanatical fans of any sport. Ask them why they feel such a strong connection to their team. See if you can match their motivations to a character in *Us Against You*.

2. Tom Hanks will be starring as the title character in a film adaptation of Fredrik Backman's novel *A Man Called Ove*. There are so many great characters in *Beartown*; who would you cast to play them in a movie?

3. Research a local or popular sports rivalry. How are their rivalries like Hed and Beartown? Are there off-the-field reasons that this rivalry is such an important one?

4. Pick a theme or scene from the book to draw inspiration from and write eight to sixteen lines of lyrics for a song that captures the emotions and tone of the scene. Look to Maya's songs in the book for examples.

A Q AND A WITH FREDRIK BACKMAN

Us Against You **is centred around hockey and one town's obsession with it. Did you grow up playing the sport?**

No. I grew up playing just about every other sport: football, basketball, floorball (it's a Swedish thing, long story), handball, table tennis, golf and whatever I could sign up for. But I was a very fragile kid, so I kept breaking stuff when I tried to play hockey. That's probably part of my love for that game, that I have an outsider's perspective, but also know first-hand just how hard it is to play.

One of the interesting things about *Us Against You* **and** *Beartown* **is that the town itself is a character. The setting is at once vital to the story, and yet it recedes into the background as the reader gets swept up in the emotional experiences of the characters. Why did you choose this sleepy, remote town as the backdrop to the story?**

Because I know it, probably. There are a million places like it, and I think I like small places more than big cities because, in the city, people can spend their whole lives without ever having to hang out with anyone who is not exactly like them. People find their groups where everybody dresses the same, talks the same, has the same political views and likes and dislikes all the same things. In a small town you don't have that choice: people there are going to influence you, whether you like it or not. It makes for better stories, I think.

Like *Beartown*, *Us Against You* highlights the extraordinary impact that sports can have on families and communities, and it isn't always good. You are a big sports fan, but do you think it has become too important and influential? Is *Us Against You* meant as a cautionary tale in some respects?

Sports is both good and evil, great and terrible, everything we really care about is always like that. We invest so much feeling into it, of course it's sometimes going to make us better and sometimes going to bring out our very worst qualities instead. In the case of these books, sport plays a big role in the town's economy and vice versa, and that means a lot of things become . . . political. And that changes the whole premise of the story.

To me one of the most important lines in the book is: 'What is a society? It's the sum total of our choices.' It's impossible to say when sports become too influential, it's just a constant struggle with ourselves to be brave enough to ask ourselves tough questions. To keep redrawing the line as we become smarter. But with all that said, I could have written this story about a small town with one very successful company at the centre of it, a company that employs everyone and in that way affects them all. The star of the hockey team could have been a genius entrepreneur. The questions would have been the same. Are we, as a society, prepared to let some people live above the law, if they're important enough to our economy and well-being?

Many of the characters in the book feel trapped either by circumstances, their careers, their marriages or their sexuality. Talk to us about that.

Well, a lot of people probably feel trapped by things in life. I think that's a universal feeling. Whenever we choose one thing we give up a lot of other things. I don't think I'm overly interested in people feeling trapped, to be honest, but I am very interested in the way our pasts shape our personalities and views of the world. When you've been hurt, you're never left unaffected, you either become harder or more fragile.

How do you write and how does the writing process work for you? Is there a place where you particularly love to write?

No. I trained myself very early on to never have a place for writing. Because I think I would get much less writing done in that case. I have two kids, and kids are sick like two hundred days a year, so if you create that perfect little environment somewhere, with the desk and the view and the lighting or whatever it is, and convince yourself that THIS is where I write, you run the risk of only being able to spend like a week every year there. It really helps to be able to write anywhere and on anything. I write on the backs of envelopes and on my phone and on my arm if there's no paper around. Most of all I always write in my head. I don't know if that's the answer you're looking for, but I don't really believe in a 'writing process'. I do, however, think it's very important to have a 'thinking process.' Give yourself time to think. A lot.

For someone who has never visited Sweden, what is the place they must see and why?

There's a pretty good coffee shop around the corner from my office. And I hear good things about the forests and the lakes, if you like that sort of thing. There's also a huge museum in Stockholm with an enormous royal warship that sank on its first journey in 1628 because it was built all wrong. That's a very Swedish thing, I think, to dedicate one of our biggest national exhibitions to something we messed up. We're bad at building boats, but pretty great at building museums.

What's next for you?

I'm writing a couple of novels and maybe a movie script. Maybe, also, a play. I always start about ten projects every year and finish one or two of them. So we'll see. I'm still waiting for people to figure out that I don't really have any idea what the hell I'm doing and force me to go get a real job. But until then!

ALSO BY

FREDRIK BACKMAN

THE NEW YORK TIMES NUMBER 1 BESTSELLING AUTHOR

FREDRIK BACKMAN

BEAR TOWN

EVERY TOWN HAS ITS SECRETS

Beartown is a small town in a large Swedish forest.

For most of the year it is under a thick blanket of snow, experiencing the kind of cold and dark that brings people closer together. Until the day a single, brutal act divides the town into those who think it should be hushed up and forgotten, and those who'll risk everything to see justice done. At last, it falls to one young man to find the courage to speak the truth that it seems no one else wants to hear.

With the town's future at stake, no one can stand by or stay silent. Everyone is on one side or the other.

Which side would you be on?

THE NEW YORK TIMES NUMBER 1 BESTSELLING AUTHOR

FREDRIK BACKMAN

THE
DEAL
OF A
LIFETIME

**It is Christmas Eve, and a father and son are
meeting for the first time in years.**

The father has a story he needs to share before it's too
late. As he tells his son about a courageous little girl
lying in a hospital bed a few miles away, he reveals even
more about himself: his triumphs in business, his failures
as a parent, his past regrets, his hopes for the future.

Fans of *Beartown* and *A Man Called Ove* will love
this festive novella.

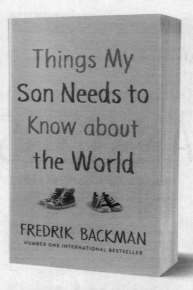

COMING JUNE 2019

Things My Son Needs to Know About the World is a
tender and funny series of letters from a new father to
his son about one of life's most daunting experiences:
parenthood.

In between the sleep-obsessed lows and oxytocin-
fuelled highs, Backman takes a step back to share his
own experience of fatherhood and how he navigates
such unchartered territory.

Part memoir, part manual, part love letter to his son, this
book relays the big and the small lessons in life. As he
watches his son take his first steps into the world, he
teaches him how to navigate both love and IKEA, and
tries to explain why, sometimes, his dad might hold his
hand just a little bit too tightly.

This is an irresistible and insightful collection
from a master storyteller.

ANXIOUS PEOPLE

The author of *A Man Called Ove* is back with a riotous comedy about a hostage situation at a Swedish apartment viewing.

A bank robber on the run locks himself in with an overenthusiastic real estate agent, two bitter IKEA addicts, a pregnant woman, a suicidal multi-millionaire and a rabbit. In the end the robber gives up and lets everyone go, but when the police storm the apartment it is . . . empty.

In a series of dysfunctional testimonies after the event, the witnesses all tell their versions of what really happened and it's clear we have a classic locked-room mystery on our hands: How did the robber manage to escape? Why is everyone so angry? And . . . What is WRONG with people these days?

n stores and

He just wanted a decent book to read ...

Not too much to ask, is it? It was in 1935 when Allen Lane, Managing Director of Bodley Head Publishers, stood on a platform at Exeter railway station looking for something good to read on his journey back to London. His choice was limited to popular magazines and poor-quality paperbacks – the same choice faced every day by the vast majority of readers, few of whom could afford hardbacks. Lane's disappointment and subsequent anger at the range of books generally available led him to found a company – and change the world.

'We believed in the existence in this country of a vast reading public for intelligent books at a low price, and staked everything on it'
Sir Allen Lane, 1902–1970, founder of Penguin Books

The quality paperback had arrived – and not just in bookshops. Lane was adamant that his Penguins should appear in chain stores and tobacconists, and should cost no more than a packet of cigarettes.

Reading habits (and cigarette prices) have changed since 1935, but Penguin still believes in publishing the best books for everybody to enjoy. We still believe that good design costs no more than bad design, and we still believe that quality books published passionately and responsibly make the world a better place.

So wherever you see the little bird – whether it's on a piece of prize-winning literary fiction or a celebrity autobiography, political tour de force or historical masterpiece, a serial-killer thriller, reference book, world classic or a piece of pure escapism – you can bet that it represents the very best that the genre has to offer.

Whatever you like to read – trust Penguin.